IDENTITY CRISIS

Book Two in the Executive Decisions trilogy

GRACE MARSHALL

Published by Xcite Books Ltd – 2013

ISBN 9781908917829

Printed and bound in the UK

Cover design by
The Design House

Identity Crisis is dedicated to that wild and wonderful and supremely unpredictable organ which keeps us alive and keeps us in love, and keeps us in hope -- the human heart.

Thank you, with all of my human heart to:

Renee and Jo and all of the lovely Ladiez at Sh! You've been a bright spot in my writing journey almost from the beginning. Not only are you a fount of information, fun and encouragement, but you're an endless source of inspiration to me. Hugs and kisses and my deepest gratitude.

The indomitable Hazel Cushion, and Liz Coldwell and all the fabulous people at Xcite Books for making my dream of the *Executive Decision Trilogy* a reality.

Melanie Garrett and Helen Callaghan, who were with me way back at the beginning, long before there was an *Executive Decision Trilogy* and have encouraged me and cheered me on through the long journey.

Lucy Felthouse, for cracking the PR whip, when necessary, and for staving off more than a few panic attacks for this neurotic writer. Thanks for all that you do. I couldn't have done it without you, EP!

Kay Jaybee, for always being there and for just being your fabulous self. The journey has been so much more fun because we've shared it. You're amazing!

Raymond, for putting up with me when I'm not my charming self and loving me anyway. Thank you for believing in me and being proud of me and easing the journey. There's no one my human heart would rather have by my side. Volim te mnogo!

Chapter One

'Excuse me.' The man sidled in next to Kendra at the bar all casual-like. 'I couldn't help noticing you sitting here all by yourself, and I was wondering if I could I buy you a drink?'

Kendra lifted her barely touched rum and Diet Pepsi. 'Thanks, but I already have one,' she said without looking up from her novel. 'And I'm not alone.' She nodded down to her Kindle. She was just getting to the good part. All she wanted the man to do was go away and leave her alone.

Honestly, she was so engrossed in her novel that she thought he'd done just that until he cleared his throat loudly and sat down on the stool next to her. 'So, whatcha reading that has you so enthralled?'

'Tess Delaney's latest, *Learning the Business*.' She kept reading. Surely eventually he'd figure out she didn't want to be disturbed. There was a time it would have embarrassed her to say that she was reading a romance novel, but now she didn't think too much about it, not when it was a Tess Delaney novel.

But apparently the man wasn't very bright. He scooted slightly closer, as though he might read over her shoulder. 'It must be really good. I mean, this is the Boiling Point. Most people don't come here to read.'

She heaved an irritated sigh and closed her Kindle. 'Yes the book's very good. Tess Delaney's best so far. And no, most people don't come here to read.' She downed her drink in one go and jammed the Kindle into her bag, making no efforts to hide her irritation. It barely registered as she slid off the stool and headed out the door past the mountain-sized bouncer that the man hadn't been bad looking. He was in a nice suit like he'd just come from some office somewhere, and if it wasn't

1

for Tess Delaney, Kendra probably could have had him in the park on that little secluded bench behind the shrubbery if she'd wanted to. That would have been a nice kinky beginning to the weekend. That was what she'd come to the Boiling Point for, wasn't it? She figured she'd dance a little, flirt a little and, with a little luck, get nicely laid. She hadn't done that in a while. Was she losing her touch?

She cursed under her breath. Whoever this reclusive Tess Delaney was, her novels were ruining Kendra's sex life with her damn romance and love and not settling for just having a tumble and a handshake. What the hell was the matter with her? A fantasy, that's all it was, just a fantasy. Nobody really got a happy ever after!

But when the man at the Boiling Point so rudely interrupted her, she'd left Lisa and David with the sexual tension sizzling between them, and she was pretty sure they were going to get laid even if she wasn't. That being the case, she sure as hell didn't want to miss out on their fun. She felt like a damned voyeur. She headed out across the park at a quick pace. It was a short walk back to Dee's. She'd order herself some nice Chinese and curl up with Lisa and David for their boardroom romp. God, what was getting into her? Was she just getting old? Harris never let her forget she was the oldest of the Three Musketeers. By two months, she reminded herself. And Harris was joking. It wasn't that she wasn't horny. It wasn't that she didn't want to start out the weekend with a sweaty romp with some hot guy. It was just that, well, she knew it would never feel like it felt when David and Lisa's anger gave way to lust and they ended up humping each other's brains out on the floor of his office. Oh, it wasn't that Tess Delaney didn't write good love scenes; they were fabulous, in fact, hot and steamy and pulse-racing. But that was just it; Tess Delaney wrote love scenes, not sex scenes. Lisa would have never had a one-night stand with some guy she just met at a bar, and David would have never gone looking. There was chemistry, real chemistry in a Tess Delaney novel, and though Kendra seriously doubted if such chemistry, such romantic feelings really existed, Tess Delaney had drawn her in and made her wish like hell that they did.

As she often did, she was house-sitting for her best friend, Dee Henning, who had been in New York on business. Well she was probably back home now, but she'd be having a very steamy romp of her own with Ellis Thorne over at his place. Against all odds, Dee and Ellis were a couple almost straight from a Tess Delaney novel. In fact, if she didn't know better, Kendra would swear that Tess Delaney had been hiding in the closet or under Ellis's desk taking notes for this novel. Wow! If this was what it felt like for Dee and Ellis, if this is what they experienced when they were together, then she was damn well jealous. She'd never admit it, of course. And as the Chinese food arrived and she scrounged in the fridge for the Diet Pepsi Dee always kept on hand for her, she found herself wondering if maybe she should stop reading those novels. It was pretty stupid, really. It only made her want what she knew she couldn't have. Dee was Dee. Dee had a way of pushing through, of never giving up, of never settling until she got what she wanted in the relationship department, or any other department. Sadly, Kendra wasn't like that. She wasn't an optimist where love was concerned. She never had been, even as a child. She knew better. But since her return from California, she'd found it really difficult to get back into the clubbing scene. That meant the only sex Kendra was getting these days was sex for one.

Dee's two red tabbies, McAlister and O'Kelly, heard the rattling of the bag from the Chinese food and came to investigate. Kendra handed over the bag to the felines and settled onto the floor in front of the coffee table to eat her spring rolls and kung pow chicken with cheap wooden chopsticks.

Just as David and Lisa clawed their way to the mother of all simultaneous orgasms, Kendra's iPhone rang, and she dropped a spring roll into her lap, then grabbed it up with her fingers while David and Lisa quickly dressed, embarrassed by all the feelings they shouldn't be having. It was Harris on the phone.

'Hi, Ken. Surprised I caught you.' She could hear the concern in his voice. 'Weren't you going to the Boiling Point?

Are you all right?'

'Fine,' she said. 'I'm fine, just having some Chinese before I head over,' she lied. 'What's up?'

'Just wondering if you can pick up some extra beer for tomorrow, maybe some soft drinks. It's supposed to be hot. Plus, with the guest list being what it is, well, I don't want to run out of lubricant.'

'In that case, better get some hard stuff too,' she said. Harris, Dee and Kendra had been best friends from high school and the bond had grown stronger during university and beyond. After all those years, they were still the Three Musketeers. Tomorrow Harris was throwing a little bar-B-Q out at his lake cabin, sort of an informal engagement party for Dee and Ellis. She'd work up a lot more enthusiasm for that little soirée if Ellis's jerk of a brother wasn't going to be there along with that Stacie chick, with whom it sounded like the two Thorne brothers had quite a history. Kendra liked Ellis. She liked him a lot, and she'd never seen Dee so happy. However, Ellis's brother and Stacie, well, they were both trouble. The two of them had bumbled about until they'd nearly destroyed the relationship between Ellis and Dee before it happened. Though that had not been their intention and they had both been very contrite, Kendra didn't place much stock in good intentions. It didn't matter, though, Garrett was still Ellis's brother, and apparently he was coming with Stacie as his date, even though she was his ex-wife. A perfectly good bar-B-Q ruined. But she supposed if Dee and Ellis could forgive the two, she would have to at least try.

After she hung up she made a quick note to herself to pick up drinks and returned her attention to Lisa, who was now coming clean with her best friend about sleeping with her boss.

Pale morning light filtered through the bedroom window, illuminating the delicate curve of Amanda's shoulder and the swell of her breasts, which rose and fell in the even breathing of sleep. For a second he wondered if he was dreaming, but then he reached out and ran a finger along her cheekbone and watched the twitch of muscles and heard the soft moan escape her lips. It was no dream and, as memories of the past night flooded back to him, he wanted her all over again.

'Damn it. It's not right. It just doesn't feel right.' For the third time in the last half hour, Garrett Thorne shoved back the chair from his desk and moved to pace in front of the French doors that led onto the balcony. It had not been a stellar day for writing, and there were deadlines looming. He was prolific. Tess Delaney was prolific. He could whip out the novels almost as fast as his publisher wanted a new one, but for some reason, there was just no flow, no chemistry between Jessie and Amanda, and fuck if he cared, to be honest! The last thing he really wanted to write was another billionaire story. But this one was an oil tycoon in Texas, his editor said. A unique approach, his editor said.

'Think kinky *Dallas* all wrapped up in a black and grey book cover,' Garrett grumbled out loud. 'Yep, that's unique all right.' He'd been joking when he brought up the idea, just joking. But hell, he didn't have any other ideas at the moment, and that was very unusual for Tess Delaney.

At the moment he just wasn't thinking like Tess, that was the problem. He was thinking like Garrett Thorne, and Garrett Thorne wanted to kick back, have a couple of beers in front of the television and … Well, actually, Garrett Thorne wanted to get laid. But he'd only been in Portland just long enough to get settled into his new house. He didn't know anyone here, and the truth was, he wasn't into one-night-stands, and he certainly wasn't anxious to put his heart out there again after what happened with him and Amy. She'd sent him a free ticket to watch her dance the lead role in *Sleeping Beauty* in New York, but of course he wouldn't go. He just couldn't ride that roller coaster again. Not for the first time, he found himself thinking that if he really were Tess Delaney, if there was such a person, she would just get on with it.

He sat back down at the desk and took a sip of the neglected glass of cabernet. Out of the stack of waste paper he saved up from read-throughs, he took a piece and began to write on the back with a fountain pen.

I've never really thought about what Tess might look like, other than to notice how deliciously comfortable she is in her own skin. And that makes her outrageously sexy. Tess doesn't really think much about romance and love and struggles of the heart. She just gets on with it. Tess is more practical than Garrett is. Tess knows that sometimes you just need to get laid, that sometimes you just want it to be easy for a little while.

He chuckled to himself and drained his glass of wine.

Tess isn't really my secret, so much as I'm hers. She can cover for me, and she does. She knows I'm the twit who wears his heart on his sleeve, and that I write all about it. Tess covers for me in a way that's far more elegant and natural than I could ever be.

Sometimes I wish she were real. I suppose this is a testament to how neurotic I am, but sometimes I wish she was my lover, tough and strong and comfortable in herself and able to slap me around a bit when I need it. Jesus, what am I writing here: Tess Delaney, Bad-Ass Dom? No denying that thought gets my attention, even if it makes me a bit uncomfortable.

Still, I suppose Tess's fans see her as far more straight-laced than that. She's hardly the kind who would fuck the lesser Thorne brother, is she? Though she might beat me into submission from time to time, she'd definitely go for the hero at the end of the day. And when she catches the public eye, she's the paragon of virtue, the teller of tales of the heart. Ah! Tess Delaney! Where the hell are you when I need you?

Beneath it, he scribbled a heart with an arrow through it, then stood to pace again. He was just ready to sit down and try once more with Amanda and Jessie when his BlackBerry rang.

It was his publicist. 'Damn it, Garrett, don't you ever read your emails?'

Garrett plopped down at his desk and pulled up his Gmail account. 'Why should I, Don? I can always count on you to call me in a panic if I need to know something.'

Don cursed, not quite under his breath. He'd been Garrett's publicist long enough not to be required to be polite, and certainly Garrett wasn't at times … Most of the time, actually. 'Tess Delaney has just been nominated for the Golden Kiss Award.' He didn't wait for Garrett's reply, but ploughed on, as he usually did, trying to get as much said as quickly as possible before Garrett hung up on him. 'You do know what that means, don't you? You do know what a big deal that is, what a coup? And if Tess wins, well, it could very well eclipse anything else she's done up until now, and I'm sure I don't have to tell you what it would do for sales.'

'The Golden Kiss? Tess was nominated for the Golden Kiss?' Garrett almost managed to let the excitement of such an honor sink in before Don was off and ranting again.

'This year, the awards banquet's in Portland. Well, that's right there for you, isn't it? And frankly, Garrett, your agent, your editor and I, well, we all think it's the perfect opportunity to out Tess Delaney as a local boy gone romantic. And I think –'

'No!' Garrett said, feeling as though the bottom had just dropped out of his stomach. 'There'll be no outing Tess.'

'Calm down, Garrett. Don't hang up. Just listen to me, and I'm sure you'll agree that it's well worth considering. Outing Tess Delaney can't do anything but help sales and if you win, well, it would be –'

'I said no,' Garrett repeated, no longer listening to Don's long litany of reasons. 'I won't out her, and you can't make me. And that's final.'

He was just ready to hang up when Don said, 'Well, actually, we can. We can make you. Your publisher is riding your editor who's riding me, and unless you're dead or dying, Garrett, they want you at that award ceremony. I suppose you could go in drag, but then to be honest, I think you'd make a very ugly woman, and I don't think you'd be keen on the chest waxing beforehand either.'

'Goddamn it, Don, I don't want Tess outed! I've told you before, I write better when no one knows, when everyone thinks I'm just Ellison Thorne's worthless brother. I don't mind going. But not as Tess. There has to be another way, or I'm warning you there'll be trouble. You know I don't have to write for Romancine.'

'Well, actually, you do. You're under contract for three more novels.'

Garrett gripped his BlackBerry tighter. 'I can make it miserable for all of us.'

Don's huff of a sigh into the phone sounded like an explosion. 'Jesus, Garrett, can't you ever just do what you're asked? This is a big deal, the biggest. It's a huge honour to even be nominated, and it would be the perfect time to let the real Tess Delaney take her bows … His bows, rather. Think how it would boost sales?'

'Sales are already good.' Garrett made a desperate reach for his wine glass only to discover it empty, and the bottle was still in the kitchen.

'Good, yes, but this could be better than even you, even Tess, could imagine. Garrett, we've thought this out, really thought this out, and there's no logical way for Tess Delaney to make her first live appearance ever without letting the world know she is really bad boy Garrett Thorne. It's like a PR dream-come-true.'

In the kitchen Garrett refilled his glass spilling a trail of wine across the granite counter top before drinking back half the glass. 'Come on, Don. What if I can't write when everyone knows I'm Garrett Thorne? Then what? Did you think about that? I mean, it's no secret what a neurotic mess I am; just ask my brother. Don? I can always get another publicist, you know?'

'All right! Damn it!' The curse was loud enough that Garrett held the BlackBerry away from his ear. 'All right.' There was a long pause, and Garrett was perfectly happy to wait. Tess Delaney books were top sellers, and the mystery of the woman behind them was discussed in more than a few coffee klatches and girls' nights out. He did have some weight to throw around where the issue of his outage was concerned, and throw it around, he would!

'OK, look. The solution is simple, then,' Don said. 'Find someone else to be Tess Delaney, I don't know, an actress, a friend, someone you can trust. Then you go as her date.'

Garrett gulped the rest of the wine and emptied the bottle into his glass. 'You're kidding, right?'

'This is not my kidding voice, Garrett. I'm serious. The way

8

I see it, this is your option. You either come as you are, and out Tess Delaney as Garrett Thorne, or you come as Garrett Thorne, Tess Delaney's bad boy date. I mean, we could get some serious PR mileage off that: Tess Delaney dating Garrett Thorne.'

'How am I going to pull this off?' Garrett said, as much to himself as to Don. He was already going down the list of women who might play Tess Delaney. The obvious choice was Stacie, but everyone already knew who Stacie was, and she had a reputation of her own to keep, as well as the fact that she was his ex-wife.

'Not my problem,' Don was saying. 'If this is how you want to play it, that's totally fine, but you'd better find someone and she'd better be good or your ass is outed. I'm sorry, man. They want to break ground by having their big name romance writer be noted as a man. They figure women will eat it up. That's what Romancine wants. The way I see it, you hire yourself a Tess Delaney or you come clean. I don't care which you do, but you have to do one or the other. Think about it. And read your fucking emails, for Chrissake.' He hung up, leaving Garrett white-knuckling the BlackBerry to his ear.

Chapter Two

'You look poorly slept with,' Ellis said, giving Garrett a hard slap on the back.

'Can't say the same about you,' Garrett said. 'Either one of you.' He gave Dee a hug and took the bottle of Sam Adams his brother offered him. He leaned back against the deck railing, glancing out over the golden midday glow of the Water Hole, as Harris's little private lake had been dubbed.

Stacie came to his side. 'It's friendlier on this half of the deck,' she said, nodding over to where Harris and Kendra huddled around the grill with Wade Crittenden. Ellis and Dee's secretaries and their spouses, along with several other people Garrett didn't know, people he figured were friends of Dee's, milled around down by the water.

'Give them some time,' Dee said, following her gaze. 'They'll warm to you.'

Garrett's gaze came to rest on Kendra Davis, dressed in a baby-blue bikini top and a pair of shorts that made her legs look like they went on for ever before they joined her luscious bottom up under what he could imagine was nice soft cotton. Damn, it would be easier to dislike the woman if she didn't look so good. Garrett's jaw still ached in muscle memory when he recalled the hard slap she had given him down in Wade's office back on the day when no one was really sure what would happen between Ellis and Dee and everyone was nail-biting to see how the two would deal with the sharks in the press waiting to accuse Ellis of sexual harassment. Falsely accuse, of course, but that never stopped them. Garrett still felt awful about the role he and Stacie had inadvertently played in that nightmare. One more item to add to his guilt list where his relationship with his brother was concerned. Dee and Ellis had forgiven them, and it was clear all was well in paradise, but Dee's friends didn't seem nearly so willing to forgive and forget. In spite of being closer to his brother than he'd been in a very long time, he still wished there was a way to make things up to him and Dee.

He watched as Kendra put her arms around Harris from behind and gave him a tight squeeze from where he leaned over the grill, tongs in hand. He'd been told they were just friends, but if that wouldn't make a man stiff, he didn't know what would. Garrett had given himself a hard-on several times thinking about Kendra Davis's enthusiastic slap. How pathetic was he? Of course, in his fantasies what followed the slap was a lot more fun for him than what had actually happened. Still, he would have liked it if she at least loathed him a little less.

'So what's up, bro?'

Garrett turned his attention back to Ellis, but before he could say anything, Stacie spoke up. 'Tess Delaney's been nominated for the Golden Kiss Award.'

'Really? That's fantastic!' Dee threw her arms around Garrett and gave him a proper bear hug. Seemed Ellis had told her about the lesser Thorne brother's secret life.

Ellis gave him another hard slap on the back. 'Congrats, Tess. You must be all aflutter.'

Garrett gave a quick glance around to make sure no one else was close enough to overhear.

'So,' Ellis continued. 'If Tess has been nominated for such a big honor, then why do you look like you've had an encounter with a freight train?'

'They want to out him,' Stacie said, sipping daintily at her Margarita. 'Tess, I mean.'

'Shut up, Stacie,' Garrett said between gritted teeth.

'Out you, what do you mean out you?' Ellis asked, and he took the stance Garrett was too familiar with, the one that said he wanted the straight answer and he would have it one way or another.

Once he was finished with the whole tale and starting on a bottle of something from one of the local micro-breweries he'd never heard of, he was pretty sure he wasn't happy with the way everyone else who'd just heard his sad little story seemed to be smirking.

'Why don't you ask her?' Stacie nodded to Kendra, who was now engaged in conversation with Wade Crittenden as though he was the most fascinating man in the whole world.

In spite of himself, Garrett couldn't keep from offering her an admiring glance.

Ellis laughed. 'Not sure he could survive a date with her, incognito or not.'

Dee elbowed him in the ribs, but even she couldn't hold back a snigger.

'All joking aside,' Dee said, 'PR is Kendra's forte and this is sort of a PR task, specialty, no doubt, but still, Tess needs someone who knows her work really well and is really comfortable around big crowds, someone who could move with the movers and shakers and blend right in. Surely that's what Tess Delaney would be able to do.'

'Tess Delaney? What's this about Tess Delaney?' No one had noticed Kendra until she stood in their midst. Her blonde hair slightly wind-blown, her bright eyes at least a couple of shades bluer than the sky, and Garrett so did not want to be thinking about the way she looked.

'Nothing.' Garrett gave them all a warning glare, grabbed Stacie by the hand and practically dragged her away. He knew Ellis and Dee would be the epitome of discretion. Stacie he was never too sure about.

'Tess Delaney is looking for some specialty PR help, apparently,' Stacie managed over her shoulder before Garrett could drag her away. Damn it, the woman had a big mouth. He was sure she'd done it on purpose.

As he escorted her briskly off the deck, he overheard Kendra ask Ellis, 'Do you know Tess Delaney?' But he couldn't hear his brother's response because Wade was suddenly asking him how he liked his new house.

'Ellis, do you know Tess Delaney?' Kendra asked again. 'If she needs help with PR I'm her girl.' She lifted her glass in a toast, way more excited about any lead that would give her a chance to meet Tess Delaney than she cared to admit.

Ellis and Dee shot each other a meaningful glance, and whatever the meaning was, Kendra had every intention of getting it out of her friend the first chance she got.

'I know her, yes.' Ellis spoke as though he wasn't overly willing to let the words out of his mouth. 'I don't know the details of what she's looking for, Garrett didn't exactly say.'

'Garrett knows her too?'

He shot Dee another glance, shifting uncomfortably from foot to foot. 'Better than I do, really. Maybe you should talk to him.'

Talking to Garrett Thorne was not something that Kendra really wanted to do, and for someone who was so good at giving nothing away at the negotiating table, Ellis certainly was not good at keeping his discomfort to himself when it came to talking about romance writers. 'What is Tess Delaney, an ex-lover or something?' she asked.

Ellis nearly choked on his beer. Dee pounded him on the back and Kendra could tell she was trying hard not to laugh. He shook his head. 'No, nothing like that. Honestly, she's much closer to Garrett than she is me. Why don't you talk to him?'

She looked over the deck railing to where Garrett was now chatting with Wade. He was the last person she wanted to talk to, but it would be really something to spend time working with Tess Delaney. And the truth was she was bored with being a lady of leisure. Though she was set for money for a long time to come, even had the funds set aside to buy a house whenever she got round to actually looking for one, a bit of interesting work, a chance to pick the brain of the woman who created such tantalizing tales would be the perfect distraction. She waited until Garrett was alone, down on the dock. He'd stepped aside to answer his cell phone. She'd just catch him when he hung up and ask him a few basic questions, then leave him to his ruminations and that would be that. It couldn't take too long.

* * *

'Now's not a good time, Don,' Garrett hissed into the phone. 'I'm at my brother's engagement party.'

'Tell Ellis congratulations for me,' his publicist said. 'This'll only take a minute, then you can get right back to the party.'

Garrett gave a gargantuan shrug. 'What do you want?'

'I just wanted to let you know that I've put it out among some of my close friends and more respected colleagues that Tess Delaney is looking for a PA.'

'You did what?'

'Well, I didn't know what else to call it. I thought I could maybe screen the candidates for you. I also know some folks who have connections with the actors' guilds and they may be able to send some possible candidates as well. I mean, we have to get on this, Garrett – that is if you're absolutely sure you won't just go to the award banquet as yourself.'

'I already told you, no. Let me do the screening. If this woman is going as my date, I need to at least like her and trust that she knows enough about my work to pull it off.' Though in all honesty he was finding it very difficult to imagine how he'd ever find someone who would understand Tess Delaney on a level that could convince people she was the woman who lived inside Garrett Thorne's mind. But then, he wasn't the one she'd have to convince, was she? She'd just have to convince Tess Delaney's fans, and writers were often quite different than their loyal fans imagined them to be.

'I insist.' He interrupted Don's list of reasons as to why he should choose the future Tess Delaney rather than Garrett.

There was a moment of silence, and for a second Garrett thought they'd lost the connection. 'All right then,' Don spoke at last. 'I'll send you the résumés of the candidates. But remember what I told you. She'd better be good, or you're outed. It's not my call. That's just the way it is.'

Garrett hung up without saying goodbye. 'Asshole,' he growled, as he stuffed the BlackBerry back in his pocket.

'So tell me about Tess Delaney.'

Garrett jumped. He hadn't even seen Kendra until she was right on him.

'Jesus,' he said. 'Do you always sneak up on people like that? Were you listening to my conversation?' The minute he said it he realized his mistake and the phantom burn from her hand to his left cheek flared with a vengeance.

She thrust her hands on her hips and glared at him. 'I wasn't sneaking, and why the hell would I be listening to your conversation?'

He thought she was going to turn around and leave, but instead she took a step closer. 'Ellis just told me that you know Tess Delaney. Is that true?'

'Why?' He stepped back dangerously close to the edge of the dock.

'Well, Stacie said she needed some kind of PR help and PR's my specialty.'

'She doesn't need your kind of PR help,' he said.

'What the hell's that supposed to mean? And how would you know anything about PR needs? I'm damn good at what I do, and if anybody could solve her PR problem, I could.'

'Oh, I doubt that,' he said. Another big mistake.

She took another step closer, folding her arms across her chest, and if looks could kill, he'd have been well dead and buried. 'Why don't you let her be the judge of that?' she said.

'Trust me on this, you're not right for the job,' he said. 'I know Tess Delaney, and she's looking for someone way more cooperative than you are.' Jesus, why the hell couldn't he keep his mouth shut?

The smile she offered him had no humor in it at all. In fact, the curl at the edge of her luscious lips was downright dangerous. 'Oh, I'm very cooperative with my clients. I promise you Tess Delaney will be very happy my work, and you know why that is, Thorne? It's because I keep my nose out of other people's business and do my job, something you wouldn't know anything about, would you?'

He felt her words like a slap, and yet, even as he was regretting it, he still couldn't keep his fucking mouth shut. 'So what are you going to do for Tess Delaney, huh? Slap her around? Throw your drink at her?'

The words were barely out of his mouth before she gave

him a hard shove. He waved his arms wildly, teetering on the edge of the dock, then, just before he went over, he grabbed her around the waist, and they both went off the end, hitting the mirror-bright water of the lake with a huge splash while Ellis and Dee and all the rest of the guests looked on.

Chapter Three

Jessie grabbed Amanda by the wrist and practically dragged her away from the party.

'What're you doing? What the on earth's the matter with you?' she half whispered, half hissed as he force-marched her through the open French doors and out onto the dock of the summerhouse. 'Let me go.'

But he held on to her with a bruising grip. He held on to her until they both stood in the fresh air under the full moon reflected off the mirrored surface of the water. He held on to her until they were away from the scent of expensive perfume and wealth, away from the clink of champagne flutes. He held onto her until they were away from James Dennison.

'I said let me go.' She pushed both of her hands flat against his chest, against the crisp white shirt of his tux, but he held her.

'Dennison –' he forced the words out like he'd eaten hot coals '– James Dennison, what's going on between the two of you?'

'What?'

'I saw the way he looked at you, like he wanted to eat you up, like he wanted to, to ...' He caught his breath.

'He asked me to dance, that's all. Not that it's any of your damn business who I dance with. I didn't realize that you were keeping me under lock and key. What, have you put out an edict that no one is to look at me?'

He pulled her to him hard and kissed her hard, and she struggled against him. He felt the anger tremble through her, rising up to meet his own, and God in heaven, he wanted her. His rage battled with his desire for her, and he pulled away, chest heaving. 'Damn it, Amanda, you're mine. I won't share you with Dennison, or with anyone else, do you understand?' He shook her none too gently. 'Do you?'

Her eyes flashed like fire in the bright moonlight, and she drew a sharp breath. 'I don't belong to you, Jessie Pennington, nor anyone else, and I don't appreciate being treated like your possession.'

All it took was a little shove, just a small one with the flat of her hand, to unbalance him and send him, tux, bowtie and all, off the end of the dock, but not before he grabbed her around the waist and took her with him.

Damn, he couldn't believe he'd actually grabbed Kendra around the waist and pulled her into the lake with him. Garrett pushed away from the laptop, breathing like he'd just finished a marathon, and sonovabitch if he didn't have a hard-on he could hang a boat anchor from. It made no sense. The woman was a total bitch. She was a banshee from hell. How could someone as nice as Dee Henning end up with someone like Kendra Davis for a best friend?

But God, the woman was hot. He'd wanted to rip her clothes off and taker her right there in the lake in front of everybody. Of course, she probably would have killed him and ripped out his still-beating heart long before he ever got any satisfaction. At least she'd been gracious enough to laugh it off in front of the onlookers and lie, something about a game the two of them were playing and they got too close to the edge of the dock. He was pretty sure Dee and Ellis and probably Harris and Stacie knew it was a lie, but at least she'd tried. When Harris showed them to separate bathrooms to dry off, Garrett was pretty sure she'd growled and bared teeth at him.

And he … Well, he'd had to take care of some very pressing business before he could be decent enough to rejoin the party. He hadn't been that turned on since … Well, he couldn't remember ever being that turned on. How could that be? Afterwards she'd kept her distance. And with everyone else she was completely charming, and God, he wanted her.

'She's a bitch,' he reminded himself out loud, trying to ignore the bulge in his jeans. 'Kendra Davis is a total bitch. I can't stay far enough away from her.'

Since Don was always nagging him for never checking his email, and he planned to ride the man hard about finding him someone to play the role of Tess, he pulled up his account, all prepared to write a "well? Have you found her yet" message. Instead, there was an email from Razor Sharp. Once again the man had managed to get beyond the Tess Delaney fan pages and find his way to Tess's private email address. Garrett knew he shouldn't read it. He knew he should just copy it to the file with the others like Detective Brewster had told him, but he'd already opened it.

Hey Lovely Lady,

Just finished reading your latest novel. A triumph, as they all are. And oh so hot. As they all are. Most definitely a one-handed read for me. Woman, what you do to me!

Rumors are flying that you've been nominated for the Golden Kiss Award. How very exciting.

I'll be watching. No doubt with one hand well occupied.

Love and heat,

R.S.

Garrett sat staring at the email until the words swam out of focus before his eyes. Razor Sharp, he was calling himself now. He had been The Razor and The Deepest Cut and several other similar names. Though the emails were creepy, there was nothing seriously threatening, so why did Garrett always feel like someone had poured ice down the back of his shirt whenever he got one? And he didn't even get them all that often. But how many people could know about the nomination for the Golden Kiss Award when Garrett's publicist had only just told him? Granted, the man could have simply guessed. Garrett pulled a deep breath and saved the email into the file for the police. Not that it would do any good. He had more important things to think about at the moment, and Tess had her share of loopy fans. He supposed that was to be expected since no one really knew who Tess was. That certainly was a big plus. Garrett turned his attention back to composing a surly email to Don.

* * *

19

What's in a name? he wondered. Do names ever fit the people who wear them? How could they, when parents choose the name they think is cute for an infant. And when people choose their own name, they can hardly be objective in their choices, can they? He pushed the chair away from the laptop, then stood to pace the floor in front of the make-shift desk. Each time he turned, his eyes caught the images flashing on the monitor. He'd turned the volume down until the sounds of sex were nothing more than background noise. He was way too excited to pay any real attention to the sex acts being performed by the two generic actors going through the motions. He was bored with them anyway. They rarely made him hard any more. But thoughts of her did. Thoughts of her always made him hard.

He ran a hand over the new growth of stubble on his head. He'd kept his head shaved all this time. But he'd let it grow now, for her. She'd like that, he was sure. He was sure she liked men with hair she could run her fingers through, and he would let her do at least that when the time came.

Everything was about to begin now. He felt it in his bones. He could be anyone he wanted to be now. She wasn't the only one who could hide away from the world until she wanted to show herself. He tilted his head from side to side and felt the pop in his neck. Lots of tension there to be released, he thought. And she was the cause of it; she was always the cause of it, the way she kept herself hidden, the way she toyed with him and teased him. Well, she wasn't the only one who could tease and toy, was she? He made his way to the refrigerator and pulled out the half empty carton of milk. On the bottom shelf, he found the last four hard-boiled eggs. He peeled them into the sink and ate them mechanically, ate them without tasting them. Outside he could hear the city just waking up. Had he really been up all night? Well, he didn't need much sleep these days. Not now when he was so close, not now when he knew it would happen soon. He could feel it in his gut, the burning, the impatience that never left him now, never let go of him, like it would gnaw him in two if he didn't have her soon. And he would have her soon. He'd spent most of the day in the cabin, their cabin, preparing it just for her. It was so perfect, so isolated. He hoped she liked nature, but then again it didn't really matter if she didn't.

When he finished the eggs, he emptied the milk carton in long, thirsty gulps, dribbling milk down his chin and onto his T-shirt. He wiped a hand across his mouth and tossed the carton into the avalanching trash bag.

He paced the kitchen floor, back and forth, back and forth. He peeked out the window at the traffic just beginning to move on the freeway, then he pulled the curtain shut. He'd already been to the gym. He'd found a seedy 24-hour place a few blocks from his apartment. It had what he needed, without the reek of perfume on made-up doxies in designer spandex. And there were no crowds in the wee hours. Not that he minded crowds, not really. He just didn't want them in his space when he was pumping iron. He'd worked out until he was exhausted, but he still couldn't sleep. He spent the darkest hours on the computer, surfing, just surfing, flipping intermittently to porn sites, searching for something, anything to hold his attention. But ultimately nothing could, nothing except her and his fantasies of what it would be like when he had her here with him.

So much information. So much. There at his fingertips, all ready and waiting for him, just like always. And every day there was more, and every day he grew closer and closer to her. He wondered if she felt it in her gut the way he did. He hoped so. He really hoped so. How could she keep from it? Whether she understood it or not, they were connected, deeply, almost spiritually, connected. If she knew, if she really understood that connection, she would be searching for him too, she would never be satisfied until she found him. Never mind, once he had her, once they were together, he could make her understand. He knew he could. That's all he'd ever wanted. To make her understand.

It seemed like he'd dreamed about their coming together for an eternity. Maybe he'd even dreamed about her in a previous life. He'd always known the time would come and he just had to wait for the right moment. It was so close now. It was so very close. And soon he could take exactly what he wanted, what he'd been waiting for so patiently.

He paced the hall a couple of times, then stripped. The T-shirt and the back of his sweat bottoms were white with the dried salt of his sweat from the gym, and his body felt sticky and damp as he stretched out on the bed on top of the tangle of blankets. Everything in him was restless, unspent, wound to the breaking point, ready to explode. Every thought, every dream, every breath was about her, about what he'd do to her when he had her. It amazed him how she could still be with him every single second, even when he couldn't touch her, even when he couldn't yet have her. There was no lying still with her on his mind, no calming down for the rest that he knew he needed, no distracting himself even for a minute with thoughts of anything else. She never, ever left him, she constantly tormented him, taunted him, tortured him. It was exquisite agony companioned by rage patiently endured, finely honed. But not for much longer, he promised himself. Not for much longer. She would be his. And soon. He felt it in the gnawing burn of his gut.

He twisted and writhed in the knotted bedding. Every cell of him ached with the want of her. He was painfully hard, feeling as though he would burst with the weight of his need. He seldom masturbated. He preferred to sublimate all that sexual energy, to save it up for her, to save it up until he could make her take it all back, until he could fill her and hammer her and break her with every single bit of lust and anger and desire that she had forced him to hold, every endless unsatisfied moment he'd had at her expense. He would make her take it all back. Again, and again, and again. Yes, he seldom masturbated, but this morning, he couldn't help himself. This morning, he could almost feel her in his arms, almost feel the silk of her skin against him, almost feel the heat of her breath against his mouth begging for it, even as she tried to deny herself what he knew she really wanted, what only he could give her.

His breathing was thick and heavy in the tiny room, roaring in his ears, drowning out the freeway sounds as he tugged and cupped at himself, as he wondered what she'd look like after all this time, wondered what she'd feel like when he entered her the first time, when he claimed his prize after all his

22

waiting, after all her teasing. It would be so good, so very good. He convulsed into the T-shirt he'd just removed, then relaxed back against the pillow, settling into dreams of all the things he'd do to her when he had her with him at last, dreaming that it would be very, very soon.

Kendra spent the better part of the next three weeks doing her homework, calling up all of her resources, researching every possibility online. It would be a total coup to work with the elusive Tess Delaney, to actually get to meet the woman behind the romance. If she hadn't been hell-bent on offering her services before her nasty encounter with Garrett Thorne at Harris's bar-B-Q, she certainly was now. Who did he think he was anyway to tell her that she wasn't right to work for Tess Delaney? He didn't know anything about her. He didn't know that she was the best in her field. But then again, he wouldn't, would he? How would he know who ran the Ryde Agency? There were less than a handful of people who'd ever seen her face to face. She had worked her miracles through the magic of IT and a kick-ass staff that was great at keeping secrets. No one knew that the head of the Ryde Agency, K. Ryde, was Kendra Ryde Davis. She had her own reasons for keeping secrets, reasons she tried not to think about these days, but nonetheless, she knew better than most how important a little anonymity could be, and she was sure someone like Tess Delaney would really appreciate her skills in discretion. Discretion was something she doubted that blabbermouth Garrett Thorne would ever understand.

There was no denying the tight squirm of pleasure she felt below her belly as she thought about him grabbing her around the waist and pulling her off the end of the dock into the lake with him. What an asshole, she thought. And yet he was a cheeky asshole with a great body, one the wet summer shorts and polo shirt revealed quite nicely. Didn't make him any less of an asshole, though. How did he get to be brothers with someone as amazing as Ellison Thorne? More significantly, how had Ellis kept from murdering him when they were kids? She was pretty sure she would have if he'd been her brother.

She returned her attention to her online attempts to connect with Tess Delaney. The woman had covered her tracks better than anyone she'd ever known – even better than she had. Not one of her substantial connections seemed to know anything about the woman or how to get in touch with her people. Still, the harder it was to find out what she needed to know, the deeper she dug. K. Ryde never gave up. She just hoped some lesser being didn't get Tess Delaney's attention before she did. It would be a pity if the woman ended up with less than the best.

It was long after midnight at the end of her third week of searching when she finally found what she was looking for, or rather, it found her. It was an email from the Bachman Agency, a PR firm Kendra had quite a bit of contact with when she was in the business. Most often they'd been competitors, though it had been friendly competition for the most part, and on occasion they'd actually helped each other out. The email was sent to K. Ryde personally. Not many people knew that address. In fact, it was pretty much an inactive account now, and yet there it was, a message from Donald P. Bachman.

Dear Mr. Ryde,

Everyone always assumed K. Ryde was a man.

I'm emailing on behalf of Ms. Tess Delaney, who would like to employ a PR person for a special project, one of a sensitive nature. Ms. Delaney requires a woman in her early to mid-30s, one comfortable with making public appearances and speaking in public, should the need arise. Ms. Delaney is looking for someone who can represent her publically and discreetly. She would need this person as soon as possible. Please send résumés on to me or contact me personally.

Sincerely yours,

Donald P. Bachman

Did she actually whoop out loud? She looked around the room to make sure no one had heard her, which was totally ridiculous, since she was all alone. She was exactly what Tess Delaney needed. Though the woman didn't know it yet, Kendra was totally certain of it. With a few short email exchanges, Kendra made sure that Donald P. Bachman knew it as well. Just before she shut down for the night she gave Mr. Bachman a call, or rather, Kay Lake gave him a call, Kay Lake with her newly created email address, Facebook page and Twitter account. Kay Lake who had studied PR at university as well as acting. Kay Lake who until just a few hours ago didn't exist. If the Bachman Agency were desperate enough to email her old K. Ryde account, then they would find Kay Lake to be exactly what they were looking for. And by the time she ended their conversation, she had Don Bachman eating out of her hand. She was going to work for Tess Delaney. She was as sure of it as she was her own name.

She shut down her laptop and headed off to bed. In her mind's eye, she could imagine rubbing Garrett Thorne's nose in just how wrong he was about her suitability to represent Tess Delaney. As she brushed her teeth, making her usual faces in front of the bathroom mirror, she berated herself for even considering Garrett's opinion. The Bachman Agency would take her at her word no matter what Garrett Thorne thought. After all, she was recommended to them by K. Ryde. If she said she could get the job done, then for all practical purposes, they could count it already done. The red Shelby Mustang parked safely in the underground car park of her apartment complex was evidence of that.

She stripped out of her yoga bottoms and her tank top and slid naked into the bed. As the sheets grazed the tips of her nipples and the cool cotton embraced her, the memory of Garrett Thorne wrapping his arms around her and pulling her into the lake on top of him made her feel wet in places that had nothing to do with lake water, places that had been tetchy since they'd made their big splash at Harris's bar-B-Q. She couldn't say she didn't like the feeling. But, God, did it really have to be Garrett Thorne who made her wet? Tess Delaney would not have palmed her heroines off on the unemployed bad boy little brother of the hot shot of the business world, she was sure of it. That was not a story the woman would write. Surely Tess would give the brilliant young PR exec a better match than that.

Damn it, listen to her. Tess Delaney wrote romance novels,

for fuck sake! She didn't write real life because nobody wanted to read about real life. The truth was that if you could give up the stupid fantasies about happy ever after and hearts and flowers, you could have sex. Sex was easy, sex was abundant. You simply had to remember that it was just that. There were no strings and there were no expectations. That way no one got hurt and everyone knew up front what the rules were. She always made certain of that, and she always made certain the rules were her own. It had worked for her all these years. It had kept her satisfied and it had kept her heart safe. And she had always been a firm believer that if you let your heart get broken, well, at the end of the day, you had no one to blame but yourself. No one but yourself.

For a long time she lay in the darkness listening to the night sounds of Portland, thinking about Garrett Thorne and Tess Delaney. Maybe tomorrow night she'd go back over to the Boiling Point. There were always interesting people to be met there, and how long had it been since she'd actually had sex? Of course, Dee and Harris thought she had it all the time, thought she had it whenever she wanted it. And she did. Didn't she? For some strange reason, she just hadn't wanted it all that much lately. She wondered if she should see a doctor. But then the memory of being pressed up close to a very wet, very aroused Garrett Thorne came back with a vengeance, nearly taking her breath away, and she slipped her hand down between her legs. Her breath caught at the feel of herself, the need that she'd usually let someone else take care of, the itch that was somehow never quite scratched even with the thrill of the chase and the buzz of the conquest. Underneath it all was the feel of her; just her, just Kendra Davis alone on her own, and honesty seemed an easier thing in the wee hours. The feel of her coupled with the thoughts that made her need, made her open and soft and achy, were all thoughts that involved being angry and wet and pulled up tight, even for only a moment, against an angry, wet Garrett Thorne. As she replayed the event in her head, she let herself remember the shape of him, then she turned and twisted the memory until, when they burst from the water, no one on shore noticed them there together in the lake.

No one noticed that Garrett Thorne was kissing her. And certainly no one could see what their hands were doing under the water, his shoving at her shorts, hers busy with his fly, yanking and tugging until she could feel him hard and warm and pressing anxiously toward her.

No one could see his tentative exploration with anxious fingers, opening her, spreading her. No one could see her guiding him home, up deep inside her to scratch that itch. And certainly no one could see him cup her bottom and lift her, pull her tight to him, coax her to wrap her legs around him.

No one could feel the friction and no one could see the rocking and pressing of their bodies, tightening and gripping and forcing the breath from each other. And no one could hear their quiet gasps and cries and groans as they came together, came together just like the lovers in Tess Delaney's novels, came together nearly drowning each other in power of their orgasms.

Kendra was alone when her orgasm snaked up her spine and trembled through her nervous system like leaves rustled by a breeze, and she was probably way too far gone to be thinking straight. Maybe she was even already asleep and she only dreamed the calling of Garrett's name. And anyway, it was just a fantasy, wasn't it, and everyone had them. She'd had fantasies about her dentist, for God's sake. Why not have fantasies about Garrett Thorne?

Chapter Four

Garrett answered his BlackBerry with a growl. 'This had better be good news, Don. Time's running out. And if that happens, things will get very ugly.'

'I'm fine, Garrett. Thanks for asking. How are you?'

Garrett growled louder.

Then Don was on his usual spiel about his difficult task, the same spiel Garrett had been hearing for three weeks now. 'It's not that easy to find someone who can act and keep your secret and knows enough about Tess and her books to go in front of an audience if need be and speak like Tess Delaney. I mean, this is a tall order.'

'Goddamn it, Don, I don't want to hear it! We barely have a week. I want to hear that you've found someone to be Tess, and I want to hear it now, or I promise you, Romancine can sue my balls off if they want to, but they'll still wish they'd left well enough alone.'

He could hear Don shuffling papers and clicking computer keys on the other end of the phone. 'There's only one way I could see to deal with this situation, and it's something I never thought I'd have to do, but I'm going to have to hand you over to the competition.'

'What the hell are you talking about?'

Don puffed a sigh into the phone. 'You ever hear of the Ryde Agency?'

'No. Should I have?'

'Not unless you're in Hollywood, and even then probably not. The Ryde Agency is the epitome of discretion in the PR world. They were the new kid on the block. We never expected them to be real competition. They came out of nowhere, and

28

the next thing we knew, they were kicking ass – ours, most of the time. They've handled all kinds of nasty PR problems for the rich and famous. You remember the accusations against Devon Barnet a few years ago?'

'What accusations? As far as I know Devon Barnet has a shining reputation, and in the past couple of years he only has to do a cameo in a film and that film's a shoo-in for an Oscar nomination.'

'Exactly,' Don said. 'K. Ryde almost single-handedly turned Barnet's career around. Very few people know this. I only know it because, as I said, the Ryde Agency is the competition, and when K. Ryde agreed to take on Barnet personally, well, the Bachman agency didn't stand a chance.

'It's a miracle I was able to get hold of him, actually. I took a chance with an old email address. K. Ryde is almost as elusive as Tess Delaney, but when the rich and famous have a PR disaster they need taken care of discreetly, it's the Ryde Agency they go to. To this day Barnet won't say a word about K. Ryde, only that Ryde's the best, that Ryde's a genius. There are no photos of them together, no text or email trails, no sightings, and God knows the paparazzi tried.

'Apparently K. Ryde no longer has much involvement in the business. They say he's retired. Maybe he's a romance fan. I don't know. But for Tess Delaney, he's willing to do what he can.'

'Look, I don't care if you've got to call God out of retirement,' Garrett said. 'I don't want to out Tess, so what can this Ryde fellow do for me?'

'Turns out he has contact with a woman who loves Tess Delaney novels, who happens to live close to the Portland area, and who's dying to meet Tess Delaney and do whatever Tess needs. Of course I didn't tell Ryde the details; just told him what we needed, and that we needed the woman yesterday.'

Garrett sat up on the edge of his chair and wiped a suddenly sweaty palm against his jeans. 'And?'

'I told Ryde that there would have to be some coaching to make sure the woman could do what Tess needed her for and that this was top, top secret.'

'Go on.'

'Well,' Don said. 'I talked to the woman last night extensively, and if she can't be your Tess Delaney, I don't know who can. If you pull up your email, I've sent you her address. You set the time, and she's yours.'

With fingers none too steady on the keys, Garrett pulled up his email and, sure enough, there was a message from Don with the address for a Kay Lake. 'Got it,' he said. Then he hung up and emailed the woman he hoped would save his bacon.

Dear Ms. Lake,

Ms. Delaney has agreed to interview you for the position. Can you meet tomorrow at 2 p.m. at the Pneuma Annex? Suite 3B.

Best wishes,

Gary Rose

Secretary to Tess Delaney

He sent the message off. It was brief. He'd found that brief was always better when keeping a secret was essential. Even when Tess was quoted in press releases, it was always very brief, very Garbo-ish. It wasn't the first time he'd used one of the Pneuma Annex offices for official Tess Delaney business and, though Ellis grumbled about it, he always kept suite 3B open for him. And Garrett had always used the name Gary Rose for Tess's secretary. Somehow it seemed right that Tess should have a male secretary. It was really only a way to give Tess Delaney and Garrett Thorne one more level of separation to protect their anonymity. He'd never had to meet anyone face to face before. He wondered if he should find someone to be Gary Rose this time too, but then that was another complication he didn't need, and time was quickly running out. Besides, if he didn't trust Don's opinion on his future female self, he sure as hell wasn't going to trust someone he'd hired off the street. After all, he was screening for the perfect Tess Delaney.

Almost immediately the response came back.

Dear Mr. Rose,

Tomorrow at 2.00 is fine for me. I look forward to it.

All the best,
Kay Lake

For a long time Garrett stared at the screen. He hoped this Ryde Agency was as good as Don said and that they truly had found him the right Tess Delaney. He was furious at being put in this position. Right now, he just wanted it all behind him, Golden Kiss nomination or not. He picked up a fountain pen and began to write on the back of a sheet of his waste paper again.

I'm not comfortable with any of what's going on. There's so little time to prepare. I don't know who Kay Lake is, and that makes me really nervous. It makes me nervous that she'll know my secret, it makes me nervous that the myth and the reality of Tess Delaney are about to collide in a very dangerous way.

But when I think about it, I suppose I've never really pictured Tess as anything but dangerous. Who could I ever tell that Tess writes my soul in a way I never could do it myself when I was younger and writing testosterone-laced shoot-'em-ups? I would have rather been the King of the Thriller. That was my dream. Then Tess shoved her way into my life, and instead, I'm the Queen of Romance. How the hell did that happen?

And another thing, this Kay Lake, will I begin to think of her as Tess Delaney? Will she convince me that the figment of my imagination who splintered and became my other half lives and breathes manifest in her body? Jesus, that's too strange to even think about. More likely she'll always be an actress to me. Well, I'm hoping after the award ceremony I can retire Tess back to her reclusive life and swear Ms. Lake to secrecy on the life of her first born.

But it'll never be the same again, will it? Someone else will know my secret, Tess's secret, and the way I picture Tess Delaney in my head will forever be tainted by Kay Lake's version of Tess.

He laid the pen aside and closed down his computer. Tonight was the night he'd be watching Amy dance the Sleeping Beauty if he'd made the trip to New York. It was over between them. He knew that. He'd known it when he'd gone

31

back to her the last time. He didn't deal well with endings, and now it felt like he was losing Tess too. He opened the French doors and moved onto the balcony. 'She doesn't exist,' he said out loud. 'She never has.' Someone a little less neurotic than he was would have let it go a long time ago. But sometimes it was easier being Tess Delaney than it was being Garrett Thorne.

He turned and went back into the house, closing the doors behind him. Tess Delaney. He had never assigned her a real physicality. In his mind's eye, she'd never looked like Amy or any of his other lovers. Strange that he had always been happy with her being physically undefined, but then she wrote the stories, she wasn't in the stories. Her boundaries were far more permeable than those of the heroines she created or those of the women he'd loved.

Kendra had spent the better part of the morning trying to find any last-minute information she could about Tess Delaney. There were rumours all right, lots of rumours. They seemed to surface and rise every time Tess released a novel, then fade into the background until there was another new release. But beyond the rumours, it seemed no one really knew anything about Tess Delaney. That made it all the more exciting for her to be the first to have contact with the elusive woman. Oh, she was sure there would be strict protocol, non-disclosure and who knew what other measures set in place to protect the woman's identity, but that didn't matter. She wasn't interested in sharing her experience of Tess Delaney with anyone. That would ruin it, actually. She just wanted to meet the woman, see what she was really like.

Though she could find nothing of any real value about Tess Delaney. She was pretty sure her knowledge of the woman's novels would be invaluable. She'd read once that all novels, in some way, were about their authors. She wondered if that meant Tess had lots of passionate lovers or only wished she did. She wondered if that meant Tess was a woman totally out of touch with reality, or if it meant that, just like Kendra, Tess wrote the life she didn't really believe in, but she loved to fantasize about. Kendra had never fantasized about romance –

ever. At least, not until she picked up her first Tess Delaney novel. She was never really sure if she should praise the woman for that or curse her. The jury was still out. One thing was for certain, the woman and her romantic notions had played havoc with Kendra's sex life. She'd read every novel Tess had ever written, and most of them more than once. She had them all on Kindle as well as in pristine hardback copies on her shelf at home. A few she even had in tattered, dog-eared paperback as well. She had played some of the most powerful passages over and over in her head, her heart racing with an ache she didn't want, and yet didn't want to be without now that she had it. Now that she'd felt it. Problem was, now that she had felt it, she didn't really know what to do with it. She couldn't bring herself to talk to Dee about it, though she probably should, since Dee was the one who would know about real romance. And what could she say to her that didn't sound totally silly and adolescent?

But Tess Delaney didn't sound silly or adolescent, and she would soon be set to find out why that was. She pretty much knew the job with Tess was hers. If Bachman had called her in for help, then it was hers. Kendra didn't get where she was in the PR world without a very finely honed attention to detail, and a scalpel-sharp memory; that, and a deliver or die attitude that always left her clients more than 100 per cent satisfied.

She hadn't had a chance to talk to Dee about the meeting because Dee was off in Paris on business, and though she wouldn't have minded picking Ellis's brain about his knowledge of Tess Delaney, he was in Spain. And she wouldn't give Garrett the satisfaction. Besides, she was pretty sure he wouldn't help her anyway. Clearly he hated her. Well, she didn't like him much either.

She flipped through her closet until she found the rose-pink linen suit that looked romantic and yet very chic and professional. It wasn't exactly sexy, but it definitely wasn't unsexy either. With a blouse and matching heels just a few shades darker and a string of freshwater pearls, she figured she looked like the perfect assistant to a romance writer. As she added the final pins to the French knot in which she wore her hair, she felt the change she always felt when K. Ryde took control. Though, in all honesty, K. Ryde never made public appearances. This time it was Kay Lake who would take the lead role representing the Ryde Agency, and she was an expert at enthralling an audience, even if that audience were only a world-famous romance writer and her secretary. By the end of the day, Kendra Davis fully intended to be in the employ of the reclusive, mysterious, much whispered about, much admired Tess Delaney. She slipped into her heels, then gave a turn in front of the full-length mirror. God, she'd forgot how much she loved the rush of adrenaline that always accompanied the challenge offered by a difficult client. She could hardly wait.

Chapter Five

Kendra had always loved the Pneuma Complex. It was one of the most beautifully designed, environmentally friendly work spaces she had ever seen. She always felt as though she was walking in botanical gardens when she visited. The Pneuma Building housed Ellison Thorne's cutting-edge company, Pneuma, Inc., the company Dee now helped him run. The Pneuma Annex provided office space for companies with a similar mind set to Pneuma Inc., as well as space for short-term rentals. The annex's green, economical design was from the fabulous mind of Wade Crittenden, the creative force behind Pneuma Inc., which meant office space could be offered for less money than similar sites. It also meant those who leased offices in the annex enjoyed the PR boost that came from being in an environmentally friendly building.

Sites in the Pneuma Annex were coveted and hard to come by, and Kendra was pleased that Tess Delaney had an office there. Though she was pretty sure the woman hardly ever occupied it. She was hoping today would be the exception. Certainly, if the desperation in Don Bachman's emails and their discussion on the phone were any indication, she'd be meeting the woman in person.

She did a quick touch-up of her make-up and hair in the restroom of the annex's sunny atrium before she made her way to Tess Delaney's office.

The recessed door of Suite 3B reminded Kendra of a grotto hidden away in the thick foliage of ferns and strange vining plants. A brass plaque to the right of the door read *Gary Rose* in bold sans serif script. Kendra paused to straighten her jacket one last time, then she hoisted her bag neatly onto one shoulder and gave a crisp rap on the door.

She waited.

When there was no answer, she knocked again. And when there was still no answer, she cracked open the door and stuck her head inside. There was a small waiting room decorated in clean lines and Zen colours, fronted by a desk, to the right of which was another door. Kendra's pulse jumped. Was the woman herself behind that door? And where was the secretary? Certainly for someone who guarded her privacy so fiercely, having the secretary as the vanguard was essential. Where was Mr. Rose?

She cleared her throat loudly and stood in front of the desk, shifting from foot to foot. It wouldn't do for Tess Delaney to think she'd been late. She paced the length of the waiting room a couple of times, then made an executive decision and knocked gently on the door by the desk.

Nothing.

Had she been stood up? Had Tess Delaney got cold feet? Quickly she checked her iPhone to see if she'd had any last-minute messages from Gary Rose or Don Bachman. But there was nothing. She shoved it back into her bag, cleared her throat a little louder this time, and was just getting ready to knock a little harder when the door burst open and she found herself almost nose to nose with Garrett Thorne.

'What the hell are you doing here?' they both said at the same time.

Then he grabbed her by the arm, hauled her into the office, and closed the door behind them. 'I'll ask you again,' he said between barely parted lips, his chest rising and falling like he'd just run a fast mile. 'What are you doing here?'

'What do you mean what am *I* doing here? What are *you* doing here?'

'Look,' he said, glancing down at his watch nervously. 'I'm expecting someone at any minute now, Kendra. I don't know how the hell you got here or what you want, but you have to leave. Now.' He tried to push her back out of the door, but she turned on him and glared up at him. 'There must be a mistake. I have an appointment with Gary Rose, set up by Donald

Bachman, from the Bachman Agency, and if this is some kind of a joke, it's not funny.'

'Hold it, hold it.' He ran a hand through his hair and the way it fell over one eye would have made her forget about why she was here if the reason had been a little less important. 'Don sent you?'

'You know Don Bachman,' she said.

'Of course I know him, he's my ...' The laser stare they gave each other probably would have been deadly if they hadn't cancelled each other out. 'Jesus, Kendra. You're ... You're not ...'

She held his gaze. 'I'm here to see Tess Delaney.' She glanced around the room, but there was no one else there. 'Where is she?'

'You're the one Don chose for the job?' He stepped back and shook his head further mussing his bedroom hair. 'That can't be right. That can't possibly be right. He promised me that the Ryde Agency never failed. He promised me that Ryde had found me just the perfect person for the job. He promised me that –'

Suddenly she felt like the floor was tilting, and her heart raced. 'Wait a minute, he promised you? *You*?' She stepped back and grabbed at the door knob to steady herself. 'There has to be some mistake.'

Her denial was mirrored by his own. 'Don said the Ryde Agency was the best. Don said Ryde would send me the perfect person, and then Ryde sends you? Is this a joke, is this the man's idea of a joke?'

Kendra took a deep breath and stepped forward, using all of her self-control to keep from punching the jerk. 'I am K. Ryde, you asshole, and you're a fine one to talk to me about a joke. Now, what the hell is going on and where's Tess Delaney?'

It was Garrett's turn to step forward, once again nearly nose to nose with Kendra, his breath hot on her cheek. 'You're looking at her, and if you tell anyone, I swear to you I'll –'

'No! No fucking way can you be Tess Delaney!' She pushed past him and paced like a trapped animal in front of his desk. 'Tess Delaney's a woman. You're not.' He didn't move, but just stood glaring at her, looking as though his chest were about to explode from his efforts to breath. 'She writes novels. You don't do anything.' She wasn't sure but what there might be steam coming out his ears. He was furious. Well, so the hell was she. 'She's famous because of her work. You're famous because of your brother.'

She turned on him. 'What was Tess Delaney's fourth novel?'

'*Golden Moments*,' he replied instantly. 'About Terri Sorenson, a woman with a rare form of cancer, and Del Hendricks, the doctor who cures her.' Before she could respond, he shot back another question. 'Who's Turk Bishop?'

'A washed-up prize fighter who falls in love with his manager's niece, Andrea Livingston, one of the few successful female boxing managers. From Tess's seventh book, *TKO*.'

'Who was terrified of elevators?' Garrett said, moving back to the nose-to-nose, Mexican stand-off position.

'Delilah Benton from *High Flyers*. She'd been trapped in one alone for 12 hours as a little girl.' She shoved her hands onto her hips and glared at him. 'Deke Arnold's drink of choice?

'Gin martini made with Bombay Sapphire,' he said. 'Sarah Masters' biggest weakness?'

'Lapsang Souchang tea and chocolate éclairs from Finnegan's Bakery.'

'Jesus!' They both spoke at the same time, then turned and paced in opposite directions.

'Why?' he asked, sounding like she had just murdered his favourite pet.

'What do you mean, why? Because I admire the woman's work.' She shook her head and rubbed her eyes. 'Admired the woman's work, and I'm the best in my field. I jumped at the chance to work for her … Well, who I thought she was.'

Their pacing became synchronized.

'You mean to tell me Kendra Davis, the queen of bad temper, reads romance novels?'

'You mean to tell me Garrett Thorne, the epitome of ambition-free living, writes romance novels?'

'And just what did you think you were going to do for me … For Tess? Throw drinks at her? Slap her around? Try to drown her?'

Once again they found themselves nose to nose, and Kendra couldn't believe the sense of loss she felt, the sense of rage that this man had, in less than five minutes, destroyed her hero. And damn, she was furious! She was actually fighting back tears. How could she have let the bastard reduce her to this? 'Fuck you.' Her voice was little more than a whisper. 'Tell Bachman to find someone else.' She shrugged her bag up her shoulder, turned on her heels, and headed for the door.

'Wait.' He grabbed her by the arm, more gently than she would have expected, and swung her around to face him. The look on his face was desperate, a look K. Ryde had seen often. Suddenly, he struggled to hold her gaze. 'Are you as good as Don says you are?'

For a second her anger flared, but the look on his face was earnest, and she held her tongue. 'Would I be here if I weren't?'

He studied her unabashedly for a moment, and she returned the favour.

'There isn't time for Don to find someone else.' He gave a desperate glance around the room and shook his head. 'I need help now.'

If there had been even the least hint of subterfuge, she would have punched him hard and left. But she'd made a living at reading people. The man was desperate. K. Ryde came to the forefront. She took a deep breath. 'All right. Tell me what you need.'

Instead of moving behind the desk, he guided her to a sand-coloured sofa flanked by a small woodland of tall plants, then he sat down on the edge of a matching chair facing her, hands folded in his lap, leaning forward into her gaze. 'I need you to be Tess Delaney for me.'

She blinked twice. 'You what?'

'I need you to be Tess Delaney.'

A pot of strong coffee and two cans of Diet Pepsi later, neither of them had moved, and Kendra had to admit that, in spite of the nervous riot of unrest raging in her stomach, in spite of the cold sweat breaking on the back of her neck at the very thought of putting herself out there again in such a public way, she was more intrigued than she had been in her whole life.

He looked like a nervous schoolboy about to ask a girl out for the first time, and she had to admit she sort of liked that look on the arrogant face of Garrett Thorne – er – Tess Delaney. 'What do you think? Can you do it on such short notice?'

She should have told him no. This was so not what she expected Tess to require of her. There were reasons, good reasons for telling him no, not the least of which was that the idea itself was insane. No doubt that's why it intrigued her. Instead, she found herself saying, almost as though her voice had ignored the rage of nerves and the fears and the bad memories and acted unilaterally, 'Of course I can do it. Don wouldn't have called me if I couldn't.' What the hell was the matter with her? She didn't need to impress Garrett Thorne. She didn't care what he thought about her. She was just about to tell him that, though she could do it, she would have to turn him down.

And then he said, 'You do have a temper.'

She smiled at the thought that he might be just a little intimidated by her. 'Kendra Davis has a temper,' she said. 'K. Ryde simply does what she has to do to get the job done. If you need me to be Tess Delaney for the Golden Kiss Awards, well, I'm up for the challenge.' No, she wasn't! What the hell was she talking about? She should be running away now! She didn't like Garrett Thorne. Let him deal with his own mess. This was not something she should get involved with. It was too much deception. That she could handle. But it was way too public a situation for her to deal with, way too soon. She couldn't guarantee how she would react, she couldn't guarantee if she could keep the past in the past and just do her job. It wasn't fair to him. It wasn't fair to Tess. It wasn't fair to anyone, and besides, the very thought of what would be involved in such a ruse scared the hell out of her.

Just when she was about to back-pedal, just when she was about to extricate herself from a situation that she really wasn't ready for, he breathed a huge sigh of relief and moved onto the sofa next to her. 'Good, then we'll have to get our stories straight. We'll have to create a life and hobbies and a past and the whole nine yards for Tess, and we'll both have to know it.'

And he had her. She knew it. Once he'd actually started scheming, once her mind had actually latched on to thoughts of how they could make it work, he had her. She was in. She would be his Tess Delaney. Besides, the past was the past. The only way to shake it off was to move forward. She breathed a sigh of her own and scooted closer on the sofa.

'No, Garrett, we don't both have to know it. You're my date. You can know relatively little about me. And Tess, being the recluse that she is, isn't likely to give very much away even if she's up on stage. All you have to do is trust me enough to let me lead the way.'

'But you don't know Tess like I do, and there's so little time.'

She reached out and touched his arm, feeling the tension pass up through his body under her hand. 'Listen to me, Garrett, the less everyone knows about the Tess you see in your head, the better. It's really fairly simple. We go to the banquet and, with any luck, we'll have to do nothing more than smile and nod, maybe have a few microphones shoved in our faces, and I'll make short, evasive answers. We'll sit through the meal smiling and nodding, then make our escape at the earliest possible moment.'

'What if someone follows us?'

'They won't. Trust me, I'll make sure they don't. Tess is not the first celeb I've had to keep away from the press, Garrett. It'll be all right.'

He didn't look like he believed her, but she'd seen that look before too.

He made a weak attempt to laugh, then he stood and moved to look out the window with his broad back to her. 'Who'd have thought this would happen? Who'd have thought I'd end up depending on you?'

She bristled but calmed herself. 'Who'd have thought Garrett Thorne was Tess Delaney?'

He turned so quickly that he nearly knocked over one of the potted ferns in his effort. 'Don't say that. Don't ever say that out loud.'

'All right.' She sat with her hands folded around a half empty Diet Pepsi can and watched as he paced again. 'Mind if I ask why not?'

'You'll laugh,' he said, dropping back onto the sofa next to her.

'Try me.'

'It's just that saying I'm her, or she's me … Well, it feels like it'll jinx it all somehow. I know that sounds stupid, but it just feels that way.'

'Doesn't sound stupid at all,' she said. 'I'm astounded you've been able to keep her a secret all this time, that you've been able to keep the world thinking you're living the life of luxury off your brother's money. How have you managed to get Ellis to agree with this arrangement? I can't imagine he's pleased with it.'

'He didn't know for a long time. Then he found out.'

'How?'

A light blush crawled up Garrett's throat, and she had to admit he was sexy when he was wrong-footed. 'Rumors got out that he was supporting me.'

'Oh?'

He shrugged. 'I might have started them. Possibly. And it really wasn't that hard for people to believe. No one knew who Tess Delaney was, and I had no visible means of support. I mean, I couldn't really do a part-time job and write like I needed to to keep up with the demand for Tess's books.'

'It couldn't have been that easy,' she said.

'It wasn't as hard as you think.' She thought she saw pain cross his face, but wasn't certain. He straightened his jacket and was suddenly all business. 'We've only got a week. I'm willing to do what we have to. I don't want Tess outed. Are we clear?'

'Very clear,' she said. She pulled out her iPhone and began

to make notes. 'I'll get Don Bachman to send me all the information about the event along with any other relevant details. Then you send me anything else you think I need to know, I don't care how minute. If you think it's important, then it probably is.'

'What if there are questions about Tess's work?' he asked.

'Trust me, Tess Delaney making her first public appearance on the arm of the enigmatic Garrett Thorne will be such a sensation that no one will be thinking about Tess's work. Besides, I have a great memory. I promise no one will stump me if they do ask.'

She looked down at her watch. 'I've got to go, Garrett. There's a lot to be done, and I'm a perfectionist. If you need to get in touch with K. Ryde, I've just emailed an address to Gary Rose. Otherwise you already have Kay Lake's email.' She stood, and he walked her to the door. 'I'll email you as soon as I have everything sorted.'

'What if I want to get in touch with plain old Kendra Davis?' he said.

'Now, why would Garrett Thorne want to get in touch with Kendra Davis?' She offered him a smile that was probably a little more of a smirk than she intended. 'After all, they hate each other, remember?'

Once she was out of the office, she made a mad dash for the restroom in the main reception area. She managed to lock herself in a cubicle before the shakes began. She collapsed against the wall, sliding down it until she was seated on the floor breathing in and out, in and out, trying to slow the mad hammering rage of her heart. Was she crazy? Was she out of her mind? She should go right back in there and tell Garrett no. No way could she do this thing. No way should she even think about doing this thing. Not now, not ever! Not ever again. Hadn't she learned her lesson? Hadn't she paid in spades for her quiet life, and here she was about to go public in the biggest possible way. She couldn't. She just couldn't. She was sorry for Garrett, but she couldn't run the risk. She couldn't put herself through it all again.

For a long time she sat on the floor of the cubicle looking

up at the ceiling through a mist of tears that was brought on by the first panic attack she'd had in a long time now. But, as her mind cleared, logic once again took over. What had happened in Santa Monica was the past. It couldn't hurt her now. She could live her life in the open again. She could do whatever she wanted. And until she did step outside the little cosy comfort zone she had created for herself here in Portland with Dee and Harris, how could she ever expect to truly get over the past? She'd stopped seeing the psychologist three months ago, but she knew that getting back on the horse was a big part of the healing process. And really there was no denying that playing Tess Delaney for Garrett Thorne was by far the most intriguing prospect she'd had in a very long time, even when she was head of the Ryde Agency, working with the stars.

By the time she was able to stand again and had found her way out of the cubicle to freshen her make-up she had convinced herself that being Tess Delaney for Garrett Thorne might be the best thing that could happen to her right now. It would be interesting work, challenging work, work that might be very healing. She could help Garrett keep Tess's identity secret while at the same time helping herself back into a world that was a little less neurotic.

Yes, she was disappointed there would be no wildly feminine romance author flouncing around her lush Victorian house, laughing wickedly at Kendra's dry wit and sharp questions. But how could she not be intrigued? All of those stories that gripped her, all of those stories that seemed to come straight from the core of everything that was powerful and vulnerable and mysterious and wild and female, all of those stories about the magnetic draw between the sexes had actually been written by a man, and one who was pretty much a jerk at that. It was the kind of challenge K. Ryde could never resist. By the time she got to the parking lot and was securely belted into the Mustang, she was already making a list in her head of things that had to be done to prepare both Tess Delaney and her bad boy date for the glitz and the glam, and for the subterfuge of the Golden Kiss Awards.

Chapter Six

Garrett went straight home from the Pneuma Annex. His head was reeling. How could anyone as explosive and impulsive as Kendra Davis be the queen of PR, and how the hell could she possibly pull off what had to happen to make sure Tess didn't get outed?

By the time he got home, just as she'd promised, he found an email address, a cell phone number, and a list of questions for him to answer that would help her determine the best way to approach her representation of Tess Delaney. He found the whole professional demeanour of the email to be irritating. This was the woman who had pushed him in the lake at his brother's engagement party. This was the woman whose powerful right arm, he was convinced, could knock out a bull moose if she was angry enough. She was volatile, unpredictable and, from all outward appearances, just as unemployed as he was. And if she held a grudge over what he and Stacie had inadvertently done to Ellis and Dee that had nearly ruined their relationship and their careers, then he was so fucked. Yet what choice did he have? Don believed this woman was his only hope, and the email he'd received from him even before he left the Pneuma Annex was just more evidence of his faith in Kendra Davis – er – K. Ryde.

The emails to Garrett weren't signed K. Ryde. They were signed Kay Lake. God it was all so confusing. What was he supposed to call her? Who the hell was she really? He changed into jeans and a T-shirt, opened a beer, and settled in at the computer. He'd barely thought about the deadline for *Texas Fire*. The stress of Tess's imminent outage weighed so heavily that writing anything serious had been next to impossible. And that wasn't likely to change until after the Golden Kiss Awards were safely behind him, and he and Tess could go back to their quiet life.

With a start, he realized the always nebulous picture of Tess Delaney he held in his head wasn't so nebulous any more. The face smiling back at him was now Kendra Davis's face. And the woman standing beside his desk in his mind's eye, whispering the story in his ear, was dripping wet. Baby blue bikini top and satin shorts clung revealingly to curves that were athletic and muscular but outrageously feminine. Her nipples beaded heavily beneath the wet top and the shorts hugged the rounded hillocks of her bottom. There were no panty lines. Oh yes, he'd noticed that when she'd turned to walk away from him the other day at the lake. By that time he was doing his best to hide the rise of his cock that had been so stunning and had happened so fast it had completely taken him by surprise. The woman was a bitch, he reminded himself. And whatever else she might be, she was most definitely not his Tess Delaney. Well, at least for no longer than it took her to play the role, for no longer than it took her to make sure that Tess's true identity was protected. And if she betrayed him, if this was her way of getting revenge … He didn't want to think about that. He couldn't. He had no choice, and frankly the woman in his imagination, the luscious wet Kendra Davis, offering him a full-lipped pout, had his complete attention. The longer she stood there, in his imagination, watching him work, the more transparent her clothing became, and the more transparent her clothing became, the more uncomfortable the front of his jeans became.

He couldn't recall his thoughts of Tess ever being truly sexual. She was him, for Chrissake! He'd never wanted to date her. He'd never wanted to fuck her. And if Tess Delaney had Kendra Davis's face – not to mention her body – and he started really seeing her that way in his head, he was so screwed!

'The woman's a bitch,' he said out loud. But as he said it, he was already busy fumbling with his zipper. As he said it he pictured her all dressed up for business. Even all professional and ready to work, she looked like something he'd like to eat with a cherry on top. He'd like to start right at her ankles, just above those pink stilettos, and work his way on up, tongue first, taking the middle path, all the way up those endless legs of hers to what was just barely hidden by her wet shorts, what looked luscious enough to keep him in very filthy thoughts for a long time to come. And it was already clear exactly where those filthy thoughts were leading. He shoved back from the desk and headed for the bathroom jeans open, boxers shoved low around his hips, stroking as he went.

Later, when he returned to his study, there was another email from Kay Lake.

Mr. Rose,

I'm ready to meet with you tomorrow. I'll need several hours of your time, at your convenience.

Sincerely,

Kay Lake

It chafed, volatile Kendra Davis emailing him all business-like and professional. He ground his teeth and emailed back.

Ms. Lake,

Shall we say 2.00 again?

Then he gave her his home address. He didn't like the idea of doing what they had to do in the annex of his brother's business, especially now he knew who she really was. He hoped that the whole distasteful situation could be kept secret as much as possible. Though he figured Dee and Ellis would ultimately have to know, he hoped he'd be able to keep it from Stacie. He wanted no more loose ends than absolutely necessary. If all went well, by the time the banquet was over, Tess Delaney could go happily back into hiding and he and Kay Lake or Kendra Davis could shake hands and never have to speak to each other again.

Don had dropped a quick text that he'd had an email from K. Ryde saying the meeting had gone well and the situation was being dealt with. Garrett wrote back a terse answer basically agreeing but not giving anything away. The less anyone knew the better. It was embarrassing, really. The woman he couldn't even think about without getting both angry and stiff was going to be Tess Delaney for an event that could turn out to be detrimental to Tess's career.

Within minutes, Kendra emailed back confirming their appointment.

Garrett had half hoped she would be at least a little bit late, but the professional PR version of Kendra Davis was right on time. She was dressed in black trousers and a light summer blazer over a silky white blouse that draped her body like its only purpose was to caress her. He felt an irrational stab of jealousy as she slipped out of the jacket and handed it over for him to hang. They were barely seated, her with her Diet Pepsi and him with his coffee, before she pulled out her iPad. 'Did you sleep well?' she asked without looking up from what she was doing. Her lips curled into a hint of a smile. 'You should sleep better now that I'm on the job.'

He forced a smile. 'I'm certainly glad one of us is confident.'

This time she looked up at him, and the smile she offered, if he wasn't mistaking, was reassuring. 'It's natural for you to be nervous about the situation and I know we're cutting it close to the wire, but believe me when I say I've handled a lot worse.'

'Why?' he said.

She blinked and the smile faded. He was sorry to see it go. 'Why what?'

'Why are you doing this? I know how you feel about me.'

She laid aside the iPad and scooted forward on the sofa. 'Garrett, this isn't personal. This is my job, and I really admire Tess Delaney and her body of work.' He thought he could see a slight blush tingeing her cheeks. 'I figured you could see that yesterday with my extensive knowledge of her novels.'

That did give him a sense of satisfaction.

'Besides,' she added, 'I really am the best in my field.'

'That's good. That's great,' he said. And it was; he knew it was. But he couldn't help feeling just a little peeved that she could turn it all on and off as though she had no feelings one way or another. He'd have never thought it possible, but he missed her anger. At least when she was angry he knew what he was up against, and why. Plus, it was hot. There, he'd actually admitted it. She was hot when she was angry. Not that she wasn't hot now too, but now it felt like she'd put some sort of plexi-glass wall between them. He forced his attention back to what she was saying.

'I've taken care of the limos to get us there and back.'

'Limos?'

She nodded. 'There'll be four, two each way. One we'll be in and one we won't. Just a distraction.'

'A distraction. Right.'

He listened carefully as her brilliant plan unfolded with all the careful arrangements and attention to detail. And then she told him his role in the plan. 'I know you have no problem looking rakish and getting the attention of the opposite sex, and we'll be counting on that Friday night.'

He burnt his tongue on his coffee. 'Excuse me.'

'Garrett, everyone knows who you are and what your reputation is. You've counted on that for a long time to distract people from the truth, so now we're going to count on it some more. You are going to be stunning and charming and every woman there, and every woman watching you on television, is going to want you.'

He braced himself for the insult that didn't come. Instead, she continued, 'And Tess is going to be totally enthralled with you, which will give the press something else to focus on rather than her appearing out of nowhere. Everyone loves a love story, right? Especially if there's a hint of scandal with it. And the very involvement of Garrett Thorne will give that hint and then some.'

He wiped unusually sweaty hands on his jeans. 'You're going to be totally enthralled with me?'

She shook her head and a wisp of a smile brushed her lips. 'Tess Delaney is going to be totally enthralled with you. You're her date, Garrett, and the more into each other we appear to be the more attention will be drawn away from Tess Delaney.'

'You really believe that?' Garrett said. He figured he could very easily pretend to be into Kendra Davis. He just wasn't sure how safe it would be.

'If I didn't believe that, then we'd be doing something different. Garrett, you have to trust me.' She ran a hand through her hair. This time she wore it loose around her shoulders. It looked silky and golden, and it was hard for him not to want to follow suit. 'Look, I know you're having trouble getting past the rough relationship we've had so far, and I can certainly understand that. But I'm a professional, and I would have never taken this job if I didn't believe we could work together.'

'You thought you'd be working with Tess Delaney,' he said.

'I am working with Tess Delaney.'

He scrubbed his hands over his face. 'God, it's all so confusing.'

She patted his arm. 'Don't worry. It'll all be over by this time Saturday, and Tess can go back to keeping her private life private.'

For a second the two sat in silence, him staring down into his half empty coffee cup, her taking notes on her iPad. At last she spoke. 'Mind if I ask you a personal question?'

He shifted uneasily. 'You can ask.'

She lay the iPad aside and smiled up at him. 'Why don't you want anyone to know that you're Tess ...?' She backtracked. 'Why don't you want anyone to know your relationship to Tess Delaney? I mean, it's got to be tough to know what people are saying and thinking behind your back when you know none of it's true.'

'Just because I'm gainfully employed doesn't make me a hero, Kendra. It's better this way, for Tess to take the credit. Besides, I get a much more intimate view of the world when no one takes Garrett Thorne too seriously.'

She held his gaze, and he wasn't sure what happened, or how, but suddenly there was no doubt it was Kendra Davis's eyes he was looking into, and it was like looking into fire. 'Oh, I take you seriously, Garrett. Believe me I do.'

The sudden urge to kiss her was visceral, almost overwhelming, and he might have very well done it if she hadn't broadsided him with a question that took him almost as much by surprise as her slap had. 'Garrett, I need to know what you want me to say if Tess wins the Golden Kiss. After all I'll be taking kudos for you … For the two of you.'

Garrett scratched the stubble on his chin. 'Honestly, I don't think there's any chance of that happening. Did you see the names of the authors Tess is up against?'

'I did, yes.'

'They don't mean anything to you? I mean, they're huge. They're the biggest names in the business.'

She blinked. 'Oh, I know that. I've researched them all, and I'll be very familiar with their work by Friday night.' She offered him a self-deprecating smile. 'I never read romance before Tess Delaney, and she's the only one I've read until now.' Before he could say anything, before he could even let his feelings about that fact sink in, she continued. 'I've researched the other four authors you're up against well enough to know that your chance is as good as anyone else's.'

There was no disguising the sense of pride he felt at Kendra Davis actually believing Tess might win the Golden Kiss, but really, how well did she know the business? 'Thanks,' he said, 'but I won't win, so we don't have to worry about that, and if we do, well, you can say whatever you want.'

She cocked her head and looked at him in a way that made him think she was expecting to find something, something he was hiding. But just when he was beginning to feel defensive, she shoved her iPad back into her bag and stood.

'All right then. That's all I need today.'

'Wait a minute,' he said, following her to the door. 'Don't we need to – I don't know – practice? I mean, I barely know you and you said we need to be comfortable with each other.'

She turned so quickly he nearly ran into her. 'You don't have to be comfortable with Kendra Davis, Garrett. You have to be comfortable with Tess Delaney, and I promise you will be.' She looked up at him with a smile that might have been teasing, might have been a smirk. Whichever it was, the small alcove where they now stood suddenly seemed even tighter fitting than it actually was. 'If it'll help,' she said, 'you can kiss me goodbye.'

'That's not very professional,' he managed, feeling like the breath had been squeezed out of him as he fumbled to help her into her jacket.

Her smile was warm, reassuring. 'Actually, in our case it's very professional.' She rose on her toes and brushed a kiss across his lips. 'Very professional indeed.'

And before she could pull away he scooped her into his arms, feeling her little gasp of surprise as he took her mouth. What had only been intended to show her he was up for it very quickly changed to something else, and suddenly they were clawing at each other, hands grabbing collars and hair and anything else to get closer. Clothing brushed against clothing until friction mounted and body heat radiated through. And God, her mouth was sweeter than anything, full lips so soft one second and so hard and demanding the next, parted to allow him access to her tongue and her hard palate, to her humid breath coming faster and faster as her fist clenched in his hair and her own tongue battled for supremacy. And her body, Jesus, her body was hard-pressed and tight and mounded and undulating and he'd never felt so much fire just beneath the surface.

But she was Kendra Davis. And just when he was ready to scoop her up and carry her off to his bedroom, just when he was ready to hold her captive there for the next three or four or more hours, she stepped back with a little sigh and caught her breath. She raised a hand to her lips, almost but not quite covering her teasing smile and said. 'You get an A-plus for practice, Garrett Thorne. You just convinced the hell out of me.' Still breathing hard, she ran a hand through his hair, brushed a quick kiss across his lips, and let herself out, leaving him leaning against the wall, barely able to stand. For the very first time, he allowed himself to think that not only might they be able to pull this whole charade off, but he might actually enjoy it.

Kendra fled Garrett's house, mentally kicking herself. Why the hell did she kiss him? Could she be any more stupid? Yes, they might have to kiss each other, and yes, they might have to hold

52

each other like they couldn't get enough of each other. But that was for Friday night. That was for the Golden Kiss Awards. That wasn't for this afternoon. That wasn't for the privacy of Garrett's house. What the fuck was she thinking? She didn't even like the man. This was her job, nothing more.

She shoved her way into the Mustang and barely managed the seatbelt with her trembling hands. But she took a deep breath, squared her shoulders, and forced herself to drive around the block out of Garrett's site before she stopped, threw on the emergency brake, and laid her head against the steering wheel, struggling to catch her breath, struggling to calm herself, struggling not to think about how badly she'd wanted to stay, how badly she'd wanted to escalate things even further. If he'd started it, she would have slapped his face or maybe kneed him in the balls. But she had started it. Her! What the fuck was the matter with her?

She fumbled in her bag and found her lipstick, trying to breathe deeply as she used the rear-view mirror to tidy her make-up. Clearly she just needed to get laid, that's all. How long had it been now? And all this the result of too many Tess Delaney novels, no doubt. Even when he wasn't consciously fucking with her, Garrett Thorne was fucking with her. God, he was a pain in the ass. Yet how could she blame him for her bad behavior? And now she'd have to face him Friday night as though nothing had happened, as though what she had done was simply a part of her plan to facilitate their desired end result. She would have never pulled anything so brazen and unprofessional with any of her other clients, and she'd had more than a few who were plenty willing, bigger names than Garrett Thorne, she reminded herself. When she was calm again and her hands had stopped shaking, she started the Mustang and headed back into Portland. She had a dress to buy and all the other accessories she could imagine a glam romance writer extraordinaire might need for an awards ceremony. And, in spite of her best efforts, she couldn't help thinking of just how her version of Tess Delaney would take Garrett Thorne's breath away.

Chapter Seven

Garrett had got lucky. He'd managed to catch Dee and Ellis between travels and meetings and wrangled an invite for dinner at Dee's place. Well, it was just burgers on the grill, but it didn't matter. He didn't care so much about the food. He just needed to talk. Dee met him at the door in cut-offs and a Sportswide Extreme Adventure T-shirt. She threw her arms around his neck and kissed his cheek. 'Hope you're hungry,' she said. 'Your brother believes in grilling for the masses.'

Her ease with him after everything that had happened always surprised him. She certainly didn't hold the grudge that Kendra seemed to hold. In fact, she'd already accepted him like family. He was outrageously glad for that. Not only because he was sure she would be the dream sister-in-law, but because she had been the balm that had, in spite of everything, eased the way for greatly improved relations between him and Ellis. That had been a gift for which he could never fully repay her.

She motioned him through to the patio, where Ellis stood over the grill in faded jeans and a black T-shirt. Garrett had to do a double take. He'd so seldom seen his brother at his ease in the past few years, and he could never remember him looking so relaxed. Ellis coughed and moved out of the line of the smoke from the grill, then turned to offer his brother a smile and a wave with a spatula. 'Hey, bro, beer in the cooler. Grab yourself one and tell us the latest.'

Dee went about the business of setting the picnic table and Garrett grabbed a beer. 'How was Paris?'

'Fast,' Dee called over her shoulder.

'And Spain?' he asked Ellis.

'*Muy bueno*,' came the reply as Ellis returned his attention to the burgers.

'Good. That's good,' he said, pacing the length of the patio, admiring the rhythm the two had fallen into with each other. He wasn't sure if they'd worked out a plan for when to be at her place and when to be at his. He didn't know if they'd decided where they would live after they married. He'd not had time to ask about the future since they officially announced their engagement. He needed to make time. It was important, maybe the most important thing ever – to see Ellis truly happy. But tonight, there were pressing issues.

'Did you see Stacie before she headed off to Japan?' Ellis asked. 'I got an email saying she was overnighting here before she left. Plans for the new gallery seem to be moving along.'

'No,' Garrett said. 'No. I missed her. So, Kendra does PR?' The words were out before he had a chance to think about them, and suddenly he had both their full attention.

'You could say that,' Dee said. 'Her degree's in marketing and PR. After she graduated she went off to California to start her own business.'

Ellis laid the spatula down and dropped onto the bench of the picnic table. 'That was why we were trying to head you off at the pass the other day at the engagement party.'

'Of course, you had no way of knowing that she loves Tess Delaney novels, and certainly no one would suspect that from Kendra,' Dee said. 'But I don't know anybody as tenacious as Kendra when it comes to getting what she wants, and once she found out that Tess needed help with PR, if anyone could figure how to get to Tess, Kendra could.'

'Could and did,' Garrett said, slugging back half his beer.

'Shit,' Dee half whispered. Then she dropped onto the seat next to Ellis. 'What happened?'

'Kendra's going to be Tess Delaney for the Golden Kiss Award, or rather Kay Lake is. I'm going as her date.'

For a second neither Dee nor Ellis said anything. They only sat looking at Garrett as though he'd suddenly grown a second head. Then Ellis spoke, holding his brother's gaze. 'Garrett, are you sure this is a good idea?'

'It's not like I have any choice in the matter, is it? I've got less than a week before the award dinner and Don hasn't found anyone but Kendra.' He waved his hand. 'I mean, I didn't know K. Ryde was Kendra, and obviously Don doesn't know either. We nearly gave each other a heart attack, Kendra and I, when she showed up at the Pneuma Annex and discovered Tess's true identity.'

In spite of herself, Dee almost managed to hide a snigger, and Ellis was biting his lip, trying to keep back a laugh of his own. 'That would have been a sight to see,' Ellis said.

Garrett glared at him. Then he turned his attention to Dee. 'Is Kendra really that good?'

'Let me put it this way,' Dee said, scooting forward on the bench. 'The Shelby Mustang she drives? A gift from Devon Barnet.'

'Jesus,' Garrett said. 'Are you serious?'

She nodded. 'A gift for a job well done. No one knows that, of course. Devon Barnet and everyone else K. Ryde ever worked for are sworn to secrecy. Well, anyone who actually ever met the real K. Ryde. She's good all right.'

'Still,' Ellis said, returning to the grill to check the burgers, 'I'm surprised she'd even consider working for you, knowing how emotionally attached she is to you.'

Garrett flipped his brother the finger. 'Kendra's not working for me. She's working for Tess Delaney.'

Dee nodded. 'Well, that makes sense. She's a ravenous reader, but not of romance, not until she discovered Tess Delaney. Kendra doesn't believe in romance.'

'Has she talked to you about any of this?' Garrett asked.

'Of course not,' Dee replied. 'Kendra loves a good bit of gossip as much as the next person, but when it comes to keeping secrets, the woman's a fortress, and when it comes to her work, the woman's a fortress with a shark-infested moat around it. In fact, she'll probably not be happy that you've talked to us about it.'

'You think she can pull it off, then?' Garrett asked.

'Of course she can pull it off.' Dee sounded like Garrett had just asked her the stupidest question ever.

'Question is, bro,' Ellis called over his shoulder, 'can you

56

let her pull it off and stay out of her way?' Then he turned and offered a wicked smile. 'I certainly hope so, because I'm guessing she'll probably kill you if you mess it up for Tess.'

Somehow Garrett suspected that might just be the case.

Kendra had never needed a lot of sleep. It was a part of what made her good at what she did. If she needed to go to a party at night and do research during the day, she could manage it on an hour of sleep and a cup of strong coffee. Back in the early days, no one would pay any attention to a young woman a little too blonde and a little too pretty to look like she knew what she was doing. But she *did* know what she was doing, and when that blonde became a brunette and took a job as the PA for the mysterious K. Ryde, she had more work than she could manage. In the beginning, that was cool. In the beginning, she juggled the roles flawlessly. And it didn't really matter because no one ever saw K. Ryde. Ryde was like Charlie from *Charlie's Angels*, only she imagined him much edgier, much scarier – that is, when she imagined him at all. K. Ryde was only male because that's what people naturally seemed to think, and that suited Kendra just fine. K. Ryde controlled the business from behind the scenes, leaving Kendra Davis free to recreate herself again and again. At first she did it only for the job, only when K. Ryde needed her incognito. But it was so freeing to be someone else. She'd never felt such power. Soon she realized she could just as easily become someone else to explore the night and the people who hung out in it. In the beginning, it was thrilling and exciting. She felt alive and free and totally untouchable. Of course, it was just an illusion. But she didn't know that back then.

At the tiny desk squished in the corner of her studio apartment, she opened her laptop. With a few clicks, she pulled up an old photo album, one that no one else would ever be able to find if they just happened to be browsing her files. She understood about alter egos far better than Garrett Thorne could imagine. She understood about secret identities, about people who didn't exist anywhere in the real world, about people who existed only in her head. There had been so many.

Most didn't really have names unless they needed to, and most were gone the next morning, the next week or two at the latest. She pulled up the picture she was looking for, feeling her skin prickle as she viewed it after all this time. It was taken by the man she'd been with that night, a man who had grabbed her phone away and started snapping photos of her. It was later that she'd learned his name. Too late. She hated photos of herself. She tried to get him to stop, but it was only on her phone so it really didn't matter. She could delete them later. She didn't know why she never did.

She studied the photo for a long time, as though she could undo it if she stared long enough, as though she could make that night and everything that happened after disappear. Of course, she couldn't. The picture she could delete, but the scars were permanent. Even she wouldn't recognize herself if she hadn't known it was her in the photo. Her hair was black, cut into a bob that just brushed the bottoms of her ears. It was short enough to show the temporary tattoo of a flock of delicately drawn birds ascending over one shoulder and up the pale column of her neck to disappear into the black nest of her hair. The outfit she wore was blood red and strapless, short and form-fitting; the black boots rose halfway up her thighs.

The man had called her the Bird Woman. He hadn't known her as anything else. He hadn't known anything about her. At least not until later, when her world fell apart.

She shivered and pulled a sweat jacket from the back of the chair onto her shoulders. After that, Kendra had moved back home to Portland, back home to the arms of her friends, back to where she could heal. Whatever the hell that meant.

The Bird Woman had been the last of the strangers who had lived their short lives out in her body. Until now, at least.

For the tenth time she went to the closet and pulled out the emerald green gown she'd bought for Tess Delaney's debut. It was off the shoulder, cut low across the collar bones to show plenty of cleavage. It made her look like a princess at court. Kendra was hardly the princess type, but she figured Tess Delaney, if she'd existed in the real world, probably would be. And, in truth, the dress looked like it was made for her.

She studied her reflection in the mirror and ran a hand through her hair. She'd been blonde since she'd returned to Portland. That was her true color. But that was Kendra Davis. She really couldn't picture Tess Delaney as a blonde, nor did she want her to be. She would take care of that Friday morning. She wouldn't have to cut it much. She figured Tess was the sort who wore her hair long.

She walked back into the darkened main room of the studio half wishing she'd asked Harris to come over for pizza and a movie marathon, but it was a work night, and Harris needed more sleep than she did. Still, he would have dropped everything to come and be with her if she needed him. So would Dee. But there was nothing wrong with her, not really, just a bit of not-so-happy nostalgia. And tomorrow, when she became Tess Delaney, it would be a part of her job, and that would make it easier. She would never go back to the dark places that had pulled her in those years in California. Everyone had their dark places, and being Tess Delaney was anything but a dark place. The woman was bright and optimistic and hopeful and full of happy-ever-after good cheer. And that was something Kendra would be glad to have. Though it certainly didn't seem like Garrett Thorne had a lot of it, unless she was badly misjudging, and that wasn't very likely.

There had been more email exchanges, each one with Kay Lake sounding totally in control of the situation, but as the time drew nearer Garrett found himself less and less sure. Sometimes he tried to blame it all on Kendra Davis. How could he trust such a volatile, unpredictable woman? How had he ever allowed himself to be talked into such insanity? At other times he reminded himself that it had, ultimately, been his idea, that he had been the one who refused to out Tess Delaney. And yet he doubted himself. Could he really pull it off? Could he really go to the Golden Kiss Awards with Kendra Davis on his arm, with her projecting out to the world her version of Tess Delaney? How could her version be anything close to how Tess really was?

Tess Delaney wasn't real, he reminded himself for the thousandth time. Kendra could play the role any way she wanted to and it wouldn't matter. That thought only served to make him more nervous.

By Thursday night he was a basket case. A glance at the clock on the nightstand informed him that it was almost three in the morning. He'd only been in bed an hour. Up until then there was no reason to even attempt sleep. The beer he'd drank to make himself sleepy had only made him have to pee, and now he lay awake, every muscle tense, staring at the ceiling. He grabbed his BlackBerry from the nightstand and texted with shaky fingers.

Are you awake?

He regretted it the moment he'd done it, but there was no taking it back. God, Kendra would probably not even see it until the morning, then she'd think he was the neurotic mess he actually was. So much for good role playing. His BlackBerry rang in the darkness, causing him to jump.

'Garrett, are you all right?' Kendra spoke without greeting, and the concern he imagined he heard in her voice made him instantly feel a little better, if a little silly.

'Fine.' He could feel the embarrassed heat rising up his throat. 'Can't sleep. Nervous, I guess.'

'There's no reason to be.' Her voice was softer than he remembered it, warmer. 'I promise it'll be OK.'

'Why aren't you asleep?' he shot back, trying to sound a little less neurotic. 'It's the middle of the night.'

'I don't need much sleep,' she said, with a chuckle that sounded a little rough, as though maybe she had been sleeping, or at least she should have been.

Or maybe it was her bedroom voice. Suddenly, his body was at full attention. He took a deep breath and hoped she wouldn't hear his heart, which was now juddering in his throat. 'Me neither. I usually write best after dark. But these days the writing hasn't been going too well.'

'Sorry to hear that. If you don't mind my asking, as a fan I mean, what's Tess writing these days?'

It pleased him more than he cared to admit that she was his

fan … Tess's fan. He felt himself smiling hard. 'Imagine *Dallas* does *50 Shades of Grey* with a hint of *Jane Eyre* and a dash of *Bridget Jones's Diary* thrown in for good measure.'

Her laugh was warm and thick and he held the BlackBerry closer as though he could feel it if he tried hard enough. 'You're kidding, right?'

'Actually, I was kidding, but my publisher loved the idea.'

Dear God, did she actually giggle? The sound was musical and suddenly it was hard for him to imagine the woman on the other end of the phone had ever slapped him or tried to drown him. 'No wonder you're … I mean, Tess is having trouble with it.' Then she added, 'Life is stranger than fiction, Garrett. You do realize you're living out a Tess Delaney plot even as we speak, don't you?'

'I had thought about it, yes,' he said, curling himself around a pillow, imagining that it was her scooped into his arms against his body. 'But then I was afraid you might resort to further violence if I mentioned it to you.'

This time her laughter was explosive, and he found himself laughing too, feeling like the darkness had somehow been pushed back.

'Oh, come on, Garrett,' she said, 'Aster Martin clocked Daniel Varner good in *Too Much Moonlight* and Al Tristan ended up wearing a whole bowl of rum punch courtesy of delicate little Heather Jackson in *Appealing to Heather*. I would think you'd be truly inspired by now.'

'You know what happens next in both of those novels?' he said, gripping the device tightly to his ear.

'Of course I know. Angry sex. Tess Delaney writes brilliant angry sex. The inspiration is certainly there. But you're … I mean, Tess is the writer. I'm just the lowly PR person.' Her voice felt suddenly closer. 'You need to get some rest, Garrett. It would hardly do for you to be falling asleep all over your lovely date's shoulder tomorrow night, now would it?'

Chapter Eight

Strangely enough, Garrett *had* slept after Kendra called him, and that without phone sex … Though he wouldn't have minded. It had been almost noon when he was startled awake by the buzz of his BlackBerry. He grabbed it up breathlessly, hoping it was Kendra. It was Don.

'I hear everything is ready for tonight. My plane just got in and I'm waiting for luggage. Kay assures me that you don't need me to come and hold your hand. She sounds amazing.'

'Jesus, Don, please tell me you two didn't discuss holding my hand.' Garrett rolled over on his back and threw his arm across his face.

'Relax, Garrett. You know I'm just concerned. Seems like the Ryde Agency has everything under control, though. Makes me a little bit nervous for my job, actually. I'm told all I have to do is show up and you'll be there with the lovely Tess Delaney on your arm.'

The rest of the day passed in a blur. Strangely enough he found himself writing down some ideas for a novel roughly based on his experience with Kendra. She was right. It was the dream story and it wouldn't be that difficult to twist and turn it just enough to make sure their own identities were protected. Maybe Tess would even put a foreword in the novel to the effect that some of it was autobiographical. That would be the perfect way to thumb his nose at his publisher. After the dust was all settled, after the award ceremony was over, who cared if Tess let it slip that maybe, just maybe it wasn't really her at the ceremony.

In spite of the hours he'd spent writing, he made sure to give himself plenty of time to get ready. If he had to be the no-account woman magnet of a Thorne brother, he wanted to make sure he did his best to look the part. OK, if he were honest, he also wanted to impress Kendra Davis, and he had the distinct impression she wasn't all that easy to impress. He'd certainly not done a great job of it so far.

He was ready 30 minutes early and, to keep from giving in to the nerves threatening to run amuck in the pit of his stomach, he settled back into writing a synopsis for the story of Tess's cover-up. He had just got to their steamy kiss in the foyer when the doorbell rang. His heart jumped. This was it. This was where he placed the past ten years of his life into the hands of a woman who didn't like him. But, he reminded himself, she did like Tess Delaney. She liked her a lot. He'd have to trust that would be enough. He swallowed his nerves, straightened his bowtie and went to the door.

The woman on the porch left him breathless. Her rich russet hair was piled on top of her head in careless but outrageously sexy curls, curls that looked as though she might have had a romp in the sheets just before she remembered she had a party to go to and then she'd had to hurry to get ready. However, the rest of her looked polished to a delicious emerald shine. The dress sheathed her like a second skin, the split high up the right side allowed her long delicious thigh to play peek-a-boo from beneath when she walked. The shoes and the jewellery were gold; the necklace sparkled with a filigreed heart resting between her breasts.

At last he found his voice. 'Your hair,' he managed, 'it's …'

'Red, I know. Didn't you envision Tess as a redhead? I could never have imagined her as anything else. But don't worry, I can be blonde again as soon as it's all right with Tess.'

It was only when she offered him a smile and nodded to the limo that he realized he'd been staring, just standing there staring. He pulled the door to and locked it, then offered her his arm, which she took. And did she actually look up at him admiringly? Well, she was pretending to be Tess Delaney after all, wasn't she?

*   *   *

63

To Garrett's surprise, they'd made it to their table almost unnoticed. He figured that was because no one knew what Tess Delaney looked like, and no one honestly expected her to show up. Don was already there with some woman whose name Garrett promptly forgot after their introduction. He could barely remember his own, as focused on just getting through the evening as he was.

At the table closest to them sat the obnoxious critic, Barker Blessing. Garrett hadn't thought to warn Kendra about the womanizing bastard, but then how could he have known? In his white tux and black bowtie, with his air-brushed hair, the man might have passed for an older version of James Bond, with a slightly slimy edge to him. Blessing's striking good looks were quickly eclipsed when he opened his mouth and graced everyone with a vocabulary that mostly involved the words "me", "my", and "I". Add to that the fact the man had the unpleasant habit of talking with his hands in the presence of good-looking women, hands that usually arrived uninvited on the more personal parts of female anatomy, and Blessing was best avoided whenever possible. Garrett could only imagine the explosion if the groping Barker Blessing's hands invaded the volatile Kendra Davis's personal space. He'd have to make sure that didn't happen.

The second Garrett pulled out the chair for Kendra, Blessing was on his feet. 'You must be the lovely, and very secretive, Tess Delaney,' he announced loudly, bending over her hand to press a sloppy kiss across her knuckles. 'At long last we meet.'

And that was it. The room erupted in a strobe of camera flashes as Kendra said something polite and then turned her attention to Don, who was also offering her his hand. It was clear he was very pleased with Kendra's version of Tess Delaney. Before Don got his greetings out, there was a Dictaphone thrust in Kendra's face.

'Ms. Delaney, can you tell us why you chose this night to make your first public appearance after ten years of enthralling the world with your novels?' the young female reporter asked.

Garrett bristled and was about to push his way in between

64

Kendra and the reporter to protect her, but her hold on his arm became a vice grip, while the rest of her remained as calm and serene as a sunset over a summer ocean. 'Why, Ms. Flannery – ' She called the reporter by name, which seemed to be a total, if delightful surprise to the woman. 'I would have thought that would be obvious. I could hardly resist being here for the Golden Kiss Awards, not when I've had the honour of being nominated. It's every romance writer's dream to be in this place with these people, you know.' She gave her a smile that had the reporter blushing like an adolescent. Oh, she was good. Behind them, Blessing was taking notes fast and furiously on his iPhone. Three other reporters asked her questions in rapid succession and she answered them just as easily.

Then the intrepid Ms. Flannery butted in again. 'Ms. Delaney, I see that you're here with Garrett Thorne. Are you two an item?'

Garrett truly had to refrain from dragging her away from the reporter. But Kendra was already as close to digging claws into his arm as she could possibly be without drawing blood. She gave him an adoring glance that softened his mood considerably, then smiled back at the woman. 'Ms. Flannery, I never kiss and tell. I save that for my novels.'

Before anyone could ask more awkward questions, the press returned to their seats and everyone settled as the ceremony began.

In all honesty, Garrett paid little attention to anything other than the woman sitting next to him. Perhaps he was just being paranoid, but it felt like all eyes were on her. On the one hand he could certainly understand why that should be, but on the other the longer they sat there under the curious gaze of everyone anxious for their first look at Tess Delaney, the more they risked being found out. He didn't like the way Don was looking at Kendra. He sure as hell didn't like the way Barker Blessing was looking at her, like she was dessert. God, he wished he'd warned her about the creep beforehand.

The entertainment was endless. Someone sang, there was some ballroom dancing, a comedian. Someone else sang. Everyone clapped politely and ate their dinner as it was served up in courses. The final announcement of the winner of the Golden Kiss Award would be given just before dessert was served.

Garrett barely touched his wine. He barely touched his food. All he wanted was to get Kendra and himself and Tess out of this place as soon as possible before the vultures could descend again. It was Kendra curling her fingers around his that drew his attention back to the present as some man on stage crooned a medley of love songs. She leaned close to him. 'You're supposed to be enjoying yourself. You're the date of the most mysterious, most exciting woman in the whole room. This is Tess's moment.' She moved her hand down to rest on his thigh. If she hadn't had his full attention before, she did now. 'Kiss me on the ear,' she whispered. 'And slip your arm around me. You're supposed to be into me, remember?'

Doing as she asked was no hardship, and it helped take his mind off the position in which they now found themselves. The fact that doing so not only made her smile, but made her blush and giggle softly went a long way to focus him on things far removed from what was happening onstage. He could feel Blessing's gaze boring into the back of his head, but that didn't matter quite so much as he dropped a kiss on Kendra's ear, then another on the glorious expanse of her neck laid bare by the off-the-shoulder dress.

And then it was time. The two MCs stood before the microphone and read the names and recent achievements of the five novelists. A big deal was made out of the fact that this was Tess's first ever public appearance. The camera zoomed in on her, where she sat smiling demurely next to him, and suddenly Kendra's lovely face filled the big display screens that had been placed so everyone could get a good view of what was going on. Garrett felt the muscles in his shoulders knot even tighter.

The reassuring squeeze of her hand against his was just beginning to calm him when the MC said, 'And the winner of this year's coveted Golden Kiss Award is … Tess Delaney!'

Chapter Nine

The crowd went wild. Garrett nearly catapulted from his chair, an act that Kendra turned into an exuberant winner's kiss for her date followed by a reassuring caress of his biceps. Then she made her way up the aisle toward the stage, and Don did his best to subtly ease Garrett back into his seat. Not that it mattered; all cameras were on Tess Delaney, all adoring eyes were on her, and Garrett wasn't entirely sure he wasn't going to throw up. He felt hot all over, he felt like his chest was about to explode and his stomach was about to implode. He wanted to run up to the stage and whisk Kendra away before she could open her mouth. Dear God, surely this was expecting too much of even her.

'Calm down,' Don hissed in Garrett's ear. 'Let her take care of it. Just smile like the adoring lover. That's right. Tess won, Garrett, Tess Delaney won the Golden Kiss. You know what that means?'

'Shut up, Don,' Garrett hissed between barely parted lips.

'Then sit down and behave yourself.' Don made no effort to disguise the warning in his voice. Garrett was sure the man would have put him in a stranglehold if he felt it necessary. Well he was certainly welcome to try, Garrett thought.

On stage, Tess took possession of the golden trophy topped with its replica of Rodin's sculpture, The Kiss. She graciously gave each of the two presenters a peck on the cheek to a roar of applause. Then she stood, smiling brightly in front of the microphone, till the room quieted. She waited for a second, then the smile broadened and became contagious. Garrett couldn't help noticing that everyone was smiling back at her. Even he was smiling back at her.

'This is such a wonderful surprise.' She looked down at the trophy. 'I can't tell you how honoured I am even to have been nominated for this award, to be in the company of such esteemed writers, writers who are my heroes in the romance world. But to actually win – well, I have to pinch myself to make sure I'm not dreaming. I don't mind saying that I was a little bit nervous when my publicist suggested that the Golden Kiss Awards might be the time to make my first ever public appearance. I mean –' she leaned close to the microphone '– it's just so very public, isn't it?'

Her captivated audience laughed their appreciation.

'As I'm sure you can imagine, I've always felt more at home behind the laptop than I do in the public eye. I guess most writers probably feel that way. I'm guessing I'm not the only one who finds myself a lot more comfortable talking with my characters than with real people, a lot more at home with the people I've created in my novels than I am with, well, people in the real world. I've always found them a bit scary, a bit intimidating. But, well –' she offered the audience a dazzling smile.

'– you all are lovely. Thank you. Thank you so much.'

There was a spontaneous round of applause, and when there was silence again, she continued, 'That I'd like to thank my publicist and my editor, and all the bookish folks who make my novels a reality, is obvious.'

She leaned a little closer to the microphone, and Garrett could swear she was looking right at him. He braced himself. Was this it, then? Was this the point where Kendra Davis got her revenge? He held his breath as she continued.

'Not so obvious are the people who inspire me and help me and encourage me in quiet ways, the people who never take the bows, even though they deserve them, even though this –' she raised the trophy for everyone to see.

'– this could have never happened to me without them. Thank you. You're truly amazing.'

Garrett was sure she was looking right at him, and he sat a little taller, and for the first time in the evening his smile was easy and genuine. There was another round of applause, and

Kendra moved off the stage. The applause continued as she glided between the tables and back to her place, back to Garrett. And it became deafening when he stood, scooped her into his arms, and kissed her. Best of all, she kissed him back like she really meant it, pulling away only enough to beam her bright smile at him and mouth the words "we won", before she yielded to his next assault.

He could have just kept on with the kissing. He could have just kept on with her there in his arms, pressed tightly against him all warm and soft and breathing hard with the excitement of victory. But Don butted in for a hug and a kiss on the cheek and his date, Julie – that was her name, Garrett remembered – did the same. And then Barker Blessing shoved his way in for a grope and a slobber before Garrett could pull Kendra possessively back to him and before everyone settled in for dessert and an onstage tribute to musicals.

It was when chocolate mousse arrived, mounded high with whipped cream and topped with a huge fresh cherry, that Blessing made his move. He forced his chair in between Kendra and Don – after all, Don was Tess's publicist, and Blessing always situated himself with the movers and shakers whenever possible. If Garrett had been Ellis, then no doubt he would have squeezed in where he could rub shoulders with him too. But clearly Garrett's reputation was well known to Blessing who, after a curt nod in his direction, turned his full attention to Kendra, who had just begun her mousse.

'My dear, I must congratulate you again. I think I speak for everyone here when I say Tess Delaney has stolen our hearts.'

Garrett was never 100 per cent sure about what happened next, though he did play the events over and over in his head many times afterward.

He read Kendra's body language before he was able to see, from his poor vantage point, what was actually happening. Her spine stiffened and tension tightened her shoulders, which until now had been completely relaxed.

'As you know, I've reviewed all of your novels very well, very well indeed.'

Bullshit, Garrett thought. He had always approached Tess's

books as he did all romance novels, as though they were the bastard stepchildren of proper literature, and the best he'd ever said about her work was that it was not bad for what it was, and that it was a pity such talent was wasted on such low-brow literature. As Blessing's hand moved up high on Kendra's right thigh, Garrett had visions of strangling the man with his bow tie.

'I'm sure my reviews were taken into consideration in these awards, Tess – I can call you Tess, can't I?' He addressed Kendra's cleavage, 'So, in a small way, I guess you could say I'm responsible for you carrying away that lovely piece of metal. And I'm willing and able to help advance your career in ways you haven't even thought of.' His thumb slid beneath the soft green fabric of her dress and his fingers followed suit, finding their way to Kendra's bare thigh.

What happened next seemed to unfold in slow motion. Garrett rose from his chair and grabbed the bastard by the back of the collar just as Kendra looked up and caught his eye, then she shook her head and mouthed the words "sit down".

He didn't. He just couldn't let the bastard touch her like that. But before he could bodily heave Blessing out of his chair, before he could do more than lay a hand on the man's jacket, Kendra, without so much as batting an eye, daintily and very deliberately dumped her entire chocolate mousse upside down onto the lap of the man's white suit, making sure to give it a good hard shove, adding a slide from side to side so there would be no easy clean-up. The whole incident might have been subtly covered up if, at that moment, one of the cameramen hadn't chosen to zoom in for a close-up of the beaming winner and catch the whole magical moment and multiply it and enlarge it on the big screens that surrounded the room, resulting in a raucous round of applause.

And that was when Garrett decided it was time they made their exit before he did the man serious bodily harm. He cupped her elbow in his hand, helping her from her chair. The applause was thunderous.

'Garrett.' She spoke between clenched teeth. 'What the hell are you doing? We can't leave before the press conference.

70

Garrett!'

'Fuck the press conference,' he growled. 'We're leaving now, before I kill the bastard.'

For a split second he was sure she was going slap him. Her eyes blazed blue fire and her lips were parted, to make room for each accelerating breath.

'Now,' he said, tightening his grip on her arm.

She blushed ever so slightly, made a little curtsey to the applauding crowd, then yielded to Garrett's none-too gentle tugging. As the room fell silent, all except for the sputtering and cursing of Barker Blessing, who was now being ministered to by a couple of the male wait staff wiping at his bemoussed crotch with white linen napkins, the two walked out of the room with all the dignity of royalty. Without a word, they quick-marched down the stairs into the foyer and out into the warm summer evening, where Garrett practically shoved her into the waiting limo, the Golden Kiss Award still suicide-gripped in her hand.

Chapter Ten

He held the remote so tight that his fingers hurt, but he didn't care. He slid from the chair onto the floor, as close to the TV screen as he could get. With the back of his hand he wiped tears. It was her! Dear God, it was her, there on national television. There for all the world to see. He had pictured her a thousand ways in his mind. He had imagined a thousand ways she might look, a thousand personalities she might have, but he knew that when he saw her he would know her like he knew himself. He would feel her like the other half of him. He knew it, and he'd been so right.

He ran a trembling hand along the image of her bright cinnamon hair piled high on her head, along the soft curve of her cheek, along the full red of her lips as she opened her mouth to thank everyone for the Golden Kiss Award. Tess Delaney, close up and personal, shining like the sun all new and bright. She was exquisite in ways he could have never imagined, even in the very best of his fantasies. She took his breath away. She made him ache all over with longing. She was a religious experience, too sacred for someone like Garrett Thorne to be pawing at. And yet she felt so comfortable, so familiar, like he'd always known her.

The fact that she was with Garrett Thorne tied his gut in a burning knot. It didn't matter, he tried to convince himself. Thorne wasn't known for staying with one woman for very long. And who could blame him for wanting to stand in the radiance of Tess Delaney's light? But he was certain Tess couldn't really feel anything for someone as shallow as Garrett Thorne. She would see right through him and it would end soon enough, and even if it didn't, it made no difference to him. He hadn't come this far to be denied the prize.

He listened as she made her little speech. Her voice was like the music of the angels to him, flowing from her lips honeyed and sweet, and flooding him with such ecstasy; not what she said, but that it was she who spoke it, breathed it, willed each word of it into the world. Dear God, how had he survived all of this time outside her radiance, outside her beauty? He watched as she waltzed down the aisle like the queen of the world before her adoring public. He watched as she returned to her seat. He watched as Garrett Thorne stood and took her into his arms like he owned her, like she belonged to him, like he could fuck her with his mouth right there in front of everyone.

The flash fire of rage in his belly felt like it would burn him to a cinder. There was a sharp pop and crack as the plastic casing of the TV remote shattered in his vice grip. Slivers of hard plastic sliced into his palm. He felt the warm wet of his blood flowing from the wound down his wrist. He smelled the sweet-metal scent of it and was instantly hard, imagining that it was her blood. Imagining that it was her blood mingled with his own, imagining the pleasure of the pain he could share with her, and how much more intense that pain would be for the way she allowed Garrett Thorne to slobber all over her, to grope at her like some animal in rut.

He ignored the soft drip, drip, drip of the blood on the carpet as he watched the beginnings of the musical number through a hot haze of tears, impatient for more of her, impatient for the press conference that was to follow, impatient to hear what she had to say for herself, for allowing Thorne's behavior, even inviting it. He watched as that damned Barker Blessing mauled her. Fuck, had she really fallen so far? Had she really lost her way so badly that she had become nothing more than a whore for anyone to fondle and rut with?

When Garrett Thorne rose behind Barker with his hand on the man's collar, he found himself hoping that he would kill the man, strangle him right there in front of the whole world on national television, make the man pay for touching Tess. And then … And then … He would find Garrett Thorne and make him pay … And then, he would take Tess, take her away, and

73

make her pay … For a very long time, he would make her pay. And then, once she was purified, once she understood, once her mind was clear again, they could truly be together.

'What the fuck?' he growled, as Tess dumped her dessert in Blessing's lap, close up and personal, covering the man's bulge in chocolate mousse. That's not what was supposed to happen. He wanted the man covered in blood; he wanted the man choking out his last breath while everyone watched in delicious horror.

'No, no, no!' he roared at the monitor, up on his knees, close enough that his breath misted the screen as Garrett Thorne took Tess by the elbow and led her from the hall to the loud applause of all present. 'No! That's not right! That's not the way it's supposed to happen! That's not the way I want it,' he raged, shattering what was left of the broken remote against the monitor over and over again, streaking it with more of his blood before rising to his feet, yanking the monitor from its stand and smashing it over and over against the wall, the sound of crumbling sheetrock, splintering plastic and metal, drowning out the electronic crackle of shredding wires.

'She's not yours! You can't have her,' he shouted as the image of Thorne and Tess Delaney disintegrated and crumbled in a shower plaster dust. 'She belongs to me. To me!'

When there was nothing left of the television monitor or the remote, he sat back on his heels and sobbed, holding his bloodied hand against the spastic jumping of his heart. It was ages before he finally stood. He wrapped his hand in half a roll of toilet paper, shoved on his trainers, and went for a run. He would not let Garrett Thorne have his Tess. In the end she would still be his, but they would both pay for their betrayal. He'd be sure of that. He ran and ran, he didn't know for how long. He didn't remember anything about it, except that the night vision of the Portland streets was filtered through the red rage that surrounded him like a fog. He wasn't even sure how he wound up back at the door of his apartment, struggling to get the key into the lock, struggling with all his might not to think about what Garrett Thorne might be doing to his Tess right now. It was unbearable. It was agony. He'd waited so

74

long. And then this!

In the bathroom, he peeled away the bloodied toilet paper from his hand. The gash had clotted clean, but reopened with the removal of the tissue. He washed it for ages under cold water, then, when he was sure it wouldn't bleed any more, he stripped off his clothes and shuffled back into the living room. Ignoring the rubble that was once the television, he went to the makeshift desk and booted up his laptop. Sitting naked, as dawn began to break grey over the city, he surfed through everything he could find in the press about last night's Golden Kiss Awards.

At last, he went to Carla Flannery's article. She was a young nobody of a journalist, who always seemed to find out what no one else could. As he read her report about the strange goings on at the Golden Kiss Awards, an idea began to form in his head. It wasn't that hard to get the attention of the media these days, and it was Carla Flannery's attention he wanted. All the reporters were watching her out of the corner of their eyes after she broke a story about an illegal landfill near John Day. She was only just an email away. He rubbed his hands together and began to type.

Once the limo pulled away from the curb, Garrett pried the award gently from her fingers, then hefted its weight. 'I'd say the bastard was damn lucky he got the mousse in the crotch instead of the Rodin upside of the head.'

Kendra forced a pained laugh, in spite of herself, and he could tell her control was near the breaking point, but he didn't care. He didn't!

As the anger dissipated slightly from her face, she took a careful breath and said, 'Garrett, you should have let me handle it. I've had to deal with gropers and droolers and all sorts, and I know what an asshole Blessing is. I was ready for him. Really I was. But you forced my hand. Damn it, you forced my hand.' Her grip on the leather arm rest was white-knuckled, and Garrett was pretty sure it was in attempt to keep from punching him good. 'You should have let me handle it. That's my job, Garrett, that's what you're paying me for, and frankly I –'

'Shut up, Kendra.' He risked life and limb by stopping her words with a hard kiss, followed in quick succession by several more. The wild and furious battle between her tongue and his came as a total surprise. When they both pulled away in a breathless gasp, he said, 'I'm sorry. I fucked up. I couldn't stand him touching you. If you hadn't moussed him I might have done something that would have required my brother to bail me out of jail, and that would have completely ruined Tess's evening.'

'That wasn't my plan, Garrett. The mousse wasn't my plan, and now we can't foresee the consequences of what I did.'

'Kendra, you only did what every writer in that room and all the writers watching from home wanted to do. I can't imagine the consequences of your actions being anything but good. You were stunning and amazing. And right now I want you so badly I can hardly stand it.'

For a second Kendra froze, her whole body tensing, her eyes locked on his. The only sound was their heavy breathing above the soft purr of the limo engine. Garrett was sure this was the point at which he got slapped again. He held his breath.

At last she found her voice. 'That makes two of us,' she whispered.

Before he had time to wonder if he'd heard her right, she scooted and wriggled her way onto his lap, scrunching the skirt of the dress, exposing the silken flesh of her thighs between stocking tops and a gold lace garter belt. He caught a flash of matching panties that were barely there. Then she straddled him, and the heat of her against the uncomfortable expansion in the front of his tux trousers was exquisite.

His mouth vied for position with the golden pendent in the soft swell of her cleavage. He nuzzled away the silken smoothness of the dress to get to the rounded hillocks of her breasts, far more silken than the dress, high and tight and crested with ripe-fruit nipples that grew impossibly erect at his caressing. And when he took them into his mouth in turn, she gave a little gasp and shivered against him, curling her fingers in his hair.

Deftly she managed his belt and his fly and shoved up so

that her knees supported her on the leather seat either side of his thighs. He wriggled his trousers and boxers down over his hips, releasing himself into the stroke and grip of her hand, which caused an involuntary groan that began low in his belly as he ground his ass against the seat beneath them.

From somewhere she produced a condom even before he could get to the one stuffed in his pocket just in case. As she rolled it onto him, he pushed aside the crotch of her panties, and she whimpered at his touch, gripped at his fingers as he stroked her open and circled the swell of her with his thumb. Then, with a shifting of her hips, she rose up into position and squatted onto him, settling down tight and wet and sweeter than anything.

For a second she sat very still atop him, fully impaled, her bright eyes burning into him in the scant light of the limo. Then her lips curled into a bow of a smile and she said, 'Here's to Tess Delaney, the winner of the Golden Kiss.' And she began to shift and undulate against him as he thrust up to meet her like his life depended on it, like he'd never get another chance, like being inside her was the best thing ever, and at the moment, that was pretty much the truth. Kendra Davis riding him hard, surely this must be the end of the world, but he could happily live with that.

They strained and shifted and grasped, bathed in the strobe of the passing night lights of Portland. The leather seat creaked in the hard friction of expensive clothing and exposed bare flesh, in the grip and release, thrust and stroke of need born of excitement and anger and some sort of wild animal magnetism. They came together, trembling and gasping and holding tight.

They barely had time to tuck and tidy before the limo arrived at his house. He didn't ask if she wanted to come in. He wasn't about to give her the chance to say no, and now that he'd been with her, he was sure one dose of Kendra Davis was nowhere near enough to cure what ailed him. To his relief, no manhandling was necessary. She followed him willingly up the porch steps, offering him a hug and a caress from behind while he unlocked.

As he opened the door and turned on the light in the foyer,

she slid a hand under his jacket to stroke his ass, which had the exact effect on his cock he figured she was aiming for. He turned and trapped her against the door, capturing her mouth with his, cupping the rise and fall of her, delighting in the hard and soft of her. In mid-kiss, she reached behind her, unzipped her gown, and let it slide down her body, almost in slow motion, as though it intended to caress each inch of her bared flesh all the way to the floor.

She wore no bra, and it was perfect that she didn't. It would have been such a shame to put any more clothing on those exquisite breasts than absolutely necessary. She stood before him in only the garter belt, stockings and panties, and the gold fuck-me heels that made her legs look like they went on for ever before they joined her body in the scant swaddling of gold and lace. Jesus, she was a sight to behold!

Still holding his gaze, she removed a gold clasp from her hair and it fell in a cascade of mussed copper around her shoulders.

He wound a soft fall of curls around his fingers and reeled her in until he could taste her breath, until he could possess her lips and her mouth and her breasts. While he traced the pathway along the well-muscled length of her spine, she shoved his jacket off his shoulders to puddle on the floor next to her dress, never missing a beat in the tango of their tongues. 'I want to undress you, Garrett. I want to see you. All of you. So hold still.'

'Christ, you're bossy,' he grumbled half-heartedly.

'You don't know the half of it,' she said as she pushed his hands away from her breasts and deftly undid his bowtie. And he obeyed her. Kendra Davis exploring him, touching him, unwrapping him like he was her Christmas present made the weight already heavy in his groin feel nearly unbearable. And yet it felt way too intriguing for him not to hold on for as long as he could, to hold on for her, until she wanted it all for herself, and he was sure that would be soon.

She undid his shirt and shoved it off, doing battle with his cufflinks until together they managed to free his arms. Then she suckled and nibbled until his nipples were raw and achingly hard and outrageously sensitive to the air that felt cool against them once they were no longer kept warm by her mouth. But her mouth, led by the scrape and nip of her teeth and the laving of her hot tongue, held his full attention as she nibbled and licked her way down his belly. She paused to probe his sensitive navel with her tongue before she undid his trousers, then squatted in front of him as she eased them down over his hips. He toed off his shoes and there, positioned in front of him, perched on suicide heels, legs open, her face only scant millimetres from his erection, she slid both trousers and boxers off one leg at a time. When at last he stepped free of his clothing, she tossed them aside with the rest of their party finery and cupped him and stroked him until he bit his lip and struggled to hold himself. Then she clasped his butt cheeks in her palms and pulled him to her, taking the heavy length of him into her mouth.

'Jesus, Kendra!' He sucked air between his teeth 'I can't stand that for very long.'

'I bet you can stand it longer than you think,' she breathed.

'Fuck,' he said, curling his fingers in her hair. 'Is this some kind of challenge?'

'Just an observation.' Her eyes were wide, her pupils dilated, and her cheeks were flushed as she pulled away and slipped off her panties from her squatting position. Then she lay back on the floor and motioned him to her.

He fumbled in the pocket of his jacket for the condom. This time, she made no attempt to help him, but only lay there watching him, shifting her hips, making sure he knew exactly what she wanted. It didn't take him long. Then he stretched out on top of her, feeling the silk of her stockings rise along his ribs as she lifted her hips. He cupped her and shifted until there was contact, right where they needed it. They both moaned as he entered her, thrusting, and she wrapped her legs around him, still wearing her shiny shoes, still wearing stockings and garter belt. And she was outrageously warm and wet and needy. She gripped him as though she would consume him, and he rode her as though he might never get another chance. A possibility all too likely, he figured, but he didn't want to think about that now, not while they were together like this, not while they were revelling in Tess's success and celebrating their own conquest of a difficult situation. He didn't want to think about that now, not while there was time to be with Kendra Davis, more vulnerable than he'd ever seen her, nor would be likely to see her again. He expected nothing else. Just now. That would have to be enough. At least, that's what he told himself.

Pizza and beer. Kendra Davis was sitting across from Garrett in the middle of his living room, floor having pizza and beer – totally naked! How could anyone be that unselfconscious? Garrett had pulled on a pair of workout shorts that didn't do a great job of coverage because he'd been at half-mast and rising ever since they had returned from the Golden Kiss Awards. And yet, it made him feel a little less exposed.

She didn't seem to mind him studying her unabashedly while she devoured a huge slice of meat-buster supreme with extra cheese. It was a good thing she didn't, because he couldn't keep his eyes off of her. It was easier when they were fucking, he supposed. When he was making love to Kendra Davis, there was no time to think about anything else, no time to be anywhere but the present, and no time to wonder what was going on in the woman's beautiful head. And, as much as he loved that she was still here with him, hours after what the two had already begun jokingly calling "Blessing the mousse", Garrett was, at his core, waiting for the other shoe to drop.

'What is it?' she said, speaking round a mouthful of pizza before she washed it down with a huge swig of beer that would have made any biker proud. 'What's the matter, Garrett? I don't mind you staring at me. I actually like that a lot or I would have put clothes on. But it's, I don't know, it's the way you're staring at me. I get a feeling it has nothing to do with my tits.'

'Will we regret this in the morning?' There, he'd said it. The words were out. And even though he was glad it was out in the open, he still felt stupid for saying it. Tess would have had a lot more finesse, no doubt.

Kendra sat the beer down on the coffee table and wiped her

hands on one of the napkins that came with the pizza delivery. 'It's already morning, Garrett. Besides, I don't have regrets. It's a waste of time I can't afford.'

'What do you mean, you don't have regrets? Everyone has regrets. How could we not?'

This time she studied *him*, just sitting there completely naked, looking at him as though she had just discovered a new life form.

'I make mistakes, then I learn from them and move on. And looking back ...' For the briefest of seconds, her face darkened and her gaze drifted, as though she saw something Garrett couldn't see, something she didn't want him to see. Then she caught her breath and forced a smile. 'Looking back and dwelling on what's already past, well, it doesn't do anyone any good, really.'

'Can K. Ryde teach me how to do that?' Garrett said. 'Because I'd really like to know.'

She offered him a smile that was almost a flinch, then looked down at her hands folded in her laps. 'K. Ryde, the Ryde Agency, doesn't exist anymore. Well, not like it did.' She looked up, her eyes once more unreadable. 'I sold the company almost a year ago. It's in competent hands and doing well, or so I hear. Don just happened to have an old email address from my Ryde days, one I'd not deactivated. And since I was already intrigued with why Tess Delaney wanted a PR person with special talents, I brought K. Ryde temporarily out of retirement.'

'You have more secrets than Tess Delaney does.'

The smile slipped from her lips and she held his gaze. 'You have no idea.'

A shiver ran down Garrett's spine, but before he could think about it, before he could question her further, Kendra pushed aside her plate and moved to sit next to Garrett, settling a kiss against his sternum, between his pecs. 'Just what part of last night are you planning to regret, Garrett? Tess won the Golden Kiss. You won. And you've managed to keep Tess's true identity a secret.' She shoved the wild fall of red hair away from her face. 'Granted, things didn't quite go to plan, but ultimately I think everyone came out just fine, don't you?' She moved to sit in his lap, legs on either side of him, and instantly he was hard. She cupped his face in her hands and kissed him, lingering, caressing with her tongue, with her lips, until he was once again in the happy haze being with Kendra Davis seemed to produce. Then she pulled away enough to meet his gaze. 'Now, Garrett, tell me what it is you regret, and I'll see what I can do to make you forget about it.'

He didn't, of course. It all seemed pretty irrelevant with an exquisitely naked Kendra Davis wriggling down onto his lap and easing her hand inside the waistband of his shorts.

Chapter Eleven

Garrett woke up in bed alone, and a tight fist formed in his stomach. It surprised him how strongly he felt Kendra's absence. He wasn't ready for her to leave just yet. He threw back the comforter and shoved his way into the shorts which lay on the floor where he had dropped them not that long ago as he'd followed her in between the sheets, literally joined at the hips. It was only when he heard a clatter from the kitchen that he relaxed – well, not really. Parts of him were very tense with anticipation.

He found her in the kitchen, leaning against the counter wrapped in his terry robe. She held a Diet Pepsi in one hand, while she scooped coffee into the coffee maker with the other. Her newly red hair hung loose and mussed around her shoulders, and she had that well-slept-with look about her as she smiled up at him.

'Morning, sleepyhead. Thought you might like some coffee.'

'How long have you been up?' he asked.

'Just long enough for my morning dose.' She lifted her soda. 'I figured once you were up we should probably call Don. I'm really surprised he didn't storm over here last night demanding an explanation, especially since we had our phones turned off. At least, I did, and I figure you did too.'

Garrett moved behind her and put his arms around her, nuzzling her neck. 'Talking with Don definitely wasn't in the plan for the evening.'

She giggled softly. 'There was a plan, was there?'

He slipped his hand inside the robe to cup her breasts, feeling himself harden even further at the press of her stiffening nipple against the glide of his thumb. 'Oh yes, woman, there was a plan.' He nibbled her earlobe and she squirmed. 'I wanted to get inside those golden panties of yours, hopefully without getting slapped.'

She shifted till her bottom rubbed against his growing erection. 'You're a cunning man, Garrett Thorne.'

'And brave,' he added. 'Don't forget brave.'

She pushed the start button on the coffee maker, then turned in his arms and smiled up at him. 'If Don had shown up, I'd have sent him packing.'

'God help him if he'd argued with you.' Garrett said, dropping a kiss onto her ear, then another one onto her collar bone where the robe gaped open, offering an exquisite view of the pale, round rise of her breasts.

She sighed and gave him a quick kiss, then shrugged out of his grasp. 'Still, I suppose we should let him know that we didn't fall off the planet.'

He took her hand and led her into the living room. His BlackBerry lay on the coffee table where he'd carelessly tossed it last night when his mind was completely taken over by the wonders of Kendra Davis. He'd barely got it turned on when it rang. It was Don. Kendra leaned close to hear what was being said.

'Garrett, are you home?' Don said without preamble.

'Yes. Why?'

'Just turn on the television. Now. Local news.'

Kendra grabbed the remote and flipped to the news just in time to catch her and Garrett in a very public lip-lock at the Golden Kiss Awards.

The voiceover was saying, 'The Golden Kiss Awards ceremony was full of surprises last night. Tess Delaney, notoriously elusive writer of some of the most popular, and hottest, romance novels on the market, made her first ever public appearance on the arm of Garrett Thorne, bad boy younger brother of business tycoon, Ellison Thorne. The two were clearly enjoying each other's company.'

There was a close-up of Garrett kissing Kendra's ear, then her neck, while she smiled and blushed happily.

'Though the odds were not in her favor to take home the coveted award against stiff competition, the underdog pulled it off and Tess Delaney took the prize.'

They watched as Tess's acceptance speech was played back in full. Even just watching it, Garrett couldn't help feel a sense of pride, as though he'd actually witnessed Tess Delaney accept the honor. The voiceover went on.

'If Tess Delaney's big win came as something of a surprise, what happened next was even more of a surprise for the audience, and especially for literary critic and announcer, Barker Blessing.'

There it was, right there for the whole world to see, Blessing groping and Kendra reacting. Not only was it being played on national television, but it was being played in slow motion with a close-up, first of Blessing's hand sliding up the slit in Tess's dress, then of Tess, deliberately and with forethought, emptying her entire bowl of chocolate mousse, whipped cream, cherry and all, right onto the crotch of Blessing's white James Bond suit. Fortunately, the cameras were too busy capturing Tess's antics to notice Garrett's grip on the back of the man's collar a split second before.

They watched in high definition, as Garrett took Tess's arm and escorted her out of the banquet hall to a roar of applause.

'Blessing could not be reached for comment. However, Andrew Day, our reporter on the street, says Tess's actions have had a knock-on effect that amount to way more than just her first public appearance on the arm of Garrett Thorne and the sharing of her dessert with Barker Blessing. Andrew.'

The screen cut to a reporter standing in the middle of a huge check-out line in Powell's Bookstore.

'What we're seeing here is pretty typical of the five bookstores I've visited so far today.' The reporter turned to a woman in the check-out line who had three Tess Delaney novels clutched to her chest. She explained to him that she had watched the award ceremony and was so intrigued she rushed right to the bookstore this morning. The same interview was repeated with four other people.

While they watched what was unfolding on the screen,

Garrett put the BlackBerry on speaker so they both could hear Don.

'That's just the tip of the iceberg,' Don said. The excitement in his voice was palpable. 'That little scene with the mousse has already gone viral on YouTube and is trending on Twitter. Kay Lake's act was a stroke of genius, and Barker Blessing is now trying to convince everyone that it was all planned. You can't expect the man not to take advantage of good PR, even if it's at his expense. He didn't get where he is by being stupid.

'What's more, there's been a massive surge in sales, and my phone hasn't stopped ringing with people wanting interviews with Tess Delaney, wanting her to endorse everything from hairspray to condoms to pick-up trucks. I have to say, Garrett, I thought you'd blown it, but the woman is a genius. I've sent an email to K. Ryde, but haven't heard back yet. And I can't get hold of Kay Lake. Any ideas where she might be?'

Garrett and Kendra shot each other a quick glance, and she nodded her OK. 'I'm here, Don,' she said, her gaze still locked on Garrett.

There was a moment of silence. Garrett could almost hear the man thinking the situation through, speculating as to whether Kendra had just arrived or if she had stayed over. Neither Kendra nor he gave anything away.

Then Don continued, 'As for endorsements, well, I understand that's a bit beyond the pale for the moment, but I think we will need to discuss interviews, Garrett. Strategically planned and done sparingly, they could keep the wave going, keep the sales rising, keep everyone on the edge of their seats guessing what Tess Delaney will do next. Certainly having her seen with Garrett Thorne was a spot of genius if ever there was one.'

Garrett bristled. 'This isn't part of the plan, Don. Tess has done what you asked of her. That was what we agreed on and nothing more.'

Don offered a nervous laugh. 'I know, buddy, I know. But you have to understand, this is way bigger than either of us could have imagined, and I'm sure that K. Ryde will agree when he gets back to me. I just think it would be foolish not to take full advantage. A gift horse and all, you know?' Before Garrett could do more than growl, he continued, 'Look, all I'm saying is just think about it. Give me a chance to talk to Ryde and get back to you, and I'm sure we'll figure out the best way to make this work to the greatest advantage for Tess.'

The line went dead, and Garrett and Kendra sat staring at each other. Garrett reached for the remote and switched off the television. 'So what do you think?' he said. 'I mean, you are K. Ryde.'

She ran a hand through her hair and tightened the sash at the waist of the robe. In the kitchen they could hear the coffee maker gurgling out the last of the coffee into the pot. 'Garrett, I work for Tess Delaney, not Don Bachman, and I think it's up to you. You've done what was asked of you. It's had better than expected results, and now I think you should do what you want. I mean, a huge part of Tess's appeal is her mystique. The more public she becomes the more she risks losing that mystique. If you do decide to have Tess make the odd public appearance, then I'll happily oblige, but the more I pretend to be Tess Delaney, the more risk we run of her really being outed.'

He tugged a strand of her red hair. 'You think I should do what I want?' He scooted closer and brushed a kiss against her parted lips. 'Because I'm pretty sure you have a good idea of what I want right now.'

She made a half-hearted effort to pull away from him. 'Garrett, this is serious business. I need to know, K. Ryde needs to know what to do next.'

He gently nipped her lip and felt her breath catch. 'I understand that, Kendra, believe me, I do.' He guided her hand to rest against the bulge barely contained by his straining shorts. 'But I can't think very well at the moment. If you could just help me out a little bit here –' with his other hand, he slid open the bottom of the robe to reveal her lush thighs and beyond '– then maybe I could concentrate on business a little better.'

She forced an irritated sigh that ended in a soft giggle as he pulled her to him, shoving the robe open still further, exposing her breasts to the explorations of his lips and the cupping of his hands as he eased her back onto the sofa, wriggling his way in between her legs. He had just worried open the sash and slipped a hand down to cup her and stroke the unbelievable warmth of her when a loud crash on the front porch caused them both to jump. She jerked the robe back around her, and he shot up from the couch like he was spring-loaded.

'What the hell?' He scrambled to the door with her right behind him, tightening the sash of the robe as she went.

'Wait, Garrett. Don't open it.'

She reached for his hand, but it was already too late. He wasn't thinking straight. How could he possibly be thinking straight when he had been just about to make love to Kendra Davis? He swung the door open wide and found himself, in nothing but his scant and somewhat bulging workout shorts, with Kendra barely covered in his oversized robe, facing a sea of reporters. Cameras flashed, the press surged, and before Garrett could close the door, someone shoved a microphone in his face, shouldering his way into the breach of the door. Garrett sought to recall his name. Mike Pittman, that was his name –Garrett remembered the irritating reporter from Dee and Ellis's meeting with the press a few weeks ago. The microphone might have been in Garrett's face, but Pittman's eyes and the lens of the cameraman's camera were focused on Kendra, hair thoroughly mussed from last night's romp, still tying the robe that was clearly his, and looking more than a little like she'd just been caught in the act.

'So it's true, then,' Pittman said. 'Tess Delaney did spend the night with you after the Golden Kiss debacle?'

Debacle! That slimy little rat! 'Get out of my face.' Garrett's voice was a dangerous growl, and he wasn't sure what would have happened if Kendra hadn't pushed her way front and centre.

'Mr. Pittman,' she said, her voice way too good-natured for what Garrett was sure she must have felt. 'The answer to that question is obvious. Where else did you think I would be on such an occasion?' As if to demonstrate, she ran her arm through Garrett's and smiled up at him.

'And what about Barker Blessing?' Pittman pressed on. 'Have you heard from him? From his lawyers?'

'I think you need to talk to Mr. Blessing about that.' She stepped forward into the man's personal space and forced him back with nothing more than the power of presence. 'If you'll excuse us, Mr. Pittman –' she shot a quick look around, and offered a smile and a polite nod to the rest of the rabble '– everyone. Coffee's getting cold.' Her smile turned wicked. 'I'm starving, and Garrett promised to make me pancakes.' Then she stepped back and shut the door in the man's face – not slammed it, just shut it – and turned to face Garrett, her back pressed against the door.

'Make you pancakes?' Garrett managed before she hijacked the conversation.

'Rule number one,' she said, before he could even utter the curse that was on the tip of his tongue. 'Don't give the press any reason to up the ante.' She shrugged. 'All right, you already blew that one last night, and this is the result.' She nodded to the shuffling and mumbling they could still hear beyond the closed door. 'This is why we needed things to go smoothly last night, and why we need them eating out of our hands now.' She made her way into the living room and peeked around the edge of the curtain at the reporters on the lawn.

'I blew it?' he bristled, following her to the window. 'You're the one who dumped your dessert in Barker Blessing's lap.'

And that was his fatal mistake. Would he never learn to hold his tongue around Kendra Davis? He could see the tension in her shoulders before she turned to face him. 'It was dessert, Garrett, just dessert. Not your fist to the man's face, not a lawsuit, not jail.' She stood facing him with her hands on her hips, her eyes bright and fiery. 'And would you have hit Pittman there, if I hadn't stepped in?'

'Oh, you're a fine one to talk about not resorting to violence,' he said, following her around the living room as she scooped together her clothing. 'You, who nearly dislocated my jaw!'

She turned on him. 'Oh pa-lease. You deserved it. You've deserved everything you got so far, and last night, well, if you'd have just let me handle it, then this –' she stabbed a finger at the door '– wouldn't be happening.' She shoved off the robe and stood naked in front of him, tugging her panties up over her hips and then fighting her way into the green dress. And fuck, it was so hard to stay focused with her doing that. Did she do that on purpose – get his cock's full attention so his brain wouldn't work? She probably did. She was a bitch, he reminded himself. How the hell could he forget the number one fact about Kendra Davis? The woman was a bitch. Interact with her at your own risk. He watched her stuff her stockings and garter belt into her bag like they were the enemy, and he was sympathetic.

'Where's the back door?' she said.

'Through the kitchen,' he replied, his brain still half occupied by her angry reverse striptease that had left him in a bad way. 'Wait a minute. Where are you going? What are you doing?' He followed her into the kitchen with her stumbling into her killer heels as she went. 'Fixing it,' she huffed. Then she fumbled in her bag for her iPhone. 'Hi, Dee. You home? Can you come get me? I'm at Garrett's.' He was pretty sure Dee got the "don't ask" warning in her voice. She'd have to be deaf and stupid not to. 'Come around back. The alley yes. Now.'

Dee lived close. Garrett hadn't planned it that way, but it was a nice neighbourhood. Kendra shoved her phone back into her bag and headed for the door. Then she turned her attention to him. 'You stay put. Don't go out until I give you the all-clear. I mean it, or you can find someone else to fix your fuck-ups.' Then she shoved her way out the back door, pulling it carefully to behind her. He'd expected her to slam it, but then K. Ryde wouldn't slam a door, would she – er – he?

It was all he could do to keep from storming out after her and dragging her back so they could settle this, but no. He wouldn't give her the satisfaction. He absolutely would not give her the satisfaction.

He half stormed, half limped over to the coffee machine,

still sporting a hard-on that reached the counter before he did, a hard-on he had no intention of taking care of. He wouldn't give it up to her even if he exploded.

He missed the cup with the coffee pot and poured steaming coffee onto the granite countertop – what he didn't manage to scorch his hand with. Damn the woman. She was a scourge to femaledom. What had he done in a past life to deserve her? He gulped coffee, burnt his tongue, and cursed out loud. He couldn't believe such a comedy of errors existed in the real world. This really was the kind of stuff that came straight from a Tess Delaney novel.

He couldn't help himself. He made his way into his study, uncomfortable in the shorts, burnt on the tongue, and pissed off as hell. He opened up his laptop and continued with the synopsis he'd started the other night after he'd talked to Kendra, back when things were civil. For a brief second, he felt his chest tighten. He hadn't wanted her angry. He had wanted her happy and sexy and pleased to be with him. He took a more cautious sip of his coffee, pushed the thought out of his head, and began to write like a madman.

He'd been writing for nearly an hour when he decided to check his email. After all, Don might have been in touch. At least that's what he told himself. What he really was hoping for was an email from Kay Lake, one he had no intention of answering, of course – unless it was an unconditional apology begging forgiveness with the offer of sexual favours. The only email there, however, got his full attention and raised the hair on the back of his neck. It was from Razor Sharp.

Congratulations, Tess!

Of course, I'm not at all surprised you won. How could you not? You looked stunning last night, by the way. I was gripped. You were like the sun, Tess, like the sun.

Until you fucked Garrett Thorne. Don't play stupid. Of course I know you fucked him. Everyone watching last night knows you fucked him.

That ruined it for me – ruined you for me.

How could you do it, Tess? Don't you know what he's like? Don't you know he's not for you? You can't go about whoring with the likes of him if we're going to be together. I won't have you being a slut! You'll have to pay, my darling. I'm sorry, but you'll have to be punished for what you did to me. Then maybe you'll understand nobody can satisfy your filthy appetites like I can.

Disappointedly yours,
R.S.

Before he had finished reading the message, Garrett called up Kay Lake's number on the BlackBerry, which he gripped to his ear almost painfully. 'Pick up, Kendra,' he breathed. 'Please pick up.'

When he only got her voicemail he said, 'I need you to call me now. It's urgent.' He hung up and texted her frantically.

Once he'd sent his text, he called Ellis. He didn't wait for his brother's greeting. 'Are you at Dee's?' He barely gave the man time for a yes before he ploughed on. 'Is Kendra there?' Another yes left him weak-kneed with relief. When he finally caught his breath, he continued before Ellis could ask. 'Listen, I need you to tell Dee not to leave her alone. I can't explain over the phone, but just tell her. And can you come over? Now. I need to see you, bro. It's urgent. And Ellis, could you park around back and come in the back door? Quietly.'

He hung up, read the email one more time. The level of relief he felt at knowing Kendra was with Dee was nearly overwhelming. He hurried to his room and got dressed.

It had been a helluva 12 hours for Carla Flannery. It had taken all the pull she could manage to get into the Golden Kiss Awards, and even then she'd still had to pay for a ticket. There'd been speculation right up till the end as to whether Tess Delaney would even show at all. Odds were against it. The editor she was working for at the moment had been so sure of it that he wasn't going to send anyone. She had forced the issue, and wow, she was glad she did!

Yes, she felt cheated that there had been no press conference afterward, but she'd been the first to figure that the couple would head straight for Garrett Thorne's house afterward. From the moment she saw the two get out of the limo together and realized who Thorne was escorting, she had made it priority one to find out where he lived. She had friends in the real estate business, and she knew the man had only recently moved to Portland. She was a bit embarrassed to admit that she had followed what went on with the two Thorne brothers and Wade Crittenden like a groupie. Who wouldn't, though? Wade and Ellis were brilliance times two, and then there was Garrett, baddest of bad boys, and hotter than hot. And now, perhaps all that groupie adoration just might pay off.

From the beginning she was pretty sure she wouldn't get anything at the Golden Kiss Awards that every other reporter there wouldn't also get, and that would never be enough, even with Tess Delaney making her first ever public appearance.

When the couple left unexpectedly, she was ready for them, and she would have had them all to herself if that damned Mike Pittman hadn't noticed her leaving and followed. Then, in the neighbourhood where Garrett Thorne's house was tucked away, she got lost in the cul-de-sacs and side streets that curved back onto themselves like a tipped-over bowl of spaghetti. She arrived just in time to see the very amorous couple disappear into the house. And damn if Pittman wasn't right behind her, followed by half a dozen other reporters.

All through the night the ranks had swollen, with other reporters coming and going, with bathroom breaks and breaks for coffee and snacks. But she had a bladder of steel. That, along with a Snickers bar and a half a roll of cherry LifeSavers, stood her in good stead for the night. She waited stoically, checking out every possible lead she could come up with on her iPad. The first glimmer of dawn was breaking, and she had just returned from a quick pee behind the car, when she got the email.

You're a stellar journalist, Ms. Flannery. Pity you don't get the credit you deserve. That's why I chose to email you with this tip.

Tess Delaney's quick departure from the Golden Kiss Awards was not what it appeared. I have it on good authority that Tess is being stalked, that her life is being threatened.

Adrenaline surged like a drug through Carla's veins. This

could be the break she was looking for. She read on.

I'm sharing this with you because I think you're trustworthy. I think you're a good journalist who believes in protecting her sources.

I'm absolutely certain of this little tip, Ms. Flannery, because I'm the one stalking Tess Delaney. And I have every intention of making her pay for everything she's done to me, for making me wait, for keeping herself hidden like she has, for being such a tease, for being such a whore. She deserves whatever she gets, Ms. Flannery. Don't doubt that for a minute.

Carla felt the fine hair on the back of her neck prickle and gooseflesh broke across her arms.

Ask Tess, when she comes out to speak with the press. And she will. She won't deny you that opportunity. I'll wager her publicist will force the issue. Ask her about the threat to her life.

Ask the question, Ms. Flannery. See what she says. What a story you'll have!

The email wasn't signed.

She felt like someone had just poured ice water down her spine. She'd had anonymous tips before. Lots of them. And several of them had paid off big time. Carla knew better than to ignore them, but damn it, this was a little bit scary. This was more than a little bit scary. In the end, it might be best for her to keep her mouth shut until she could talk to her editor about it. She shifted in the seat and tried to stretch her aching back. Her editor had the news instincts of a damp paper towel. And she was here and now and ... She looked around the neighbourhood as the dawn light paled around her. Garrett Thorne's house was completely silent. She imagined the couple were still sleeping it off. It could be hours before there was any movement, before there was any possibility of a story. That gave her time to consider whether or not to talk to her editor about it. And, in truth, she could always just send a text at the last minute.

Thanks to that ass, Pittman, the place was crawling with reporters and the possibility of getting anything unique was almost non-existent – except for this tip, this nasty little tip that made her skin crawl.

She searched for any stories that mentioned threats to Tess Delaney. There were none, because until last night no one had ever even seen Tess Delaney. That in itself would bring all the nutters out of the woodwork. Tess Delaney, out in public for the first time, with a real face and a real personality, would now be subject to all the craziness every other celebrity was. Carla couldn't keep from wondering why the woman hadn't just stayed tucked away in her private hideaway and let the loonies find someone else to badger. Of course, she was happy about the chance for a story, but really, this email was just creepy. She considered calling one of her buds down at the police department, but then she knew that would be a wasted call. It was just one more prank among many, they'd say. And they were right. She'd wait and see. That's all she could do at the moment. Wait and see. God, she'd give her right arm for a cinnamon roll and a cup of coffee about now!

Chapter Twelve

Kendra had had a quick shower and now sat in yoga pants and a tank top from the stash of clothing she always left at Dee's for when she house-sat. McAlister, the red tabby, lay curled up in her lap on the sofa, his tail twitching from side to side. Ellis and Dee sat in the two wing-backed leather chairs across from her and listened to the whole sordid story. They offered no judgmental "I told you so". She really appreciated that, especially since she knew she deserved it.

'You had sex with Garrett,' Dee said, holding her gaze. Jesus, was she really going to make her repeat it?

Kendra nodded. 'It just happened. We … We weren't ourselves, I guess.'

Ellis was trying hard not to snigger, and she really appreciated that too. She'd certainly have been sniggering if it had happened to someone else.

'So what are you going to do?' he asked. 'The two of you.'

She shifted under the heavy weight of the cat, scratching his thick ruff and eliciting a half-hearted purr. 'Well, I think we'll to have to make a statement. I mean, if Garrett wants Tess to keep out of the limelight, I think we're going to have to give the press at least something. Then after that, I think Garrett's going to have to be super-protective of his girlfriend.' She lifted the cat off her lap and stood to pace in front of the sofa. 'Maybe him being surly like he was this morning and dragging Tess away like he did last night is just the ticket.' She stroked her chin. 'Maybe that's our way out.' She was talking more to herself now than to Dee and Ellis, who sat with coffee cups in hand and watched her pace. 'I mean, who wouldn't believe that he's protective of his lover's privacy, if his lover's the ultra-reclusive Tess Delaney, especially. He just has to keep up the cover until the initial excitement dies down a bit and people get bored with the story. You know how quickly people get bored. It wouldn't take more than a day or two, especially if we give them an interview to placate them. Then, I'd guess by the middle of the week at the latest, we could leak something to the press, I don't know, something about the two of us breaking up. We could just say that Tess has gone away someplace private to write and mend her broken heart.' She ran a hand through her still-damp hair. 'It means I'd have to stay at Garrett's for a little while. I don't see how we can avoid that now, since Tess literally has no place to go, and we can't risk the press finding her at my place. Plus they already know we were – together last night. We're now an item, whether we like it or not, and at the moment, I think we need to at least convince the press that we like it.' She waved a hand as though she was fending off a swarm of mosquitoes. 'I mean, it can be stormy, of course it can. Most relationships involving celebrities are, and I can't imagine one with Garrett being anything but stormy.' She stopped mid-soliloquy and turned her attention to Ellis. 'Sorry, Ellis, I know he's your brother and all.'

Ellis only smiled and shrugged as though she wasn't telling him anything he didn't already know.

'Do you think you two can manage that without killing each other?' Dee asked.

'We'll have to, won't we? If we want to keep Tess's identity safe. OK, last night was a mistake, I'll admit it. Last night was unprofessional and I – K. Ryde – owes Garrett an apology for my unprofessionalism. Nothing like that has ever happened before and there's no excuse for it. None. I'll see that Garrett, that Tess, doesn't have to pay for K. Ryde's mistake, and I'll make it right. That's all, I'll make it right.'

Just then Ellis's BlackBerry rang. He picked it up from the coffee table. 'Garrett? What's up? What do you … Yes, she's here.' He shot Kendra a quick glance. 'Do you want to talk …?'

Both women stared at Ellis, but the remainder of the

conversation consisted of, 'Yes … All right, I can do that … Now …? OK, I'll be right there.'

He hung up and blew out a sharp breath. 'Garrett wants me to come over. He says it's urgent.'

Kendra refrained from saying that he probably just needed some hand-holding. 'Please, Ellis, don't let him go outside, even if you have to tie him to a chair. I don't want him in the public eye until we have a working plan in place. Can you do that for me?'

Ellis offered a smile that made her stomach do a little somersault as she realized just how much it reminded her of Garrett's quirky grin. 'It'll be a pleasure to keep the twit in line,' he said.

He glanced down at his watch, then motioned Dee to walk him to the door, Kendra figured for a little private cuddle, and hell, the two had earned it, hadn't they? She felt another stab of anger at Garrett for what he and Stacie had nearly destroyed.

Ellis offered Kendra a reassuring smile. 'Don't worry, I'll take care of him.'

While Dee was saying her goodbyes to Ellis, Kendra checked her email. Just as she'd expected, there was a message from Don for K. Ryde. After his glowing praise for Kay Lake's portrayal of Tess, the email was a basic repeat of what he had said to Garrett this morning, urging K. Ryde to try and convince Garrett to let Tess do some interviews and some endorsements.

Kendra stared at the message. Was the man an absolute idiot? Was he really so greedy that he couldn't see every time she made a public appearance, Tess was that much more likely to be outed?

Beneath it was an email from Garrett asking her to call him, saying it was urgent. There was also a text that said nearly the same thing.

She wanted to ignore him. He'd called his brother, for fuck's sake! The big baby. She wanted to let him suffer. But she couldn't. It might be business. It might be something else with the press. He did say it was urgent. She texted back.

What do you need?

Then she added, *Is everything all right? Ellis is on his way.*

She was just about to call him when Dee returned, so she shoved the iPhone back in her bag.

'You OK?' Dee asked.

Kendra flopped down on the sofa and shook her head. 'It's a mess, Dee. I've made such a complete fuck-up of the situation.'

Dee handed her a Diet Pepsi and settled in next to her with her iced tea. Kendra could never remember being at Dee's house and not finding her friend with her perpetual glass of tea close at hand, even if she was drinking something else too.

'When Garrett told me that you were going to be Tess for him, I was shocked that you'd even considered the position after everything that's happened,' Dee said. 'I was worried about you. I couldn't decide if you were very brave or very stupid.'

Kendra forced a smile. 'I'm leaning pretty heavily toward the stupid side right now. When I found out that Garrett was Tess Delaney, I should have turned around, walked out the door, and never looked back. I should have run away fast. But no! I was so damn sure I could handle anything he could throw at me. And I could have. I could have if ...'

'If you hadn't slept with him?' Dee said.

'No! I mean well, maybe ... But –'

'Ken.' Dee stroked her shoulder. 'I know you. You don't mix business with pleasure. You've never had sex with any of your clients, have you?'

'Of course not!' Kendra tried to be offended at even the idea, but then she had broken the number one rule by jumping Garrett before they even got back to his house.

'Is this situation any more difficult than any other you've ever dealt with as K. Ryde?' Dee asked.

Kendra huffed. 'It's a waltz in the park. This barely qualifies as a problem compared to some of what K. Ryde's had to face.'

'So what are you so uptight about? You already know what you have to do. OK, it may not be ideal having to spend so much time with Garrett, but I'm sure you've had more unpleasant tasks.' For a second, Kendra thought she was going to offer that wicked smile, but Dee was nothing if not diplomatic. She remained neutral, for which Kendra was thankful. 'Besides, Garrett's an all right guy, actually, once you get to know him. Though I guess you have got to know him, haven't you?'

'Shut up, Dee,' Kendra growled.

Dee was first and foremost her best friend, and the situation had now transformed itself into girl time. 'So come on, Kendra, tell me and, be honest, because I'll know if you're not. Why did you have sex with Garrett if you dislike him so much?'

God, she hated it when Dee cut to the chase. She slugged back half her soda for courage. 'He looks like a slightly wilder, taller, darker version of Ellis. I mean, who could not like that about him?'

'People can look really good and still be such assholes the thought of fucking them is repugnant.' Dee observed. 'But Garrett's not one of those people, Kendra. Admit it. You two just got off on the wrong foot.'

Kendra glared at her. 'He hurt you.'

'That wasn't his intention. In fact, his intention was the opposite.'

'Yeah, well, good intentions are bullshit, Dee. You know that.'

'Ken, why did you have sex with him?'

Kendra found her heart suddenly in freefall at the very thought of being naked in Garrett's arms. She shut that picture out of her head as quickly as she could. 'He's fun to work with, and he's not arrogant, not like I thought he'd be. And really –' She bit her lip. 'How could I not be intrigued with a man who looks like he came straight from one of my wet dreams and writes the most amazing romance ever? I mean, what's that all about? What man writes romance? What man knows the heart of a woman well enough to do that? Clearly he isn't gay, and I'll vouch for the fact that he knows what to do with the equipment.' She fanned herself with her palm. 'Jesus, does he know what to do with the equipment.'

The smile Dee offered made Kendra think knowing what to

do with the equipment must be a shared trait of the Thorne brothers.

'It was good, Dee, really good.' Kendra shook her head and wrapped her arms tightly around herself. 'Don't you see? That's the problem. I got involved where I shouldn't have. I let my libido and my curiosity rule my brain and now look at the mess I'm in.'

Garrett was on his BlackBerry, sitting in front of his laptop when Ellis arrived. He'd felt better after Kendra had texted him, though he was pretty sure it was K. Ryde doing the texting. Still, she had at least answered. He'd polished off the last of the coffee Kendra had made and was trying to find out more about Razor Sharp, but was having no luck.

He hung up and tossed the device onto the table. Before Ellis got the door closed behind him, he asked, 'How's Kendra? Is she OK?'

'She's fine. I just left her with Dee, and Dee promised she won't let her out of her sight. Now, you want to tell me what's going on?'

Garrett pulled up the email and nodded Ellis to the computer. While his brother read, he paced the kitchen floor.

'I just got it this morning,' he said. 'After Kendra stormed out.'

'Is it the first time?' Ellis asked.

'Tess has got emails off and on from this guy for several years now. At least, I think it's the same guy. He changes his name and email address periodically, but his name always has to do with something sharp, something dangerous. Knife Edge, Stiletto … I think he was Blade Bearer once. That sort of thing.'

'Did you talk to Brewster about it?' Ellis asked as he read.

'That was him on the phone. No more helpful than I'd expected.' Garrett settled in the chair next to Ellis. 'I talked to the police right from the beginning, and, well, he's the only one I felt I could trust with Tess details. As much as he can manage it, he has a no-pry policy. But the police couldn't do anything. I mean, it's just an email, isn't it? And mostly they've just been irritating. This is the only one that's ever felt really threatening. Thing is –' Garrett ran a hand over his stubbled chin. 'This one is the first I've received since the Golden Kiss Awards and …'

'And the man now has a face to put with the name,' Ellis finished for him.

Garrett nodded. 'Kendra's face, Ellis. It's Kendra's face. Damn it! None of this would have ever happened if Romancine hadn't forced the issue. And then I … Well, I asked her to stay, or she wouldn't have. I practically begged her, actually, when I found out who she was, and what she did for a living. I was desperate. Jesus, Ellis, I didn't expect this. I never would have put her at risk.'

'I know that,' Ellis said.

'I thought about just firing her. You know, just telling her I'm terminating our working relationship. But he's seen her, hasn't he?' He nodded to the computer monitor.

'Garrett, after last night's award ceremony, millions of people have seen her, and you. For all we know he could be emailing from clear across the country, even across the world.'

'But he knows she spent the night with me last night.'

'Anyone watching the way you dragged her out of the awards could have guessed that easily enough,' Ellis said.

'I should have sent her home. I should never have taken advantage.'

'You don't know what would have happened if you'd sent her home, Garrett.' Ellis pushed away from the table, found the coffee, and went about making a fresh pot. 'Chances are if he knew she was here with you, he would have also known if she'd gone on home. And if he does live close, well, then who knows what he might have done. I mean, he saw you at the award ceremony with her. If he's the jealous type that would have been enough to set him off.'

'Damn it, Ellis, I don't want anything to happen to her because of me.'

'Do you have the other emails?' Ellis asked.

Garrett nodded. 'I saved them all in a separate file as they came in. Brewster said that was the thing to do, though I was doing that anyway. Even when the police said they couldn't do anything, I kept on, just in case.'

'Well, if the police can't help, then what do you want to do?' Ellis asked.

Garrett sat back in the chair and rotated his neck. 'I want her here with me so I can keep her close.' He ran a hand through his already dishevelled hair. 'Can you give me the number of your security service? I want to hire someone to discreetly keep an eye on the place.'

Ellis nodded his agreement. 'Of course. That's a good start.' He pulled out his BlackBerry and began to type. 'Martin is the man you want to talk to. I'll send you his information. He's discreet, thorough. He's the best in the business. He'll take care of it for you.' He sent the message, stuck his BlackBerry back in his pocket, and looked up at Garrett. 'You've got to tell her, you know? She needs to know what's going on.'

Garrett nodded. 'She's not going to like it.'

Just then the key in the lock turned and Kendra shoved her way in with Dee right behind her. Dee caught Garrett and Ellis's gaze behind her back and offered a helpless shrug. Then she turned to Ellis. 'What's going on?'

'What is it?' Kendra added.

Garrett stepped forward toward her cautiously, always careful to stay out of the reach of her bad-ass right hand until he had gauged her mood. She'd been anything but Sally-smiley-face when she'd left.

'While you were away –' He nodded to the computer. 'I got … I mean, Tess got a threatening email.'

'Let me see.'

'Kendra, no, don't.' Dee reached for her but it was too late.

Kendra shoved into the chair in front of the computer. 'Threatening emails aren't that uncommon for celebrities, you know. It probably means nothing.'

Garrett watched the muscles in her shoulders and neck tighten as she read, and he caught the slight acceleration in her breathing. She was good at hiding things, but he was good at finding out what people were hiding. It was one of his gifts, he supposed, but when the colour drained from her flushed cheeks, he found himself surprised, and more than a little concerned, that nerves-of-steel Kendra Davis would let her fear show through in such an obvious way. He took a step closer and dropped into the chair next to her. 'Are you all right?'

She made no response. He could see her pulse beating fast in her throat. When she'd finished reading the email, she pushed back from the computer and sat breathing hard with her eyes still locked on the screen. 'It's probably nothing,' she repeated. But her voice, no matter how hard she tried, wasn't all that convincing. 'Just some over-zealous fan. Is this the first one?'

She listened as Garrett told her about Razor Sharp's history. 'I'm sorry,' he said at last. 'I should have told you. It's just that up until now they've never been this threatening, and up until now, Tess Delaney didn't have a face. I talked to the police –'

'They can't help,' she interrupted. 'There's nothing they can do until … Until something happens. Like I said, this sort of thing's not all that uncommon with celebrities, and Tess is a celebrity, and you can't go crying wolf every time someone gets a little pissy or a little …'

'Kendra? Are you all right?' Garrett asked. 'Kendra?'

She stood, then stumbled and nearly fell before Garrett caught her, engulfing her in his arms. He guided her back into the chair, which Ellis had turned around for her. Once she was seated again, she dropped her head between her knees and began to shake.

'I'm sorry,' she whispered between gasps for breath. 'I'm sorry.'

Dee disappeared into the bathroom and returned with a damp washcloth, which Garrett grabbed away from her and placed across the back of Kendra's neck.

'Ken.' Dee pushed in on the other side of her friend and stroked her back. 'Ken, you know it's not –'

'No! No, it isn't. I know that.'

'It's not what?' Garrett said, gripping Kendra's hand nearly hard enough to break bone. 'What's going on?'

'Kendra had a stalker before and –'

'Shut up, Dee,' Kendra managed between gulps for breath. 'It's not him. That's over with. It can't be him, and you know it.' She forced herself to sit up, still gripping Garrett's hand for dear life. His insides twisted in anguish when he saw the pale transformation of her face, the haunted look in her eyes. 'This man has had contact with Tess, always contact with Tess. He doesn't know who I am. He just thinks I'm Tess, that's all. It has nothing to do with what happened before. That's not possible.'

'What happened before?' Garrett dropped to his knees in front of her on the floor, both her hands gripped in his. He couldn't stand the thought that anyone could transform the indomitable Kendra Davis into such a state.

She jerked her hands away and shoved to her feet. The washcloth fell to the floor with a muted plop. 'It doesn't matter what happened before. It has nothing to do with what's happening now. I just overreacted because I'm a little neurotic, that's all. And my friend there –' she nodded to Dee '– has a very big mouth.'

Dee made no response other than to offer a concerned gaze.

Ignoring her, Kendra took a shaky breath, steadied herself on the back of the chair and began to pace. 'In the meantime, we still have a major mess to clean up.'

Garrett braced himself for accusations that didn't come. Instead, she continued as though she was a football coach planning a play. He figured that was a pretty good analogy.

'I'd imagine the crowd out front is gone for the moment,' she said. 'I called in a favour from a friend, who's just had a sighting of the sneaky Tess Delaney and Garrett Thorne over at the Heathman. Escaped through the back door, you know?' She smiled, and Garrett could see a little bit of the old Kendra Davis beginning to surface again. He had to admit, it warmed his heart.

'I've called in the troops,' she said, still pacing. 'I've noticed the cupboards are bare, and since our movement is going to be a bit restricted for a while, I've got someone bringing in groceries and supplies. Lots of coffee, lots of wine, lots of Diet Pepsi. I figure we'll need all the liquid courage we can get. I'm sorry, Garrett, I had to guess at what you like. There wasn't time to put together a gourmet grocery list.'

He smiled. 'Anything's fine with me, thanks.'

She smiled back and, to Garrett, it felt like the sun had just come out. She continued, 'Harris is bringing my clothes. He's thrilled about that.'

In spite of herself, Dee sniggered.

'All of that should be happening within the hour, which is about all the time I figure we'll have before the hordes descend again. Garrett, you'll have to pretend that I'm holed up here writing. I think that's our best bet. I'm afraid we'll be stuck with each other until things blow over. Nothing to worry about. There's always something sensational to grab the attention of the gossips. I doubt if it'll be a long siege. And we'll have to go before the press. We'll make one quick appearance together to appease the masses.' She raised a hand as she saw him bristle. 'Be nice, and tell them something, I don't know, something that will at least temporarily satisfy them and keep them off our backs. Once the groceries have arrived and I have something besides yoga pants and a well-partied-in evening dress, we'll draft something, make some kind of plan.

'That –' She nodded to Garrett's laptop on the table. 'I'm wagering that's nothing. In fact, I'm wagering whoever keeps track of Tess's fan mail and website will get a few more nutters weighing in with their opinions before the whole Golden Kiss adventure is laid to rest and Tess can go quietly back to her ivory tower. But the police won't help. They can't. Please don't call them again without consulting me first.'

This time, Garrett happily risked her wrath. He came to stand nose to nose with her and grabbed her by the shoulders. 'If I think we need the police, we'll call them, and you can't stop me. Get used to it.' He nodded to Ellis. 'I'll have a security team here before the afternoon is over, and you're never to go anyplace without one of them or me, I mean it, Kendra. I'm fine with you doing your job. You're amazing at doing your job, but there's no way I'm putting you at unnecessary risk, so just deal with it.'

To his surprise, she didn't slap him, she didn't even argue. She simply blew out a sharp breath and, holding him in that incredible bright-eyed gaze of hers, nodded her consent.

Chapter Thirteen

Garrett had dealt with the press before, usually as Ellis's misbehaving brother, and seldom very gracefully. He hated having the microphones shoved in his face, and he hated being stared at. He usually reacted badly. But the press, they were nothing compared to an angry Kendra Davis, so he would do his very best to smile and behave himself.

'Are you sure about this?' he called up the stairs to where she was getting ready in the guest room. He was still hopeful he could get her to change her mind, though why he imagined he'd have that kind of sway over her was beyond him.

'Positive,' Kendra called down.

He wasn't keen that she was settling into the guest room. That wasn't where he wanted her, but since her return this morning, she'd given no indication that she had anything in mind other than the professional arrangement they had struck when she agreed to be Tess Delaney for him. Damn it! Could she really completely turn it all off that easily? He still couldn't be in the same room with her without his cock getting tetchy in his jeans. Was she really that cool and indifferent toward him? It certainly hadn't felt like it last night, or this morning before they discovered the press camped out on his front porch.

He'd been pacing the floor of the living room dressed in his best jeans and a blue cotton shirt she had insisted he iron. When he'd hinted that he wasn't very good at ironing, she only glared at him and nodded to the ironing board. He'd had help to do that sort of thing in New York, but he'd not got around to hiring anyone yet. He paced once more and then suddenly found himself looking up at her descending the stairs, and his full attention was riveted to her luscious long legs leading the way from underneath a sundress that hugged her body in shades of turquoise and gold. And how she could even walk in the shoes with the nosebleed heels was beyond him. But she wasn't just walking, she was practically floating.

She wore her hair loose around her shoulders and the fact she was actually smiling at him rather than growling, as had been the order of the day so far, went a long way toward easing the discomfort he felt at having to face the press. The whole damn lot of them had once again rudely made themselves at home on his front lawn after they discovered that the sighting of Tess Delaney at the Heathman was a false lead.

'It's just that I worry,' he said, nodding toward the kitchen and the laptop with the email.

'Don't,' she said. 'Don't worry. These things happen.' A lovely blush crawled up her throat and onto her cheeks. 'I overreacted, that's all. I'm just neurotic; something you should be warned about if we're going to be spending time in close proximity.'

But it was more than that. He was sure of it. Way more. And that's what really frightened him. He was pretty sure that whatever had driven Kendra Davis to her knees was not likely to be something easy. Now wasn't the time to approach the subject. But he would approach it. There was too much at stake not to.

He returned his attention to what she was saying. 'There was no press conference last night at the Golden Kiss Awards. We cheated them. That's not a wise thing to do to the press. If we want to pull this off and get Tess back, first into their good graces, and then back to her solitude, we've got to give them what was promised, and we've got to do it graciously.'

'I didn't promise anything,' he grumped.

'Yes, you did, Garrett,' She reached up and brushed an unruly lock of hair out of his eyes. 'You did when you – when Tess penned the very first Tess Delaney novel.' She nodded to the front door, out to the crowd camped on the lawn. 'You promised them romance, and you've always delivered it. Now's no different. Now's even more important in a lot of ways. They get to meet their heroine. No one wants to be disappointed by those they look up to. So let's give them something worthy of looking up to, shall we?'

It was crazy, but suddenly he wanted to take her in his arms and kiss her, just kiss her, and hold her there. How could someone who could be such a bitch see into his heart so easily?

He took a deep breath and let it out slowly, not taking his eyes off her edible smile. 'Then let's do it,' he said.

They walked arm in arm to the front door. On the other side they could hear the chatter and shuffling of the reporters. She offered his arm a reassuring squeeze, which he figured also served as a reminder of just how hard she would pinch him if he fucked up, but suddenly it didn't matter. Suddenly he knew he wouldn't fuck up, because at that moment, there was nothing he wanted more than to please Kendra Davis. He wasn't sure why that was, but it just was. She gave him a nod, and he opened the front door.

As usual, the annoying Mr. Pittman was the first to lunge at the couple. But this time, it was Garrett who stepped forward, forcing the man back – gently and politely, but forcing him back nonetheless. He could feel Kendra bristle next to him, but he offered her his warmest smile, then he turned his attention back to the reporters.

'If I could just get you all to step back off the porch and give Ms. Delaney and me a little breathing room, we'd be happy to answer your questions.'

Kendra offered him a quick glance of surprise as the reporters, mumbling quietly amongst themselves, did as Garrett asked.

When they'd all settled, he offered his brightest smile – for her; not for them – but they didn't have to know that, did they? 'I believe that I robbed you all of a press conference last night, and who can really blame me for wanting the stunning woman of the hour all to myself.' He offered Kendra an adoring look.

The women all smiled that wistful smile women got when they were wishing their guys were so romantic to them. And the men all nodded their agreement – that they would certainly feel the same way as Garrett if they had Tess Delaney on their arm. All the men, that is, except for Mr. Pittman, who seemed completely focused on getting a story.

'Mr. Thorne, I'm wondering, would you have hit Barker Blessing last night at the awards ceremony if Ms. Delaney hadn't dumped her chocolate mousse in his lap? Or was it, as Blessing suggests, a publicity stunt?'

The subtle pressure on his arm and the slight threat of Kendra's nails served as a reminder to be nice. He forced a smile.

'You were there. You saw what happened, Mr. Pittman, and what I might have done if Tess hadn't decided to share her dessert with the esteemed Mr. Blessing is a moot point, don't you think?'

A middle-aged woman who worked for the *Oregonian* elbowed her way past Pittman. 'Ms. Delaney, clearly exciting things were going on at your table last night, things that led to Mr. Thorne dragging you away, and there isn't a person who saw that performance who doesn't want to know what really happened.'

Kendra stepped forward, offered everyone her award-winning smile and then a modest blush. 'In all honesty, last night was a bit overwhelming for me. Remember I told you that I'm not much for public appearances. I was terrified I was going to fall over my own feet on my way up to accept the Golden Kiss Award. I'm a bit of a klutz, really, and here's shy, reclusive me in front of the whole world, and then winning the Golden Kiss and all. I never expected that.' She bit her lip and her eyes welled with emotion. Garrett was stunned again by just how good she was. Several of the reporters nodded their understanding, and Garrett could almost feel the swell of sympathy.

'Anyway, I was mortified when my dessert fell into Mr. Blessing's lap. We all know the weight the man carries in the literary world and how respected he is. And here he was paying attention to me, and then I go and dump my dessert in the man's lap, and him in a white suit.' Someone at the back sniggered. Garrett bit the inside of his cheek to keep from doing the same. Kendra took a bosom-heaving deep breath. 'Well, as you can imagine, I was horrified, and all my plans for being graceful and impressive went right out the window. That was sort of the straw that broke the camel's back.' She leaned close to Garrett as though she needed his support, and he slipped an arm around her, which was no hardship at all. In fact, he wasn't acting when he pulled her protectively to him. 'I really am a very private person, painfully shy, actually, and right now I'm working very hard to meet a tight deadline. And all the excitement and everything, well, you can imagine the stress it caused. I was simply overwhelmed, that's all.'

'You seemed fine to me,' Pittman said.

Kendra's fingers dug into Garrett's ribs in warning. She batted her eyelashes and offered her most sincere smile to the bastard. 'Well, I was supposed to seem fine to you, Mr. Pittman. That was why I was surrounded by Garrett and my lovely publicist, Don Bachman. They both agreed that getting me out of a stressful situation was essential.' Her face became suddenly serious. 'Honestly, I can't even think about what might have happened if they hadn't acted so quickly.'

Everyone else nodded sympathetically, but Pittman still didn't look convinced.

A reporter spoke up from the back. 'The news this morning is that Tess Delaney novels are flying off the shelf after last night, and yet you say what happened wasn't a publicity ploy?'

Kendra shook her head. 'No. Just me being terribly clumsy and terribly neurotic, and Barker Blessing being terribly kind trying to protect me.'

Someone else sniggered, but Garrett got it. Garrett understood that no one doubted what had happened. Everyone had seen exactly what Barker Blessing was pulling. Yet, in spite of the man's lechery, Tess Delaney was letting him off the hook, and they already adored her for it. Garrett suspected that Kendra Davis would have filled the man's lap with scalding coffee if left to her own devices. But they didn't need complications. Not if Tess were to return to quiet reclusiveness. And accusations were definitely complications. Again the woman's control was astounding.

She continued, 'I'm very sorry that I left before the press conference. It's embarrassing finding it so difficult to put myself out there in front of everyone, but you have to understand, I've never done this before, and I certainly never dreamed I'd win, and all I wanted to do last night was get away before I humiliated myself further.'

'And you spent the night here with Mr. Thorne,' came the question from one of the gossip rag journalists close to the front.

'Of course I did,' Kendra said. 'I was a nervous wreck. It took poor Garrett hours to calm me down.'

No one looked very sympathetic toward poor Garrett, and a few of the men looked downright envious.

She shot Garrett an adoring glance that made his insides tumble in a very good way. 'I don't know what I would have done without him,' she said.

'Mr. Thorne,' a reporter from the back spoke up. 'How long have you and Ms. Delaney been an item, if you don't mind my asking?'

'Not nearly long enough.' This time it was Garrett's turn to play the part. He lifted her chin on a curl of his index finger and brushed her lips slowly, seductively with his. Cameras flashed; the shifting in the crowd was a mix of discomfort and ain't-that-sweet. It was clear he'd caught Kendra off her guard. Quickly, she rested a hand against his chest, and for a second he thought she was going to push him away. Instead, she fisted her fingers in his shirt and pulled him still closer, to a smattering of applause from the crowd.

She pulled away with a happy sigh and turned to face everyone, her fingers still curled in Garrett's shirt, either seductively, or as a threat of what was to come behind closed doors. Clearly everyone in the press was convinced that what was going to happen behind those closed doors was going to be pretty fine. Kendra looked around the lawn, taking in everyone with her most charming smile, then she said. 'If it's all right with all of you, I really do have work to do, and later this evening –' She looked at her watch. 'Garrett has a nice bottle of champagne chilling to celebrate, so if you don't mind ...' She nodded toward the door behind them.

'Please, Ms. Delaney, just one more question, if I may.'

Garrett recognized Ms. Flannery from the award ceremony as she pushed her way forward from the back, and the others seemed to clear a path for her. There was a sudden whisper among them, as Kendra gave the nod that it was OK.

The woman was small of build and dressed in clothes that looked slept in, like most of the press. She had a mass of unruly dark curls hanging nearly to her shoulders. Her voice was gravelly and sexy for someone so young. 'Ms. Delaney, I've heard a rumour that Mr. Thorne has brought you here to keep you safe.' A murmur rose like a fast-moving breeze among the rest of the press that let Garrett know none of them had heard such a rumour. The reporter continued, 'Rumour has it there have been threats levelled at you, and I notice there's security around the property now that wasn't here when we left on our wild goose chase to the Heathman.' Again there was shuffling and mumbling among the other reporters. Clearly they hadn't noticed the security. 'Can you comment on that?'

Garrett felt Kendra stiffen against him. Instinctively, he tightened his grip. 'The security is just a precaution,' she said. 'I'm told I'm a hot commodity now, and I need to be kept safe.' There was a trickle of a laugh from the press, but they didn't seem very convinced. 'That's all.'

'Then there is no threat,' the surly Mr. Pittman chimed in.

'Just a precaution, like I said,' Kendra answered. Garrett noticed the tiniest bit of edge in her voice, but he was certain no one else did.

He didn't wait for further questions. He spoke up. 'Now, if you'll excuse us. Ms. Delaney has a deadline looming.' He took her by the hand and led her back into the house, managing to close the door behind them before there were any more questions.

Carla didn't feel good about confronting Tess, and she might not have had the guts to go through with it if she hadn't noticed the security around the house. They tried to blend in with the press, but her father was ex-military, and he now ran a security company. She knew things weren't always as they appeared, and she knew when security was trying to blend in. It used to be a game she and her father played – spot the hidden security. OK, perhaps a strange game for father and daughter bonding but, like most kids, she'd taken what she could get. She'd put out feelers to make sure that no one else had noticed. They hadn't. But she did, and she understood the implications.

Even then she might not have brought the subject up if Barker Blessing hadn't called her in a total panic. Barker Blessing! Calling her! Her excitement was short lived when the first words out of his mouth were, 'Dear God, Ms. Flannery, Tess Delaney is being stalked, and if the anonymous email I received is any indication, then the woman could be in serious danger. Heavens! No wonder she wasn't herself last night.'

It had taken only a phone call to her editor from Blessing, insisting that he be interviewed and that it be by her. It had been remote, but that didn't matter. It was her interview, her scoop. That was something no one could take away from her. And when Blessing had passed on the email he had received, the cold knot of dread she felt in her chest convinced her that it was the same man. She pulled it up.

I know why Tess acted so erratically last night, why Thorne whisked her away so unceremoniously. She's being stalked, Blessing. Her life is in danger. And I would know this because I'm the one stalking her.

You need to call Carla Flannery. You need to tell her that you suspected the woman was in danger all along. Talk to Flannery and only Flannery, no other reporters! And don't talk to the police, Blessing.

Carla always considered herself an opportunist, but she knew Blessing was renowned for never missing out on free publicity. And within a half an hour, her boss had remote cameras set up, and an oh so anguished Barker Blessing had shared his deep concern for Tess's safety.

The whole situation gave her a bad feeling. But then she always had a bad feeling when she uncovered the best stories. Her father called it her spider sense. He said it ran in the family. She wondered again if she should call the police anyway. But then she doubted if they could do anything she couldn't do on her own. Besides, who knew? Maybe at the end of the day he was just another nutter having his moment in the sun.

She was just about to give her friend, Al Brewster, down at the police station a call when she got a text. She nearly dropped her iPhone when she read it.

I'm in front of TV waiting with bated breath for your report, Ms. Flannery. Was Blessing good? I'm sure he thought he was.

Her hands shook as she read the text a second time. This wasn't good. How did the man get her cell number? Before she could fully consider her next move, there was another text.

If you do as I say, you'll be a hero. If you don't, just remember how easily I found your cell number, Ms. Flannery. Keep everything in perspective, and your reputation will be greatly enhanced and all will be well.

Chapter Fourteen

'How the hell did she find out about the security?' Kendra said. 'They were supposed to be plain clothes. They were supposed to blend in with the party on the lawn.'

'They are plain clothes. I can't tell them from the press,' Garrett said, locking the door and securing the deadbolt. 'I have no idea how she knew. And do they actually know about the email?'

'It could be a bluff,' Kendra said, 'an effort to try and get something. I mean, most celebrities have security. It's essential. And the press would know that.' She already had her iPhone out, making a call. 'Hello, Stella, I need you to find out about a Carla Flannery. Reporter, yes. In Portland, that's right.'

Garrett scooted close to her to try and listen in the conversation. But it was over before he really heard anything, and Kendra was pulling up an email. 'She's a freelancer.' She read from the iPhone screen. 'Mostly works for webzines, but apparently has instincts that have got her several breaking stories the mainstream media has missed. She's got a reputation for being a real bulldog. Ellis would probably know her, actually. She was instrumental in breaking the story about the illegal landfill over by John Day last winter.'

'Fuck.' Garrett scrubbed a hand over his face. 'Just what we don't need right now, a bulldog of a reporter.'

'Well, the one thing we don't want is to make her our enemy,' Kendra said. 'If worse comes to worst, we might have to bring her into our confidence.'

'What?'

'I said if worse comes to worst. At the moment, it's just a rumor. No one can prove anything, and there's nothing to prove.'

He grabbed Kendra's arm. 'But what if she knows something we don't know, what if there are threats we don't know about?'

'For God's sake, Garrett, don't borrow trouble. It's going to be hard enough wading our way out of this without letting our imaginations run wild.'

'Not imagination, Kendra, just being cautious. This is not funny and I don't like it.'

He barely got the words out of his mouth before his BlackBerry rang. He grabbed it. 'It's Don,' he said.

'Answer it,' Kendra ordered.

Before he could even so much as offer a growl, Don spoke. 'Turn on your television. Local news again, and put me on speakerphone.' This time he didn't sound happy.

Garrett found the remote and tuned in just in time to see the view of Kendra and himself from his front porch. The bastards hadn't wasted any time, he thought. But what the anchor was saying made him forget everything else.

'In a new development in the Tess Delaney story, it appears that events at last night's Golden Kiss Award in which Ms. Delaney was captured on film dumping her chocolate mousse into the lap of literary critic, Barker Blessing, were not as they seemed.

'Reports are coming in that Ms. Delaney's quick exit from the gala of the year for romance writers, after winning the coveted prize, may have been for the writer's own protection.

'Though reporters were told that beefed-up security at the home of Garrett Thorne, who has now admitted to being Tess Delaney's lover, is only there as a precaution, the whole situation has got public attention. Some are saying it's all been just a publicity stunt. Police are not involved as far as we know, but with the reclusive nature of Tess Delaney being legendary, secrecy is bound to be the order of the day.

'Reporter at large, Carla Flannery, spoke to Barker Blessing a little while ago at his home, and he had this to say …'

The screen cut to a shot of Blessing sitting bare-chested and well-waxed in front of a swimming pool with palm trees in the background. If someone had sliced the man's wrist, he would have bled sincerity and concern. Then the screen split to include a picture of the young reporter, looking as determined as Blessing looked sincere.

'Did you suspect anything during the bizarre goings-on last night at the Golden Kiss Awards, Mr. Blessing?'

'I did, actually, Carla. Almost from the beginning I was certain there was something the matter, but there was just nothing I could put my finger on.'

'Except my fucking leg,' Kendra growled. Garrett shushed her. Blessing continued.

'Yes, I was worried from the outset; right from the beginning, something didn't feel right. I mean Tess is always so lovely and so sure of herself, and she was shaken, clearly very shaken. Not at all herself. Not at all.'

'As if the bastard would know,' Garrett grumbled.

Kendra raised a hand to silence him.

'That there have been threats on the poor woman's life explains so much. Dear God, I just can't imagine how anyone could threaten such a delightful woman, and such a talent. Such a talent.'

Garrett wouldn't have been surprised to see tears in the man's eyes as he looked into the camera.

'I'm very concerned for her, and I certainly hope Garrett Thorne can offer her the protection she needs.' He heaved a Gallic sigh. 'No doubt Thorne's brother, Ellis, will see to her protection at his brother's request. Under such circumstances, I suppose that should make us all feel a little better.'

'Bastard,' Kendra said.

Before Garrett could thoroughly enjoy the pleasure of Kendra taking his side, Don spoke up.

'Is any of this true?'

'The whole thing was blown out of proportion,' she said.

'Is there security?' Don cut to the chase.

'Yes,' Kendra said, 'but only as a precaution.'

'Garrett, I want to know what the hell is going on, and I want to know now.'

Garrett couldn't remember ever hearing Don so upset. He

caught Kendra's eye, and she gave him a nod. So he told Don about the email.

'Fuck,' Don whispered when Garrett finished. 'Are you all right, Kay?'

'I'm fine. These kinds of things aren't unusual with celebs,' she said.

'I know. I know,' Don said. 'But still. You didn't sign on for this.'

'We've got it under control,' she said. And though she sounded convincing, Garrett couldn't help thinking how she had been after she'd read the email. She continued. 'We weren't expecting the question from the press, and we certainly weren't expecting it to be blown all over the news, but we'll adapt.'

'She's staying with me,' Garrett said, maybe a little more forceful than necessary. But his mind was made up. He'd have no argument from either Kendra or Don. 'Just to be on the safe side. Besides, we really had planned that anyway until we could get the excitement from the award ceremony behind us. That may take a little longer now,' he added.

'This is a major inconvenience for you, Kay,' Don said, 'Are you sure this is all right with you? With Mr. Ryde? I mean, there are other arrangements we can make if you'd prefer.'

Garrett bristled. 'This is the best place for her, Don. And anyway, just a few hours ago you were wanting her to go public and start endorsing hair colour.'

'That wasn't exactly what I wanted, Garrett, and certainly the situation is different now, isn't it?'

'The situation's not different. It's no big deal,' Kendra said. 'This sort of thing happens all the time. How the press got their ideas, I don't know, and of course, Blessing just ate the whole thing all up, didn't he?'

'Well it's better than him wanting to sue our asses,' Don said.

'Yeah, better,' Garrett grumbled. 'Now, if there's nothing else, Don, we're busy here. We've got plans to make.'

He cut the connection before Don could say goodbye.

When Kendra shot him a questioning gaze, he shrugged. 'He's hot for you.'

She nodded. 'I got that from the email he sent to K. Ryde.'

Garrett sniggered. 'That's an interesting way to find out what a guy thinks about you, I guess. All you have to do is be two people.'

'And you would know something about that, wouldn't you, Garrett?'

'Kendra.' He reached out and took her hand and was relieved when she didn't pull away. 'I'm sorry I involved you in all of this. Nothing's quite worked out like I'd planned.'

She offered him a smile and curled her fingers around his. 'It never does, Garrett. That's part of what made running the Ryde Agency so much fun.'

He held her gaze. 'If it was so much fun, why did you sell it, the business I mean?'

The smile faded, and for a brief second the sadness in her eyes was deep enough to drown in. 'All good things have to come to an end.' She stood and headed toward the kitchen. 'I need a Diet Pepsi,' she called over her shoulder, once again her cheerful self. 'And I'm starving. You?'

He sat for a second catching his breath, trying to figure out what had just happened. He never imagined when she waltzed into Wade Crittenden's office at the Pneuma Building a few weeks ago, tossed her drink at him, then bitch-slapped him until his ears rang that she was so complex, so intriguing. Eventually, the rattling of pots and pans drew him to the kitchen. Well, actually, it was the woman rattling the pots and pans that drew him. At some point, he couldn't remember exactly when, he had stopped pretending she didn't draw him to her, stopped pretending he didn't want to be close to her – as close as she would allow him to be. The knot in the pit of his stomach that had been there since the email arrived, since Kendra's reaction to it, was a pretty good indication she wouldn't allow that closeness easily.

'Do you cook?' she said without looking up from breaking eggs into a bowl. 'I can just about scramble eggs without it becoming a disaster.'

'I can do a decent bolognaise,' he replied.

'Ah yes, the one male recipe to impress the chicks.'

'Shall I do it for you and we'll see if it works?'

She laughed and began whisking the eggs briskly. 'Gonna take more than a mean bolognaise to impress me, Garrett Thorne.'

'Then what?' Unable to resist any longer, he moved behind her and slid his arms around her waist. 'What will impress you, Kendra Davis?'

She offered a little murmur of surprise and the whisk clattered on the side of the bowl, splattering egg over onto the countertop.

'Garrett.' She tried to wriggle free, but he held her, his lips brushing the flutter of her pulse in her throat. 'Garrett, I work for you. We can't do this. It's already got us into trouble.'

'No,' he whispered against her neck, pushing aside her hair to nibble down to her shoulder, his other hand splayed flat and low on the rise and fall of her belly. 'You work for Tess Delaney, and you've asked me to pretend I'm her lover, so let me play my part.'

'But I'm not Tess.' She wriggled to turn in his arms until she faced him, pressed to the counter by the weight of his body, which was already blatantly, shamelessly betraying how badly he wanted her. 'I'm Kendra. And I don't like you, and you don't like me either, remember?'

'Memory seems to be failing me at the moment,' he said. Her breath was fast and sweet on his face, and the press of her breasts against him made him ache all over for more of Kendra Davis. He curled his fingers in her hair and drew her mouth close to his own. 'Just tell me you don't want me, Kendra, and I'll stop.' The last word was pressed firmly to her parted lips, then pushed in between with the tip of his tongue, greeted by her tongue and swallowed up by her own powerful need.

'Garrett, you're trouble,' she sighed into his mouth. 'So damn much trouble. I should have run away fast the second I realized who you were.' Then she bit him on the chin, on the jaw, on the throat; bit him hard enough to elicit a gasp of surprise and a sting of pain that translated itself to pleasure down where his jeans rested tight around his fly.

With the flat of her hand on his chest, she pushed him back, but followed, still nipping and biting and teasing his mouth. She pushed him again and again until he half fell into the kitchen chair where she had been earlier when she'd had her panic attack. Once he was seated and gasping for air, she eased the hem of her dress up until he could see the dark cherry red of her panties, until she could get her legs far enough apart to straddle his lap.

Then, without settling onto him, she moved in close, close enough to offer him a long and lingering kiss, while her fingers deftly dispensed with the buttons of his shirt. Then she slid her hands inside, first to pinch his nipples, once again just enough to hurt, just enough to make his cock surge in his jeans, and then she eased her hands down over his ribs, causing him to catch his breath with a deep gasp before she took his mouth again and settled firmly onto his lap, the lace of her panties unable to hold back the thick, wet heat inside. He just had time for a sense of satisfaction at knowing she wasn't nearly as cool as she pretended to be, and then she began to shift and undulate on his lap, the shape of his erection pressing a tight trough between the swell of her, deeper and deeper with each rocking, with each pressing, until he grabbed her by the hips and held her still, struggling to keep control. 'Kendra, I'm not about to come in my jeans, so stop teasing me.'

With fingers made useless by arousal he could barely contain, he fumbled in his pocket and would have dropped the condom if she hadn't caught it.

She giggled softly. 'Always prepared, are we?' She took the condom from him and began to unwrap it while he wrestled with his fly.

'Hope springs eternal,' he managed, then he hissed a breath between his teeth and lifted his ass from the chair enough for her to worry down his jeans and his boxers until his erection was free. She deftly rolled on the condom, lingering briefly to cup the weight of his fullness. Once he was sheathed and feeling like he would burst, she raised her bottom only enough to pull the gusset of her panties to one side and open herself with two fingers. He caught just a glimpse of her before she settled onto him slowly, torturously, deliciously.

For a long moment, she sat very still, breathing hard, her nipples pearled in an adamant press against the fabric of her dress, her grip like velvet iron around him.

When he could breathe again, when he was sure he wouldn't humiliate himself beneath her, he grabbed the hem of her dress and lifted it, and she raised her arms so that he could slide it off over her head. In one nearly seamless movement he tossed the dress aside, slid his hands to her breasts, which were braless in the sundress as they had been in the evening gown. Then he took the height of her nipples in turn into his mouth, feeling a delicious sense of triumph in the little whimpers that escaped her throat as he suckled and tugged and nursed, as she held him to her, fingers curled tightly in his hair.

Then she began to shift and move against him, and fuck if he didn't feel like he'd found his way home. She fit him. She fit him so well. And she made every nerve ending in his body sit up and pay attention. The power of the woman was breathtaking, hidden somewhere beneath Kendra Davis's quick temper and K. Ryde's distant professionalism, somewhere in the layers of richness and complexity that left him completely and totally at her mercy. But then he wondered if there'd ever been a time when he hadn't been at her mercy.

She wrapped her legs around the back of the chair and tightened her grip on him. Her eyelids fluttered as he nibbled at her breasts and her throat and at the striated path down her sternum. The sounds that came from her mouth were wild, animal, hungry. She wasn't quiet in her lovemaking, and that made him hotter than anything – that someone who could fight like a wild thing and rage like a wild thing could bring all of that heat and anger and fire into the sex act as well. She was a primal force, riding him hard, riding him to the edge of his endurance and backing off just enough to hold him there. And he held on tight. He had no intention of going over that edge until he could take her with him.

He grabbed her thighs and slid onto the floor, nearly upsetting the chair behind them, but she rolled until she was on top of him again, and they were like two wrestlers fighting for supremacy. He figured either way they would both win. He felt the cool tiles on the floor bruising his butt as she settled down onto him hard, her knees drawn up close to his ribs.

He slid a hand over her belly until his palm rested against her tightly trimmed pubic curls and his thumb stroked and circled her clit. The sound that erupted from her throat was dark and rich as he pinched and tweaked and fondled her until she was like silk over pebbles, all dark red and gaping and hungry.

He wasn't sure either of them could remember how to breathe any longer, and he was pretty sure there would be pulled muscles and bruises, and that something could quite possibly break with the power of her thrusts against his, with the desperation of his rising up to meet her, of his efforts to get still deeper into her.

He rolled once again and pushed up until she was scrunched beneath him, bottom raised, ankles locked high around his ribs. The floor abraded his knees, but it didn't matter. The pain only registered somewhere remotely, as though it belonged to someone else. He cupped her buttocks and kneaded and caressed as he pushed into her harder and deeper, and she pushed back.

'I have to come, Garrett.' Her words were barely more than a harsh breath. 'I can't wait any longer.' She curled her fingers in his hair, and pulled him down to her. 'Come with me. I need you to come with me.'

It wasn't permission, but it felt that way. And for a bright second that flashed like lightning, he realized he'd been waiting for just that, for Kendra Davis to give him permission, and Jesus, it felt like he'd waited for ever. He scooped her still closer, if that were possible, felt her gasp at the force of his thrust, felt her give and collapse and sigh, just before her whole body convulsed around him in waves of shudders, and he followed suit, feeling like he would never stop coming, feeling like all that existed in the world was Kendra orgasming in his arms, Kendra giving him permission to come with her. And he did. And God, it was amazing!

Chapter Fifteen

He was irritable, stressed. He felt like his skin would crawl off him if he didn't do something soon. He'd missed his morning workout to buy a television. Then he'd waited for hours watching for news updates, waiting for Flannery and Blessing to inform the world that he was pursuing Tess now, that no one could keep her safe now. Of course they didn't know that's what they were doing, but he did, and that's what mattered.

He was desperate to work out. He got twitchy when he didn't. He got a little crazy. But what choice did he have? He waited. He just waited.

He knew that eventually Tess and Thorne had to make their public appearance. Tess's publicist, if he was worth the money she paid him, would make sure of that. What drove him insane was knowing why he'd had to wait so goddamn long. They'd been in the house fucking like rabbits, Tess and Thorne. The very thought made him sick. He wanted to go to the house and drag them out bodily, naked and covered in each other's filth. He wanted to make them greet their public as they really were; dirty, rutting animals. That would make the fucking press stand up and take notice. That would show those stupid reporters their true colors, and God, how he wanted them to be humiliated, how he wanted them to suffer!

When at last they did come out to answer the press's questions, they were all freshly scrubbed, looking like they owned the fucking world. He had to restrain himself, to keep from throwing the television out the window, but this was his secret debut, really. He controlled this news release. It belonged to him. This was the beginning. He watched Barker Blessing's well-groomed face ooze sympathy on the new television as he spoke to Carla Flannery's less than pristine visage in a nice split-screen arrangement. It was good to be able to see both of them close up. Carla looked like she'd been up all night pursuing her story. He liked that about her. She was dedicated. And he'd see that she had a great story when he was finished. Blessing looked like butter wouldn't melt, even in his feigned concern for poor threatened Tess. The bastard never missed a chance for a little free publicity. Still, Blessing was useful at the moment. That's what mattered.

He turned up the volume just as Blessing said, 'Dear God, I just can't imagine how anyone could threaten such a delightful woman, and such a talent. Such a talent.'

That Tess was talented, he couldn't argue, but he knew who she really was down deep inside. She was a slut first and foremost. He had no doubt that would delight Blessing. He knew the man was happy to diddle anything with tits. No, Tess was not delightful. He could barely stand to sit there, watching her fawn all over Garrett Thorne. He wanted to rage. He wanted to go right over to Thorne's place right now and rip both of their throats out. But he had to be patient, he reminded himself. What he had planned would be much more satisfying in the end. No, Tess was not delightful at all. Tess was a little whore, right there for the whole world to see, and the stupid public ate it all up, like she was a goddess or something. But she was just a whore. She needed to pay for how she'd made him suffer. She needed to learn her lesson. And he was the one who would teach her. He listened as Blessing continued.

'I'm very concerned for her, and I certainly hope Garrett Thorne can offer her the protection she needs. No doubt Thorne's brother, Ellis, will see to her protection at his brother's request. Under such circumstances, I suppose that should make us all feel a little better.'

He respected the other Thorne brother, Ellison Thorne. The man worked hard for what he had, and for anyone else he would be a formidable challenge. But security or not, even if he could afford the best, there was nothing Thorne could do to keep him away from Tess. He would have her. When the time came, he would have her and there'd be no keeping him back.

Giggling and laughing, they cleaned themselves as best they could, lying in the middle of the kitchen floor in the afternoon sunlight. Garrett had managed to do his best to hold onto her as long as he could, fighting back the strange panic he'd felt their first time together, the feeling that if he let go of her, she might never let him hold her like this again.

'I have a very large shower,' he said, nipping her ear and her nape as he spoke. 'Care to join me?'

She shook her head. 'Not until after we eat. I'm starving, and I might just pass out in the shower if you don't feed me first. Where would be the fun in that?'

'Woman, the only way I want you passing out in the shower is in waves of total ecstasy.' He was way happier than he cared to admit that at least she hadn't said no. He pulled her to her feet, and she stood with her arms raised, allowing him to slide her dress back on over her head, allowing him to give her breasts a good fondling before he tugged the hem of it into place. 'All right,' he said. 'Let's eat. Then we'll have a nice hot shower and see what comes up.'

It didn't take long to whip up toast and eggs. Garrett made a fresh pot of coffee and Kendra worked her way through another can of Diet Pepsi. She never bothered with a glass, just tossed the can into the recycle bin and grabbed another one.

'That stuff's not good for you,' he said, when she went to the fridge for another.

'Lots of stuff's not good for me, Garrett. This –' she lifted the can in a salute '– is pretty far down the list.'

He was slathering a piece of wholegrain toast with raspberry jam when he realized she was studying him over the top of her drink can. It was usually the other way around. It was usually him stealing glances at her, and he found himself a little nervous about being under Kendra's scrutiny. 'What?' he managed around a mouthful of toast. 'Do I have egg on my face?'

Her lips curled into a smile that looked like it might be turned slightly inward, and she shook her head, making the tangle of red hair that fell around her face shimmer in the sunshine that streamed through the skylight. 'Just wondering how you do it.'

'I know, it's amazing, isn't it?' He stroked his fly suggestively and winked. 'Guess I'm just gifted.'

She balled her napkin and tossed it at him. 'Though you're not bad –' she shrugged teasingly '– that's not what I was talking about.'

'What then?' he asked.

'How you write romance.'

He cocked his head. 'Is this a trick question? Lots of people write romance. I just happen to be really good at it, that's all.' He shoved more toast in his mouth and washed it down with a gulp of coffee, feeling way more defensive than the situation called for. The sex he could joke about. The writing was a much more sensitive area for him. Besides, there was something about being questioned by Kendra Davis that made him feel exposed in ways that had nothing to do with his state of undress. 'What? You think men can't be romantic?'

She leaned forward, and he could have happily drowned in her broad smile. 'Of course men can be romantic, though I never heard of a man writing romance before. But then I never read romance before my first Tess Delaney novel.'

'Well, men do write it,' he said. 'But usually you can tell if it's written by a man. No one knows with Tess, though.' He found himself blushing. 'What, you think writing romance makes me less masculine?'

This time the laugh that bubbled up from her throat was guttural and went straight to his fly. 'Oh Garrett, if you were any more masculine I wouldn't be able to handle you, and I can handle a lot of man, trust me.'

And suddenly it was very hard for him to breathe, very hard for him to think. She always managed to wrong-foot him when he least expected it. But before he even had time to bask in her comment about his manliness, she wrong-footed him again. 'Is that why you keep Tess's true identity secret, because you're afraid people will think you less masculine for writing romance?'

He folded his arms across his chest; suddenly he felt like he was on trial. 'I chose a pen name because women buy romance novels written by women. My publishers insisted that I find a female name before they'd buy my books. I suppose I might have been a little bit afraid of how writing romance novels would affect my manly reputation. I was writing detective novels before Tess. But the sales of Tess's first novel dwarfed the sales of all my Brad Dennis detective novels in the first three months. Manly or not, I liked the money. Besides, I like the way Tess writes. She's fun.'

She nodded as though his answer met with her approval. He was glad for that.

'Were you still married to Stacie when you started writing as Tess?'

Christ, there she went, wrong-footing him again! 'No. We were divorced long before Tess came into the picture.' He braced himself for … For what? He didn't really know. Did he expect her to play the part of the jealous girlfriend? He pretended not to notice Kendra's scrutiny. The woman never missed anything.

She sipped her Diet Pepsi thoughtfully. 'Well, it's not like I can make any real comparisons. Like I said, Tess is the only romance writer I've ever read.'

Did he actually heave a sigh of relief that she hadn't pursued the Stacie line of questioning any further?

Before he could think too much about it, she had already moved on. 'Oh, I did skim several of the novels of the writers Tess was competing against for the Golden Kiss Award, but I don't know. They just didn't do it for me. They just didn't make me feel it like Tess does.' She waved a hand abruptly. 'No, that's not it either. They didn't make me believe it like Tess does.'

OK, so he might be full of himself, but he was still completely taken aback that Kendra liked Tess Delaney novels, so who could really blame him if he wanted his ego stroked by the woman with whom he'd just had mind-blowing sex, and hoped to have more of the same very shortly. He scooted closer and captured her hand. 'What do you mean, Tess makes you believe it? You mean like the plot is believable? You believe the characters?'

She looked down at his fingers curled around hers and ran her thumb along his. The color in her cheeks rose. The beating of her pulse became visible against her throat, and the scent of her, earthy and dark, mixed with his own; the scent of their lovemaking was nearly intoxicating, making his own pulse race, making him want her again, if anything even worse than he'd wanted her before.

'No. It's not that. I mean the characters, the plot, they're all fine, and with the other authors too. Just fine.'

'Then what?' he said, scooting still closer.

For a second she studied him, as though he might be something she should run away from, and he tensed and sat very still, willing her to stay with him, willing her to tell him, willing her not to shut him out. She puffed out a harsh breath and forced a smile. 'Tess makes me believe romance might possibly be – real.'

She was having trouble meeting his gaze suddenly, and the acceleration of her breath, he knew, wasn't from arousal this time. Certainly the clench in his chest was not the response of lust he'd had a split second ago. It was sharper edged and far more uncomfortable.

'Kendra.' He scooted so close that he sat next to her, his thigh brushing hers, and he lifted her chin so she couldn't look away from him. 'Kendra, romance is real, maybe the most real thing ever because of what it can lead to, where it can take us. And it's wonderful. Look at Dee and Ellis.' The minute he said it, he wished he hadn't. He knew that what she saw as his betrayal of his brother and Dee was the reason why she disliked him so much. But to his relief, she didn't bring that topic up.

'For them, yes. They're the couple that get romance and love because they deserve it, because they fit together so well, like no two people I've ever known, other than those in Tess's novels, I mean.' In an evasive manoeuvre that took his breath away, she slid her hand free, stood, and began to clear the table. 'But it's not real, Garrett. Those people in Tess's novels, they're not real. Their lives aren't real. Their struggles aren't real. No one really gets a happy ever after. That's for fairy tales. The most any of us can really hope for is a good fuck now and then.' She stood with her back to him, rinsing the remains of their meal down the sink. 'And marriage and kids, all that, ultimately it's all just about settling, isn't it? It's all about taking what you can get because at some point you have to come to grips with the fact that you'll never have what you really want. No one does. And if you're lucky, you get someone who's stable. And faithful. If you're lucky. If you're not, then you have to either live with it or walk away. That's what you did, isn't it? You walked away. At least when it's just sex, you know what you're getting and you have some control. No one gets hurt and no one ends up miserable. You don't have any illusions about what you want or what you deserve. It's just sex.'

'Kendra.' He moved to stand behind her feeling like his heart would explode from his chest, feeling her longing as though it would break him to pieces, feeling his own longing to make her understand, to make her feel what Tess made her feel. He placed his hands on her shoulders, and turned her to face him, then he guided her clenched fists, still dripping from the dishwater, to rest balled against his chest. 'Kendra, do you think you don't deserve romance?' He cupped her cheek and ran his thumb along the exquisite line of her jaw. 'Because you do, you know? Everyone deserves romance.'

For a second she struggled to bring her gaze to his, but then he found himself once again scrutinized by her. 'Have you had romance? Did you have it with Stacie?'

'Of course I've had romance, Kendra, and yes, I had it with Stacie. Kendra, haven't you had romance?'

She ignored his question. 'Then why are you alone?'

It felt almost as though she had slapped him again, and the sting of it went way deeper than his face. But he took sharp breath and held her there. 'It didn't work out well for me. At least not yet.' The smile he managed felt fake. 'But I'm hopeful. I couldn't write what I do if I weren't. And you –' He smoothed the hair away from her face and pulled her wet hands tighter against his chest. 'Jesus, woman, I'd think your life would be full of romance.'

The smile she offered this time was tinged with sadness, or at least, that's how he saw it. 'I have sex, Garrett. I don't have romance or love. It's safer that way.'

'Kendra, I can't believe –'

'You know –' She gently pushed him away and extricated herself from his embrace. 'I think I'll take a rain check on that shower if you don't mind. I saw a nice big bathtub in the upstairs bathroom. My flat only has a shower. Would you mind if I have a wallow?' Before he could respond, she laid a hand on his shoulder. 'I need some time to think and plan our next move, and let's face it, Garrett –' she gave him a salacious raking with her eyes '– you're very distracting.'

She left him standing at the kitchen sink, aching with an ache he'd never felt before, one that was sharply defined in the space inside him, and shaped very much like Kendra Davis.

There were lavender and geranium aromatherapy bubbles in the cupboard in the guest bathroom. Kendra wondered if they belonged to one of Garrett's romances that hadn't worked out. It surprised her to feel the pang of jealousy at the thought. It wasn't that someone else might have had sex with Garrett on the kitchen floor in the middle of preparing a meal; after all, the man had been married to Stacie at one time. What she was really jealous of was that Garrett had had romantic relationships, that Garrett had taken the wild risk of marrying the woman he was crazy about. She was jealous that Garrett had somehow felt it was worth the pain to try again when the marriage fell apart. That was a bravery she couldn't understand. 'More like a stupidity,' she whispered beneath her breath. But then he hadn't had her parents, had he? No doubt his views on romance would have been very different if he had.

She squeezed a generous amount of bubbles into the tub and turned on the water, stepping out of her rumpled clothes, inhaling deeply the pungent scent Garrett had left on her body, in her body, and the scent that was her body's hungry response to him. She was glad she hadn't bathed it away too soon. His body fit hers so well, and God, did he know how to make that

132

fit work for her. She shook her head, not wanting to think about that right now as she stepped into the hot summer scent of the tub and settled into the rising foam. She should have never had sex with him. No matter what he said, they both knew he *was* Tess Delaney. And Tess Delaney made her feel things she'd never felt before, made her ache more deeply than she thought possible, made her fantasies wild and uncontrolled, and sex was only a part of it.

They were stupid, teenage fantasies, she scolded herself. And at the end of the day, it wasn't Tess Delaney who had made her feel all those things; it was Garrett Thorne, the man downstairs cleaning up in the kitchen, the man she couldn't get enough of. The man she should ultimately be running away from. She was beginning to suspect he was far more dangerous than any of the ghosts from her past could ever be. What the hell had she got herself into? She'd learned her lesson long ago. She'd learned by example, and her parents were the very best example as to what a lie it was, the fantasy of romance and happy ever after, what a lie it was that giving up control of your heart to anyone else could ever lead to anything but pain.

She turned off the water and sank to her neck into the bubbles, eyes closed, relaxing, drifting, remembering the beginning of the end of her illusions about happy ever after, about romance. The memory came unbidden, something she hadn't allowed it to do in a long time. She remembered because it was just before her 11th birthday.

It was the crash that woke her up that night, and the sound of something shattering. At first she thought she'd only dreamed it, but then she heard her father's voice, and she held her breath to listen.

'Marianne, stop it. Shshsh! Sweetheart, you'll wake up Keni. Now hush! We can deal with this. Downstairs.'

'Deal with it? Like we always do, Aaron? Hmm? You'll say you're sorry and I'll believe you and forgive you until the next one of your little whores comes along?'

'Shshsh! Marianne, shush now, shush.' Her father's voice had been so even, so calm, as though he had been the reasonable one, as though he was calming an angry child or soothing away a nightmare. Her mother's voice was only slightly less than hysterical and, for a split second, Kendra was frightened for her, frightened that something serious had happened, that her mother was sick or injured. She had slipped from her bed and peeked around the edge of her door. She could hear her mother's muffled sobs. She could just make out her back, wrapped in the lilac chenille bathrobe her father had got her for Christmas. Her father was still dressed in his suit. He still looked immaculate, like he always did. And so handsome. She remembered how handsome her father looked, how powerful. She remembered because that was the night she stopped thinking of him as handsome. On the floor in shattered bits, Kendra could see the Tiffany lamp that had always sat on the hall table.

'Please, Marianne, sweetheart, I know you're angry, and rightly so, but let's discuss this downstairs. Let's not do this here.' Even as he spoke, he slid a powerful arm around her mother's shoulders and guided her down the staircase. And Kendra knew then that he had won, no matter what her mother said from that point on.

Quietly, on tiptoe, Kendra had eased herself outside her room and into the hall, careful to avoid the shards of glass on the carpet. They were so caught up in their discussion they hadn't even thought she might eavesdrop. She's followed silently down the stairs, holding her breath, listening, not wanting to hear and yet not able to turn and run back to the safety of her room. What was the point? There was no unknowing what she now knew. From the foot of the stairs just around the corner, out of their line of sight, she listened, hands clenched in tight, painful fists at her side.

'It was Sadie, wasn't it?' her mother was saying. 'Sadie Myers. I know it was, I saw you with her, and people talk. God, Aaron, I'm not stupid. You used to try to hide it, so at least I wasn't humiliated in front of all our friends and neighbours.'

From around the corner in the stairwell, Kendra watched as her father stooped to kiss her mother. 'I'm sorry darling. I'm so sorry. I'm not strong like you are. I'll make it up to you. I promise. It won't happen again.'

But it did. Of course it did.

'Mom, why do you let him do it?' she'd asked once when the bastard had actually had the balls to bring one of his bimbos home and pass her off as a colleague. 'Why don't you leave him? You've got a degree, you can find work. You don't have to put up with it.'

Her mother had pulled her into her arms and offered the sad little smile she always did. 'He's a good provider, Keni, and he loves his family. He just needs a little extra, that's all. More than I can give him. Someday when you get married and have children of your own, you'll understand, sweetheart. It's not always as simple as what you read about in those novels.'

Simple? It had never been simple. Kendra always knew that. Kendra always knew who had the power and who was willing to sacrifice what. It was like a game of advance and retreat. There was an endless stream of women, and Kendra and her mom got things – a new car, holidays in Spain, nice clothes, new furniture. There was never a lack of things. Ever. And Kendra knew, as well as her mother did, how to manipulate her father for a new outfit, a new computer, new boots. It was control. The only control she had, and she used it. Even when there was nothing she needed, even when she had her own money from her after-school jobs, she never, ever let him forget he owed her, he owed both of them.

As for her mother, well, Kendra was always apathetic toward people who didn't stand up for themselves. Her mother was weak. Her mother was willing to settle. Kendra promised herself early on that she never would. Kendra promised herself she would always be the one in control. And she had always kept that promise until last year, until she'd been forced to sell the Ryder Agency and flee. Even as terrifying as the whole situation had been, it was still the loss of control that bothered her more than anything else. It was the memory of walking away when she didn't want to, of being frightened, truly frightened for the first time ever, and not being brave enough to stand and fight, that tore at her. For a moment, for a dark, despairing moment, she had been her mother's daughter, and it had been the worst moment of her life.

Chapter Sixteen

Garrett always wrote when he was frustrated or when he was suffering. And as much as he hated to admit it, Kendra Davis was making him suffer – much more so than if she had simply bitch slapped him. But then again, it wasn't all about him, was it? And whatever had happened at the table, whatever had started out as a simple discussion about why he wrote romance, had turned inward to a place that Kendra was clearly not willing to share, a place that clearly caused her pain.

Outside, he could still hear the shuffling and mumbling of the press, now spurred on by the scent of a hot story about Tess Delaney's stalker. Christ, he wished he knew how word had got out. Even more, he wished he knew if there was any truth to it or if the email from Razor Sharp was just a prank. He'd certainly been happy to believe that, until Kendra came into the picture. He couldn't bear the thought of something happening to her because of him. Perhaps he should just come clean, just confront the press while she was still in the bathtub and tell them that he was the real Tess Delaney and Kendra only worked for him. He could be finished and the whole thing over with before she even finished her bath.

And he'd do it in a heartbeat if he could only be certain that it really would be over, that Kendra could walk away clear and clean and safe. OK, he had to admit he didn't like the idea of her walking away from him. But that didn't matter as long as she was safe.

He kept writing. Battling with the problems of Jessie and Amanda, who were now huddled together under a blanket in the boathouse, kept his mind off his own problems, off sharing the tight confines of his house with a woman he could barely keep his hands off of. Writing had always been Garrett's way of dealing with his emotions, and at the moment if he didn't write, he feared he'd shove his way into the bathroom, drag Kendra out, and make her finish what she started. She ran away, damn her! She ran away, and he wasn't finished with her. How could he let her walk away believing romance wasn't for her, believing love wasn't for her? If it was ever for anyone, it was for her. How could she not see that? He wanted to prove it to her, he wanted her to feel it, experience it for herself, understand how much it mattered. And yes, if he were honest, he wanted to be the one to take her there.

He found his balance in front of his laptop, and even he had to admit the story seemed to be flowing much better since Kendra had arrived, since he knew she was in the very next room. And now, strangely, the Amanda in his head looked like Kendra and Jessie, well, clearly that was him. And when Jessie wrestled Amanda down onto the floor of the boathouse, when he positioned himself and pushed into her, and when she wrapped her legs around him and met him thrust for thrust, Garrett knew that it was really himself with Kendra he was writing. As the scene unfolded it felt as though there was some nearly mystical connection between the woman lounging in his bathtub and the creative process going on in his head, a process that suddenly seemed to be going on in his body in equal measure.

Jesus, why did he torture himself this way? And even as the story flowed, even as it gained momentum and power that it hadn't had since he began it, it was no less torture. He didn't really want to lock himself in his bedroom and rub one out. What he wanted was Kendra, but he wanted more than just to be inside her body again, and he wanted to give her more than just sex.

He heard the bathroom door open and felt his shoulders tense and his pulse accelerate, knowing that she was so close. But then he heard the door to the guestroom close, and there was silence. Was she still thinking and planning? Was she sleeping? Or was she simply trying to avoid him?

*   *   *

Kendra slipped into Garrett's robe, the one she had worn – was it just this morning? It seemed a long time ago. It smelled like Garrett, and the scent of him caused little tremors low in her belly. How could she have got so used to his smell, almost addicted to it, in such a short time? She jerked the sash tight around her waist and slipped out of the bathroom. In the hall, she could still hear the press outside. Now that Barker Blessing and the web reporter had given them the scent of fresh blood, they weren't going anywhere until there was a new and better story to pry them away. Just down the hall, she could hear the tap-tapping of Garrett's laptop, and she resisted the urge to see if he was in Tess Delaney mode, to watch Tess at work. No doubt that would only muddy the waters further, and they were already muddy enough.

Instead, she moved quietly down the hall to the guestroom. She had some work to do and some research of her own. But even if she didn't, she still needed a bit of space before she faced Garrett again. She needed time for him to forget about their ill-fated conversation, time for her to feel a little less exposed. And even though a huge part of her wanted to linger, wanted to be close to him, she went into the guest room and closed the door behind her.

She dug the iPad from her bag and stretched out on the bed with it beside her. Then she closed her eyes. Just for a few minutes. It was never her intention to do more than that. She certainly hadn't planned to fall asleep.

She woke with her heart juddering madly, feeling as though each serrated breath was turning to ice in her lungs. The afternoon light had gone, and the street lamp from outside bathed the room in garish red-black shadows. The rest of the house was dark and silent. She was just about to call out for Garrett, when she sensed more than saw that she wasn't alone. The red blackness was thick and heavy, like a bloodied mist floating in the room. It was the flash of a cell phone camera and the voice that brought it all back to her in one horrific moment. She hadn't heard that voice in over a year now, but there was never any mistaking it.

'Come on, Bird Woman, let me see what you've got. I

know what a show you can put on when you feel like it.' He moved out of the shadows and came to sit on the edge of the bed next to her, the tattoo of a cobra coiling around a skull practically pulsing from beneath his tight black muscle shirt and over his biceps. He reached out and opened the top of the robe until her breasts were mostly exposed. She shoved him and fought back the urge to scream. 'Don't touch me,' she managed before his hand settled around her throat, big enough to choke off her airway, big enough to leave bruises in a circlet along the line of his thumb and up to his index finger. He had huge hands.

'You can't stop me, Bird Woman. I'll do what I want. You couldn't stop me then, and you can't stop now.' He moved in so close that his face was practically touching her, and there was nowhere for her to go, nowhere to back away from him. His breath was hot and wet, and she fought back the urge to gag. He only laughed and kept talking. 'Really, it doesn't matter what I do to you.' He took another picture of her exposed breasts and then shoved the robe open further. 'It doesn't matter who I share you with, since you don't even exist.' He moved in closer still, his thumb pressing hard against the soft spot where her pulse hammered like a warning bell. With a deft move, he slipped the knot on the robe and the camera flashed again. 'We both know Bird Woman won't even exist in a few more days. She doesn't even have a name, does she? You never gave her a name because you knew how short her life would be.' His gaze felt abrasive as it raked over her body.

She wanted to move, she wanted to scream for Garrett, she wanted to run away, but he held her there effortlessly, the hand around her neck now moving down to grope and stroke and make way for the camera's accusing eye.

'Leave me!' She managed to push the words up through her raw throat. 'Go away and leave me alone. You're not here. You can't be!'

'Aren't I?' His face was suddenly scant inches away from hers, his eyes obsidian black in the poisonous light. 'When Bird Women is gone, when you have no further use for her and you discard her like you did all the others, just remember, I know who you really are, Kendra Davis. I know what you do, what games you play. I knew you couldn't give it up. Does he know? Does Garrett Thorne know who he has playing his Tess Delaney? What a sickening, whoring coward she is? What a liar she is?'

He brought the camera close to her mouth, so close she thought he was going to force it down her throat, but instead he took a picture of her lips, then, with his thumb and forefinger on either side of her jaw, he forced her mouth open and the camera flashed into her mouth. 'Ah, the pit of lies, the pit of evil. This mouth –' He brushed his lips against hers then took another picture, the lens up close to her teeth. The pressure of his fingers on her jaws was bruising and the nail of his thumb drew blood just below her cheekbone. 'This mouth knows nothing but lies and deceit. This mouth deserves no tenderness. This mouth is a pit, deserving nothing but to be filled by the vilest of cocks.' The camera phone kept flashing photo after photo until the after-image of him was like a dark and gaping wound.

'Kendra Davis, I know who you are. Kendra Davis, you're not fit for anything else,' the cobra on his arm hissed.

'Kendra Davis, you don't deserve anything else.' The mouth of the skull moved in agreement.

The camera flashed, and she screamed and drowned out the sound of her name, her name he was never supposed to know. Kendra, Kendra, Kendra …

'Kendra, goddamn it, wake up! Wake up!'

She woke with a gasp of blessed air. It felt like an eternity since she had breathed, and she found herself sobbing, folded tightly in Garrett's arms.

In an effort to free herself from the last vestiges of the nightmare, she threw her arms around his neck in a near stranglehold, and he returned the   avour around her waist. 'It was a dream,' she managed between efforts to breathe. 'A dream.'

'I got that,' he said, smoothing her hair and reaching with one hand to turn on the bedside lamp and bathe the dusky room in welcome light. 'Must have been one hell of a nightmare. You nearly raised the roof, and I thought you were going to flatten me before I could get you to wake up.'

'I'm sorry! I'm sorry.' She pulled away slightly and looked into his eyes. 'Did I hurt your?'

He offered a wry chuckle. 'Not this time. Though I'm not sure you're rendered any safer when you're unconscious. Is there any time when you *are* safe?'

She managed a weak laugh that sounded more like a kitten mewling. 'I'm never safe, Garrett. Don't you know that yet?'

He dropped a warm kiss onto her ear. 'I have nerves of steel, Kendra. You can't scare me, so you might as well stop trying. You want to tell me about it?' His voice was velvety soft against her ear.

'What I want is to get out of here. Don't get me wrong, your house is nice. I love your house, but being cooped up like this with the press out front is driving me nuts.' She pulled away enough that she could look him in the eyes. 'Do you dance? I mean, I know you do ballroom, Dee told me, but can you – you know, dance?'

He raised an eyebrow. 'You've talked to Dee about my dancing abilities?'

'It came up in one of the conversations we had, yes. One in which she was being a good future sister-in-law, trying to convince me you weren't the total asshat I thought you were.'

'Bonus points for Dee,' he said, offering her a pout she could have happily eaten off his face. 'And yes, I can dance any kind of dance you want to dance. What did you have in mind?'

She smoothed the lock of unruly hair back away from his face. 'A night out incognito that I think we could both pull off without ever being missed or found out.'

'I'm listening.'

'You'll need to wear a tracksuit – preferably a ratty dark one with a hood.' She ran a hand down the lapel of his shirt. 'Or is everything you have designer?'

He stood and pulled her to her feet. 'I can look as ratty as you need me to look, Kendra. Trust me.'

'We'll see about that,' she said. She looked at the clock on the nightstand. 'Timing's perfect. We'll go in early, and we won't stay too late. But we should have plenty of time to burn off a little energy, you know, let our hair down, relax a bit, blow off a little steam before the crowd descends. And we'll be back home before anyone even misses us. You go get changed and give me about a half an hour.'

'Where are we going?' he asked.

She was already shuffling through her bag for what she needed. 'Ever been to the Boiling Point?' she called over her shoulder.

'No.'

The chuckle she offered him was practically evil. 'Then you're in for a real treat.' She shooed him out with a wave of her hand. 'Now go get ratty, Garrett. I would guess that's something a chick magnet like you isn't used to, so it may take you a while. Better get to it.'

Chapter Seventeen

Garrett felt like a naughty teenager as they sneaked out the back door, through the gate of the privacy fence, and down the alley. He wore a shapeless tracksuit with the black hoodie pulled up over his head and a scruffy pair of Converse sneakers that weren't exactly designed for dancing. And Kendra, well, she hardly looked ratty, in his opinion. She wore low rider jeans, and where they weren't hugging her body like a second skin, they were full of threadbare, flesh-revealing holes. The black sweat top she wore was cut short enough to show a tantalizing flash of her navel and hip bones when she moved just right. It slid off one shoulder to reveal the thin, lacy strap of a red bra. She wore all of her russet locks tucked up under a leather beret. Her fashion statement was topped off with black ankle boots. She looked very, very dangerous. And hot. Of course, she didn't need to dress the part for either, he thought. He was already certain on both counts.

'You live a little closer to The Boiling Point than Dee does.' She took his hand and nodded to where the alley.

T-ed with the street, and then gave way to the park on the other side. 'She never goes there, of course. Well, she did once, but that was just for Harris, then he hated it.' She giggled. 'God, I wish I could have been there for that.'

'Am I going to hate it?' he asked.

She shook her head. 'Probably not. You're much more of a bad boy than Harris is, or is that all an act?'

The long line of shiny chrome Harleys out front of the squat cinderblock building gave Garrett the first clue that this was not *Dancing with the Stars*. Kendra waved them away absently. 'The Boiling Point's not really a biker bar, but it's kind of the warm-up act, I suppose you could say. Lots of bikers start off here before they head on to their usual haunts. Makes for an exciting mix. Later in the night there are almost no bikers. But there are always lots of interesting people.'

Any other time, Garrett would have been up for meeting interesting people, but tonight he couldn't imagine anyone interesting him more than the woman on his arm. He paid the fee at the door and a surly man the size of a small house with fire-engine hair and a scruffy beard stamped their hands with a red ink TBP.

Inside, a live band had just begun to play to a full, but not yet crowded house. 'The place gets raided from time to time,' Kendra said. 'I don't know what all goes on. I just come here because it's interesting.'

'A good raid and us carted off to the police station will really give the press something to talk about,' Garrett observed.

'Don't worry.' She yelled to be heard above the band's bass-heavy version of *Highway to Hell*. 'They just got raided last week. They'll be good to go for a while now. We can relax and enjoy ourselves.' She pulled him onto the dance floor. 'Best dance while there's room. In a few hours it'll be a real tit squeeze.'

Kendra Davis was just as stunning dark and dangerous as she was golden and romantic, as she was naked in his kitchen, and she definitely knew how to move on the dance floor. But it made Garrett more than a little nervous that he wasn't the only one who seemed to be noticing the way the woman could shake her booty. He thought about asking her to try not to draw too much attention to herself, but he wasn't even sure it was possible for Kendra Davis not to draw attention.

The place smelled of leather and beer, and sweat. Already there was a thick haze of pheromones invisible to the eye, but everyone there breathed them, gave them off, and revelled in the dark anticipation of what the night might bring. The look in Kendra's eyes was bright and wicked, like she would do anything, try anything, like all the boundaries were suddenly negotiable.

And fuck, as amazing as she was like that, as much as he

wanted to lose himself in the place, in the experience, there was no way he could keep from thinking about who might be watching her in that crowd, about who might be waiting for just the perfect opportunity.

As though she was reading his mind, she pulled him to her with a hand curled around his neck and spoke against his ear. 'Oh, would you relax, Garrett. Do you really think this is the kind of hangout Tess Delaney would frequent?'

Then she slid both arms around his neck and let him pull her into a deep, hungry kiss. When it ended with an aggressive flick of his tongue, she offered a throaty giggle. 'Marking our territory, are we?' Before he had a chance to respond, she returned the favour, plunging her tongue in deep, and tightening a fist in his hair to pull him closer.

He moved a hand to the small of her back and gave her the full frontal rub-up, enough to be sure she knew she'd got his cock's attention. 'You see where this is leading if you keep that up?'

She pulled away and gave his crotch some breathing room as the music settled into a heavy metal beat that filled the dance floor with lots of heavily booted bikers and their spandex and leather women. Garrett was surprised to find more than a few men in pressed jeans and designer polo shirts bellied up to the bar in the mix that looked like it was probably mostly low-brow. He wasn't the only man who looked like he'd just come from a workout at the corner gym and Kendra's shredded jeans seemed to be the fashion statement of more than a few women among a smattering of Goth and grunge and plain old redneck jeans and T-shirts with baseball caps.

With each song the band played, the dance floor became fuller and fuller. The strobe light flashed and the disco ball bathed the floor in sparkles as people rocked and strutted and sweated, and it became more and more difficult to tell who was dancing with whom. Garrett was about to grab Kendra by the hand and reel her back in so they could stay connected when a biker in a ZZ Top T-shirt that smelled like an ashtray and looked like it might have been painted across his bulging pecs managed to slide in between them, turn his back on Garrett,

145

and focus his full attention on Kendra. And suddenly all Garrett could see was his broad back.

'Kendra,' he called, but his voice was drowned out in the roar of Def Leppard. And that might have been OK if the man hadn't been so fucking big. Kendra was certainly entitled to dance with whomever she liked. But he couldn't see her. He fucking couldn't see her! Not even her feet between the man's shuffling boots. 'Kendra!' He called again. Louder this time. That at least got the man's attention, but when he turned to see what Garrett wanted, and he could see beyond the biker's bulk, Kendra was not there! The woman the man was dancing with had cropped blonde hair and a leather bustier several sizes too small.

'Kendra!' Garrett called out, louder this time, shoving his way past the biker, who pulled the blonde to him protectively. Frantically Garrett scanned the burgeoning crowd on the dance floor, scanned the women with hats. There were cowboy hats, police hats, even a few stocking caps, but there were just too many people, too many lights, too much noise. In his mind he could only think of Razor Sharp's horrid email and Kendra's response to it. Why the hell hadn't he forced the issue? Why the hell hadn't he made her tell him why she was so upset, made her tell him about the stalker Dee had mentioned? And fuck! Why had he let her talk him into bringing her here?

He shoved and pushed his way to the edge of the dance floor, fumbled in his pocket for his BlackBerry, and punched in Kendra's number. It rang endlessly with no response until Kay Lake's voicemail picked up. 'Where the hell are you?' he growled into the phone, then shoved it back into his pocket and resumed his search. A tall woman in a red jumpsuit and a cowboy hat tried to entice him back onto the dance floor, then flipped him the finger and an insult about the size of his dick, which he only caught part of as he shoved past her, wishing they'd shut off the damn strobe light so he could see, wishing the band would take a break and clear the dance floor. Had she gone to the restroom? Surely she would have told him if she had. He cornered one of the biker women coming out of the bathrooms. 'Excuse me, have you seen a tall woman in a black beret in the restroom?'

She shook her head and walked a wide path around him like he was some pervert, and she wouldn't have told him anything.

He had just pulled out his cell phone to call again, when he looked up to find Kendra standing at the bar with a drink in her hand, and his knees nearly gave from relief. One of the designer fashion boys was chatting her up. And immediately the relief was replaced with something a lot more tetchy. He shoved past a knot of Goths who mumbled and gave him a few nasty looks, but he was way past being polite at the moment.

'The Porsche outside, it's mine,' Fashion Boy was telling Kendra, preening with one hand while he held a beer in the other. 'Bought it with my bonus from last year. It's one helluva ride.' He moved in closer. 'If you're interested.'

'I'm not.'

'She's not.'

Both he and Kendra spoke at the same time.

The man raised his hands and backed away, and Garrett grabbed her by the arm, none too gently, and marched her toward the door. 'Where the hell have you been?' he said, half shoving her out into the warm summer air, past the curious gaze of the bouncers.

'What do you mean, where have *I* been?' She yanked her arm away. 'I was dancing. I looked around and you were nowhere to be found. So I went to the bar to wait. I figured that would be the first place you'd look for me, and why are you so angry?'

'Why am I so angry? You scared the shit out of me, that's why I'm so angry.' He jerked her closer to him. 'One minute you're dancing with me and the next minute the Incredible Hulk steps in between us and then you're gone.'

'Where are we going?' she said, pulling back.

He jerked her forward. 'Home, damn it. We're going home, where it's safe.' He half marched, half dragged her through the parking lot across the road and to the edge of the park before she gave him a shove, pulled away from him altogether, and turned on him.

'Fuck you, Garrett! I haven't done anything wrong and even

if I had, you're not my father. I'll go home when I'm damn good and ready.'

'So what? You want to go back and ride banker boy's Porsche, do you? Is that it? He buys you a drink and you let him give you a ride.'

That she didn't slap him was the first shock; the second was that she didn't turn back to the Boiling Point, but that she headed on into the park at a pace that a racehorse would have struggled to keep up with.

'I bought my own drink, you asshole. And I came with you. You're the only one who gets to give me a ride.'

'Kendra, I'm sorry. Kendra, wait!' He struggled to catch up with her. 'I just panicked when I couldn't find you. I'm sorry, OK. I panicked.'

'And you just assumed that I was on the make. Fuck you, Garrett! Fuck you!'

It was then that he realized she was leading him off the main path into the darkened edge of the park. 'Kendra, where are you going?'

She didn't respond, so he kept following her up a winding path deeper into the centre of the park.

At the top of the hill, in a grove of hawthorn trees and rose bushes in fragrant full bloom, there was a bench. The leaves of the trees admitted a tiny pool of light from the street lamps just above it. 'Kendra, where the hell are you going?' He grabbed her hand, and she turned on him so quickly that he thought for sure this was when she would slap him – certainly, he couldn't blame her – but instead she fisted both hands in the front of his hoodie and pulled him to her in an angry kiss, then one hand migrated into the front of his track bottoms, and inside his boxers.

'God, Kendra, what the –?'

She swallowed up his words, biting his lip, sucking his tongue, licking at the back of his teeth and his hard palate until he couldn't breathe. Her fist around his cock was a stranglehold, and even in its discomfort it felt like he was in heaven. 'Kendra, I can't …' He tried to push her hand away, but the other hand snaked in and jerked his bottoms and boxers down over his ass until he could feel the night air on bare flesh. He wriggled and squirmed, his heart racing in his chest. 'Jesus, Kendra, you can't be serious. This is a public place. What if someone –?'

She bit his lip hard enough that he wondered if she'd drawn blood, and his cock surged so strongly in her hand that he feared he'd come right there.

'Shut up, Garrett,' she growled against his mouth. 'I need you to fuck me, so just shut up.'

He heard the crackle of foil and, with a sleight of hand that nearly took his breath away, she sheathed him in the condom. Then, with hands that seemed as full of anger and need as the rest of her, she ripped open the fly of her shredded jeans and shoved them down. Christ! There were no panties!

'I need you, Garrett.' She struggled to breathe. 'I need you to fuck me right now. I can't wait. Right now. Right now!' She turned her back to him, still shoving and pushing at the jeans until they were down around her thighs and the rounded heart shape of her bottom showed in the pale light. Then she bent over and rested a palm onto the seat of the park bench. With the other hand, she reached behind her, grabbed his hip, and pulled him up close until his cock pressed into the valley between her buttocks. 'Do it, Garrett. I can't stand it any longer. Do it now!' She wasn't trying to be quiet. She wasn't trying to be subtle. She didn't care that there were other people still using the park, that they might get caught, and Garrett felt like he'd burst at the very thought of what they were doing – and where.

She opened herself to him and shifted her hips, while he, with one hand low on her back and the other on his cock, fumbled and manoeuvred until he slid home. She grunted a curse and pushed back onto him hard, and they both cried out as they began to thrust.

Her beret tumbled off behind the park bench and he grabbed at her ponytail as it fell free, reining her in with it. He yanked her back toward him like it might help him control her somehow. He yanked her back until he could bury his mouth against her neck, rake her pulse point with his teeth, suckle and

149

nip until the sounds coming from both their throats were feral groans and grunts.

With a quick movement, she unhooked her bra, grabbed his free hand, and guided it to the bounce and the fullness of her breasts, nipples tight and puckered against the rake of his thumb. Then she grabbed his hand from her hair and brought his fingers to her mouth, licking and nibbling before she shoved them down between her legs, down to the heavy strain of her clit.

They were both too far gone to hold back much longer, and it took little more than a stroke between her legs before she came, growling and straining and nearly collapsing onto the bench as he came, juddering in hard waves inside her.

It was only as their breathing began to return to normal that he could hear her sniffles. As he pulled out, she stood and wiped her nose on the back of her hand, then jerked her jeans up as though they'd made her angry somehow.

She stuffed her bra into the pocket of his hoodie with a hard shove, bent to retrieve her beret, and was already heading down the path before he could deal with the condom and get settled back into his track bottoms. He hurried to catch up. 'Look, I'm sorry. I shouldn't have jumped to conclusions back there at The Boiling Point. It's just I was so scared when I couldn't find you, and I saw the way everyone was looking at you earlier.'

Amazingly, the tension dissipated from her shoulders and she shot him a sideways grin. 'You jealous?'

'Yes.' He didn't even have to think about it. Of course he was jealous. And suddenly he could tell she was studying him in the dark, a situation that was never very comfortable for him.

At last she spoke. 'Garrett, you had no reason to be jealous. Don't you know you were by far the most interesting man there?'

He fought back a wave of confusion. Kendra Davis had wrong-footed him again. 'No. I didn't know that.'

'Well, I knew it.' She slid her arm through his, leaned in on her tiptoes, and settled a kiss on his cheek. 'And so did every other woman who saw you there tonight. The lust was rampant,

Garrett, totally rampant.'

He pulled her to him and kissed her on the mouth. 'Oh, now you're just toying with me. You wanted to slap me again. I could see it on your face. You wanted to do … Well, probably all sorts of unthinkable stuff to me.'

'And you deserved it,' she said, as they continued their walk. 'Problem is you might have liked it a little too much if I'd slapped you, and I was too angry to give you something you might like.'

This time he laughed out loud, causing a couple walking a pair of corgis to start and glance over their shoulders before hurrying on down the lit path. 'And you think what happened up there –' He nodded to the hill they had just descended, and the hawthorn grove. 'You think that wasn't something I like?'

'That –' She glanced over her shoulder. 'That wasn't for you. That was for me.'

'Maybe so, but it worked for me on a lot of levels.'

He could see the corners of her mouth turn up in that quirky smile that always made him wonder if she was laughing at him or at herself. 'Guess you got lucky, then, didn't you?'

This time she let him slide his arm around her, slipping his thumb down into the waistband of her low riders just enough to stroke the swell of her hip, and she returned the favour, stroking his back beneath his hoodie. A part of him was disappointed that the walk back to his house wasn't a longer one, but the closeness of her, the wild restlessness of her, was already making him horny again by the time they slipped up the back steps and into the kitchen.

Chapter Eighteen

While he locked the door, she tiptoed into the living room and peeked out into the front yard between the heavy drapes, which had remained drawn with the discovery of the press. 'Looks like the night watch is in place,' she called back over her shoulder. 'Somebody's even out there in a damn motorhome.'

By the time she'd returned to his side, he'd extricated the remains of last night's pizza from the refrigerator and was chomping on a cold piece.

'Starving.' He spoke around a mouthful. 'You can nuke it if you want.' He nodded to the microwave.

'I can't wait that long.' She slapped his hands away from the box and grabbed her own piece. 'Besides, I get really grouchy if I don't eat regularly.'

'That would be a shock,' he said.

She flipped him off, and he blew her a kiss.

He pulled his BlackBerry from his pocket and checked it. 'Missed call from Don, missed call from Don. Text from Don to check my email. Missed call from Don. Jesus, the bastard's a bore,' Garrett said.

She pulled out her iPhone and nodded as she scrolled down. 'Yep. I see what you mean. Still, I suppose we should at least make an effort. I mean, he may have a great new feminine hygiene product lined up for Tess to endorse; more money for both of you.'

He pulled her into his arms and she offered a little yelp as he lifted her onto the counter. 'There's nothing Don can possibly have to say that can be worth missing out on what I've got right here.' He ran a hand up under her sweatshirt and cupped her bare breasts in turn. Her bra was still stuffed in the pocket of his hoodie, and God, was it a turn-on to watch the frontal action when Kendra's breasts were free.

She wrapped her arms around his neck and lazily nibbled on his bottom lip. 'Better call him,' she said as she pulled away with a flick of her tongue. 'Then we can get on to better things.' She nodded down to where his cock was beginning to tent his track bottoms again.

While he pulled up Don's number, Kendra grabbed a couple of bottles of Mirror Pond Pale Ale from the refrigerator, opened them, and handed one to him just as Don's voice boomed over the speaker phone.

'Where the hell have you been?'

Garrett looked at Kendra. 'I've got you on speaker phone, Don.' He winked at her. And they both smiled at the shuffle and huff of embarrassment on the other end of the device.

'You doing all right, Kay?' Don asked.

'Fine, thanks. I'm fine.'

'Now, where have you two been?' Garrett recognized the forced politeness in Don's voice. He didn't use it on him very often. He and Don had long ago moved past the need to be polite.

'Dancing,' Garrett replied, pulling out a chair and settling at the table in front of the BlackBerry. 'We've been dancing.'

'Dancing, right. And how did you manage that without the press finding out?'

'Well.' He pulled Kendra down onto his lap and ran his hand back under her shirt. 'Kay's very creative. We went incognito to a place not far from here. Sneaked out the back.'

There was a long silence at the other end of the phone, and they could hear Don's forced sigh. 'Isn't that a little bit dangerous? Have there been any more emails from your stalker?'

'I'll get the laptop and we can find out.' Before Garrett could grab her, Kendra was off his lap and halfway up the stairs. She returned in a few seconds with his computer and plopped back down onto his lap while he manoeuvred around her, sloppily brushing her breasts on purpose as he pulled up his email.

153

Kendra saw it first, and the little hitch of her breath was enough to knot his stomach. 'There's something here from him, from Razor Sharp.' Garrett barely managed to keep his voice steady, not wanting to make matters worse. He tightened his grip around Kendra's waist as he took a deep breath and opened it.

You're a whore, Tess! I'm only just now realizing how much of a whore you really are.

Kendra flinched on his lap as though she'd been slapped.

'Read it to me,' Don demanded.

Garrett could barely hear his own voice over the loud fluttering of wings in his ears. 'Don, we'll call you back.' He reached for the BlackBerry.

'No.' Kendra laid her hand against his. 'It's all right. I'll read it.'

Before he could stop her, she read in a voice that was distant, mechanical.

You're a whore, Tess! I'm only just now realizing how much of a whore you really are. Sadly, when I'm honest with myself, I always suspected that you were. I always suspected that no one could write sex like you do without being a dirty little slut herself. And the way you let Garrett Thorne fuck you, that worthless excuse for a human being, the way you play the whore with him, only confirms that you aren't worthy, that you deserve to be punished. And when I get you to myself, Tess, when it's just you and me and no Garrett Thorne, no interfering press, no one else, then I promise you, I will punish you, and you will repent of your wickedness and beg for my forgiveness. It's the only way we can be together, Tess. And we will be together. I only hope it's not too late.
Yours in deepest love,
R.S.

'Damn it, Garrett! This isn't funny. Kay, are you –?'

But Kendra wasn't listening; instead, she fought her way off Garrett's lap and made a mad dash for the bathroom, slamming the door behind her.

'Garrett, what's going on? Don't you think maybe you should –?'

'I'll call you back.' Garrett broke the connection and ran after Kendra.

Kendra wasn't sure how long she sat on the bathroom floor with her cheek pressed against the cool tiles of the wall, fearing if she moved she would throw up, fearing if she moved all the nightmares would come racing back, fearing if she moved she would unravel a thread at a time until there was nothing left of her but the knot of panic threatening to devour her. It could have been seconds. It could have been years.

At some point, out of the dark mist that surrounded her and danced like shadows across her vision, Garrett knocked softly on the door. When she didn't answer, he opened the door a crack. 'Kendra? Can I come in?'

She might have nodded her head the tiniest bit or not, but for some reason he felt he had her consent. For a second he stood in the open door and took in the situation, her sitting, against the wall, close enough to the toilet that she could get there if she needed to retch, but close enough that the tile could cool the heat of rage and frustration and sick fear that threatened to tear her apart.

Then he moved to the sink, filled a glass with water, and sat down next to her. 'Can you drink this?' His voice was like light pulling her back from the dark. 'Because if you can it'll help you feel better.'

When she reached for it, her hands were too unsteady to hold it, but he held it for her, tipping it to her lips so she could drink. And when she'd had enough, he set the glass aside and eased her gently into his arms. It felt better there. For a long time he didn't say anything. He just held her, and the nausea disappeared and the world righted itself and she could breathe again. It was still a long time before she could risk speaking, before she felt she could manage it without sobbing. Only Dee and Harris had ever seen her sob. Only Dee and Harris loved her anyway. 'I'm so sorry,' she finally managed.

Garrett smoothed her hair away from her face and kissed her forehead. 'For what?' He asked. But before she could apologies for what a coward she was, for how weak she was, he continued, 'What happened, Kendra?' He nodded toward the door. 'I know that email isn't it.'

There was a time when she would have rather cut out her own heart than told any of her secrets to Garrett Thorne, than told any of her secrets to anyone. Now that time seemed very long ago, indeed.

She fumbled with her iPhone, flipped through it with fingers that were still none too steady until she came to the picture. Then she handed it to him. She could tell by the look on his face that he didn't recognize her, and she waited until she saw the light dawn in his eyes.

'It's you,' he said breathlessly. 'I would have never guessed.'

She reached for the water glass and drank the rest of it back. 'No one would have. That was the point. And I never thought of her as me. I never thought of any of them as me. Just like I didn't think of myself as Tess Delaney at the Golden Kiss Awards.'

'I don't understand,' he said. 'This was a role you played for another client?'

'No, Garrett. That –' she nodded to the image on the iPhone '– that was a role I played for me. One of many.' She took a deep shudder of a breath. 'The Bird Woman, that's what he called me, because of the fake tattoos. The Bird Woman was the one who cost me everything.'

She could tell by the drawing of his brows that he still didn't get it. Of course he didn't. How could he? She took a deep breath and continued.

'I told you I don't need much sleep. I never have. The Ryde Agency demanded a lot of time and energy from me but not nearly all of it, especially since I found the work so stimulating. And early on, once I figured out what I had to do to make it work, money was never a problem. The Ryde Agency was a cash cow long before my skill was anything other than dumb luck and a huge ego.

'I figured out early on with everyone thinking K. Ryde was a hard-assed PR guru, a man surrounded by his stable of PR nymphs who could pull off miracles for a price, I could be whoever I wanted to be. I had the money, and I had, I don't know, this way of emptying myself when I wanted to and reinventing myself as another person. At first, I did it only for work. I was K. Ryde's PA. I was an actress K. Ryde hired to play someone's secretary or someone's mistress, someone's sister. I was K. Ryde's wife, even, at times. And if I could be anyone I wanted to be at work, why not at play? So I started dressing the part. I'd go out someplace far enough away from my own stomping ground, someplace I was unlikely to meet up with anyone I knew. I'd change my hair color, my cut, my make-up.' She cupped her breasts. 'My tit size. I even went out as a man a few times.' She shrugged. 'I wasn't so good at that. I could never quite get the walk and the mannerisms right. But anyone else I could be for a night, for a week. If I met someone interesting I would keep the persona I had when I met them as for as long as it took me to get bored. That was never more than a couple of weeks. And since I was the Ryde Agency, the way I looked was never an issue at work. Even the people I did hire to assist me never saw the real me, and they never saw each other. No one knew anyone in the real world. So whenever I decided I wanted to get to know someone, spend some time with someone, it was easy.'

'You mean with a man.' Garrett struggled with the words. 'Spend some time with a man.'

She nodded. 'Yes, with a man. Well, at least most of the time. Occasionally it was just an interesting group of people that I wanted to know more about, that I wanted to get a feel for. But my sexual partners were always men. Not that I wouldn't have considered a woman. It just never happened, that's all.'

'And you had sex with all these people? The people you met?' The muscles along the top of his jaw clenched and his shoulders looked like they were made of iron.

'Not all of them, and not always. It was more about the control I had, about the freedom I had as a nobody, as a person who didn't really exist. Because I was good at my job, it was never hard to win people's trust, and it was always easy to manipulate my way into the centre of things. Garrett, I could have sex whenever I wanted it. That was never an issue. That's not why I did it.'

'Then why?' he asked.

'Don't tell me you've never wanted to be someone else? I mean, you are someone else, and you've pulled it off at least as well as I have, you and Tess.'

He squirmed and straightened his back against the wall, but said nothing.

She nodded to the photo. 'I was Bird Woman when I met the man who ... The one who stalked me. There was a woman I'd partied with a few times. We just ended up together, Lila was her name. We ran into each other at a really ratty bar in Santa Monica one night. She was with him. She called him Edge. That's all, just Edge. She was fucking him, and she told me he wanted to do a threesome with me. She was really strange about it, almost like she was desperate to involve me. I told her no. There were too many elements in a threesome I couldn't control, and after seeing the two of them together, I was pretty sure I couldn't control him, pretty sure he was dangerous. That was the night he grabbed my phone away from me and took this picture.' She looked down at the image. 'It's the only picture I have of any of them, any of the people I used to be. I wouldn't allow photos, but this was on my own phone, so it didn't seem to matter, and I didn't want to upset him. He was flirting with me, and she was watching, sort of, I don't know, she was just acting really strange. I was just trying to be polite, be nice and get the hell out of there. It wasn't comfortable. When he asked me outright if I'd like to have sex with them, I politely declined. I thought everything was cool. I made a quick stop to the bathroom on my way out when I heard noises in the alley. And he was out there, beating the shit out of her.'

She shivered, and Garrett tightened his hold around her and chafed her arms. 'I wasn't thinking. I started yelling at him, I told him I'd call the police. I told him I had a gun.' She shrugged. 'I didn't. I didn't have anything, but he just shoved her against the wall and stared at me. And he said, "I hear birds don't live long, Bird Woman." Then he left.

158

'Two weeks later Lila was dead.'

'Jesus!' Garrett pulled her closer. 'He killed her?'

'No. He didn't kill her, at least not outright. She committed suicide. Though, looking back, I've no doubt he drove her to it. I didn't even know she was dead until he emailed me the link from the paper and her obituary. I have no idea how he got my email, how he discovered who I was when no one else could. In the beginning, he seemed all broken up about Lila, and I was sympathetic, but distant. I figured he'd lose interest and if he didn't I'd change my email address and that would be that. K. Ryde had lots of email addresses and lots of identities. I figured it couldn't be that difficult to handle.'

'But it was.'

She nodded. 'It was. Then the expensive gifts and flowers started showing up at my door, *my* door, not K. Ryde's office, my home which no one knew anything about. I couldn't send them back, I had no address. I emailed and asked him to stop and he got angry. And the gifts got unpleasant. Rotting fish, a dead snake, horrible, horrible pictures. I don't know if he took them or just downloaded them off really sick internet sites, but it got worse and so did the emails, more and more threatening. Awful stuff. I changed my email. It didn't help. I moved. It didn't help.'

'Didn't you call the police?'

'Of course I did, but there was nothing they could do. Even when the death threats started, there was still nothing they could do, not really. He had my cell phone number and he called me dozens of times a day. I got a new phone and it started all over again. Then he found out that I worked for K. Ryde. I don't think he ever learned that I was K. Ryde, though I can't imagine how he didn't know that. He knew everything else. But when he found out that I worked for the Ryde Agency, he found out about a client I was working with at the time, a very secretive client. He told me he'd turn his attention on the client. That's the only time I ever turned a client over to the Bachman Agency. And I knew I couldn't continue, that K. Ryde couldn't continue without putting clients and people I cared about at risk.'

She lowered her head into her hands and tried to breathe, tried to get her heart to slow down. 'I couldn't take it anymore, Garrett. I left. I sold the Ryde Agency for a lot of money and I moved back to Portland.'

'Fuck, Kendra! And I involved you in all this.'

She shook her head. 'Garrett, it can't be him. I hired a detective to find out who he was, to find him and get him off my back. I mean, I had to do something. The police were of no use. I gave them everything I knew, even went so far as to hang out in the places where he used to be with a wire.'

'Jesus, Kendra! Were you crazy?'

He pulled her to him with such force that she groaned and wriggled for breathing space.

She offered a ghost of a smile. 'I probably was. I certainly couldn't have been far from it. All I knew was that I wanted my life back, and I wanted this bastard to leave me alone.

'In the end, I sold up and left California. The stress was doing a number on me, and the detective thought I'd be better somewhere safe and out of harm's way.'

'So what happened?' Garrett asked.

Kendra wiped at her eyes with the backs of her hand. 'It was almost like the minute I took back my identity, my real identity, and came home to where I belong, the threats, the phone calls, the emails, everything stopped. I lived on eggshells for several weeks. Harris and Dee took me in, took care of me until I was fit to rejoin society again. Then, when I'd been home about a month or so, the detective agency got in touch with me. They'd found the man, a Frederick Parks. Called himself Edge. Apparently, I wasn't the first woman he'd stalked.'

'Did he go to jail for what he did?' Garrett said.

She shook her head and shoved the hair back over her shoulders. 'He was dead. They think he fell asleep with a cigarette, he was probably drunk or on something, and burnt his own house down around him.'

'God,' Garrett whispered. 'And they were sure it was him?'

She nodded. 'The ID was positive. So there's no way this Razor Sharp can be my stalker. You said it yourself. He's been emailing Tess for a long time now. And I still maintain that it's probably nothing. I just … I never expected to react quite so strongly.'

'Fuck, Kendra! Why the hell wouldn't you react strongly? I mean, the man made your life a living hell. The nightmare. It was …'

'It was about him, yes.'

For a long time, the two sat in silence on the bathroom floor, Kendra resting her head against the wonderfully steady beating of Garrett's heart. At last she sighed. 'I really need a Diet Pepsi, and maybe some more of that cold pizza.'

Later, when they had both eaten and had worked up an email to send Don that was evasive enough about what happened to protect Kendra's privacy but they felt offered enough to satisfy his curiosity, exhaustion set in.

Garrett pulled Kendra to her feet and guided her to the stairs. 'Shower in the morning,' he said, then he nuzzled her neck gently. 'Together. Rain check and all, you know?' She smiled and nodded her agreement.

At the top of the stairs, he didn't let go of her hand at the guest room door, but slid his arm around her and guided her to his room. 'If you think I'm letting you sleep alone tonight after the day you've had, then you'd better think again.' When she started to protest, he covered her lips with his and shushed her. 'I won't take no for an answer.' He slid the shirt off over her head, then went to work on the fly of her jeans. 'And don't worry, I'll behave.' He nipped her earlobe lightly. 'Unless you want me to misbehave. I'm fine either way.'

He helped her out of her boots, then her jeans, and settled her into his big bed, the one they had romped in together – was it just last night? It took him all of two seconds to shed his track suit and his sneakers, then he slid in next to her and pulled her tightly against him into a spoon position. 'Get some sleep, Kendra. Tomorrow we'll both see things more clearly.' He kissed her ear. 'And if you dream, I'll be right here. I'm not going anywhere.'

'Garrett.' His name felt good on her lips in the darkness.

'Hmm?'

'Thank you.'

He kissed the back of her neck and cupped her breast in the curve of his hand. She could feel the press of his erection against her butt, and she would have loved to take care of it for him, but she was asleep before she could do more than think about it. This time it was the deep, dreamless sleep of exhaustion, sleep in a safe place, a comfortable place. Quite possibly the most comfortable place in which she had ever slept. In the arms of Garrett Thorne.

Chapter Nineteen

Dawn was paling when Garrett woke, feeling confused. For a brief moment he didn't remember where he was or what his circumstances were. It was the muffled moan that came from the pillow next to him and a length of exquisite thigh extending from beneath the comforter that brought everything back to him, and he was suddenly wide awake, holding his breath, listening, listening to Kendra sleep. But after a moment of intense scrutiny, he relaxed and raised himself on one elbow to look down at her. She wasn't dreaming. Thank God! There was no rapid eye movement, and her breathing was deep and even, completely relaxed.

He studied her blatantly, lying there sleeping, vulnerable, unable to avoid his gaze, unable to turn the tables on him. The red hair was a far cry from the creamy blonde she'd been only a few days ago, and the cut, the style, all different from the Kendra Davis he knew. Even in her portrayal of Tess she had emptied herself. She had become as nobody in order to embody the woman he had become as nobody to create. Jesus, what a pair they made! Did either of them even know who they really were?

He couldn't remember a time when he hadn't been Ellis's kid brother, even though there was less than a year's difference in their age. He couldn't remember a time when he hadn't felt inadequate to the task, the task of living up to the standards Ellis so effortlessly set from the time he was a little boy. Garrett was the other Thorne – the one who never amounted to much, the one who always found a way to disappoint. He swallowed back his bitterness. He might as well be Tess. At least Tess was somebody. It certainly wasn't Ellis's fault that

163

he was the disappointing brother. Ellis was wonderful, Ellis was true and steady and always, always there for him, even after everything that had happened, even after all the pain he had caused.

He reached out a finger and traced the soft spiral curve of Kendra's ear, exposed from the fall of her hair. He understood her. He understood her far better than she could imagine. He understood how much power one wielded when one was nobody, when one could simply fade into the woodwork and not be taken seriously. The invisible can manage so much in their anonymity. Did Kendra live in the shadow of an older sister or brother? He seriously doubted it. How could anyone so powerful, so exquisite, so brave ever live in anyone's shadow? And yet how easily, how perfectly she had embodied Tess. To the rest of the world, she was Tess Delaney.

'But not to me,' he whispered, bending to brush a kiss across her hair. She stirred slightly and sighed. 'You'll never be Tess to me,' he said. 'You're Kendra Davis, and that's way more of a challenge than Tess could ever be.'

She stirred again and wriggled into the spoon position. The lovely naked arc of her bottom, pushing back against his usual morning stiffness, brought his cock to full attention and made his heart race.

'You awake?' she mumbled. The sound of sleep in her voice was outrageously sexy.

He tried very hard to hold still, to ignore the irresistible urge to shift his hips until his erection nestled tighter in the cleft between her buttocks, pressed there hopefully, eagerly. 'You should go back to sleep.' He brushed her throat with a kiss, and his insides leapt with excitement as her lips curved into a smile, heavy lashes fluttering over her still-closed eyes.

'Make me,' she whispered. Then she ground her bottom against his hard-on, and he gasped his surprise. She fumbled beneath the covers to where his hand rested on her hip and guided it first to brush across her breasts with their begging nipples full and distended. It was only a brief tease of a detour on the route to the soft curls of her pubis. They were golden curls, he recalled with great satisfaction. At the core of her, she was still Kendra Davis, and no matter how hard she tried, she could never really be otherwise. For a second she allowed him to stroke and caress her there, then she wriggled and shifted, guiding his fingers until the middle one brushed the marbled rise of her clit, causing a kitten-like whimper and a hitch of her breath. Then she rocked, first back to rub against his cock, then forward onto his fingers, which wriggled and squirmed and burrowed their way into the valleys and rises of her, desperate to tweak and probe her humid depths. Already he could smell her heat rising. Already she was open and yielding, her body gripping at the push and shove of his fingers like a nursing infant. Already he felt the weight of his own arousal surrounding and enfolding him.

Over her grumble of a protest, he pulled away and reached for a condom from the nightstand. And when he was sheathed, he slid down next to her. He eased her thighs open from behind and she pressed her bottom back toward him, meeting him, opening to him, yielding as he manoeuvred his way home. As he pressed up into her, she released a long, quavering breath.

With one hand splayed low on her belly, he pulled her tighter to him, pulled her closer and deeper onto him until he could feel the full grip and release, grip and release of her need against him.

The press and strain and the rock and shift would have been barely noticeable to anyone looking on from above the comforter, but Garrett felt the gripping warmth of her, the caress of each undulation all the way to the crown of his head, and the buzz of being inside Kendra Davis was better than any drug, any drink he had ever experienced. He nibbled and caressed her neck and her nape and her shoulders. He thumbed and raked at her nipples. He ran his hand down the flat slope of her belly to stroke the softness of her tight curls, to tweak the hardness of her clit, to feel her fast, furious pull for breath low in her abdomen, to feel the tight edge of her imminent orgasm barley restrained, barely held back by her desire, by both of their desire to make it last.

Holding tight, holding his breath, holding to every last shred of control, he waited for her, waited expectantly, anxiously, needily, until at last her voice found its way up through her efforts to breathe. 'Garrett, make me come now. I need you to make me come.'

It only took another sharp thrust and she convulsed into orgasm, gripping him tight enough to send him as well, shuddering and growling against her.

And when they could breathe again, she reached behind her and patted his ass with her palm. 'That's better. I'll go back to sleep now.' And she did. They both did.

Even though her father's was a very small motorhome, it still dominated the street in front of Garrett Thorne's house. Carla wasn't sure how long she could park in the neighbourhood before someone called the police and she'd have to ask her dad to come get it and bring her car back. It was still smaller than some of the news vans, she told herself, though she didn't expect that to carry much weight with the police. Even though she could barely turn around without hitting her nose on the opposite wall, at least now she had the luxuries of a bathroom and a mini refrigerator. She could last for weeks if she had to with her father bringing her supplies. And he loved a good mystery as much as she did, so he had been all too happy to oblige.

Still, this mystery frightened her. This mystery made her feel there was way more at risk than a great story.

A tinny rendition of *Duelling Banjos* suddenly filled the tight space and she jumped and uttered a little yelp of surprise before she managed to retrieve her iPhone from the makeshift Formica table.

'Carla, Barker Blessing here.'

There was only one reason she could think that he might be up at this hour. Her insides roiled at the sound of his voice, and it was suddenly difficult to breathe. 'Have you heard from him?' She hoped he couldn't hear the nervous flutter in her voice.

'No,' came the breathy reply.

She slumped, feeling the tension drain away from her shoulders. Even though they really could use another message from the stalker about now, it was still a relief not to have one. There was an uncertain sounding pause, and she could hear Blessing take a deep breath. 'Then there's – nothing new?'

'No. Nothing.' She said, continuing her web search for stalkers in the Northwest who were notable enough to get the police's attention. There were also some websites her father had given her links to. His resources were often at least as good as the police.

Blessing laughed nervously. 'I didn't wake you, did I?'

'No. I was awake.' She peeked out at the front of the Thorne house, bathed in the early morning sun. Her eyes felt like they were full of sand, but she was awake.

'You haven't told anyone, have you?' he said. 'I mean, he did say not to and we can't put poor Tess at any more risk than she already is, can we?'

She rolled her eyes. 'Of course I haven't told anyone.' Well, she had actually told her father, but the stalker hadn't said she couldn't and her dad had wheedled it out of her in exchange for the motorhome and help with the links he had access to. Besides, her dad was a resource she couldn't afford to overlook. 'I'm just doing a little research on my own. You'll let me know if you hear from him, though, right?'

'Yes, yes,' he said. 'Perhaps you should come over to my place, maybe for brunch, and we could discuss everything that's happened. I'm sure you must have more questions about my time with Tess at the Golden Kiss Awards. Plus it would be nice to meet the woman in person who interviewed me.'

Jesus, was the guy really hitting on her? 'Thank you, Mr. Blessing, but at the moment, I can't get away.'

'Are you still staking out Thorne's house?'

'Mmm-hmmm.' A few of the press were now out of the vans, milling about. Some had cups from the local Starbucks, some were eating doughnuts. Her stomach growled.

'Any sightings of our illustrious couple?'

'Nothing since the press conference. I would imagine they're still in bed.'

'You suppose she really is writing?' His voice was low, suggestive. 'Thorne has a reputation, you know.'

'I don't know what she's doing, Mr. Blessing. At the moment you know as much as I do.' That was a lie, but his pumping her for information was a waste of her time if he had nothing he could offer.

For a second, there was silence on the line. An email from her father popped onto the screen of her iPad. She opened it to discover links to reports of recent sex-related murders, and her stomach churned at the sudden escalation in her research. She nearly forgot about Blessing until he forced an impatient little sigh.

'You all right?' she asked at last.

'Yes, fine. I'm fine. It's just that yesterday was a rather harrowing day, wasn't it?'

'Sure was,' she said. 'Look, Mr. Blessing, I really need to get back to it. I need to stay focused, you know? Thorne and Ms. Delaney could come out any time.'

'Stay focused, yes, of course you do. I'll just … I'll just let you go, then. You will call, right?'

'I will, I promise, Mr. Blessing,' she said as she cut the connection. He might be famous, but he was irritating as hell when she was trying to work. This was the fifth time he'd called her since the press conference.

She laid her iPhone aside and began to sift the data her father had sent her, double checking to make sure all the doors to the motorhome were locked. Of course they were, and yet, she still couldn't fight back the feeling that she was being watched.

She'd just poured the last cup of coffee from the Thermos her father had brought her when, out of the corner of her eye, movement caught her attention. She looked up to see a blue-grey Lexus pull in front of Thorne's house. As the door opened, she set her coffee cup down onto the table, slopping it across the shiny surface as she grabbed her Dictaphone and shoved her way out of the motorhome, slamming the door behind her. This was just too much for even her to believe!

The sun was streaming through the bedroom window when they both were startled awake by a commotion from the press already gathered on the front porch. Then they heard the turning of the lock and the opening of the front door.

'What the …?' Garrett catapulted out of bed and practically fell on his face getting into his track bottoms. 'Stay here, Kendra. I mean it,' he called over his shoulder. He was halfway down the stairs before Kendra could shove her way into his robe. Outside, she could hear the press attempting to engage whoever was shoving their way into Garrett's front door. But they were getting no joy. She raced out of the room and nearly ran into Garrett where he stood halfway down the stairs, and then she saw the reason why.

'Stacie? What the hell are you doing here?' Garrett's voice was low and dangerous.

'Your ex? Your ex has a key?' Kendra felt a tug of jealousy in the pit of her stomach, and mentally kicked herself for caring one way or another.

The woman was locking the door behind her and checking the deadbolt. She was dressed to the teeth in a pinstripe power suit and matching navy stilettos, and damn, she looked way better than Kendra wished she did. Especially when she could only imagine what she looked like. She had gone to bed with Garrett without bothering to take off her make-up or run a comb through her hair. She wasn't sure she could have stayed awake long enough to do either.

'Sorry, Garrett, I didn't mean to wake you,' she called over her shoulder. 'I just got into PDX after a very long flight. What the hell's the press doing out there anyway? I thought they were going to tear me –' She stopped mid-sentence when she turned to find Kendra and Garrett standing on the stairs, clearly just out of bed.

Everyone stood freeze-framed in the moment that it took the situation to register. The silence was broken only by the press, who sounded like they were ready for blood.

'She has a key?' Those were the first words out of Kendra's mouth, and fuck if they didn't make her sound like some kind of jealous bitch. She wasn't jealous, damn it! She wasn't!

Garrett ran a nervous hand through his hair and huffed out a harsh breath. 'Stacie, you are the queen of poor timing. Have you been on another planet or something? Are you the only one who doesn't know about Garrett Thorne absconding with the winner of the Golden Kiss Award and hiding her away from her adoring public?' He pulled Kendra to his side and slipped an arm around her. She resisted the urge to elbow him good and hard in the ribs.

'I've been in Japan negotiating for an exhibition of antique kimonos and armour from the time of the Shoguns. I haven't heard anything.'

'They don't have CNN in Japan?' he asked.

'They do, but not where I was.' She was speaking to Garrett but her eyes were locked on Kendra. 'Tess won?'

He nodded.

'Congratulations.' She folded her arms across her chest and offered Kendra a wicked smile. 'Don't know how you managed it, Garrett, but Tess certainly looks radiant.' She cocked her head and returned her attention to Garrett. 'No bruises, near-drownings? Other injuries I should know about?'

'Shut up, Stacie,' he growled.

She only smiled and looked from one of them to the other. 'I'm assuming the guest room is unoccupied, so I'll just stash my bag, and I'm starving. How about I make pancakes? You have stuff for pancakes?'

'No,' Garrett said.

'Yes,' Kendra said. 'Full larder. You make pancakes?'

Stacie nodded. 'The best.' She offered them a knowing smile. 'Why don't you two go slip into something a little less comfortable, and I'll get cooking.' She waved a hand to the wheelie bag sitting on the floor by the door. 'I'll stash that later.'

Kendra pushed Garrett's arm off her shoulder and shot him an evil look. 'I'll help you in the kitchen,' she said.

Stacie shrugged, and Kendra thought she heard Garrett say a few unsavoury words under his breath. Then she sauntered down the stairs, tugging the sash of the robe as though she was making every effort to cut herself in half with it, and led the way into the kitchen.

She already had a Diet Pepsi open for courage and was

beginning a pot of coffee when Stacie came in behind her, and easily found her way around to gather ingredients.

'I'm not sleeping with him,' Stacie said as she bent to get eggs out of the fridge. She said it as casually as if she was discussing the weather outside. 'We haven't fucked in a very long time now, sweetie. And we were friends long before we were lovers, so that part of us has stayed.'

'None of my business,' Kendra said, starting the coffee pot.

'True, but I could tell you wanted to know, since clearly you're sleeping with him, I can't blame you. I certainly would if I were you. Garrett's good in bed.'

'Jesus,' Kendra whispered under her breath.

'I stay with Garrett when I'm in Portland since he has a house now. It's just nicer than a hotel, and it gives us a chance to catch up.'

'You don't seem surprised we're having sex,' Kendra said, trying not to feel self-conscious in her underdressed state. Upstairs, she could hear the shower running and remembered she had planned to fuck Garrett senseless in their morning ablutions.

'Not surprised that you're having sex, no. I mean, when two people are at each other's throats the way you two were at Dee and Ellis's engagement party, sex is pretty much the next step, isn't it? I am a little surprised you haven't killed each other in lieu of post-coital bliss.'

Kendra nodded to the press beyond the door. 'We've had to put acts of random violence temporarily behind us and fight the good fight.'

Stacie offered a throaty giggle as she perused the contents of the refrigerator for what she needed. 'Oh, this just keeps getting better and better, tell me more. I'm dying to catch up and I –' She gave a little gasp and laid a hand against her ample cleavage. 'You have blueberries.'

'Yes.' Kendra replied. 'So?'

'Do you like blueberry pancakes?'

'Better than almost anything,' Kendra said. 'And if there's maple syrup then they're almost –'

'Almost better than sex?' Stacie walked to the pantry and

171

pulled out a bottle of maple syrup.

'God, yes!' And suddenly both women were giggling.

Stacie kicked off her shoes and pulled out an apron, noticing Kendra's look of surprise. 'The syrup and the apron, I bought. I cook for Garrett occasionally when I'm here because that's one thing I can manage without bodily injury.' She shrugged 'That and suss out the best art in the world for my galleries. Otherwise, I'm a bit of a klutz, I'm afraid.'

Kendra watched in fascination as Stacie began to whisk together the ingredients like a pro. She couldn't resist. 'Were you really engaged to Ellis when you married Garrett?'

'Yep,' the woman said without looking up at her. 'I was very young and very stupid, and very sorry very soon.' She glanced over her shoulder. 'They were my two best friends. You can't imagine the loss, and how much I regretted it.'

'Your two best friends. Really? How did you meet?' If she sounded like she was giving the woman the third degree, well, she supposed she was a little bit.

'I moved in next door to the Thornes when I was 12. And my telescope was better than Ellis's.'

'You were into astronomy?'

'I was, yes, and my father helped me build my own telescope. That made me very popular with Ellis. His parents were both professors, but neither had any interest in astronomy, so he'd had to save birthday money and money from paper routes for his.' She began to spoon the batter onto the griddle. 'Soon after that, Garrett got interested too, and we became fast friends. In the end, the friendship was strong enough to survive Garrett and my stupidity, something I'm very grateful for. Good friends are hard to come by.' Before Kendra could comment, she turned the conversation back to her.

'So, tell me what happened. How did Garrett ever convince you to be his Tess Delaney? To be honest, I'm surprised he could even convince you not to shoot him on sight.'

'I don't own a gun,' Kendra said, finding a colander to rinse the blueberries.

'Better for Garrett. Now, tell me what happened.'

And, strangely enough, Kendra found herself quite

172

comfortable talking to Stacie. She had told her everything except for the part about the emails and was setting the table when they both turned to find Garrett standing in the kitchen door, freshly scrubbed, hair still damp, with his arms folded across the unbuttoned, untucked black cotton shirt, and God, he looked hot.

Stacie smiled up at him. 'Sit down. Breakfast is served.

'Smells great. Thanks, Stacie,' he said, but his gaze was locked on Kendra, like it wasn't Stacie's pancakes he wanted to eat.'

'I see you two haven't killed each other,' he said.

Kendra shrugged and moved to pour him coffee. 'How was your shower?'

'Not as good as it could have been.' He raked her with a hungry gaze.

All the way through a delicious breakfast, Stacie regaled them with her adventures in some of the more remote regions of Japan in search of exhibits for the grand opening of her New World Gallery West. She owned New World Gallery in New York City, and was now expanding to the West Coast.

'Since there's a large Japanese influence in the Northwest, I thought that would be a wonderful way to open New World West,' she said, cradling her coffee cup between her hands. 'That would be half of the exhibition, and the other half I'm hoping to dedicate to the natural beauty of the area itself. I want to exhibit some of the best wildlife and nature photography, photographed by local photographers.' She nodded to Kendra. 'I'd like to get your friend Harris Walker to display some of his work. In fact, I'd like to have him be the main exhibitor. Problem is he won't talk to me now that he knows who I am.'

Kendra nodded. 'You mean after what happened with Dee and Ellis.'

'A little surprised you'll talk to me, actually.' She held Kendra's gaze. 'What happened was totally unintentional, you know.' She glanced at Garrett. 'Neither of us ever wanted anything but the best for Dee and Ellis.'

'I know,' Kendra said, laying her fork down and folding her

173

hands in her lap. 'But you have to understand, the three of us are close. Really close, and we're really protective of each other. We have been for a long time.'

Stacie and Garrett shot each other a knowing look. 'We do understand,' Garrett said. 'If anyone understands, we do.'

The conversation was light and easy, a thing Kendra hadn't expected. There was nothing between Garrett and Stacie that felt in the least like lust. The relaxed way the two were together reminded Kendra a lot of how she was with Harris.

It was the ringing of Garrett's BlackBerry that interrupted their relaxed chat. 'That would be Don.' He sighed. 'I hung up on him last night. Surprised it's taken him this long.'

'You'd better answer it,' Kendra said, sorry for the interruption of such an unexpectedly pleasant morning.

Garrett didn't even manage a hello before he shot Kendra a glance that said this was not a happy call, and the shit storm was well on its way. 'Christ,' he cursed out loud, not bothering to put his hand over the phone. 'He says to turn on the damn TV again. I knew I should never have had the stupid thing installed.'

Kendra could make out only Don's garbled displeasure on the other end of the device as they all three left the table and crowded onto the sofa in the living room where Garrett switched on the TV.

'How could he do this to her?'

A woman in a book store clutching a hardback copy of Tess Delaney's latest to her chest practically yelled into the microphone the reporter thrust at her. Her eyes welled with tears.

'I mean, I knew it wasn't a good sign when Tess Delaney showed up at the Golden Kiss Awards on Garrett Thorne's arm. Everyone knew that. OK, it's true the man is gorgeous, but everyone knows he's not worthy of her.

Stacie cursed.

Next to Kendra, Garrett stiffened, and she could see the muscles along his jaw tense. She felt her insides clench in empathy, and fought back the sudden urge to throw something heavy at the television.

174

The woman continued, 'Then, even while poor Tess is bravely slaving away under death threats from a stalker, as if the poor woman doesn't have enough to deal with. Then this!'

'Death threats, what death threats? What stalker?' Stacie was practically bouncing off the sofa. Both Garrett and Kendra shushed her. And the woman on the television sniffed back another sob.

'As if she isn't under enough stress, that – that beast brings in his ex-wife!'

'Fuck,' Stacie cursed, just as the camera cut to earlier scenes in front of Garrett's house and Stacie's arrival, with plenty of close-ups of her, dressed to kill, pulling her wheelie weekender along behind her.

Skilled in interaction with the press, Stacie had only smiled and pushed her way gently to the door. The reporter gave a brief voiceover.

'Stacie Emerson, owner of the New World Gallery in New York City, has a long-running relationship with both Garrett Thorne and his more famous brother, Ellison Thorne, CEO of the cutting edge company, Pneuma Inc. With the ex-wife showing up, bag in tow, it would appear that there's trouble in paradise. As the saga of reclusive author Tess Delaney's first public appearance at the Golden Kiss Awards unfolds, adoring fans meeting their heroine for the first time, only to discover that she has received death threats from an anonymous stalker, are not pleased with the younger Thorne brother's less than stellar behavior.'

'Oh shit,' Stacie said. 'Oh Garrett, I'm so sorry. I had no idea.'

'They want to crucify you,' Don said. At some point Garrett had put him on speaker phone.

'I can see that, Don,' Garrett said.

The noise in front of the house crescendoed and suddenly the scene on the television cut back to the front of Garrett's house. This time the view was live.

'Damn,' Kendra said. 'Is there a mob gathering?'

'Oh my God.' Stacie's voice was little more than a whisper. 'I'm so, so sorry. I didn't know. I'll leave.'

'No!' Kendra grabbed her arm and pulled her back onto the sofa. 'You can't leave.' She nodded to the TV where someone in the growing crowd threw an egg, then another.

'Garrett, what the hell were you thinking?' Don growled over the speaker phone.

'It's not his fault,' Stacie said. 'He didn't know I was coming, and I have a key. I always just let myself in, and there's nothing going on between us, Don. You know that.'

'I know that,' Don said. 'But they don't.'

On television a woman in the mob thrust a sign in front of the camera that read *Garrett Thorne, Devil Spawn*.

'Devil spawn,' Kendra said. 'You're kidding me.'

Garrett only shrugged and sat staring at the television.

Just then Kendra's iPhone rang. She'd grabbed it up when Don had summoned them all, once again, to the television. There were already several urgent emails for K. Ryde, as she had expected, and several texts for Kay Lake. They were all from Don. But it was Harris calling.

'Ken, thank God!' The concern in his voice was palpable. 'Are you all right?'

'Fine. I'm fine, Harris, don't worry.' She slipped off the sofa and moved to stand in the hallway where she could still see and sort of hear the television, but could have a little privacy in which to speak to Harris.

'You watching TV?' She could hear at least a little bit of the tension drain from his voice.

'I'm watching,' she replied. In the background she could hear traffic noise. 'I'm on my way over. I'll be there in about 20 minutes.'

'No, Harris. That's not necessary. Really, everything's all right.'

'Not all right, Kendra. Not all right at all. I'm on my way, and Dee and Ellis are on their way back from Seattle. They'll be there as soon as they can get there.'

'Harris, please, it's not a big deal. Really, it'll be all right. Please don't.'

'Ken, I'm coming and that's that. End of conversation. I don't trust Garrett Thorne, and well, after everything that's happened to you, I'd just feel better if I were there.'

'Harris, all that's over. I'm fine, really. This is just part of negotiating the PR maze.'

'I don't care if it's all over. Ken, I know what you went through. I was there, remember? There's no way in hell either Dee or I will let that happen to you again, and frankly I'm shocked Thorne would drag you into this.'

She rolled her shoulders and massaged the base of her skull and the onset of a tension headache. 'He didn't know, Harris. It wasn't his fault. It was my fault.'

'I don't care whose fault it is, I'm still coming. Deal with it.'

She nodded, even though she knew he couldn't see. Another complication she didn't need. 'Park a couple of blocks away and come in the back,' she said.

'See you soon,' he replied.

She hung up just in time to hear Don saying. 'Look, I'm at the airport. I was flying back this morning, but with the threats and now this mess with Stacie, I think it best if I stick around. How are you holding up, Kay?'

She slipped back onto the sofa. 'I'm fine. Please don't come, Don. We have everything under control here.'

'Threats, what threats?' Stacie said.

'Threatening emails,' Garrett said. 'I've been … Tess has been getting them for ages, but now that Tess has a face, they've got worse.'

Stacie shot Kendra a horrified look. Kendra only shrugged. Then she had an idea. She picked up her iPhone and K. Ryde sent a very quick email.

'Hold on,' Don said. 'I just got an email in from K. Ryde. Damn, I wish the man had a phone. He's got to be furious with all this going on. Anyway, I'll be there as soon as I pick up another rental … Oh, wait a minute.'

Everyone leaned over Garrett's BlackBerry as though they could see the email from K. Ryde. But really only Kendra knew in advance what it said. 'Read it,' she commanded.

Bachman. This mess has put my girl at risk. Now I'm taking care of it. If you feel you need to stay in Portland, that's up to you, but stay away from Thorne's house until I've dealt with this. I don't want you interfering with my plans. If you do, I'll pull Kay and you'll have to figure your own way out of this mess. By late this afternoon, I'll have it sorted. Now back off. Are we clear?'

'Shit,' Don cursed. And just as a chant outside Garrett's house started – "Tess rocks, Thorne sucks, Tess rocks, Thorne sucks" – K. Ryde got an email from Don Bachman agreeing to back off.

'I'll find a hotel room, then,' Don said. 'I'll be here if you need me.'

He cut the connection, and the three were left to watch a woman in a poison green tracksuit two sizes too small lob an egg at Garrett's house.

Kendra stood and yanked the robe tight around her. 'Harris is on his way. I couldn't stop him.'

'Shit,' both Garrett and Stacie said in unison.

'I don't want to hear it, all right.' Kendra's control slipped. 'We have a mess to clean up here and I've bought us a little time. I think Harris might be just what we need.'

'I don't see how Harris Walker could possibly be just what we need, and what the hell do you mean, you've bought us a little time?' Stacie asked.

Garrett shifted uncomfortably on the sofa and nodded to Kendra. 'Stacie Emerson, meet Mr. K. Ryde.'

'Fuck me,' Stacie breathed.

Kendra offered her a nothing-for-it-now shrug. 'Harris won't be here for another 30 minutes. He forgot about the construction on I-5. He always forgets. Now, if you'll excuse me. I need a shower.'

She left Stacie pumping Garrett for information about the events of the last 48 hours.

Chapter Twenty

'Wow,' Stacie said as they watched Kendra storm up the stairs. 'She's K. Ryde. That I would have never guessed.'

Garrett nodded, his eyes still locked on Kendra's legs as she disappeared up the stairs. 'You know K. Ryde?'

'Well as much as anybody does, I suppose. He, I mean she did some fabulous PR work for me a couple of years ago. But this I didn't see coming. The threats. Are they serious, do you think?'

Garrett turned off the TV with the remote, his gaze still locked on the stairs where Kendra had just disappeared. 'I honestly don't know. I just know she wouldn't be in this mess if I hadn't practically begged her to be Tess for me.'

He could feel Stacie studying him, and the woman never missed a thing. 'K. Ryde has dealt with lots worse stuff than this, Garrett. Lots worse.'

'That may be. But it feels like it's Kendra Davis I'm putting through all this. Not K. Ryde.'

'And besides, it's not K. Ryde you're in love with.'

Christ! Did he actually flinch? Stacie had a way of bringing the most outrageous things into conversation as though she was discussing her shopping list. Before he could tell her how wrong she was, before he could tell her it was none of her business, she continued.

'You're not really going to let her shower alone, are you?' She waved a hand toward the kitchen and the back door. 'Don't worry, if Harris Walker gets here before the two of you are finished, I'll let him in and entertain him.' She rolled her eyes as though that would be a task and a half. Then she nodded to the stairs. 'Go. I'll do the dishes and hold back the angry mob.'

He wanted to protest. He wanted to tell her he'd already had a shower and was happy to leave Kendra to it, but she'd know he was lying. Stacie could always read the Thorne brothers like books.

'You sure you can handle Walker?' He was already halfway to the stairs.

'Of course I can.' She waved him on. 'Just go.'

He shouldn't be here now. Dear God, he shouldn't. What was he thinking? This wasn't his plan. This wasn't supposed to happen, but he couldn't stay away. He just couldn't. The woman was like a magnet. No fucking way could he stay away from her! It would be the easiest thing in the world to end it all now. All he had to do was go into the bathroom, open the shower door … A simple snap of her delicate, slender neck, and no one could stop him. No one would even know until after he was long gone. He felt giddy with the power of it, the control of it. Her very life was literally in his hands right now, and she didn't even know it. No one in the house, no one outside in the yard, not the press, not the security, no one knew it but him. Her life in his hands. The thought made him hard, made him drunk with the power of it. He flexed his hands in the latex gloves.

He could hear the shower running. She was there. Just on the other side of the door. His heart raced like he'd been running, like he'd been lifting heavy weights. The prize was within his reach. With hands dead steady, in spite of the jumping of his heart, he carefully, ever so carefully, curled his fingers around the doorknob, took a deep, steadying breath, and slowly, patiently tried it with a silent sigh of satisfaction. Exactly as he'd suspected, it wasn't locked. He could hear Thorne downstairs, talking to his slut of an ex. He heard the mention of the shower and was just about to turn and flee when Thorne's cell phone rang. He relaxed his hand on the door, and stood quietly listening, holding his breath. When he was certain it wasn't going to be a short conversation, he began to breathe again. Then he pushed the door opened slowly, ever so slowly.

* * *

Kendra leaned her forehead against the cool tiles of the shower, letting the hot water course over her, desperately struggling to calm down. She hadn't expected to take it so personally when the people on the television had started in on Garrett, like they knew him, like they understood what drove him, like they understood anything about him. Of course they were only aping the same sentiments she had felt only a few days ago. But that was before she knew him, understood who he really was on the inside. Still, how could he stand it? How the hell could he just sit there and take it? And how could he have sat back and taken it all these years? She couldn't have. She couldn't have taken it for one minute. It was all so unfair, so wrong. And here she was trying to help him continue the farce.

And damn it, this was a job! Nothing more, this was just a job, she reminded herself. Garrett Thorne had hired her to be Tess Delaney for him. It was just another one of those delicate PR tasks that K. Ryde was famous for handling so exquisitely. So why the hell was she behaving like some lovesick teenager? She was a pro. She was the best, and this situation was a walk in the park. This situation wouldn't even phase K. Ryde. That it didn't go by the book, well, nothing ever did, did it? That was why K. Ryde was so good. She could think on her feet, she could fix it when it didn't go to plan. This was no different. This was just another situation that didn't go to plan. And the emails, well, Garrett himself said Tess had got lots. They were nothing, really, and she was ashamed of her overreaction, but that had nothing to do with the mess they found themselves in now, did it?

Ultimately it was Garrett's mishandling of the Golden Kiss banquet that screwed everything up. Lest she forget, K. Ryde would have given him an ultimatum to shape up or she'd walk. So why was she still here? Why was she trying to clean up the mess that kept getting worse and worse, first with Garrett, and now with Stacie showing up? And why the hell was she letting this situation get to her so much?

It was as she turned in the shower and lifted her face to the hard spray that she saw him standing there in the open door. Her heart skipped a beat and everything inside her went warm and liquid. She could just see the shape of him, the dark of his jeans, intimations of the broad expanse of his chest; the rest was lost in the rising steam and the mist on the glass. She should tell him to go away. She knew she should. Garrett Thorne was trouble when she first met him, and Garrett Thorne was still trouble. The last thing on earth she needed was more trouble, more complications. She should tell him to go away. But she didn't.

'Well?' she said. He took a step closer.

'Are you going to take off your clothes and join me or are you just going to stand there and get a good steaming?'

He felt like the heavens had opened and the holiest of light had descended into the steam of the bathroom. She, the woman who had invaded his sleeping and his waking, every second of his life for as long as his life had mattered, was inviting him to join her, to make love to her, to join himself to her. This was the stuff of his deepest, most moving fantasies.

The mist and the steam played over her body as though she was doing a sensuous veil dance for him, revealing, concealing, and revealing again. The alabaster curve of a hip, the luscious fruit mound of a breast, the delicate arch of her back, and God, she was exquisite, she was heaven on earth calling out to him as he had always dreamed she would.

The sound of her soft laugh was like the music of the gods. 'Come on,' she said. 'The water's great. All right, I know you've already bathed, but there are other things we can do in the shower besides bathe.'

It was a bit jarring, her being so brazen. But he could understand, after all this time of waiting, how desperate her need for him must be, and he wouldn't punish her for that when his need was at least as great. With his heart racing in his chest, he took another step forward and reached out his hand.

'Hurry up, Garrett, we don't have all day. It won't be much fun for Stacie or for Harris if he shows up and you and I are still busy fucking in the shower.'

And it was as though she'd poured ice down his spine, but the cold gave way to hot, burning rage in the pit of his stomach, and agony that was nearly unbearable, the brutal, bitter reminder that she was still first and foremost a slut. That she expected it to be that bastard Thorne coming to whore with her, that she didn't even for a second consider it might be him, it might be the one she was meant to be with. He felt it all like the stab and the twist of the knife, agony that ripped at him like sharp teeth. For the briefest of seconds, he thought his agony would drive him to his knees, but he couldn't let it. He couldn't let the want of her cloud his mind to the truth. He eased his hand onto the door of the shower and took a deep breath. Just a sharp twist to the neck, that was all that was needed, and she would torture him no more.

'Garrett?' A sudden chill rose up Kendra's back and a clenching down deep in her chest that had nothing to do with arousal. She grabbed for the wall, feeling disoriented and muzzy-headed. 'Garrett, what's going on?'

There was a smell, a scent that wasn't Garrett's. She could barely make it out over the steam and the soap. She could almost believe she was imagining it. Almost. It was more feral, darker, and it clawed at the back of her throat like it was desperate to get inside, to lodge there unwanted. It was all so sudden, so confusing. There was a charge in the air, a charge that she could almost hear in Garrett's silence. It crackled around the room like heat lightning, making her feel like something crawled beneath her skin on tiny barbed feet. 'Damn it, Garrett, whatever you're doing, it's not funny. Now, are you coming in or not?'

Just as she reached a trembling hand to turn off the water to see what the problem was, the smell of something different, something that caused her heart to pound, something that had nothing to do with sex nearly overwhelmed her. Then she gave a little gasp of surprise as Garrett turned and practically ran out of the bathroom, closing the door behind him.

'Fuck you,' she said out loud, standing in the warm steam, fighting back tears. It's not like she expected anything from him, or even wanted anything from him, but she didn't appreciate him toying with her, playing games with her. For a long time she stood just breathing in and out, forcing her emotions to calm. This didn't matter. This was just Garrett Thorne being Garrett Thorne. They had more important things to deal with than the fact that he was too chicken shit to shower with her when his ex was downstairs.

By the time she turned off the water and stepped out of the steam, she had resolved not to mention it to him. She'd let him bring it up. She wasn't about to let him think that it mattered one way or another.

He stood a safe distance from all of the press vehicles and watched the gathering mob around Thorne's house. It had taken him ages to regain his equilibrium. He had vomited his breakfast at the end of the alley after he'd made his escape. That was simply his body's way of reminding him how close he'd come to ruining all of his carefully laid plans, his body's way of purging itself of being so close to her powerful lust, being so close to her wicked influence, being inundated by the filth with which she now surrounded herself. If only he had found her sooner, then perhaps he could have made things easier on her, but not now. Now it was much too late for the easy path. A snap of the neck was a clean death, a hero's death, a death of virtue. She deserved no such thing, and he had, all of his life, believed that people should get what they deserve. It was right. It was what should be. It was the reset button for the balance of the universe.

On trembling legs, he leaned against a privacy fence at the end of the alley and watched Carla Flannery in her silly little motorhome. She was priceless. She was a godsend, she and Barker Blessing. They would serve him well before everything came together and he had his glorious triumph with Tess Delaney at his side. He felt better now. He felt his balance returning. He was glad he had the strength to pull back in the presence of such outrage. He was glad that his control had not broken. He would be patient a little longer. That was all that was needed. Just a little more patience and then the prize would be his, and he would savour it as he had savoured nothing in all of his life.

Though she would have liked to linger, though she would have appreciated a little more time before she had to face Garrett again, Kendra didn't take her time getting ready. She knew how uncomfortable Harris would be if he got there and found himself entertained by Garrett and Stacie. There was no love lost between the three of them, and she'd not had the chance to talk to Harris about what was going on between her and Garrett, though she was sure he'd figured it out when he delivered her clothes to Garrett's house. He wouldn't approve, but he'd have figured it out. Still, she didn't want to make it more difficult for him than necessary.

She was halfway down the stairs, dressed and made up as Tess, when she heard the knock on the back door. She found only Stacie in the kitchen.

'Garrett's in his study working,' she said, as she wiped her hands on the dish towel and scrambled for a quick exit. 'I'll be catching up on some of my own work in the guest room if you need me.' She gave Kendra's hand a squeeze.

'If all goes well, I'll probably need you both in a little while, and Don too.'

Stacie only had time for a raised eyebrow before Harris knocked again, and she scurried off up the stairs, choosing retreat over staying to hear Kendra's plan. Just as well. Kendra figured best break it to them in small groups. Divide and conquer. And the hardest sell, by far, was about to walk through the kitchen door. If she could enlist Harris's help, then she figured the other two would be a cakewalk.

Kendra took a deep breath and opened the door only to be bodily scooped off her feet into Harris's muscular embrace. He said nothing, only held her there close to the rapid beating of his heart, surrounding her with arms and abs and chest made hard from kayaking, his sport of choice. He was good at it, and his body reflected his skill.

Not for the first time she wondered what might have happened had they not met so young, had they not became fast friends so early. But then again, Harris's friendship, along with Dee's, were the two most precious parts of her life. They were her constants in a world that had been anything but, and she doubted either of them could imagine just how much that had meant to her over the years. She could fuck anyone, but she could only love Harris in the way she loved him, in the way he loved her back. In the way she most needed him.

At last he brushed a kiss over the crown of her head and released a tight breath. 'You all right?'

She nodded against his chest, surprised to find how close to tears she felt. 'Better now that you're here.'

He pulled away enough that he could lift her chin with the crook of a finger, forcing her to meet his bright gaze. 'What's he done?'

There was no question who the "he", spoken with such distaste was. She'd have to work on that. She really wanted Harris and Garrett to like each other. Strange how quickly her feelings for the man had come full circle. Dee had told her from the beginning that Garrett was an all right guy. She should have known. Dee rarely misjudged anyone's character. And neither did Harris, but Harris didn't know Garrett. He didn't know the man's heart like she did.

'He hasn't done anything, Harris,' she replied. 'It was all just poor timing. Stacie showed up just back from Japan. She had no idea what's been going on, and now somehow the press is imagining the mad orgy with Garrett and his sex-crazed ex right in front of the poor long-suffering Tess.' She realized he was staring at her. 'What?'

His smile was cautious. 'It's just that you really do look different. I've never read a Tess Delaney novel, but I read the back cover of the one you had in your bag, and you look just like I would have pictured the woman who wrote it.' He curled a lock of her hair around his finger. 'I like you better blonde, though.'

She squeezed his hand. 'Kendra Davis is blonde. Tess Delaney is a fiery redhead.'

His smile went from cautious to stunning. 'Well, at least she shares the fiery bit with Kendra Davis.' He looked around the kitchen. 'Where are they?' The word "they" sounded like something nasty he needed to spit out of his mouth.

'They're both catching up on some work.' She grabbed a

much-needed Diet Pepsi from the refrigerator and offered him one. He seldom drank any kind of soft drink, but he made the exception for her from time to time. He took the offered beverage and followed her into the living room. They both settled on the sofa.

Once again, she could feel him studying her. This time she didn't have to ask. She knew it was coming.

'You shouldn't have slept with him, Ken. What were you thinking?'

She bristled and was about to tell him who she slept with was none of his business, but he didn't give her the chance.

He cocked his head. 'Are you falling in love with him?'

She felt as though he had gut-punched her, especially after the little incident in the shower. But she'd made a living bluffing. She squared her shoulders and forced herself to hold his gaze. 'I don't fall in love, Harris. You've known me long enough to know that.'

'I've known you long enough to know that you haven't fallen in love yet, but you're just as vulnerable as the rest of us, Kendra, whether you want to admit it or not, and he –' he nodded toward the stairs '– well, he's trouble. Surely you can see that by now.'

'I see a lot of things, Harris. A lot of things that you don't, so please, don't lecture me.'

He raised his hands in defeat, which she knew only too well was only feigned. She braced herself for his next assault.

'Have there been any more emails?'

'Last night there was one,' she said, then she hurried on, not wanting to hear his response. 'They're nothing, really. They're not a problem.'

He shifted on the sofa and set his drink on the coffee table. 'Dee told me what happened when you read the first one, Jesus, woman, you think I don't remember what it was like for you after you came home from California? Don't tell me it wasn't a problem. How could it not be?'

'All right! All right.' She puffed out a hard breath and clenched her drink can for courage. 'I'll admit, it was a bit of a shock at first, and I didn't handle it very well. But that was me reacting to my past and not to the situation at hand. Harris, believe me when I say I've seen this sort of thing dozens of times. This is just some dip-wad getting his kicks, that's all. Nothing more. It's not a problem. But what is a problem at the moment is the press making Garrett the villain in all this. It puts him at risk and it could put Tess at risk too.

He held her gaze. 'Tess doesn't exist.'

'Right now, for those people out there, she does, and Garrett is enemy number one where they're concerned.'

'Yeah? So?'

'Damn it, Harris. I'm sorry you don't like him, but this is my job right now, and if Tess is at risk, I'm at risk, and I need your help.'

He still held her in a cast iron gaze that made it very difficult for her not to squirm. 'There was a time, just a couple of days ago, when you didn't like him either.'

'Yeah, well, that was a couple of days ago! Harris, are you going to listen to me and help me here or are you just going to be a pain in the ass?'

His gaze softened. He released a deep breath and took her hand in his. 'Ken, I'll do whatever I can to help you. You know that. Just tell me what you need.'

And she did. And he wasn't happy about it.

'You want us to do what?' Stacie said, looking first at Kendra then at Harris. 'You're kidding, right?'

Harris sat on one end of the sofa with his arms folded defiantly across his chest. 'Believe me, it's not my idea of a good time either.'

Kendra had a sneaking suspicion that Garrett wanted to snigger at the two, but he had the good graces to keep his mouth shut, which was just as well because she wasn't in the mood to put up with any more bullshit and the last thing she needed was for him and Harris to be at each other's throats.

'I'm not talking about a good time,' Kendra said. 'We're already way past that here. I've told Dan to leak to the press that we're all about to make a statement. Harris, no one knows you're here, and since you're a bit of a hero with the press after your photos and write-up in *Wilderness Vanguard* from your Valderia trip with Ellis, your rapport will make it easier for the rest of us. Stacie, you've already said you wanted to feature Harris in your gallery opening. We don't have to lie to make this one work. All you two have to do is act like you might be able to work together, and act excited. Can you do that?' She gave Harris's arm a gentle shake. 'Harris?'

He squared his shoulder, still locked in a glare-down with Stacie. 'I can if she can.'

Stacie offered him a smile that could have cut glass. 'Don't you worry, Photo Boy, I can. I promise.'

Kendra released a slow, even breath, an effort to cover nerves that were so not characteristic of K. Ryde on the job. 'Good. Now I'm going to go freshen my make-up. Remember we want Tess to look bright and shining and the ex to look a little jetlagged.'

Stacie offered a pout. 'That's really very cruel of you, Kendra, and here I thought we were friends.' Then she smiled. 'Of course, it's going to be a real effort for me to look jetlagged.' Did she actually wink at Harris? The blush that crawled up his throat suggested that she most definitely had.

'What about him?' Harris said, nodding to Garrett, who sat on the other side of Kendra.

'I get to be Tess's adoring lover.' Garrett said with a smile that looked more edible than chocolate. Kendra wondered how the hell he could sit there all sweetness and light after the shower incident. She expected at least a little brooding on his part.

Harris growled. 'You get rewarded for fucking up.'

'Harris.' Kendra elbowed him. 'Shut up. I told you it wasn't his fault.'

Garrett returned his growl. 'I don't need you to defend me, Kendra,' he said.

'Then fuck both of you,' Kendra stood and headed for the stairs. 'I'm touching up Tess's make-up, and if I come down here and either of the two of you are anything but polite and docile, I'll march right out the back door and leave the lot of you in Don's tender care. Am I clear?'

They both nodded. Stacie sniggered, and Kendra flipped all three of them off as she headed up the stairs hoping the two men could hold off on a brawl until after their confrontation with the press. And to be honest, she wasn't entirely sure but what Stacie might be the best brawler of the three.

When she returned in a clingy summer dress that showed plenty of cleavage in its off-the-shoulder sea foam décolletage, the response she got was stunned awe, which was exactly the response she hoped she'd get from the press and the mob as well. And as much as she hated to admit it, in spite of the fact that this was work, Garrett's look of appreciation made her feel a little giddy.

'Don just called,' he said. 'They're expecting us.'

'Then let's do it,' she said. Her eyes locked on Harris. 'You sure you're OK with this?'

He nodded and came to his feet, taking her in his arms. 'I'll do whatever you need me to do, Ken.' He shot Garrett an acid glance. 'Whatever it takes to protect you.'

But Garrett rose from his seat too, and pulled her away from Harris. 'You don't need to worry about protecting her, Walker.' He crushed her to him possessively. 'I promise you that.'

She couldn't say she didn't like it, Garrett being so possessive of her, and something about knowing he'd be by her side made her feel better. She reminded herself once again that this was just another job for K. Ryde – and an easy one at that. Whatever happened upstairs in the shower, well, he seemed to be over it, so she needed to let it go too.

Harris, true to his word, offered Stacie his arm and forced a smile. She batted her eyes at him and returned a smile that was all flowers and bunnies as she folded her arm over his. Jesus, what a bunch they were, Kendra thought. As she reached for the door, Garrett brushed her ear with his lips. 'You're amazing, you know that?' He squeezed her hand. 'Now, let's do this.' He opened the door to a chorus of boos from the mob and the reporters. But when they saw their Tess the boos turned to cheers. And the cheers became a mumble of confusion when Stacie came out onto the porch on Harris's arm. Harris they liked. Even before Ellis guaranteed their goodwill toward him, with the exclusive for *Wilderness Vanguard* magazine from deep in the Valderian forest, Harris had a reputation among the green people in Portland, and that was a good percentage of the population. Harris they respected. Kendra could already see people recalculating in their heads.

Everything was going according to plan, until Garrett stepped forward to a muffled whisper among the reporters and mumbling and shuffling of the mob beyond. Kendra's stomach knotted. What the hell was he up to?

'I'm very disappointed,' he said. And the crowd fell silent. Kendra dug her nails into his palm, but he didn't even flinch. 'I'm very disappointed that you all thought I would do anything to hurt the woman who has completely stolen my heart.' He raised her hand to his lips and brushed a kiss across her knuckles, forcing her nails away from his palm. 'I'm disappointed for anything I've done to make you believe such a thing of me.' He turned to Stacie. 'As you all clearly know, Stacie Emerson is my ex-wife. But apparently what most of you don't know is that not only are Stacie and I still good friends, but Stacie and Tess are friends as well.'

The shuffling and muttering from the crowd increased. Kendra nodded her agreement, and Stacie stepped forward, offering her thousand-watt smile.

'Garrett's right. I've been away in Japan, deep in negotiations for several exhibitions for the opening of my West Coast gallery. I had no idea what all had gone on with Tess and Garrett when I arrived this morning, jetlagged and exhilarated by my time in Japan. I only stopped by on my way to see this gentleman who you all know very well, I would imagine.' Kendra was sure she nearly blinded Harris with her smile. Stacie continued, 'I'm sure I don't have to tell you, Harris Walker is one of the best wildlife photographers in the Northwest, maybe the world.'

There was an impromptu round of applause from the mob. Harris forced a smile that looked a little bit like a grimace. Stacie pulled him forward. 'I came to negotiate with Mr. Walker. You see, I love the Northwest. I grew up here, and I'm so excited to be opening a gallery here in my home state in my favourite city on the planet. I hope to counterbalance the exciting Japanese exhibits from the time of the Shoguns with photographic exhibits of the natural beauty of the Northwest. I'd like to feature local photographers, and in particular, I'd like to feature Mr. Walker's wonderful work. He's the real reason I'm in town. I'm hoping to make his work the centre of New World Gallery West's grand opening exhibition.'

One of the reporters spoke up. 'Mr. Walker.' Of course it was the irritating Mr. Pittman from the front row once again. 'Is this true? Are you going to be exhibiting your work in Ms. Emerson's gallery?'

'That's what we're negotiating.' Harris managed a genuine smile and even managed to sound congenial. Kendra loved her friend even more when he offered Stacie a smile that really could have passed for genuine. Kendra knew he had done it just for her.

'Ms. Delaney,' Carla Flannery chimed in from the back. 'Is it true that you and Ms. Emerson are friends?'

'Yes, it's very true.' Kendra offered a warm smile which Stacie returned in kind. 'All of this …' She raised her hand to indicate the reporters and the mob. 'All of this is very touching, that you all feel so deeply for me. It's wonderful to feel so loved. But I promise you there's absolutely nothing to be concerned about. I'm very happy for Stacie's visit. It was a wonderful surprise to cap off an amazing weekend. And Garrett is more than happy to offer his place for Stacie and Mr. Walker to meet.' A bald-faced lie if ever there was one, but then not very much about the past two days wasn't a lie when it came right down to it. 'I promise you all is well with Garrett and me. Very well, indeed.' She offered him her best smitten by love smile, and he returned one with equal radiance. Some of the Tess fan club clapped and cheered. 'I'm hard at work on the next Tess Delaney novel, and Garrett is taking very good care of me while I write. Very good care.' She kissed his cheek and someone wolf-whistled. 'Now please, everyone. Please go home. I need to be able to work in peace. Stacie and Mr. Walker just want to get on with their negotiations. If you could

192

do that for me, if you could just go home to your families, I'd be so grateful.'

'Ms. Delaney.' The reporter from the *Oregonian* spoke up. 'What about the threats on your life?'

'There are no threats on my life. There never have been. I get an occasional email from an overzealous fan, like every other writer or actor or anyone else who has a public profile, but there are no threats on my life, so you can all rest easy tonight that I'm safe here with Garrett, happily writing away, and that the next Tess Delaney novel will be in your book stores very soon.'

'If that's true, if there are no threats on your life, then why are the security people still here?' Mr. Pittman put in.

She smiled sweetly. 'Mr. Pittman, my publicist is always a bit paranoid for my privacy at my request. That shouldn't come as any surprise. Plus I'm sure I don't need to remind anyone that Garrett's house has just been well and truly egged. I believe there might have even been a tomato or two. Just a precaution. That's all.'

'That's a lot of security for just a precaution,' Pittman said.

Carla Flannery spoke up again. 'My sources assure me the threat is real.'

God, they were tenacious, Kendra thought. But she only smiled and said, 'Just a precaution, like I said.' Then they all turned and walked back into the house according to plan.

Chapter Twenty-one

He hadn't intended to watch them. He rather liked seeing the reports on television, knowing that in a way he was orchestrating the whole thing. And Garrett Thorne's ex-wife showing up was just icing on the cake, that was all. Oh, what a mix it was. He had hoped when he'd heard of her arrival that Tess would come to see what a worthless excuse for a human being Garrett Thorne was. He had hoped against hope that the man had had his fill of Tess and was dumping her for his ex. But even as he hoped that, the rage that ran through him nearly choked him, that anyone in their right mind could jilt Tess, that anyone in their right mind could even look at anyone else. And for the briefest moment he had fantasized about how he would punish Garrett Thorne for hurting his beautiful Tess. But none of that was true.

Bile rose at the back of his throat as he watched the two couples fawning over each other in front of the press, as Thorne pawed and preened and all the while his ex looked on like he was God himself come down to save the day. Well, he wasn't! He wasn't.

And what the hell was the matter with Carla Flannery? She barely got one question, and a weak one at that. She was supposed to be an ace journalist. She was supposed to be young and hungry. Hell, he could have hired a kid off the street to do better than she had.

As the four disappeared back into Thorne's house, he yanked his cell phone from his pocket and texted.

You can do better than that, Ms. Flannery. I'm very disappointed in you.

He sent it with a hard press of his index finger, then, as an afterthought, he texted again.

By the way, nice touch, the motorhome. Makes you seem important. But really, the kaki T-shirt is too tight. It makes you look like a slut with a military fetish. Daddy's little girl, maybe?

They barely made it into the house before Garrett's BlackBerry rang. He shrugged his resignation. 'No doubt that's Don calling to see how it all went.'

Everyone nodded agreement and waited for him to connect. Kendra grabbed a much-needed Diet Pepsi and passed around drinks from the fridge.

Sure enough it was Don, so, as they all settled around the kitchen table, Garrett put him on speaker phone.

'Is Kay all right?' Don offered no greeting, no "how did it go?" His voice was tight and breathy in a way Garrett had never heard him before. Everyone's gaze turned to Kendra, who froze in her seat.

'Yes.' Garrett said, his stomach knotting dangerously at the tone of Don's voice.

'Thank God,' Don breathed. 'Look, just listen to me. I've forwarded you an email I just got from this Razor Sharp bastard.'

Garrett nodded to Stacie, who was already heading up the stairs for his laptop. Before he could say anything, Kendra spoke up. 'What happened, Don? What did the email say?'

'Shit, Garrett, you have me on speaker phone?'

Kendra stiffened in her chair. The bright color that Garrett had noticed always tinged her cheeks when she was making a public appearance, when she was doing the job she did so well, was suddenly gone and her face was porcelain pale. Harris scooted his chair close to her and slid an arm around her, and Garrett was jealous. That should be his job. But the angry glare Harris levelled at him was a reminder of whose fault it was that Kendra was in this position to begin with. As if he needed reminding. He swallowed back the burn of his guilt as Stacie returned with the laptop.

'Pull it up,' Kendra said, moving closer to Garrett. 'I want to see it.' Stacie stood behind her with both hands resting on her shoulders.

Just then, there was a knock on the back door. Stacie opened it and Dee and Ellis shoved in, caught the mood of the moment, and moved close to Kendra and Garrett close enough to look over their shoulders at the email.

'I don't think that's a good idea,' Don was saying. 'Listen, Kay, it might be better if –'

'I said pull it up.' Her voice was hard and distant.

Willing his hands not to shake, Garrett did as she asked. There were two new emails; one just forwarded from Don, and the other one, just below it, was from Razor Sharp.

Garrett took a deep breath and opened the email.

Clearly you can't control your bitch, Bachman. You're her publicist. It's your job to protect Tess's reputation. FAIL! Don't you know what she's doing in there with Garrett Thorne and his whore of an ex and Harris Walker? The press may believe their lies, but I don't. If you can't control her, I will, Bachman. And I promise you, I'll make sure she behaves herself.
R.S.

Everyone's eyes were on Kendra. Garrett was sure everyone's hearts were in their throats, just as his was, everyone aching for her, everyone fearful. But this time, she didn't run for the bathroom. This time she didn't hyperventilate. This time her blue eyes were like ice and the air around her was electric with her control. She squared her shoulders and glared at the screen, raking her teeth across her bottom lip. Garrett was once again amazed at just how tough, just how brave she was.

'I got it just a few minutes ago,' Don said. 'I've never got one from him before. I passed it on to Ryde. Does he know about this, Kay? Have you heard from him?' Don asked.

'He knows,' Kendra replied. 'Open the next one.'

This time the color rose in Kendra's cheeks. Harris cursed out loud and Dee moved to flank Kendra next to Stacie.

'What does it say?' Don asked.

'Jesus, you callous bastard,' Garrett said, 'you can't really

196

expect me to read it out loud! I'll email it to you.'

Before he could forward the message, Kendra pushed his hand away and began to read aloud. Her voice was distant and without emotion. There was no trembling, no wavering. Just hard, cold resolve.

You're a whore and a liar, Tess Delaney. You may be able to fool the press with your innocent radiance, but I see right through you. Whores go to jail when the police catch them, Tess. I promise I won't let you off nearly that easily.
R.S.

'That sonovabitch,' Ellis said softly, laying a hand on Dee's shoulder. He had his BlackBerry out.

'What are you doing?' Garrett asked.

'Getting in touch with Wade,' he said. 'If the police can't help, maybe Wade can. Send him the emails, Garrett, and I think we all need to make a trip down the Pneuma Building. I've got Jeffries waiting in the alley with the limo,' he said.

When Dee saw the look of surprise on everyone's faces, she added, 'We figured the two of you would be getting pretty claustrophobic by now. Not that Garrett's house isn't nice, and all, but, Ken, I know you don't like being in one place too long. We were just going to drag you back to Ellis's place for a little break from all of this, but I think our first stop now definitely needs to be Wade's dungeon.'

'Pack what you need,' Ellis said. 'You're not coming back here tonight.' He gave a glance around. 'There's plenty of room for everyone. I'll have Galina throw an extra bean in the pot and make the beds up in the bunk house.'

'It'll be a slumber party.' Dee squeezed Kendra's shoulder in an obvious effort to cheer her up.

But both Harris and Stacie shook their heads.

'I have a very early meeting down on the Malheur Reserve tomorrow,' Harris said. 'We're planning some migratory shoots. But if you need me, Ken –' he took his friend's hand '– I'll cancel.'

'I have a feeling she doesn't need either one of us,' Stacie said, lightly touching Harris's arm. 'But I echo Harris's sentiments.'

Kendra shook her head. 'No. Do what you both have to do. I'll be fine. I still think it's all just idle threats. Every celebrity gets them.' She forced a smile that didn't look too convincing.

Stacie nodded. 'I have meetings with my lawyer and the realtors to finalize the papers on the gallery,' she said. 'I can stay in the house if you want me to, Garrett. That way it won't be empty.'

'Don't be stupid,' Garrett said. 'This asshole clearly doesn't like you very much either. There's no way you're staying here alone.'

'Garrett's right,' Dee said.

Stacie nodded. 'Well, I haven't stayed at the Heathman in a while. I think I'd quite like a few days of being spoiled. And Dee, Garrett, Ellis, you all have my number if you need me.'

Harris went to the living room and peeked out the drapes at the front yard to where they could still hear the reporters shuffling and mumbling. 'Ken –' he called back over his shoulder '– why don't you and Garrett get what you need and get all set to go.' He turned his attention to Stacie. 'Is your rental car still out front?'

She nodded. 'Might be covered with eggs, though.'

'We can handle eggs, I think.' He said. 'How about if we draw the press's attention while you all make a fast getaway?'

Stacie nodded agreement.

'I'll keep the security here,' Garrett said. I'll phone and see if a couple of them can just hang out in the house so it feels like we're still inside, what do you think?' He slipped his arm protectively around Kendra. 'That way maybe they won't go looking for us.'

It had taken Carla ages to stop shaking. She sat in the motorhome with the doors locked, trembling like a leaf, with the final text from the stalker wavering in and out of focus in front of her eyes. She wanted to look away. She wanted to run away actually. She wanted never to hear from this sicko again, but where could she go?

She needed to tell her father about this. He would know what to do. *Daddy's little girl*. She stared down at the email and shivered. He had researched her, then. If he knew her father, he had researched her. He hadn't just picked some random reporter from the crowd. He had chosen her specifically. Her hand was shaking so bad that she dropped her iPhone, and it skittered across the floor of the motorhome. 'Bastard,' she said beneath her breath. Daddy's little soldier. They'd called her that in school, teased her mercilessly. He couldn't have actually known about that. How could he have reduced her to this in just one short text?

She scrambled to pick up the phone. When she could get her fingers to stop shaking enough to cooperate, she texted.

Where are you?

The response was almost instant.

Never far, Carla. Never far. Didn't you think I'd check up on you to see how you were doing?

'Jesus!' She caught her breath with a little sob, and looked frantically out the windows of the motorhome, but there was a jumble of people. Lots of them now leaving after Tess's little appeal to the mob. He could be anywhere. He could be anyone. He could be a she, though she was pretty sure he wasn't.

Why are you doing this? She forced her fingers to type.

Because Tess is a lie. Tess isn't who you think, Carla. Tess isn't who anyone thinks, and she should pay for her slutty ways.

She gulped the dregs of a cup of instant coffee she'd made just before Tess and friends had spoken to the press then she texted again.

Tell me. Tell me who Tess is, then, and how do you know?

This time there was no response. She waited for what felt like an eternity, and when she was pretty sure he was done playing with her, she stood on legs now a little bit more steady and shoved the door to the motorhome open. She could see Mike Pittman standing on the sidewalk in front of Thorne's house, typing frantically onto his iPhone. He gave her an absent nod when she came to stand by him.

'Did you see anyone suspicious?' she asked.

He offered a bored grunt. 'You've been standing here in the same crowd of loony-tunes I have, Flannery. If I'd seen anyone suspicious, how the hell would I have known?'

The man was right there, she thought. She stood staring at the front door of the house, and for a second she was tempted just to march right up there, knock on the door and force the issue. For a second.

Thirty minutes later, they were all four tucked neatly into the back of the Pneuma Inc. limo with Garrett and Kendra facing Dee and Ellis.

Kendra had been the ice queen since Don's phone call with the news of more emails from Razor Sharp. Frankly, under the circumstances that worried Garrett a lot more than her hyperventilating or losing her breakfast. He knew she couldn't have completely shaken off all of those feelings, all those memories every email from that bastard must bring back to her, and yet she seemed to have shut it all away. How could anyone have gone through what she had and not taken it all badly? And yet she was cool, distant.

Across the seat from him, Garrett could feel his brother studying him over the top of his glasses like he always did when he was about to ask a question Garrett was sure he didn't want to be asked. 'What?' he said.

Ellis smiled his slow, lazy smile, the one that seemed much more freely given since Dee came into his life. 'Just worried about you, bro. That's all,' he said. 'They were pretty rough on you out there.'

Garrett shrugged. 'I'm fine. That was nothing I haven't had to handle before.'

'And you handled it well,' Kendra said. 'I didn't get the chance to tell you that after we talked to the press.'

'I have no doubt he did,' Ellis said. 'Like he always does. Needlessly.'

Garrett bristled. 'I really do appreciate your concern, but I don't really need this lecture again, Ellis. Not right now.'

'He's right, though,' Kendra said.

Across the seat, Dee still held Kendra's hand in a grip that could have never been misconstrued for anything other than fiercely protective. Garrett was amazed there wasn't a broken finger or two. And he felt a huge sense of relief when the look Dee offered him was warm and empathetic, so much more than he deserved, but then Dee had always given him so much more than he deserved. God, he could understand why his brother loved the woman. She was so good for him. What the two of them shared was the very essence of what he tried to capture in Tess's novels, what he was certain every person longed for down deep. He did. He longed for it so badly that at times the ache felt as though it would rip him apart – to have come so close so often, to have almost been there. He studied Kendra out of the corner of his eye. What had happened that she had so shut out even that longing, something that seemed so basic to the human psyche?

Kendra's iPhone buzzed a text, and she pulled it out of her bag. 'It's Harris,' she said. 'Looks like our little performance dispersed the angry mob, but the reporters haven't budged.' She nodded to herself. 'They still think Tess's life is under threat, no doubt.'

'Reporters aren't stupid,' Dee said. She raised a hand before Kendra could speak. 'I don't give a damn what you think, Ken, what K. Ryde thinks. To me those emails constitute a threat. And even if they are nothing more than some neurotic fan, I know how you respond to those emails no matter. And that's not something I can let pass, you know that.'

Garrett bundled Kendra close to him and smiled at Dee. He wouldn't want to be on the wrong side of either of Kendra's friends. He was pretty sure it would be fatal. At the moment, he still wasn't sure Harris wouldn't happily yank his heart from his chest and make him eat it if he got half a chance. But all of that fierce loyalty, all of that deep love was for Kendra, just because she was Kendra, just because she was amazing and they knew her better than anyone. That made him feel better somehow, lest he forget it was his fault she was in this mess to begin with. And he really wasn't likely to forget that, was he?

There wasn't much traffic late on Sunday afternoon in Portland, so the drive to the Pneuma Building didn't take long. Kendra wasn't sure why Ellis and Dee – and Garrett too, for that matter, were so keen on her seeing Wade Crittenden, like he was some god or something. OK, she knew the man was a genius, and she owed him big time for unleashing evil Kendra on Garrett in his office several weeks ago. Though it hadn't seemed to bother him too terribly much, as she recalled. She admired that about him from the start.

They parked in the underground garage, away from prying eyes, and took the elevator down to Wade's dungeon. Kendra had laughed when she'd first heard the man's nerd king laboratory referred to as such. Harris had elbowed her into silence, and it was clear that Wade was completely oblivious to the double meaning. Either that or he just didn't care. With Wade it was never easy to tell. And in truth, she had only seen the lounge of Wade's domain. Who knew, maybe he did dabble in BDSM somewhere down in the bowels of the Pneuma Building. She couldn't help but smile at the thought.

They found the man in the inner sanctum, also known as his boudoir. God, surely the man couldn't miss out on all of the double entendres, even in his insulated little world. He was hunched over the keyboard of a computer with a very large monitor.

'I've got Flannery and his men on it, but I think the stalker's a journalist,' Wade said, without looking up from what he was doing, without offering a greeting.

'Flannery?' Kendra said. 'Any relation to the Carla Flannery who's been grilling us over at Garrett's place?'

'He's her father,' Wade replied, still tapping away on the keyboard. 'Ex-military, and a kick-ass detective and security man. He's worked for Pneuma for years. I've heard his daughter is a real pit bull. Ellis certainly has a lot of respect for her.'

'So why do you think that Razor Sharp is a journalist?' Garrett asked.

'Because of the timing,' Wade said, shoving the sleeve of his sweatshirt up to reveal a well-muscled forearm that surprised Kendra. She wondered if he actually worked out, perhaps in the dungeon she'd imagined, the one with whips and cuffs. She could picture him wielding a whip across the bared bottom of an adoring groupie, or a willing secretary. And frankly, it wasn't that hard to picture. Kendra knew that still waters often ran very deep and very kinky. Every time she'd seen Wade Crittenden, he'd been swaddled in sweatshirts and hoodies. Even at Harris's party he wore a shapeless hoodie. But if that bulging forearm were any indication, she figured the man wouldn't look half bad in leather or tight jeans.

She forced herself away from the welcome distraction of speculating about Wade Crittenden's secret life and back to what the man was actually saying. 'If you look at the dates of the last few emails, including the first one you received after Tess Delaney made her first public appearance, they all happened very soon after situations involving the press.' He scrolled up to the first one. 'Look at the time.' He said. 'You didn't see this email until the next day, is that right?' He glanced up at Garrett.

'That's right,' Garrett said.

'Granted, the Golden Kiss Awards were on television live, but even with your early departure you wouldn't have been home when this email was written. It was written while the event was still going on. Could have been a fan who was very angry at your absconding with his idol before he could fully indulge in the experience.

'And this one.' He scrolled down to the next email. 'What time did the two of you confront the press?' he asked.

'It was afternoon,' Kendra said. 'Somewhere around three, I think.'

'Was any of your talk with the press carried live?' Wade asked.

Kendra shook her head. 'Not that I know of. Though it was broadcast very shortly after.'

Ellis chimed in, 'It probably would have been blogged about and certainly tweeted.'

'I've considered that,' Wade said. 'But nonetheless, the bloggers and tweeters at this stage would have been people at your impromptu press conference, so still a journalist. Certainly the email came almost immediately after you two first spoke to the press, possibly even simultaneously.

'And again.' He pulled up the last two emails, the one Don had received and the one Garrett had got a scant two minutes later. 'There's no way this man could have known all of these things unless he was right there, either in the mob or the press, and the mob wasn't there when the earlier emails came through.'

'Christ,' Garrett whispered. 'Then there's a good chance this man is there with the press at my house and has been the whole time.'

Kendra's legs gave and she dropped into the chair next to Wade's desk. 'You're sure, Wade?'

'I can't be sure, but it makes more sense than anything else at this point.'

She blinked away spots from behind her eyes and forced back the fear and the panic. 'There's a way we could be sure,' she said. 'We could have another press conference. We could make up something that will give it away. I don't know; it would be easy enough to come up with something. Then we could have someone inside the house on the computer checking when the email comes in.'

'No! Not gonna happen. I don't want you exposed anymore,' Garrett said, grabbing her hand.

She ignored him and kept talking. 'Maybe we've been going about this wrong. Maybe we need to give Tess more exposure, you know, draw him out.' Before Garrett or anyone else could protest, she stood and began to pace. 'Look the worst thing that could ultimately happen is that the world finds out Tess Delaney has hired someone to play Tess Delaney to keep her identity secret.'

'We're not having this discussion, and that's final,' Garrett said.

'But –'

'I agree with Garrett,' Ellis said, and Dee and Wade both nodded. 'The less risk, the better.'

Wade handed Kendra a BlackBerry. 'This is for you.'

'Thanks, but I already have a phone,' she said.

'Not one like this one, you don't,' Garrett said.

'It's a Pneuma Inc. special,' Dee added. 'Ellis has one,

Wade has one, I have one, the executive secretaries have one. Garrett has one too.'

Kendra picked it up and turned it over in her hand. 'Looks like an ordinary BlackBerry to me.'

'Looks can be deceiving,' Garrett said.

Wade typed in something on his computer and pulled up a satellite map of the whole Western Seaboard. Then he typed in Sandra Blain, Dee's secretary. And the view of the map zoomed in until it was focused on a small logging road off US-26 on the flank of the Cascades opposite Mount Hood. It focused down to an older Dodge Ram parked at a pull-out in a heavily forested area. 'Ah yes,' Dee said. 'Sandra told me she and her husband were checking out the huckleberries today.'

'The woman makes the best huckleberry muffins in the whole world,' Ellis added.

'She's been told a dozen times not to leave her device in the car. Can you talk to her again, Dee?' Wade said.

Kendra looked down at the Blackberry in her hand. 'Wow!'

'Exactly, wow,' Garrett said. 'Even when the device is off, it's not really off. Wade knows all, sees all.'

'Sounds very entertaining for Wade,' Kendra said, and she thought she saw a blush crawl up the neck of his sweatshirt followed by a twitch of a smile.

'I'm not that hard up for entertainment,' Wade said. 'It's just a safety precaution. You can't do what we do here at Pneuma Inc. and not have a few enemies. Besides, both Ellis and Dee are all over the globe. This helps me keep track of them if I need to get in touch with them. Especially if they're in someplace questionable. Now, give me your iPhone,' he said.

Kendra balked 'But I like my iPhone.'

'And you can have it back when you're Kendra Davis again,' Wade said. 'Give me a minute to transfer all the data and you'll be set.'

Kendra handed over her phone. She had the very distinct impression that arguing with seemingly mild-mannered Wade Crittenden might not be a good idea. And in all honesty, after everything that had happened, even though she still believed that the emails were not a danger to her, she still felt better knowing Wade and everyone else in the room could keep an eye on her.

Chapter Twenty-two

'Galina's a fabulous cook.' Garrett leaned against the stone wall of the patio drinking Mirror Pond ale and watching the stars come out over the open field behind Ellis's house.

'She's the best,' Dee replied. 'Without her, I think Ellis would be reduced to take-outs and peanut butter sandwiches. Afraid I'm not much help either in the cooking department. If I can slap it on the grill I can cook it, otherwise I can't be bothered.'

'Besides, when do either of you have time?' Garrett asked.

Galina had laid on a fabulous spread of Mexican food New Mexican style because she knew that was Garrett's favourite. And nobody in the whole world made *tres leches* cake better than Galina. The meal had been served on Ellis's fabulous patio with the view of Mount Hood fading beneath a fiery sunset, making it easy to believe that the mountain, like all of the Cascade Range, was once, and could very easily be again, an active volcano.

The conversation had been light and easy, and there was not the usual rush Garrett so often had felt with his brother in the past. This was a leisurely meal, something Garrett was sure, until Dee came along, his brother had not experienced in a lot of years.

Now Ellis was in his study finishing up last-minute details for a meeting in Denver tomorrow, and Kendra was settled in the atrium working on PR in K. Ryde mode. He figured a lot of that involved calming Don down. K. Ryde Agency still existed and was now owned by several of Kendra's former employees who were very talented. Kendra still had plenty of connections and she knew how to use them. Garrett could see her profile at the table amid the ferns and vines that filled the sunroom. She was still convinced there needed to be another press conference to see if they could flush Razor Sharp. Garrett would be happy if they never had to have anything to do with the press again.

Dee followed his gaze and sipped at her own beer. 'She's a force of nature, Kendra.'

He smiled at the woman hard at work. 'Don't I know it?' Then the smile disappeared and he felt the familiar fist-like clench at his heart. 'I'm sorry this happened, Dee. I'm so sorry. You have to believe I would have never ever done anything to put her in harm's way.'

'Hey.' Dee took his hand and gave it a squeeze. 'It's Kendra we're talking about here. She makes her own choices. She makes her own rules. You're not to blame for any of this. No one is.'

'If I had just let her walk away when she found out it was me, that Tess is … If I'd only just let her walk away. She wanted to. I'm so sorry.'

She guided him to a heavy pine lawn chair and sat down in one next to him. 'I'm not.'

He caught his breath and looked up at her.

'I mean yes, of course I'm sorry about everything that's happened, about this nutcase, Razor Sharp, about the press fiasco, but I'm not sorry you came into her life.' Her smile became mischievous, and she chuckled softly. 'I mean after I got over the fear of her sending you to the hospital in traction, that is. Garrett –' She scooted closer. 'You're the best thing that's ever happened to her. You're the first man I know that she's ever let in. That's huge. You can't imagine how huge.'

'Why, Dee? Why am I the first? The woman's amazing, she's talented, she's funny, she's sexy, she's … she's so strong. She could have any man she wants. Why? Why doesn't she let anyone in?'

'And why are you so damn nosy?'

Both Garrett and Dee turned to find Kendra standing in the door with a Diet Pepsi clenched in her hand.

'And why are you always sneaking up on people?' he asked.

'I didn't sneak. You two were just so caught up in gossiping

207

that you didn't hear me, that's all.' She was smiling that wonderful smile that he always wanted to kiss until it evolved into something more demanding. He reached out his hand to her and she came onto the patio and settled on his lap.

Dee looked down at her watch. 'It's an early morning for Ellis and me tomorrow, so I'm going to hunt him down and coax him off to bed.' She glanced up at the two of them and then at the darkening sky. 'Should be good sky-watching tonight. The moon's just past new. I bet you could get Galina to fix you a Thermos of hot chocolate, and if I'm not mistaken, she made ginger snaps yesterday. She knows Ellis loves them. That should give you the strength for some serious stargazing.' Garrett was sure Dee knew it wasn't stargazing they'd need strength for.

He shoved the hair away from Kendra's face with an index finger. 'You up for it?'

'Very,' she said with a smile.

'Dee told me about this place,' Kendra said, as Garrett spread the blankets onto the grass and then pulled her down next to him. 'She said the two of you watched a meteor shower from here one night. And that –' She pointed to the dome that housed Ellis's telescope. 'Will we use that?'

'Not tonight,' Garrett said. 'Not sure Ellis would even let me play with his prize toy without him present to participate. Anyway, it's a fairly complex piece of equipment, and I don't want to think that hard. At least, not about anything but you.' He pulled her into his arms so that her head rested on his shoulder. 'Shall I give you the grand tour?'

'Please do,' she said, resting a hand low on his belly, just above the waistband of his jeans. It was a position that instantly made him think of things other than stars.

He laid his hand against hers. 'For someone who doesn't believe in romance, you do a pretty good job of going through the motions.'

'What? This?' She wriggled her fingers against his waistband. 'This is about lust, Garrett, not romance.'

He hadn't planned it. It was the epitome of poor timing, but

208

the question was out before he could stop himself. 'So why don't you believe in romance? You never did tell me.'

She slid a finger beneath his waistband, and nipped his earlobe. 'What? You want romance *and* scorching hot sex? You greedy, greedy man.'

Just as her fingers made contact with his pubic curls, he sucked a tight breath and captured her hand with his, moving it up to rest against his chest just above where his heart had suddenly gone mad. 'I am a greedy man. Very greedy, and I'm nosy. Tell me what I want to know and I might let you have what you want.' He nodded down to his fly.

This time her giggle was wicked. 'What makes you think I want it that bad?'

He raised her knuckles to his lips and kissed them, then captured her index finger and ran his tongue over the length of it. She caught her breath in a quick jerk.

'Because I know you, Kendra Davis. You're insatiable, and I haven't fucked you in hours.'

She pulled his hand to her mouth and returned the favor, sliding her tongue over his index finger then turning her head just enough to nip the pad of his thumb. He felt himself harden. 'All right,' she said. This time there was a slight edge in her voice. 'It's no secret, really. I don't want to follow in my mother's footsteps.' She forced the words out fast, like maybe if she said them fast enough and ran them together, maybe he wouldn't get what she'd just said, maybe he would be too polite to ask her to repeat it. But she should have known better.

'All right, you don't want to follow in your mother's footsteps. What exactly does that mean?'

She sat up next to him, and for a long moment looked out into the woodland in front of them. Just when he thought she wasn't going to say anything else, she spoke. 'Garrett, did your parents love each other?'

'Of course they did. They adored each other, actually. Ellis and I were lucky that way, I suppose.'

'And you want what they had, then? You and Tess. That's why you write what you do. That's why you believe in happy ever after.'

'Well, I don't want exactly what they had, but something along those lines, yes. Why?'

She pulled her knees up under her and turned to face him. Though he couldn't see her eyes in the dark, or her expression, he had the feeling she was studying him. She released a soft breath. 'My mother was a romantic. She had a room full of romance novels, you know the ones that come once a month, four or five in a package, all delivered to her door. Not just those, though. She read all kinds of romance novels. And DVDs, she had a huge collection of those, and even videos. My mom owned every romance, every romantic comedy, every classic love story ever made.'

'Lots of people do,' Garrett said. 'That's what keeps Tess in business.'

'No, you don't understand. That room full of novels, those DVDS, that *was* romance for my mother, Garrett. My dad cheated on her almost from their wedding night. She told me that, years later, when she needed me to commiserate and feel sorry for her.'

'Jesus, Kendra, I'm sorry.' It was a hell of a thing to put on your daughter, he thought.

She waved his sympathy away and continued, 'He said he couldn't help himself, my dad did. He said he needed that little extra that mom couldn't give him. But he said it didn't mean anything. He said it was still her he loved, her he needed, that he needed his family. And she believed him.' She laughed a humourless laugh. 'My dad had his own version of romance, you see.' She curled a tight fist into the grass, pulled up a tuft, and tossed it aside. 'And my mom believed him until the day she died. And when she died, she died without a shred of self-respect, and without a shred of respect from anyone else, including me.'

'I'm sorry, Kendra,' he said.

'Don't be. I wasn't.' The air practically sizzled with her anger. 'And Dad. He had the balls to show up at her funeral with one of his women, one who couldn't have been much older than I was. He said he needed someone. He said he couldn't bear the pain of his loss alone. His loss!' She spat the last words out as though they were vile. 'I haven't spoken to him since. Mom and I weren't enough for him. His family wasn't enough for him. But he never had the guts to walk away either, just in case. He knew when his chicks got tired of an old fart pretending to be young, and everything crumbled, he could always come home. And he could always count on Mom to forgive him, give him a place to brood and pout and lick his wounds until the next girl came along. Well, in the end he wasn't enough for me either. He wasn't enough of a father. He wasn't enough of a decent human being.' Garrett could hear her breath, fast and furious in the darkness. 'So no, I'm not a big fan of romance because it never is what it really is. It's an excuse. It's make-believe. For me it's just one more form of fantasy, one more type of escapism. That's all. I'd die alone before I'd ever let anyone do that to me, treat me that way.'

'My God, Kendra.' He pulled her back down into his arms and held her tight until she relaxed. 'No one would ever do that to you. Not you. Not ever.'

She rose on one elbow, enough to meet his gaze. 'Not as long as I'm in control, they won't, and I'm always in control.'

'No you're not,' he said, running a hand over her cheek. 'You've not been in control for a while now, Kendra, and you know it, and it scares the hell out of you, doesn't it? And now I understand why.'

She pushed his hand away. 'You don't understand anything. There is no sweetness and light, no hearts and flowers. That's a pipe dream. That's for people like Ellis and Dee, people who live larger than the rest of us, people who dream big and then make it happen. It's not for people like me. I know how dark it really is out there, and I can't pretend just because Tess Delaney writes pretty words that the darkness doesn't exist.'

'No one's asking you to pretend the darkness doesn't exist. Of course it exists.' He reached for her and she pushed him away again.

'Look, I don't want to talk about this anymore. I'm going back to the house.'

But as she started to stand he pulled her back down next to him. 'No, you're not. You're not running away this time,

Kendra.'

She jerked back against him, 'Damn it, Garrett, I said I'm not playing, now let me go.' She jerked again. He lost his grip on her wrist, and the momentum sent her back on her butt onto the grass, forcing the breath from her lungs. She let out a little yelp followed by a curse, but he was on her, straddling her, trapping her arms above her head with one hand holding her wrists. He took her mouth viciously, hard, the only way he could take her while she fought him, coming dangerously close to kneeing him in the kidney and toppling him off.

'Garrett, damn it, stop it!' The fury in her voice was exhilarating, and frightening, and he'd never behaved this way with anyone. He never would have. He took her mouth again and she bit him and bucked hard beneath him.

He bit her back. 'You can't control me, Kendra. If you want to share power that's fine, but right now it's my turn, and long overdue.'

'Damn it, Garrett.' She shoved and kicked and tried to roll out from under him. 'You're an asshole! You're a jerk! You deserve what you get! You deserve it! You deserve everything,' she sobbed.

'Tell me, Kendra,' he gasped, forcing her legs apart with his knee and wriggling in between to nestle down tight against her. 'Tell me what I deserve.'

'You deserve … You deserve …' The bucking became shifting and raking, and her tongue darted into his mouth and they ate at each other until neither could breathe. 'You deserve better than this.' Without warning, she collapsed back onto the ground, threw her arm across her face, and broke into angry sobs.

'Jesus, Kendra! No!' He pushed her arm away from her face and cupped her chin, forcing her to look at him. 'How can you say that? There is no better than this, than you, than us together.' He kissed her throat, feeling her swallow back a sob. 'How can you not see that? How?'

He held her there beneath him, her legs open to the press of him, her wrists cuffed in his hands until he felt her relax, felt the tension drain away, felt the shudders calm. And when he was sure she would no longer fight him, he released her arms.

She lay beneath him unmoving, looking up at the sky. Then he kissed her throat again, and her nape and the lobe of her ear. 'I won't let you have control, Kendra. It's ours to share, and that can be good, that can be so good. I'm not your father, and you're not your mother. You're Kendra Davis and you're stunning, and I can't get you out of my head, not even for a minute. I don't know how the hell you did it, but you did.' He eased his weight slightly to one side, giving her space, letting her breathe, giving her room to come back to him from the dark space where she kept herself way too often.

He didn't know how long they lay there together surrounded by the night sounds. A great horned owl hooted somewhere in the trees. There was a very slight rustle of the evergreens in the breeze, and there was the sound of their own breath, in and out, in and out. At long last, he felt her fingers tracing the line his collar against his neck down to where it opened against his breastbone.

'Are you all right?' he whispered.

She only nodded, but he felt it, felt the reassuring in and out of her breath, felt the softness of muscles relaxed beneath him.

'Garrett.' She breathed his name. 'Garrett, will you make love to me?'

He felt as though his chest would burst with the relief of it, with the knowing that she wanted him still, that she had come back to him, and to no one else. He forced his words around the tight knot of emotion in his throat. 'There's nothing I'd rather do right now, Kendra.'

With hands made unsteady by the catharsis he hadn't expected, he unbuttoned her blouse and pushed it aside to kiss down her collarbone and onto the swell of her breasts rising and falling above the lace cups of her bra. She arched her back to bring herself closer to his lips. She lay beneath him, open, completely yielding as he had never seen her before. He eased the straps of her bra down, and with it the cups, until he could nurse on her nipples, already raised and tight. She sighed and gave a little grunt as he stroked his way down the flat of her belly, tight with her efforts to breathe. He toyed with her waistband only briefly before he opened her jeans and slipped his hand in to caress her soft curls. The shift and grind of her bottom raised her pubic bone into his caresses, and opened a path to her clit, resting heavy and tight at the apex of her. Another shifting of her hips and he could wriggle fingers down between her velvety folds, warm and slippery and opening to him. Her breath hitched, expanding her chest, pressing the rise of her breasts closer to his mouth. She curled her fingers in his hair and held him to her, held him against the place where her heart felt like the wild flutter of wings. And he was sure that if he listened hard, if he concentrated just a little more, he could hear the racing of the blood in her veins.

'Please, Garrett,' she whispered. 'I can't wait. I need you inside me. Please.'

He eased her jeans down until she could kick one leg free. She was already shoving his jeans and boxers over his hips. He managed a condom from his pocket and worried himself into it, less gracefully than he'd have liked, his efforts made clumsy by so much more than just arousal, so much more than just need. The vulnerability of the woman in his arms, and the gift of that vulnerability, was sobering. There was nothing he wanted more than to give her something in return, to give her the release she needed, to somehow give her more. Though he didn't really know how, or what that more might be.

But there was not the time, nor the wit left to dwell on it. She lifted her hips, positioning herself for him, opening herself with one hand while the other took hold of him and guided him into her with a catch of her breath and a flutter of her eyelids. And God, it felt like heaven! It felt like he'd come home as she lifted her legs around his waist and locked her ankles behind his back and thrust up to meet him.

She came before he did, sobbing and convulsing, fisting tight fingers into the back of his shirt, gripping him with all her might until he could hold back no longer, until he came too. And it felt like he would never stop coming, like he wanted to fill her with all he was and make her understand that she wasn't alone in her dark places.

* * *

214

'That's Cygnus, the swan.' Garrett pointed to the cross of stars above them. 'The bright star at the head is Deneb. The Big Dipper, you know. And over there, that one that looks like a sideways M, that's Cassiopeia.'

'It's beautiful,' she whispered. 'I never knew the stars could be so bright.'

'Ellis chose this place because there was no light pollution and the view of the night sky is stunning.' But it wasn't the night sky he was looking at.

'Do you think maybe we could just stay here?' she said. 'Right here in this spot on the grass, next to the woods, just stay here until the whole thing with Tess and the press blows over?'

'It's supposed to rain tomorrow. That might make the spot a little less pleasant,' he replied, relishing the fact that he could stare at her endlessly in the dark and she wouldn't squirm, wouldn't be uncomfortable. Of course he really couldn't see her, but he felt her. He felt her like she took up all the space in the field, all the space in the night sky, all the space inside him, and he would have gladly stayed there with her, even in the rain.

She sighed and snuggled closer to him. 'I suppose so. Too bad, really. I like it here.'

Too bad, indeed, he thought. Any place where he had Kendra Davis's undivided attention in such a delicious way, he was sure he'd gladly be willing to stay for at least ten or 15 years. He stroked her flank, then cupped her bottom. 'But then again, if we stayed out here in the rain I might finally get that shower you promised me.'

She nipped his chin and settled a kiss on his throat. 'That's your fault. You could have joined me this morning. I wouldn't have turned you away. The door was unlocked, but you know that, don't you? I mean, I know you'd already showered and all, but you came right on in. You were standing right there at the bathroom door staring at me. All you had to do was take off your clothes and join me.'

Garrett felt a sudden chill climb his spine and clench at the nerves low in his belly. 'Kendra, what are you talking about? I

215

was going to join you, but my editor called, ragging on me about *Texas Fire*. I never made it upstairs, and if I had, I'd have done a helluva lot more than stand and stare at you.'

She pushed away from him and sat up quickly, pulling her shirt around her as though she was suddenly cold. 'Garrett, you were standing right there in the door. I saw you. I asked you to come in and join me and you just stood there and stared. Then when you left, I figured you were mad at me.'

'Kendra –' He sat up and took her gently by the shoulders. 'I swear to you, I didn't come upstairs at all while you were in the shower. Are you sure? Are you absolutely positive there was someone?'

Suddenly, she was shivering. 'I'm positive. Jesus, of course I'm positive. I mean, the glass was steamed, yes, but when I heard the door open, I turned and I could see … Well, I thought it was you. There was a man. I could see him, Garrett. I swear he was there. He was your height. I didn't think … How could it have been anyone else? How?'

He pulled her tight against him and fumbled with his BlackBerry, punching in the number for the head of the security team at his house. 'Gabe, yes, I need you to do something for me. I need you to check the windows upstairs. I think we might have had a break-in.'

Kendra pulled away and began dressing; he heard her more than saw her in nothing but the light of the BlackBerry. While he waited, he struggled to pull his jeans up with one hand while holding the device with the other. 'You all right?' he asked her.

'Fine.' Her voice was breathy, like she'd been running. 'Put it on speaker phone, I need to hear.' Still, in spite of everything, K. Ryde came to the forefront. K. Ryde, he thought, K. Ryde was just one of the many amazing facets of Kendra Davis. She wasn't a different person, no matter how hard Kendra tried to keep the two separate, and no matter what she chose to call herself, no matter how tough she pretended to be, he knew better. But he wouldn't let anyone hurt her. He wouldn't! Ever.

At last the security man's voice came onto the phone. 'Mr. Thorne, there's nothing amiss. There's no evidence of forced entry, and nothing in the house out of place that we can see.'

'Did you hear anything else, anything that might have seemed out of the ordinary?' Garrett asked Kendra.

'No.' She chafed her arms. 'Wait, wait, there was a smell. It didn't smell like you. It smelled, I don't know, disturbing. But then, before I had a chance to think about it, the man was gone.'

'What about Ms. Emerson?' Gabe asked. 'Could it have been her you saw?'

'Of course not,' Kendra said. 'This was a man and he was wearing jeans. Look, I know what I saw.'

'Besides,' Garrett added, 'Stacie never left my side while you were in the shower, and even if she had, she would have never barged in on you. And while you were planning with Harris, she was in my study pumping me for more details about the situation. That's where we both were when you called us down. You got ready in the guest room, for the meeting with the press. Did you notice anything strange then?'

'Honestly, I wasn't paying any attention, Garrett. I was too busy thinking about talking to the press.'

'Fuck!' Garrett ran a hand through his hair and yanked Kendra close to him, ignoring her little gasp of surprise. He returned his attention to the security man. 'Both of the bedrooms look out onto the back yard. He must have come in from there.'

'If there had been someone there,' the man said, 'we would have noticed. The back is being patrolled as well as the front. I don't see how anyone could have sneaked past us. But frankly, that guestroom window's very vulnerable. Easiest thing in the world to shimmy up that trellis.'

'And you're just now thinking about that?' Garrett lost it. 'Ellis told me you were the best. Tess could have been kidnapped or killed, and you would have never known the difference.'

'I'm sorry,' the man managed before Garrett ploughed on.

'Fat lot of good that does!' He was just settling into rant mode when Kendra suddenly grabbed his arm in a bruising grip and shushed him.

'Shut up, both of you! Listen!' she hissed. 'Someone's out there.'

'Probably just a deer,' Garrett said. 'They come up all the –'

Then he heard it, the crack of a twig, the brush of a limb, and what sounded like soft footfalls. Holding his breath, he squinted into the woods, but it was full night and there was no moonlight. Even the ambient light of the house was blocked out by the steep undulation of the hill leading to the field where they sat.

For a second there was silence. They both held their breath, and Gabe, on the speaker phone, must have been holding his too. Kendra slid back on her bottom and fumbled in the backpack that had contained the blankets and snacks. Carefully, as quietly as she could, she pulled out a flashlight, and when the next crackle of undergrowth broke the silence, she flicked it on. The sound that escaped her throat was one of rage mixed with fear. Adrenaline shot up Garrett's spine and felt like it would explode through the top of his head.

For a split second, in the periphery of the circle of light, there was something running away, and the woods was suddenly alive with the crackle and crunch of the undergrowth as whatever it was made its escape.

'Fuck! It was a man! Garrett, it was a man, didn't you see him?'

Garrett catapulted to his feet, shoving Kendra. 'Stay here. Don't move, Kendra. Gabe –' he yelled back at the device '– call Ellis, and get someone down here, now!'

He grabbed the flashlight from her and tore into the woods, undergrowth slapping at his calves and thighs, brambles catching his jeans. He could hear both Gabe and Kendra calling after him to stay put, but he couldn't. He just couldn't. He had only seen movement, but something was definitely there. Something, and if some bastard was after Kendra, he just couldn't sit meekly and do nothing. Suddenly, the sound of escape in front of him was mirrored by the sound of pursuit behind him, and he knew Kendra had ignored him. He would have shouted at her to go back, but that would only give whoever was out there more information. That would only make him aware that Kendra was there, ready for the grabbing. The hair on the back of his neck prickled and he shoved forward, nearly tripping over exposed roots and uneven ground. A thin branch thwacked him low on the cheek with the force of a whip and he felt warm blood trickle down his jaw. He ignored it and pushed on. He tried hard to concentrate, to hear the sound of Kendra stumbling through the undergrowth behind him and the sound of whoever it was in front growing fainter and then suddenly stopping. The shiver snaked up his spine. He didn't know if whoever it was had moved out of the woods or if he had stopped, or if he was waiting, waiting for Kendra. He could be anywhere in the pitch black just outside the spastic slash of vision Garrett's flashlight afforded. And suddenly he couldn't hear Kendra either. He stopped dead, listening, struggling to breathe quietly while his lungs felt like they'd burst. But he heard nothing ahead of him and nothing behind him. Goddamn it, why couldn't the woman ever listen? Why couldn't she stay safe?

It felt like an eternity that he stood there, his lungs bursting from the need of air, his ears straining for the sound of her, for any sound, for any whisper, but there was nothing. At last he crept forward, trying desperately to keep quiet, but twigs crackled and pine straw schussed beneath his feet. It was high summer and the woods were dry. He was desperate to call for her, desperate to know where she was, desperate to know that she was safe.

Suddenly, from behind him there was the bounce, bounce of multiple flashlight beams, and the undergrowth came alive with the crackle and pop of branches and twigs. There was a hand on his shoulder, and before he could brain the owner with the flashlight, a competent male voice said, 'Security, Mr. Thorne. Go back out of the woods. We'll take care of this now.'

'Kendra,' he managed. 'I need to know where Kendra is.'

'I haven't seen her, Mr. Thorne.'

He could tell the security man was making an effort to keep his voice calm and to keep the irritation at Garrett from showing. He didn't give a shit. He just wanted to find Kendra.

The man gestured toward the opening beyond the trees. 'She's probably back in the field, Mr. Thorne, where you need to be too, so we can do our job.'

Ignoring the grab of brambles and the slap of overzealous saplings, needing to see her, needing to make sure she was OK, he hurried back into the open, back to where the blankets were spread onto the grass. She wasn't there!

'Kendra! Kendra!' He swung the flashlight wildly, bathing thin strips of woodland in yellow light, light that danced over skeletal branches and hanging moss, light that caught macabre shadows that slunk over tree trunks and burst from behind rhododendrons. In the woods he could hear the security man fanning out, searching. He could see the flicker of their lights.

This couldn't be happening. Dear God, this couldn't be happening! She was the bright spot. She was the centre pushing back his own darkness, and he couldn't lose her. He couldn't lose her!

'Kendra!' He yelled for her until his throat was raw. 'Kendra, answer me!' Why the hell didn't she respond?

Almost before he knew it, Ellis and Dee were on either side of him, both with flashlights. Ellis was carrying a baseball bat.

'I can't find her,' Garrett managed between gasps for breath. 'Jesus, I can't find her! She was there one minute next to me. I could hear her and then she was gone.'

He headed back into the woods, ignoring Ellis's call after him to wait.

He had just reached the point where the world was swallowed completely in darkness other than the swath cut through by his flashlight when he saw her, lying face down on the pine straw, and his heart stopped. And the world stopped. And it was all his fault. He raced toward her, feeling like he was moving through quicksand, feeling like everything had downshifted into slow motion, feeling like everything was conspiring to keep him away from her. He stumbled over an exposed root, practically falling on top of her.

Then he heard her moan, and everything launched back into real time. 'Kendra! Kendra! Jesus Christ! Kendra, are you all right?' He slid in next to her on his knees just as she forced herself up into a sitting position and coughed and gasped.

'I'm all right,' she assured him. 'Fell. Winded myself. 'I'm fine.' Her last words were swallowed up in a little gasp as Garrett pulled her to him.

'I told you to stay,' he whispered. 'I told you to stay. Damn it, Kendra! Don't ever, ever do that to me again!'

'I couldn't stay,' she managed between his rain of kisses. 'Not when you were out here alone.' She touched his cheek. 'Garrett, you're bleeding! What happened?'

'Just a branch,' he said. 'It's nothing.' He pulled her still tighter to him, forcing another breathless grunt. 'Jesus, woman, what am I going to do with you? What am I going to do with you?'

'I don't know.' She wrapped her arms around his neck as he eased her up onto her feet. 'What you did back there on the blanket a few minutes ago, that seemed to work pretty well.'

They barely cleared the woods before Dee broke into a run and grabbed Kendra in a fierce hug. 'I'm sorry,' she whispered against her friend's neck. 'I'm so sorry. We thought you'd be safe here. I swear we both did.'

Kendra pulled away and ran a hand through Dee's sleep-mussed hair. 'I am safe,' she replied with a smile that was way more confident than anything Garrett could have expected under the circumstances. 'Don't worry, Dee, I promise, I'm fine.'

Dee pulled her back into a rib-crunching bear hug with a laugh that was more of a sob. 'God, I was so scared.'

'There was someone out there,' Kendra said, as Garrett came forward and pulled her back to him, not yet ready to let her go, lest she vanish again. 'There was.' She nodded fiercely. 'You saw him didn't you, Garrett?'

'I saw something,' he said, wishing like hell he'd got a better view.

Just then Ellis joined them with the head of his security team. He gave Kendra a tight hug and surprised Garrett by giving him one too. Then he rummaged in his pocket and handed Garrett a handkerchief for his bloodied face.

'It's possible,' the security man was saying. 'There could

have been someone out there.'

'There was,' both Garrett and Kendra said in unison.

The man nodded politely. 'There's just no real way of knowing until we get some daylight and can go back and do a better search. If he was there, he's long gone by now. We'll go out at first light, before the rain sets in, and if he left so much as a hair on a branch we'll find it,' he said.

'You make sure you do,' Ellis said. 'This is my home, damn it. It's safe, off limits to the world. I hire you to keep it that way. Now take care of it.'

Chapter Twenty-three

He shoved his way into the Ford Focus, not bothering to take off his wet boots. They were only a minor discomfort, barely registering in the scheme of things. The forced march down the hill had cooled his rage and left him exhilarated, feeling justified, purified, and almost untouched by the whoring he had just witnessed. He had reminded himself all the way down that he had known what he'd find, that he had known what the two of them would be up to there on the ground behind Ellison Thorne's mansion, and it wasn't star-watching.

Oh, he'd seen the whole thing, from their arrival with blankets and goodies, to their little argument, to the first thrusts and moans of their passion. He had forced himself to watch. And with the night vision goggles, he could see every detail. He had forced himself to watch and he had forced himself to hold his lust, to sublimate it, to save it back for her. It wasn't time yet. It was an exercise in patience, in waiting, in pushing his feelings back far enough that he could do what he had to do and not let emotions interfere. It was also his way of reminding them that he could get to them anywhere they went, even on the private property of Garrett's powerful brother. It was a reminder of how helpless they were and how completely in control he was.

He started the car and headed back toward Portland. His work here was done. The time was getting closer, but he wasn't quite ready yet. As he drove the car down the winding road, he replayed the view of the two of them stumbling blindly through the woods, unaware of the fact that he could see everything. Everything. It delighted him that he had been so close behind her when she fell. She sensed him there and had just looked over her shoulder when she tripped. He saw it all happening, saw the root she caught her foot in, saw her lurch forward just as he had reached out to touch her.

A bold move on his part, and he would have done it, could have done it, just brushed her shoulder, maybe her cheek; just let her hear him breathe before he vanished into the dark. She would have been terrified, and totally blind to the danger she was in. The thought made him hard, and he absently laid his hand against the fly of his jeans where his erection stirred. The whole incident had aroused him so, even as the sight of Thorne fucking his Tess had enraged him. But this time he held his control. This time he didn't falter. His time would come. She would pay, and pay dearly.

When she had fallen and winded herself, he decided on discretion. There was so little challenge in frightening her when she couldn't run, when she was helpless. There was no sport in that, and besides, he had got what came for. He'd proven his point. She was his for the taking. And when the time was right, he would take her. And no one could stop him.

By the time security stumbled into the woods, he had already found the stream and, just to be on the safe side, had waded it back down to the road below where his car was. The woods had been dry. There had been no rain for several days. There would be no tracks, nothing for them to find. And even if they did it wouldn't matter. They'd never find him in time.

He pulled his hand away from the absent stroke, stroke, stroke of his hard-on and took deep, even breaths. He was in control. Complete control, and even his lust he could hold until the time was right.

When he was calm again, and his arousal had settled to the soft buzz of satisfaction from a task well done, he stopped at an all-night grocer as he entered Gresham. He bought eggs, milk, and a couple of steaks. He was pretty sure there was a skillet in the apartment. He was starving, and the steaks would be a treat, a way of celebrating how close he was, a way of savouring the night's encounter.

Kendra found Garrett in the bathroom leaning over the sink. At first she thought he was being sick until she saw the blood. It was all over his shirt and drying on his face. He was gingerly examining the cut along one cheekbone. She'd cleaned herself and changed into her yoga pants and a T-shirt Dee had let her borrow.

'You all right?' she asked. A stupid question, but it made him aware of her presence, and they were all a little jumpy after what had happened tonight. She hadn't wanted to sneak up on him.

'Jesus, Kendra, don't you ever knock?' The irritation in his voice surprised her.

'The door was open, and here you are bleeding over the sink.'

'The door was open because I thought I was alone, and I'm not bleeding any more. Not much.'

'Sit down.' She nodded to the edge of the bathtub.

'I don't want to sit down,' he protested. 'I want you to leave me alone.' He jerked his arm away from her and she felt his words like she'd been slapped, but she squared her shoulders and nodded to the side of the tub again.

'I don't care what you want, now sit down and let me look at it.'

'Goddamnit, leave me alone!' He shoved her away. 'Can't you ever just let it be? Can't you ever just let me do what I need to do?'

She stepped back with her hands up, a wave of angry confusion washing over her.

'Don't you get it? You could have died because of me.' He stood bleeding in the middle of the bathroom floor with both hands clenched at his side in tight fists. Even beneath the drying blood and the dust, she could see the tensing of muscles along his jaw and down the sides of his neck.

'You're the only one here I see bleeding,' she said, trying to sound calmer than she felt. 'Now please, Garrett, sit down and let me take care of that.'

He stood staring at her as though he was struggling to understand what she wanted of him, then he dropped onto the edge of the tub with a wounded-animal growl. He sat passively while she undid his shirt and slid it off his shoulders, running a hand down his chest across his sternum. He tensed beneath her touch and his eyelids fluttered. God, she could never keep her hands off him, not after the first time, not after she had been in his arms. He caught her hand and gave it a tight squeeze before letting her go.

Then she found a washcloth, soaked it in warm water, and carefully wiped the blood away from his cheek and from the cut. 'It's not deep,' she said, unable to hide the tremor of relief in her voice at knowing that he was safe here with her, at knowing that his wounds were minor. 'Doubt there'll be a scar.' She offered him a tease of a smile. 'Too bad, really, scars in just the right place can be so sexy.'

He grunted what might have been a chuckle, what might have been a growl. 'Sorry to disappoint. I'll try for a bigger branch next time.'

As she turned to rinse out the washcloth in the sink, he pulled her to him, between his legs, wrapping his arms around her waist, resting his head just below her breasts. He held her there, his breathing accelerated, his pulse a wild fluttering at the soft spot beneath his ear. She pulled him close, viewing the crown of his dark head through a mist of tears, fighting the fierceness of the emotions that threatened to unravel her. She told herself it was just the events of the night. Nothing else. They just needed the comfort of each other. They just needed the reassuring closeness of being together.

He tightened his grip until she could just barely breathe, and she returned the favour, letting the washcloth fall into the bathtub behind them. Neither of them moved. And frankly she didn't care if they never moved again, here in the bright, safe warmth of Ellis's house, wrapped in each other's arms. She'd been in a lot of places in her life. Some of them had been amazing, once-in-a-lifetime places, some of them had been horrendous nightmares of places, but none of them had ever been better, or more frightening than this, than being held in the arms of Garrett Thorne in this moment, in this quiet second when the rest of the world was locked outside.

But the moment passed, and at last he spoke into her

sternum. 'I've changed my mind, Kendra. I'll have Don arrange another chance for us to speak to the press.'

'Good.' She pulled away, retrieved the washcloth, and continued her ministerings to his wounded face. 'Glad we agree. This should help us get some idea if Razor Sharp is with the press outside your house.'

'Kendra.' He grabbed her wrist, stilling her hand against his cheek. 'I want Don to call a press conference so I can tell them that I'm …' He took a deep breath. 'I want Don to call a press conference so I can tell them that I'm Tess Delaney.' The words seemed painful as he forced them up from his throat.

'Garrett, you can't be serious.' She lifted his chin and forced him to meet her gaze. 'This can't be what you want.'

He pulled away. 'I don't see what a big deal it is anyway. I mean, you think I should come clean about Tess, and I know Ellis and Stacie do.'

She shook her head slowly. 'Not like this, not because you feel forced to. And you can't really believe it would keep me safe or make any difference in the situation.'

'I can't protect you when you do things like you did tonight,' he said. 'If I come clean and we get you out of here, I don't know, maybe somewhere abroad for a few weeks, maybe longer. Maybe we could change your appearance before you come back. Clearly that's easy enough for you to do.'

She sat down on the edge of the tub next to him. 'This is my home, Garrett. I don't want to be anywhere else. I don't want to run away again. And I don't want to be anyone else either.'

'You're being Tess,' he said.

'I'm being Tess because that's my job. You hired me.'

'That's my point, Kendra. I hired you. I put you at risk because I didn't have the balls to own up to being Tess.'

'Damn it, Garrett!' she gave the bloodied washcloth a hard lob into the sink. 'You know what you are? You're a coward. You don't want to be Tess and you don't want to be Garrett Thorne either. Who the fuck do you want to be?'

'Well, I'm not very good at being either, really, am I?'

'Who on earth told you that? Where did you get such a stupid idea?' She held his face in her hands, forcing him to

227

look her in the eye. 'What? Is it because you're not a very good Ellis? Well, guess what, Ellis would make a lousy Garrett. The very thought makes me cringe, and he'd make an even worse Tess, so stop feeling sorry for yourself and stop blaming yourself and let's just get on with it. Let me do what I do best. That is what you hired me for, isn't it?'

He pulled her to him so hard that the vertebrae in her neck popped and she offered a little gasp. 'I need you safe, Kendra. I need that more than anything else. I need you safe.'

'I'll be safe, Garrett, and I'll be a lot more likely to stay safe if you stop feeling guilty for protecting Tess, for doing what you felt you had to do.'

Galina had hot chocolate waiting when they were both cleaned up and dressed. Harold, Ellis's butler, had built a fire in the fireplace, and they joined Dee and Ellis around it. It was high summer. They didn't need the heat, but it warmed places that had nothing to do with anything physical. Garrett sat with his arm wrapped around Kendra possessively. He'd been that way ever since he found her in the woods. She was never in any real danger. At least, she hadn't thought she was, but if it had been him, if she had lost him, even for a minute … She shivered at the thought and settled still closer to him. Tomorrow she would worry about that, about how she couldn't let him go into the woods alone, about the cold knot she'd felt in her chest at the fear of him going in and not coming back.

They had told Ellis and Dee about Kendra's shower experience and the police had been notified, even though it was clear there was nothing they could do. Ellis had more faith in his security teams and the detectives he always used when he needed that sort of help.

'God, Kendra.' Dee shivered. 'I can't believe this guy was right in the house with you, right in the bathroom. What stopped him? What made him leave? Do you have any idea?'

Kendra shook her head. 'I thought it was Garrett. He just stood there for a few seconds, watching me, I guess. Obviously I couldn't make out the details of his face or I would have known it wasn't Garrett. Then, after a little while, he turned

228

and left.'

'Security has searched the house and the back yard as best they could in the dark,' Garrett said. 'So far they've found no evidence of the man.

'But he was there,' Kendra said. 'He was there all right.'

'If this is the same man you saw in the woods,' Ellis said, 'I just can't imagine how anyone could have known that you were here.'

'He could have made a guess,' Kendra said. 'I mean, Garrett's your brother and this is a place where we'd have more privacy. It wouldn't be a difficult deduction to make.'

'Through the woods is the only way onto the property without security knowing it,' Ellis said. 'And that's not an easy route unless you know it. I never wanted that kind of protection,' he added as an afterthought. 'I never wanted my home to be a fortress, but I've made some pretty powerful enemies in the past few years, and both Beverly and Wade insisted. I never expected that it would ever really be necessary.'

'I'm sorry I brought this to your home,' Garrett said.

'Don't be ridiculous, Ellis replied. 'You're family.' He shot Kendra half a smile. 'You both are, and the main thing is that you're both safe.' He held Kendra's gaze for a second, then said, 'Harris knows and so does Stacie. We felt they needed to know. Besides, I wouldn't have wanted to deal with either of their anger if they thought we'd kept it from them.'

'And Wade,' Dee said. 'We called Wade. He'll be out in the morning to check out the woods, and he may want to check your house too, Garrett. If the security people miss anything, Wade's the one to find it.'

Ellis glanced from one of them to the other. 'You both need to get some sleep. We all do. Dee and I have rescheduled our meetings and arranged things so we can work from home tomorrow,' he said. 'I don't think it's a good time to leave the two of you.' The look he shot both of them made it clear there was no need arguing with him, that the decision was final. 'There's nothing that can be done right now, and the bastard's not likely to come back tonight. Though if he does he won't find the house nearly as accessible as the woods.'

A dream of falling from a high place woke Kendra with a start. With her heart racing, she reached for Garrett, called his name. But she was alone in a huge bed in the strange room. It took her a second to remember that she was at Ellis's home in his palatial guest suite. As the nightmare of the past 12 hours came back to her, she sat up in the bed, chafing her bare arms from something far more than cold.

That the first thing she had done when she woke up was reach for Garrett meant nothing, she assured herself. After what had happened tonight, after the discovery of what had happened when she was in the shower, of course she would reach for him, for comfort. That was all. For comfort. Nothing more. Her stomach felt like it turned to stone every time she thought about what could have happened in the shower, and her all the time thinking it was Garrett come to join her, and her feeling hurt and angry when he didn't. She shivered again and looked around. It didn't matter if it was just for comfort. She still didn't want to be alone. Not just that, but she knew how Garrett blamed himself for what had happened. It wasn't his fault. She wished she could convince him of that, but knowing how well Garrett did guilt, she didn't much want him to be alone either.

She found his shirt still lying at the foot of the bed where he'd shed it when he had tucked her in and crawled in next to her. She had pulled him as close to her as she could get him, then she had climbed on top of him, to find him ready for her, needing the comfort of her as badly as she needed the comfort of him. His touch was tender as he explored her, caressed her, and yet it was possessive in a way it hadn't been before. That should have disturbed her, but they both needed comfort, she told herself. Tonight they both needed to possess each other.

And when they had both come, and as their breathing slowed and their bodies dozed, she'd fallen asleep there on top of him, with him still nestled inside her body, with her feeling the rise and fall of his chest against hers, feeling the press of his belly making her certain that when she woke up again she'd want more of him. So much more.

She slipped into his shirt and followed the anemic trail of light to the spacious study that was more like a small library just off the sitting room. He sat at the big oak desk, hunched over his laptop, tapping away on the keyboard. For a second, she stood at the door just watching. This was Garrett Thorne in Tess Delaney mode. He sat with no shirt. He wore only his boxers. His always mussed hair was more mussed than usual, like he'd just left the bed. She smiled when she thought of what had happened in the bed he'd just left.

His fingers flew over the keys. His face was a study in concentration. She wondered what he was writing, what Tess was writing. She pulled his shirt tight across her breasts, taking in the scent of him, wrapped around her so tightly. A lump rose in her throat, and she saw him through a soft mist. He was Tess Delaney. There was no jinx in that at all. Without Tess, he wouldn't be the man she couldn't stop thinking about, the man who had barged his way into her life and left his mark on her, the man, the only man other than Harris, who had seen her at her worst and stayed by her anyway.

A wave of panic washed over her. This was too much. This was way more than she'd bargained for. She should have never said yes to him. He frightened her like she'd never been frightened before. She was just ready to run back to the bedroom, maybe even move to the bedroom next door, to try to re-establish a little professional space when Garrett turned and saw her. And the smile he offered made her completely forget to run.

'You all right?' he said, pushing back the office chair and reaching out a hand to her.

'Fine. I'm fine.' She came into his arms and curled up on his lap. 'I woke up and you were gone.'

'Tess is a hard taskmaster,' he said. 'When she wants to write, there's no arguing with her.'

She ran a light finger over the fresh cut along his cheek made from the tree branch just a few hours ago. 'Does it hurt?'

'Stings a little. Not bad, though. It's nothing.'

'You all right?' She returned the question.

'I woke up with *Texas Fire* running through my mind.' He settled a kiss on her ear and pulled her close. 'Believe it or not, I've been inspired lately. I think it's going to be a pretty good read after all. Who'd have ever thought that Kendra Davis would be my muse?'

'Glad I could help.' She ran a hand over his chest and shifted on his lap, feeling the beginnings of a hard-on in his boxers. 'Garrett, what happens when you become Tess Delaney? What changes inside you, what shifts over enough so that you can access the Tess side of you?'

He stroked her arm and she could see color climb up his throat. He was beautiful when he was wrong-footed, when he was embarrassed by how amazing he was. She wished it didn't embarrass him, though. She wished he could own the beauty and the talent of who he was, because it was in that talent, in that beauty that he was more himself than she suspected he even knew he could be.

He nodded to the laptop humming quietly on the desk. 'It's not anything so simple as a shift; I mean, there's no split personality or anything like that. Tess Delaney started out as a pen name, just a way to get my romance into print and get the nice check that it promised. But still, the person who writes Tess Delaney novels is different than the person who wrote Brad Dennis novels.' His face was suddenly sad. 'The person who writes Tess Delaney novels knows more, has more life experience. The person who writes Tess Delaney novels broke his brother's heart by stealing his fiancée and then had his own heart broken when he realized that his wife still loved his brother, and then he'd lost his wife, his best friend, and his brother.' He brushed his fingers over the keys. 'Who knows, maybe Tess was my penance, maybe Tess was my healing.' He smiled up at her and the blush returned. 'Then again, maybe it was just the inspiration of a really good steady income.'

'So.' She shifted in his lap and tightened her arms around his neck. 'If there is no shift, then it's as much Garrett Thorne at the keyboard as it is Tess Delaney, more so, really.'

'It doesn't feel that way, at least not any more. It feels like when I'm writing a Tess Delaney novel that I'm in a place that's somehow a little more grounded and a little more real.'

She leaned in and kissed his ear. 'Do you ever fantasize about her?'

'No!' he said. 'It's never like that. It never has been. It's more like she's my muse. It's more like she watches and guides me. I don't even know what she looks like. I've never had the inclination to visualize her face or her body. That seems like cheating somehow.'

'Did she have red hair?'

He smiled up at her and shook his head. 'If you're asking if she looks like you, no. And no, you've never been Tess Delaney to me. You've always been Kendra Davis, the one who slapped the hell out of me in Wade's office and the one who tried to drown me in Harris's lake.'

She giggled. 'Both of which you deserved.'

He slid the shirt off her shoulders and cupped her breasts in turn, raking his thumb over her nipples, and she arched into his touch. 'I'd endure it all again to have you here on my lap like this, to constantly be thinking about the next time I see your face.' He placed a kiss on one nipple, then the other. 'About the next time I can hear you laugh, the next time I feel your touch.' He slid his hand down the slope of her belly to stroke and fondle her pubic curls, and her whole body tensed with anticipation, as it always did when Garrett touched her, as it always did when she knew he wanted her the way she wanted him.

With the other hand, he shoved his laptop to one side, then hoisted her, in a wave of giggles, onto the desk, opening her legs so that he sat in the office chair, between them.

For a moment, he just looked at her, his gaze moving down her body from her face, over her breasts, and down between her legs. His studying of her made her feel more than just sexy. The way he sat between her legs, the way she opened to him, made her feel worshipped, adored. She'd never felt that way before.

At last he moved to run the tips of his fingers over and around each nipple, to knead and caress the weight of her excited breasts in the cup of his palm. With the other hand, he lifted her feet onto the arms of his chair. It was a position into which she had to move forward, shifting and rearranging her bottom until the tilt of her hips, the position of her open thighs, the flat press of her feet gave him a perfect view of the splayed swell of her, and he didn't deny himself the pleasure of that view. He started with the cup of his hand against her perineum, then he shivered his fingers upward to open her, pausing to slide first one, then two inside her, where she was slick and anxious and tetchy.

She sucked a tight breath and shifted again, rubbing and gripping at his welcome invasion. But he didn't linger. He moved his fingers, now slippery with her lust, up to splay her further as he hunched forward to get a better view, his hand shifting and opening, his fingers opening and spreading and shoving until all of her, every bit of her was fully exposed. She could feel his breath against her clit, she could feel his gaze against all of her; hot, hungry, curious.

He glanced up at her face, his pupils dilated, lips parted. 'I've never seen anything so exquisite,' he whispered. Then, still holding her gaze, he lowered a hot, wet kiss onto her clit. She gasped and squirmed, but he held her there, exposed, displayed against the desktop, as the kiss became a suckle, and the suckle gave way to long, circular lavings with his tongue.

It took her a minute to realize that the keening sound, the breathy, soft hum was coming from her own throat, that it was somehow a replacement for speech which she could no longer remember how to use. His hands moved up the inside of her thighs, opening her still wider before they moved to cup her buttocks, to knead and stroke, to pull her onto his mouth until his whole face was nestled deep and tight and wet against her, and his thumbs raked at her and then circled and stroked the gripping bud of her bottom. And the soft, breathy keening became deep, throaty groans and grunts that rocked her to her core as he grazed his teeth up over her clit and nibbled and nipped. The harder she squirmed and wriggled beneath him the tighter he held her, captive to the will of his mouth, until, held immobile in his powerful grip, she practically cried with relief when the first wave of orgasm broke, and there was nothing to do but feel it, feel it flood her, ripple through her, wash over her like ocean waves in rhythmic ebb and flow. And once again she found her voice. 'Garrett, Garrett, Garrett.' She whispered his name to the tidal flux of her own body.

When she had calmed, when she could breathe, when the world seemed someplace where she might have lived once upon a time, he lifted her into his arms and carried her back to the big bed.

When he entered her, she felt his own need, patiently restrained until he had pleasured her, now unleashed like a wild thing to devour her and ride her and ravage her until she was too caught up in the power of it to distinguish where he ended and she began. It was something she hadn't wanted, something she should never have allowed, something that terrified her, and yet, folded in his arms with him on top of her, all around her, inside her, it was hard to think that there could ever be any other place. Ever.

Even with his own need driving him, threatening to break bones and pull muscles with each thrust, he sent her again, tumbling over, grasping and clawing and clinging, then he followed her. He followed her deep. So very deep.

Chapter Twenty-four

'I've just got off the phone with Don,' Garrett said. Dee and Ellis both looked up from their coffee. He checked over his shoulder to make sure Kendra was still upstairs asleep. Then he blew out a sharp breath. 'I'm ... I'm outing Tess to the press today. I've made up my mind.'

Ellis sat down his cup, and he and Dee shot each other a quick glance. Then he addressed Garrett in the way he did when he chose his words very carefully because he knew his brother wouldn't like them. 'Look, Garrett, I've thought you should do this for ages now, you know that. But it's not what you want, and that's way more important than what I think. And do you really believe it'll protect Kendra?'

'If I didn't I wouldn't be doing it,' he said. 'Honestly, I can't stand what this is doing to her, the stress she's under because of this Edge guy from her past. I don't know how she's held it together like she has, knowing what she's been through.' He struggled to keep his voice calm, even. He struggled not to betray the panic he felt whenever he thought of something happening to her. 'I think once the stalker realizes the woman he's obsessing over doesn't exist, he'll either find someone else to obsess over or –'

'Or come after you,' Dee said.

'Or come after both of you for deceiving him,' Ellis added. Before Garrett could respond, he said, 'You didn't see the man in the woods last night, did you?'

Galina came into the breakfast room and gave him coffee in a travel-mug. The woman had the measure of him, he thought to himself. He thanked her and returned his attention to Ellis and Dee. 'It doesn't matter if I didn't. Kendra did. And I did hear something.'

'The woods are full of deer, Garrett, and lots of other things that can rustle the undergrowth when startled.'

'Kendra's not a flighty person,' Garrett said. 'You both know that. She's steady as a rock.'

Dee nodded. 'If she says she saw someone, I believe her.' She glanced out the window. 'It's been pouring since just before dawn, and the wind has been horrible. Any evidence security or the police might have found will have been washed away or blown away ages ago.'

For a second they all three stared out the window into the dark, rainy morning. Then Dee spoke again. 'She won't be happy about what you're doing. In fact, I would want to be in the next county when she finds out if I were you.'

'I know,' he said, staring glumly into the pouring rain. That's why I need you to keep her here until the news breaks, until I can gauge what'll happen next.' He raised a hand before either of them could speak. 'I know she won't like it. I don't give a shit what she likes. I just want her safe.'

'This is not your choice to make,' Ellis said.

'Yes! Yes, it is my choice to make. I hired her. I convinced her to work for me, and now I'm firing her. My choice. All my choice. Look, all I need is for you to keep her here until after I've made the announcement to the press, then once that's done, I'll come back and deal with the consequences. If I have to kidnap her and take her away someplace I will, but first I need to take care of this.'

Dee blew out a long breath. 'Keeping her here may involve lots of rope and locking her in the wine cellar.'

'That's fine. Whatever it takes. I just can't put her through any more of this. I can't.' Garrett looked down at his watch. 'Look, I need to go before she wakes up. With any luck I'll have it all over with before she knows what's going on.'

Neither Dee nor Ellis looked like they believed that for a minute.

'I won't lie to her, Garrett.' Dee held his gaze. 'She's my best friend. But I will hogtie her if I have to.'

'Thanks. That's all I'm asking.' Garrett nodded his

appreciation to both of them, then turned to go.

'Garrett,' Ellis called after him. 'Be careful.'

Carla had managed an awkward sort of half shower in the confines of the motorhome bathroom while keeping an eye out the crack of the door to the front of Garrett Thorne's house just in case there were any further developments. Her father had brought her clean clothes and coffee and a half a dozen maple bars from her favorite bakery, which she had polished off in short order, minus the one he had eaten.

When he'd asked if everything was all right, when he commented that she looked pale, she'd been evasive. She was overly tired, she said. She just needed a good night's sleep. When he'd asked if there were any developments, she'd lied, something she had never done to her father before. Nothing of any consequence, she'd told him, even as she ached to tell him the truth.

She was still toweling her hair when the email arrived that made her wish like hell she'd come clean with him. It was from the stalker, who had still never given her his name.

I find it stunning just how dense the press can be at times, Carla. Even you. I would have thought you would have suspected something was afoot. Once again, you disappoint me. I don't like being disappointed.

So here is something I think will interest you. Tess Delaney and Garrett Thorne were not on the premises last night. They sneaked out the back to spend the night in the lap of luxury over at big brother's mansion. I know this because I saw them there. I know this because I watched them fucking like goats in the field behind Ellison Thorne's estate. While they were supposed to be watching the stars, I was watching them from the woods. I was so close I could hear them breathing, so close I could smell their rut.

Carla, dear, I was so close to Tess, I could have slit her throat, so close I could have snapped her neck. And she knew I was there, oh, she knew it. I made sure she did. But she couldn't see me, couldn't touch me. She could only speculate as to what I would do while Garrett Thorne stumbled around in

238

the thicket like a madman looking for me. Ask them about it when they return, Carla. Ask them. Of course Garrett's powerful brother called in security, but I was back home having a midnight snack by the time they could manage more than a cursory search. Ask them, Carla. I think it won't be much longer until they'll have to admit Tess is being stalked, that Tess Delaney is in serious danger. Make no mistake, Carla, Tess's life is mine for the taking. And it won't be long. Not long at all now. Oh, and if you really want to get the jump on the rest of your Neanderthal colleagues, wait for the frightened couple in the back yard. They should be home any time now. I'm sure the limo that just left the property is our happy couple.

The back yard, Carla. Wait for them there. And don't disappoint me again.

It took her a second to steady herself, a second to stop feeling like she might throw up the maple bars she'd just eaten. She was just beginning to get the shakes under control, when her editor called.

'Thorne is about to make a press statement without Tess.' He didn't bother to say hello. 'Strange, really. It was Tess's publicist, Bachman, who called it in. I don't know what the hell this is all about, Flannery, but it sounded pretty damned important. Get what you can and make it good.'

He cut the connection just as a red Ford Explorer pulled up in front of the house. It was a rental, Carla could tell, and the man who got out was Tess's publicist, Donald Bachman. He was a tall California blond who looked as though he might have been a surfer in his younger days, but he cleaned up all nice and Wall Streety.

She grabbed her Dictaphone and a pad and pen and shoved her iPhone in her pocket. Then, as an afterthought, grabbed the big golf umbrella her father had also dropped off this morning and headed into the downpour. Reporters were already beginning to gather near the front porch of Garrett Thorne's house.

'Mr. Bachman.' Mike Pittman stuck his Dictaphone in the man's face. 'Can you tell us what's happening? Do you know why Thorne wants to speak to the press?'

Bachman offered only a hint of a smile. 'Whatever Garrett Thorne has to say you'll all hear shortly. Now, if you'll excuse me.' He shoved his way onto the front step and rang the bell.

As the door opened just enough for him to get inside, cameras flashed and, for a second, all eyes strained for a glimpse of the inner sanctum, the place that had gripped them all for the past three days. Carla wondered what the hell was going on.

Inside, Garrett paced the floor like a caged lion. For a long moment, Don stood dripping on the carpet and stared. 'I don't need your help.' Garrett said.

'Yes, you do,' Don said. 'Who the hell is going to believe that you're Tess Delaney if I'm not there to back you up? They'll laugh you off the porch, if they don't crucify you first.' He looked around. 'Kay's not here?'

Garrett shook his head. 'After all that's happened, what do you think? She's with Ellis and Dee.'

Don slipped out of his wet jacket and hung it on the pegs by the door. 'How did you manage that?'

'I sneaked out before she woke up. How do you think I managed it? The woman's exhausted even if she won't admit it.'

Garrett ran a hand through his hair and returned to the living room without inviting Don, but Don followed.

'Garrett, are you sure you want to do this?' Don sat down next to him on the sofa. 'I mean this will, no doubt, send book sales still higher than they already are, and it'll be a media circus deluxe that we can make serious mileage off PR-wise, but I'm not stupid. I know this isn't what you want. And I know why you're doing it. I just don't know that it'll help.'

'Goddamn it, Don, I have to do something!' Garrett slammed his hand against the coffee table, causing the man to jump. 'I got her into this mess. I have to get her out, so I'm coming clean, and I'm firing her. Then when the press is gone, I'm going to hogtie her and take her somewhere far away from here.'

'You're assuming she'll go. And that without even talking to K. Ryde, and ultimately he is her boss.'

Garrett bit his tongue to keep from telling Don the truth, but it was Tess he was outing, not Kendra. 'It's still my choice to make. I let you bring the Ryde Agency into this, and I'm now terminating their services.'

For a second, Don studied him as though he might find something hidden in Garrett's behavior, but Garrett had pretty much always been above board with his publicist. That's why their relationship had worked. Then he spoke carefully. 'Perhaps you should let me take Kay away from here. I've got lots of contacts and I'll see that she's kept safe.'

Garrett held his gaze. 'Don, I'm sleeping with her.' He rushed on before the man had a chance to respond. 'It's a complication neither of us needed, as she frequently reminds me, but you need to know that if anyone takes her anywhere it'll be me.'

Don dropped his gaze to his hands folded in his lap and nodded slowly. 'Not that I didn't suspect.' He looked back up at Garrett. 'You love her, don't you?'

The words hit Garrett like a sharp knife in the middle of his chest and suddenly he missed Kendra Davis with every fibre of his being, suddenly he wished desperately that he had told her just that last night when he made love to her, when things were raw and open and she was vulnerable like he'd never seen her before. 'Yes,' he replied, feeling his heart hammering its way through the word. 'Yes, I love her, Don.'

'Thought so,' the man said. 'Well, then, we should probably get this over with, because Kay Lake doesn't seem the type to be fooled for long, and I'm betting if your brother and his fiancée aren't willing to tie her up and lock her away, she'll be here in a little while and she'll be pretty damned pissed at you.'

Garrett closed his eyes and took a deep breath. Then he squared his shoulders and stood. 'All right. Let's do it.'

'I can do it for you, if you want me to,' Don said, his eyes still locked on Garrett as though he didn't really trust him to do what had to be done. 'Might make it easier.'

Garrett shook his head. 'No. It won't. Nothing will make it

easier but the knowing that it might help keep Kendra safe.'

Don raised an eyebrow. 'Kendra?'

'Never mind, OK? Let's just do it.'

Carla stood under the large umbrella, waiting in the downpour like the rest of the press. She could feel the skin along the back of her neck prickle. He could be watching her – the stalker. Jesus, he could be watching her! He certainly never seemed to miss anything. She half expected to get an enraged text from him any minute demanding to know why she hadn't followed his advice, why she hadn't gone around to the back yard. But she was a journalist first, and if Garrett Thorne was going to give an interview without Tess by his side, and if Tess's PR person had shown up, then there must be something major kicking off. She needed to know what Thorne had to say.

Next to her, Mike Pittman's iPhone buzzed with an incoming text and she nearly jumped out of her skin. Jesus, Tess's stalker had done a number on her. Had he really been lurking in the woods behind Ellison Thorne's mansion last night? There was no way of knowing without questioning Garrett or Tess. Not for the first time she wondered if maybe that's exactly what she should do.

The front door of the house opened and Carla forced her attention front and centre as Garrett Thorne stepped onto the porch next to Tess's publicist, Don Bachman. As dapper as Don looked, Garrett looked pretty poorly slept with. Were he and Tess breaking up? If what the stalker said was true, Tess could be on a flight to anywhere by now. There was a muttering among the soggy press and everyone pushed forward to get closer.

Garrett Thorne stepped to the railing around the edge of the porch, and stood just out of the assault of the rain. For a second he closed his eyes, and Carla was afraid for him. He didn't seem well. He seemed like wherever he was, it wasn't a good place to be. Then he hauled a deep breath into his chest, cleared his throat, and suddenly everything went silent except for the pattering of rain against the roof and against the tops of the umbrellas. 'I'm sorry to bring you all out into the weather,'

Thorne said, 'but I promise what I have to say won't take long.'

Don Bachman leaned forward and spoke quietly in Garrett Thorne's ear, and no matter how everyone in the press held their breath, there was no making out what was said. Thorne shook his head and took another step forward until he was leaning out over the rail of the porch, oblivious to the rain.

Mike Pittman was his usual rude self. 'Where's Ms. Delaney?' He spoke above the rain. 'And why isn't she here with you?'

The tight silence of anticipation was broken by the rev of an engine and the screech of tires as a blue Audi jerked to a stop in front of the house. The door burst open and Tess Delaney practically catapulted from the seat looking way more casual than Carla, or anyone else, had ever seen her in the brief time she'd been in the public eye.

'I am here.' She spoke in a loud, clear voice. For a second, she stood facing the two men on the porch, ignoring the downpour around her. There was a muttering of awe as the press parted and Tess literally ran up the sidewalk and onto the porch. She was completely drenched by the time she reached Garrett Thorne. She pushed her way in close, grabbed him by the lapels and kissed him hard.

It was frustrating as hell. Once again, no one could hear what Tess whispered to him, but she practically manhandled Garrett back into the house, with Bachman mumbling an embarrassed apology before he followed them in and shut the door.

Inside, Kendra wasted no time. 'Don, stay here,' she shouted over her shoulder as she led Garrett, her hand still fisted in his shirt, to the kitchen. 'I need to talk to Garrett alone.'

Once they were in the kitchen, she slammed the door that separated it from the rest of the house and turned on him. But he beat her to the draw.

'How the hell did you get here? Ellis and Dee promised me they would keep you there, that they would keep you safe.'

'Don't ask people to make promises they can't keep.' Her

voice was a low growl. But that was about as calm as it got. 'You sonovabitch!' She slapped him hard enough to make his ears ring. 'You left me! You left me without so much as a fucking word!' She would have slapped him again, but this time he caught her arms and pulled them in close to his chest.

She jerked away and stood with her fists tight at her side, chest heaving with rage. 'Look, if you absolutely feel you want to tell the press Tess's secret, I can't stop you, but goddamn it, you pulled me into this in the first place to protect her identity.' She shoved a pointed index finger at his chest. 'You don't back out without telling me. Do you understand? If you want to fucking fire me, then do it, damn it! Just do it. But until that happens I'm in charge and we do it my way.'

'Kendra, Kendra! This has nothing to do with who's in charge and you know it.' He reached for her, but she jerked away. 'I don't give a fuck who's in charge and I don't care how angry you are, I'm not putting you at any more risk. I'm going out there to tell the press who I am, and then, even if I fucking have to hogtie you, I'm going to take you someplace safe, someplace away from here.' He reached for her and she jerked away so hard she fell back against the table.

'I quit, Garrett.'

She could have kicked him in the gut and he would have felt it less. 'Kendra, wait. Listen to me, please.'

'I said I quit!' She hoisted her bag higher onto her shoulder and jerked open the back door before he could jerk it away from her and slam it shut, then she slapped him again.

And he kissed her. He pressed her up hard against the granite counter, holding her wrists none too gently, ignoring the painful nip of her front teeth, grunting hard as a loose elbow hit him in the ribs. 'Damn it, Kendra, stop it. Just stop it and listen to me.'

'Fuck you,' she said, her voice nothing more than a breathless hiss before she grabbed him by the hair and pulled him into a kiss he wasn't sure he would survive. Then she was shoving and ripping at his fly, growling and cursing like fury itself. 'Damn you, Garrett Thorne. I hate you! I fucking hate you!'

He hoisted her onto the counter top, forcing the short denim skirt up over her hips and pushing the crotch of her panties aside. 'No, you don't. You don't hate me.'

She grabbed at his hair again, fingers curled so tight it felt like he was being scalped. 'I hate you, I hate you.' She forced the words up through her chest that heaved as though it would explode. With the other hand she brutalized him in her efforts to get to his cock, and how he could be erect right now made no sense, but he was. 'I hate you,' she gasped, as he gripped her buttocks and pulled her onto him so hard that her gasp was surely one of pain.

'I'll do what I have to, Kendra, so just deal with it.' This time he pulled her hair, forcing her to look him in the eyes, forcing her to face him and not look away, and he thrust as though he would split her in two, as she kicked him hard in the kidneys with her legs locked around his waist. 'Get over it, because I'll do what I have to. I'll keep you safe.' Each thrust was painful, each thrust felt like it would gut him, felt like it would break her in half, felt like it would tear the world apart.

She sobbed her orgasm as though her heart were broken, in hot tears of rage and frustration and who knew what else. God knew she would never tell him.

He felt like everything he was he suddenly spilled inside her, and there was no going back. There'd never be any going back. 'I love you, Kendra,' he whispered against her ear. But he wasn't sure she heard him when his BlackBerry was ringing from where he'd tossed it on the kitchen table when he'd come in earlier this morning.

'Get it,' she managed between efforts to breathe. 'It might be important.'

He settled her onto the floor and grabbed for it. 'It's Wade.' He put it on speaker phone.

'Wade, it's Kendra. What's going on?'

'I'm here.' Garrett spoke before Wade could ask. Then he settled onto the chair next to Kendra.

'Glad you're together,' he said. 'I figured you would be. We've found the stalker.'

The sound that came from Kendra's throat was like

someone had wounded her. Quickly she covered her mouth and swallowed back a sob, and Garrett thought his heart would break for her.

'Police have taken him into custody. His name is Bill Gleason. He works over at Web-Z.'

'How did you find him?' Garrett asked.

'I pulled a few strings,' Wade said. 'Convinced some of the friends I know in media that it might be time to check for porn on the computers of their employees. They got my meaning.'

Garrett knew that as low key and mild-mannered as Wade Crittenden appeared to be, the man had friends in high places and endless resources of the human kind, of the technological kind, and of the kind that came with Pneuma Inc.'s very deep pockets.

'You're sure it's him?' Kendra asked.

'All of the emails were there on his computer, and he's admitted to writing them.'

There was a timid knock on the kitchen door and Don stuck his head in. 'You two need to see what's on television,' he said.

'Keep me on,' Wade said. 'I'll watch from here.'

Just as they settled onto the sofa in front of the big screen TV, Kendra's Blackberry rang. It was Dee. 'Thank God! Ken, are you all right' Her voice was breathless, urgent. Kendra owed her a huge apology. She'd literally stolen the Audi when Dee was in the shower. Before Kendra could respond she continued, 'Did Wade call? Did he tell you they've caught the stalker?'

'I'm fine. Garrett has him on speaker phone now. I'll call you back,' she said, as she looked up to see a man being taken away from the Web-Z offices in handcuffs, his face covered by a jacket he had pulled over his head. She shut off the device and laid it on the coffee table next to Garrett's, her attention now riveted to the voiceover.

'Bill Gleason was arrested early this morning for threatening the life of romance novelist and winner of the Golden Kiss Award, Tess Delaney. Since Tess's first ever public appearance at Friday night's award ceremony, rumors have been rife about her early and mysterious exit from the ceremony with Garrett Thorne, younger brother to Ellison Thorne, CEO of Pneuma Inc. Since that time, Ms. Delaney has been holed up at Garrett's house insisting, during several conversations with the press, that her stay with Thorne was nothing more than him providing a quiet place for her to finish writing her next novel. Speculations arose early on the first day of Ms. Delaney's confinement that there was a threat to her life, speculations confirmed by presenter and literary critic, Barker Blessing. Those speculations were denied – no doubt for the protection of Ms. Delaney.'

The same reporter at large, who had been on hand the first day Kendra had awoken in Garrett's flat, was once again back in the bookstores, asking how people felt about the stalker's arrest.

'I'm so relieved they found him. It must have been so terrifying for Tess.'

'How could anyone do such a thing?'

'I suspected that something wasn't right after that interview with Barker Blessing.'

There were several more similar one-liners from the bookstore frequenters, many with Tess Delaney novels in tow. Then the report returned to the voiceover.

'So far Tess has made no comment, though she was seen arriving in a blue Audi a short while ago looking rather distressed.' Sure enough, there was footage of Tess piling out of the Audi and forcing Garrett and Don back into the house.

'The press is hoping for a statement from Tess Delaney and Garrett Thorne soon.'

'You're sure?' Garrett asked Wade.

'This is the man who wrote the emails, yes,' Wade said. 'He hasn't admitted to breaking into your house or being in the woods behind Ellis's house, but the police are still questioning him.'

Carla's fingers cramped from the cold rain and from the murderous grip she had on her iPhone. When her editor picked up she said. 'Phil, is it true about Gleason?'

Phil Gibbs puffed out a breath that sounded like a small explosion against her ear. 'Dena Parish found the emails,' he said. 'She was using Gleason's computer to send a quick message. I mean, we were going to check everyone anyway. Request by Wade Crittenden. Didn't even know he knew Tess Delaney, but then he does know Ellison Thorne's brother, so I guess that's how he fits into this. Wade's a police force within himself, you know? He's the go-to man for most of the police departments in the Northwest, even though criminology's not his thing. Still, he's Wade Crittenden, isn't he? If he says make it so, no one's going to argue. Turns out he was right again. It was someone in the press.

'Anyway, like I said, Dena found the emails by accident. Gleason said it was nothing, but they didn't sound like nothing to me. Scary shit, Flannery. Scary shit. Hard to believe he was right here in our midst spewing out all that horrible stuff all along and we didn't know it. I mean, I thought he seemed awfully interested in what was going on with the Tess situation, but then who wasn't? Jesus, he was even out there with you quite a bit, wasn't he?'

Carla felt ice snake up her spine. 'All day yesterday.' Quickly she calculated the time, and ... 'Phil,' she spoke slowly, mostly to be able to hear her own voice above the fluttering in her ears. 'Phil, Gleason was with me until the rain started at four this morning. We were playing cribbage. I sent him home, told him I'd call him back if anything happened.'

Carla was a freelancer; it wasn't unusual to have some of the real Web-Z staff on stories with her, and Gleason was decent with a camera. Web-Z usually went for more fluff and human interest than she did.

'So?' came the reply she barely heard.

'Nothing. I've gotta go.' She disconnected and held the umbrella gripped between her neck and shoulder to steady it as she began to text. She wasn't sure why she did it. She must be insane. With her fingers unsteady from more than just the cold, it took her three attempts at the text, but eventually she managed it and read it back, wiping residual rain from the screen. Then she sent it. To the stalker, hoping against hope that it had all been a lie and that Gleason had just been pulling her chain too.

What time were you at Thorne's mansion last night?

The reply was almost instant. So much so, in fact, that she jumped and uttered a little yelp that caused Mike Pittman to glare at her like she was some nutter.

Not long after dark. I told you, I was home in time for a midnight snack. Oh yes, I saw the news, Carla! Who knew that our dear Tess had so many admirers?

Almost before she actually knew what was happening, Carla broke ranks from the soggy front lawn vigil and ran to the motorhome, slipping and sliding on the mud-slickened lawn and drawing the attention of several of the press in her less than graceful departure. She crawled into the driver's seat and started the engine. How she managed to get out of the neighbourhood without hitting someone or something was beyond her. In her peripheral vision she could see Mike Pittman, now standing on the sidewalk at the edge of the lawn, no doubt trying to decide whether or not to follow her. At the moment, she didn't give a fuck what he did. This was way more than just a story.

As she hit the freeway faster than her dad would have approved of her driving in his motorhome, she punched in the Pneuma Inc. switchboard on her iPhone. She still had the number from when she was working on the story from John Day. When the operator picked up, she didn't wait for a greeting.

'I need to talk to Wade Crittenden. It's urgent.' She sounded like she'd just run a marathon.

'I'm sorry, but Mr. Crittenden isn't available at the moment. Could I take a message?'

She nearly hung up on the woman, but thought better of it. 'This is Carla Flannery, I'm a journalist. I need to talk to him about Tess Delaney's stalker. I'm serious. It's urgent.' She recited her cell number, then repeated it. 'It's urgent. I mean it!' she said, then she hung up and stepped on the gas.

Chapter Twenty-five

He switched off his cell phone. He didn't want to be interrupted, not even by Carla, busy playing her little detective games. Though she was entertaining, she was just a diversion, just someone he could toy with until he got what he wanted. The fact that someone else would be getting the blame for some silly little email threats was also irrelevant. Whoever it was could be of no real consequence or he would never have got caught. He wasn't jealous that someone else had got the attention. It wasn't the attention he wanted, at least not yet. It was nothing, really. Nothing at all compared to what he was about to do. The man would be totally eclipsed for his petty little dabblings when the world discovered what he had planned. In the background, the television whispered. Her television. He only had it on to listen for the latest news as the Tess Delaney saga unfolded. He could hardly contain himself when he thought about the next chapter, the one no one could have ever guessed in ten lifetimes, the one even she couldn't guess.

As he walked from room to room, he took in the scent of her; sweet, so sweet. He had caught that sweet scent in the woods the other night, but then it was contaminated by the reek of sex, by the stench of Thorne. Here, in her private space, in her flat, it was the pure, distilled, exquisite essence of her. Not of Tess Delaney, not of K. Ryde, not of the Bird Woman or any of the other people she had been in her deceptive life, but of Kendra Davis, raw, laid bare, Kendra Davis in the place where she would have never brought anyone for sex. He was sure she'd never brought Thorne here. He would have known if she had. This was the place she would keep from everyone, maybe even her closest friends. And he knew her well enough to know that here, in this place, on her home turf, she did have friends, powerful friends. But even they were no match for him. They only made the game more interesting. They would only make the final chapter more satisfying.

It was a small place, much smaller than she could afford, but then she wasn't all that concerned with material things. He had always liked that about her. She was more concerned with ordering other peoples' lives and the challenge they presented in their disorder. The place was as Spartan and as distilled as her essence that hung in the air. He was sure, remembering who she was, how she was, that everything, every little thing had a purpose. She was not sentimental. She was not a collector of mementoes. When he knew her, she lived in the moments she created, lived as a creature other than herself. He had never known her as herself. When he knew her, she was a mystery like none he'd ever tackled before, a mystery worth studying, worth waiting for. And now he would know her more fully than he had ever dreamed possible.

He moved into her bedroom and was delighted to find that her bed was made, meticulously made. Of course she probably had someone do it for her. She could afford it. But then again, he couldn't really imagine her letting a stranger touch her personal things, not even in something as mundane as making her bed. Carefully, almost reverently, he sat down on the edge of it, on the side she slept on, he could tell by the books, by the reading lamp, by the alarm clock. Then he took a deep, shuddering breath as though he was about to reverence the divine, as though he was about to step onto holy ground, onto a place that wasn't quite safe to step. Welling with emotions he had held inside himself for over a year, he laid back on it, pressing his body gently into the place where she slept and dreamed. He didn't put his feet up; that would have been wrong, like he was invading her privacy, like he was desecrating a sacred place. But the pillow! Oh, dear God in heaven, the pillow smelled so powerfully of her. It smelled of her sleep, it smelled of her dreams. And oh how he wondered what she dreamed. Did she ever dream of him? He'd tried so hard, when he knew her before, to make sure that she would remember him in her dreams. He wanted that more than anything else from her; that she would dream of him, that even when she slept she would never be rid of him. Oh yes, he wanted that! He buried his face in her pillow and inhaled as though he could take her very essence into himself, as though he could capture her spirit that way. But really, no hocus pocus would be necessary. He would need no magic. It would be easy. So very easy.

His hand strayed to his fly, which was now tight and uncomfortable. How could it not be when he was in her home, in her bed, surrounded by her essence, surrounded by her things? For a second he lay in a foetal position, very careful to keep his feet off the bed, and rocked against himself. The feel of her was almost more than he could endure. He cried out and stood quickly, breathing deeply, closing his eyes, focusing – focusing. Not yet. The time wasn't right yet. He could control himself just a little bit longer. He could save himself for her.

When he was sure he wouldn't disgrace himself, he made his way back to the desk in the tiny living room. Her laptop sat closed in standby mode, and he couldn't resist a message to her, a single message for old time's sake. It would be the sweetest gift. It would make her ready for their coming together as nothing else could.

He opened her email account, paying no attention to the messages that were there. They didn't matter to him; nothing else mattered to him about her past. There was only now, this moment, and he would extend it to include her, and this would be the beginning. He began to type an email.

For a long moment Kendra, Garrett, and Don sat in front of the television as the news ended with a recap of the arrest of Tess Delaney's stalker. At last, Garrett flicked the off switch on the remote and the silence came back into focus, hindered only by the soft drumming of the rain.

'It's over then,' Kendra said at last.

Both men nodded. And for another long moment they sat in the rain-pocked silence as though the remote had somehow switched them all off as well, as though the whole world had gone into standby.

It was Kendra who broke the silence. 'Good.' She shoved to her feet and grabbed her BlackBerry from the coffee table. 'Then I'm out of here.' She headed toward the front door.

'What the ...? Kendra, where are you going?' Garrett pushed off the sofa to follow her, ignoring Don. 'Kendra, what are you doing?'

At the front door, she stuffed the device into her bag, which she hoisted onto her shoulder. Then she turned to him, and the look on her face was cold, distant. 'I quit, Garrett.' She nodded to the door. 'I'm not speaking to the press. I don't care what you tell them. That's up to you. But I quit.'

He felt like the floor had fallen away from under his feet. He reached for her arm. 'Kendra, no, you can't, you can't leave now. We're not finished.'

She jerked away and wiped at her welling eyes with the back of her hand. 'We are finished, Garrett. There's nothing else for us to do, and I don't work for people who don't listen to me.'

'Jesus, Kendra, this is not about work, it hasn't been about work for a long time now, you have to know that.'

She raised a hand and grabbed the door handle. 'I don't know that, Garrett. I don't know anything anymore.' She glanced at the door. 'I'm going. Don't make a scene. It won't do you or Tess any good.' Then she turned and walked out the door, startling the soggy press with the unexpected visitation.

He started after her, but before he could clear the door, Don grabbed him in a firm hand and pulled him back, slamming the door shut as he did so, and Garrett was on him, fists first. 'Get off me. Get off me! I can't let her go, goddamnit!'

He landed a blow to Don's jaw and Don would have gone down if he hadn't caught himself with a hand against the wall. He shook his head, hard, then grabbed Garrett by both shoulders, risking another onslaught.

'Garrett! Garrett, listen to me! Let her go. She's right. Leave it. You can go after her later. Hell, I'll even drive you if you want me to, but you have to drop this until cooler heads prevail.'

'She's angry at me for doing exactly what she would have done if she'd been in my shoes,' Garrett yelled. 'The woman ran into the woods after me like some crazy lady, like she could save the world, like, like, like …'

'Like she wanted you safe, I know,' Don said. 'Like she was afraid of losing you.' He eased his arm around Garrett's shoulders and guided him back to the sofa in the living room. 'She's scared. That's all, she's scared. I could see it in her eyes. Give her a little space, Garrett, and let her breathe. Just let her breathe.'

'I can't lose her, Don.' His control broke. 'Fuck this! I'm going after her!'

He sprang from the sofa just as his BlackBerry buzzed an incoming message. He grabbed it up and felt his whole body tense as he viewed the screen.

'It's from her. Wait a minute. Something's wrong.' Garrett fiddled with the device, nearly dropping it before he figured out what was going on. 'This is Kendra's BlackBerry. She took mine, then. She's probably emailing to say she has mine and …' His words died in his throat and the world fell away as he opened the email.

Hello Bird Woman,

I'm back at long last, and I've been missing you terribly. Surely you knew I'd find you. I know, I know. You thought I was dead, but honestly, darling, a love like ours can't be conquered by death. Surely you know that. You'll never guess where I am, loveliness. I'm right here in your delicious little apartment, and I'm writing this message from your laptop, even from your address. It's so much more personal that way, don't you think? Of course I won't be here when you leave that horrid Thorne. But don't worry, I'll find you when the time is right. And this time, Bird Woman, I won't take no for an answer.

My Deepest Love,
Edge
P.S.: LOVE the Mustang!

Garrett was still reading the message as he frantically tried to call Kendra on his land line.

'She probably isn't picking up,' Don said. 'Let me try.'

There was no response. Garrett forwarded the email to Wade, along with a text saying he was on his way to Kendra's house.

'Dear God, do you really think she'll catch him there?' Don asked.

'Probably not, but she's still not safe, and I have to find her.'

'What do you want me to do?' Don said, following Garrett to the front door.

'Call the police. Tell the press what's going on. Maybe they can help, and keep trying to call her.'

Garrett shoved his way through the rain-soaked press and into his Jeep, which hadn't been driven in two days. The tires spun up a wild spray of rainwater as he accelerated out onto the street.

Kendra felt like someone had gutted her. And she felt scared, scared like she'd never been before. She drove down I-84 at break-neck speed, not really caring if she got stopped, not really caring about anything but getting home. Harris was right. It was a mistake for her to sleep with Garrett Thorne. It was a mistake for her to have anything to do with him. He was trouble. Already he was trying to control her life. Even when she was the boss, even when she was in charge, he had to take that away from her. Well, she couldn't have it. She couldn't! She would never allow herself to end up like her mother, controlled by some man who only used her, controlled by some man who always had room for one more when he got a little bored. There had been no sense of pride, no sense of self-worth, and in truth, she would have done anything for Garrett. It had got to that point. So close, so close. It was only when he walked out of Ellis's house this morning and tried to do what he did that she really realized just how close to losing control she was, just how close to losing what she'd fought so hard to win. And she couldn't have that. She just couldn't.

What was really terrifying was that, for the first time in her life, she understood. She understood exactly how her mother could feel so deeply for a man, so deeply that she would abdicate all control to him, that she would be willing to suffer all humiliation, willing to do whatever it took just to keep him by her side, just to have his affection from time to time. Jesus, she understood! And nothing, nothing in her whole life had ever been more terrifying. She didn't want to understand, damn it! She didn't want to empathize, and she hated Garrett Thorne for opening her to such self-loathing, to such weakness.

She wanted to get home, have a hot shower, then take the Mustang out for a good hard drive. It had been too long, and the Mustang always made her feel better. The Mustang always reminded her of who she was, of how tough she was, of how she could handle anything if she had to. She could handle anything, even Garrett Thorne. The thought made her eyes well. Goddamn him! Why couldn't he have just let her walk out the door in the beginning? And why had she been so hell-bent on connecting with Tess Delaney? Why couldn't she have just left well enough alone?

As soon as she could breathe again, as soon as she was a little more calm, she'd give Dee a call and see if she could have one of Ellis's drivers come and get the Audi. She practically stole it when Dee had gone for a shower and Ellis had been distracted in his study by a phone call. She tried to cheer herself with thoughts of an outing to The Boiling Point next weekend, but all she could think of was being there with Garrett. Well, there were certainly other clubs she could go to. The Boiling Point wasn't the only place to shake her booty. It wasn't even the best place to shake her booty. So why did she still feel so fucking miserable? Dee and Ellis didn't have to go clubbing to find each other. Dee and Ellis didn't try to control each other. And Garrett was Ellis's brother.

She tried to shake thoughts of him out of her head. He was Tess Delaney; he was Garrett Thorne, so different from his brother, so different. But she didn't care who the hell he was. He was not her problem anymore.

She pulled Dee's Audi into the underground parking garage in the space right next to the Mustang. Her lovely Mustang.

She gave the well-polished candy-apple red flank a stroke, as she locked up the Audi and headed for the elevator. A hot shower, that would be a good start. And then maybe she'd just drive on over to the coast, maybe to Lincoln City, and spend a couple of days driving the Mustang on the coastal highway. Surely that would take her mind off – things. She stepped into the elevator and let the doors shut behind her before she punched in her floor.

Chapter Twenty-six

'Where are you?' Wade Crittenden's voice huffed out of Carla's iPhone into her ear. There was no greeting.

She nearly cried with relief. She had been terrified the man would just write her off. 'I'm nearly at the parking garage of the Pneuma Building,' she managed, making no attempt to sound any less scared than she was. She wasn't sure she could have if she wanted to.

'Park in the reserved section on the ground floor,' he said. 'Take the elevator to the basement. I'll meet you there. And hurry up.' Then he hung up.

She'd heard Wade seldom bothered with pleasantries. He wasn't rude. He was just busy. And, frankly, this was no time for pleasantries anyway. Her father liked him, and that was good enough for her. She exited the street into the parking garage, miscalculating the turning ratio of the motorhome and driving the back wheels up across the curb with a loud *kathunk*. She didn't have to worry about finding the reserved spaces. Wade Crittenden himself was waiting in front of them, pacing back and forth with his arms folded across a dark blue hoodie that looked like a Wal-Mart special. She had also heard he wasn't exactly the king of dressing for success.

With him directing her, she managed to take up only three parking spaces, before he practically yanked the door open and looked up at her with wide eyes. 'Give me your iPhone,' he said.

She didn't argue, but handed it over. 'You know, then.'

'I know,' he said, nodding her in the direction of the open elevator. 'Garrett got an email. Well, Kendra did, actually, but they got their BlackBerries mixed up.'

'Who's Kendra?' she asked.

He ignored her question. 'Clearly this is not from Gleason, and Kendra doesn't know what's going on. She has her device turned off. Fortunately, she has Garrett's BlackBerry, so I can still track her with the satellite, but that still doesn't tell us where this guy is or if she's safe.'

'Who the hell is Kendra?'

'At Pneuma, I ask the questions,' he said as he herded her into the elevator. 'Not you.' He pushed a button that was not labeled, and they began to descend.

'You don't like journalists?'

'That's another question you've asked,' he said. 'I have no feelings one way or another about journalists. We'll just get more accomplished if I ask the questions.'

He was probably right. While he fiddled with her iPhone, she stood quietly next to him for the rest of the descent, which took a lot longer than she would have expected. She wondered how far underground they were. She'd heard Wade's domain was called the dungeon. Was that why?

'You're the one who exposed the mess at John Day,' he said, without looking up from her iPhone.

She found herself blushing. 'Yes.'

If she was expecting a compliment, she didn't get it. 'How did you get in touch with this man, and why didn't you tell anyone?'

She stiffened at the accusation in his voice. '*He* got in touch with *me*. And I'm a journalist, so you know why I didn't tell anyone, Mr. Crittenden.'

He looked up at her as the door to the elevator opened. 'And yet here you are. Why?'

God, the man was irritating. 'Because I know the person who wrote those first emails, and this is not him. If this asshole is anything like he sounds, Tess Delaney's in real danger.'

'You realize your life is in danger for coming to me with this?'

Suddenly her knees felt weak and she leaned against the wall to steady herself. 'I get the feeling my life might have been in danger anyway if I didn't do exactly what he wanted

259

me to do. Look, like I said, I didn't contact him. He contacted me. I have no idea why, but he did; me and Barker Blessing.'

Wade grunted. 'And Blessing is already wetting himself demanding police protection.'

'Has he been contacted again?' She switched into journalist mode instinctively. 'He promised he'd tell me.'

'If he had been contacted, he'd be squawking about it. Loudly.'

The elevator doors opened and they exited. At the end of a long hallway, Wade opened a set of double doors and motioned her through. Two more sets of double doors and a maze of twisting hallways later, Carla found herself standing nearly nose to nose with Ellison Thorne and his fiancée, Dee Henning. The look on Dee's face was agonized.

'It's the same guy,' Wade said without making any introductions, though at least on her part, none were needed.

Dee gave her a forced smile, but Ellison Thorne offered her his hand. 'Carla, it's a pleasure to meet you in person. I wish the circumstances were better.'

Before she could enjoy the fact that Ellison Thorne, *the* Ellison Thorne, knew who she was, she noticed Harris Walker sitting in front of a very large computer screen.

'Damn it, Wade, if he's not lying,' Walker said, 'if he is Edge, how can that be? He's supposed to be dead.'

'Kendra's not the only one who's good at reinventing herself,' Wade said.

'Who the hell is Kendra?' Carla asked, but she had pretty much already figured that Kendra must be Tess Delaney's real name.

'From the look of these emails and texts, I have no doubt they're written by the same man,' Wade said, handing Carla back her iPhone. 'I've got police in Santa Monica investigating and I've contacted the detectives Kendra used to find this Edge as well as some of my own contacts in the area. At the moment, though, I think it's a pretty good bet this is Edge.'

'She's still not answering.' Dee said. 'I've called her house, but there's no answer. I only hope she's gone somewhere else, anywhere else. She'll touch base soon because she has my car, but in the meantime, she might go out to Harris's place. That's often a place where we run away to, all three of us.'

'If he knows her, he'll know that,' Harris said. 'Thing is, Kendra's unpredictable. She might just take a flight to Spain and call us when she gets there.'

'I wish to God she would,' Dee said. 'At least she'd be away from him.'

'Not necessarily,' Wade said. 'If he's been in her house, we can't predict how much else he knows or how easily he can track and follow her. Best find her ASAP.'

The elevator had only gone one floor when Kendra punched the stop button. For the first time she could ever remember, she didn't know what to do. When her anger at Garrett had dissipated a little bit and it sunk in that the stalker had been caught, that Tess Delaney could go back to her life without Kendra as a front person, that Garrett really didn't need her any more, she suddenly felt awash in a sea of emptiness. He didn't need her, that's what it all boiled down to. Now everything was over, he really didn't need her. And she wanted him to. Dear God, she wanted him to. Ellis needed Dee. He'd announced it right in front of the whole world. And Dee needed him back. There was nothing wrong with that. It's exactly what every person in the world wanted, what Garrett believed everyone could have. He really did believe it. And he'd wanted her to believe it too. He told her she deserved romance. Then she'd run away scared.

Maybe she'd just take Dee's car back home. Then maybe she would talk to her friend, the one who would know something about being brave enough to go for the happy ever after, the one who would never lie to her and never steer her wrong.

She shivered and, for the first time since she'd left Garrett's, realized just how cold and wet she was from her mad race to and from the car in the rain. She pushed the button on the elevator and it began to ascend again. She'd just change clothes, then she'd call Dee.

It was only as she turned the key in the lock she realized

that she had Garrett's BlackBerry instead of her own, and there were at least a dozen messages, and that many missed calls and texts from her device. She smiled down at the screen. Perhaps it was fate. She'd have to get in touch with him now. Anyway, when she moved back to Portland, when her world fell apart around her, she had made herself a promise, that she'd never run away again. She'd come pretty damn close to breaking that promise just now. She was just about to send him a text when the first text from her device came up.

Kendra, don't go to your apartment! I repeat DO NOT GO to your apartment.

You're ...

She never got to finish the text.

'She's at her apartment,' Wade yelled into the phone to Garrett. She just got there. I've got police on the way over. And it looks like you're about ten minutes out or so.'

'I know! I know where I am,' Garrett yelled back. 'I'll be there as soon as I can.'

'Carla Flannery is here and her emails and text from the man match what you got.'

'Dee and Ellis?'

'They're here, and Harris,' Wade said.

Garrett white-knuckled the steering wheel and drove faster. 'Wade, if she gets in touch with you first or anyone there, I need you, all of you, to tell her something for me.' He didn't wait for Wade's response, but ploughed on. 'Tell her I love her.' He ignored Wade's uncomfortable sputterings at the other end of the phone and continued, 'Make her listen, Wade. Make her listen and don't let her be afraid. There's no reason to be afraid. Tell her I need her to know. Tell her that, and the very second I see her again I'll tell her in person.'

He disconnected and tried to breathe around the tightness in his chest. He wished to God he had ignored Don and marched right out into the rain after her. How could he have let this happen? Hadn't he loved her almost from the beginning? He just didn't want it to be her; he just didn't want to give her the satisfaction. And now, there was no one in the world he wanted to love but her, now there was no one else he wanted to give that satisfaction to. He couldn't lose her. He couldn't! He'd waited his whole life for Kendra Davis and he would do whatever he had to do to have her safe and sound and back in his arms.

He hadn't expected her or he wouldn't have lingered. But when the key turned in the lock, when he knew the inevitable was about to happen, everything in him went calm. It was fate, wasn't it? Fate had delivered her into his hands early, a reward for all of his patience, for all of his hard work.

She wasn't looking at him. She was looking at her cell phone. He was slightly out of her line of sight, still sitting in front of her laptop where he had been gorging on everything he could possibly discover about Kendra Davis – not the reinvented one, not the one pretending to be someone else, but the real one, the genuine article, the woman beneath all those layers, and oh, how he had longed to know her, to uncover her, to lay her bare to her very core.

And this, this was that magical moment, that split second in time before the world changed forever. This was the tipping point. She still didn't know he was there. She still thought she was alone and safe, and because of that, she was still so completely, so exquisitely at her ease that he wished he could freeze-frame the moment, he wished he could somehow capture it for posterity, so that he could bring it back and relive it time and time again long after he was finished with her.

But of course it couldn't last; the second would pass, and soon enough she would know. He watched with his heart in his throat, he waited for that instant when she knew. And when it happened it was a subtle thing, so minute at first that he almost didn't catch it, so miniscule the change that he sat frozen on the edge of the seat, not even daring to breathe, sat until his eyes burned from not blinking. And then he saw it; her agile fingers on the BlackBerry faltered. Her shoulders tensed. She sniffed and caught her breath. Her eyelids fluttered and her lovely full lips parted in a little gasp of surprise, as though she had just remembered something – something terrible.

For a second, the world shattered around her into a million shards of disbelief and horror. For a second, her mind rebelled, denied that this could be happening, denied that he could actually be sitting here in her home, in her space, that he could actually be – real. For a second, her body threatened to rebel as well, to allow itself to be overwhelmed by fear, to pass out on the floor, there at his mercy, to vomit the fear that raged through every cell of her body, to completely shut down. For a split second, she tried to wake up, certain it was a dream. But it wasn't. It was the nightmare she would have to deal with. And that all of this could happen in her head in less than the time it took to draw a startled breath would have astounded her in different circumstances.

She had but a second before she lost control. She knew he'd take from her as much as he could. She knew what she did in that second she had left could keep her alive.

He's here.

With the last shred of calm she could manage, she sent the text, took a deep breath, then turned and grabbed for the door. But she had locked it behind her, a habit her mother had hammered into her head from the time she was little, and he was on her before she could get it open. His breath too hot, exactly as she remembered, his scent both acrid and sweet, cloyingly sweet, exactly like before, his grip harsh, deliberately cruel, the horrid tattoo on his biceps swelling as he pulled her to him. As he tackled her from behind and pinned her arms to her side, she fought back the urge to gag at the scent of him. It hadn't been a bad scent when she first met him, it had meant nothing, but it soon came to mean fear and threat and despair. And worse than anything, it came to symbolize loss of control. *Think, Kendra, think!* she yelled inside herself. She had to stay focused. That was all she had; the only control left to her was not to panic, not to let him choose what went on inside her head. She relaxed in his arms and, with a hot palm, he smoothed her wet hair away from her ear and stroked her neck. She could feel the heat of him, too humid, too close.

'Not Bird Woman any more, I see.' He curled his fingers in

her hair so tightly that it almost hurt. 'And now, you're not Tess Delaney any more either, are you? I heard the news. Tess is rid of that horrible email stalker. I was so relieved when I heard. I knew with him out of the way, I'd have my Kendra Davis back and all to myself very shortly.'

'I'm not your Kendra Davis,' she half whispered, managing to sound much calmer than she really felt.

'Oh, I think you are. There's no one here but you and me, darling, and I'm much stronger than you.' As if to demonstrate, he bent her arm up behind her back until the joint of her shoulder popped and she sucked a sharp breath of pain, but held very still. 'And if you don't do exactly what I say, I also have a very sharp knife, and it doesn't matter to me, Kendra, it doesn't matter to me how I have to carve you up to make you behave yourself, to make you sorry for leaving me like you did, you'll still be beautiful to me, and I'll still want you, no matter if a few … parts are missing and I've left my mark so neither you or anyone else will ever again doubt that you belong to me.'

He levelled a wet, breathy kiss at her ear and she dug her nails into her hands and forced herself to breathe deeply. None of that had happened yet, none of those things he threatened. Garrett knew she was here. Garrett knew where she was, and she was as sure as she was of her own breath that he'd find her.

'I like your place,' he said, tightening his grip around her waist. 'Though I find it a bit claustrophobic. But then I suppose you don't spend much time here, do you? Out at all the clubs, are you? Being someone different every night? Hmmm?' The hand twisted her hair tightened but she refused to flinch.

'I'm more of a homebody these days,' she managed, uttering a gasp as his grip tightened and her scalp prickled with pain.

'I don't believe that for a minute, Kendra Davis. You could never be satisfied in one space in one body or fucking just one person for very long, not someone like you.' He nodded to the door. 'I saw the Mustang. Not a car a homebody would drive, would you say?'

'It was a gift,' she replied. 'That's all, it was a gift.'

He chuckled and his breath felt like it would scorch the skin off the side of her face. 'But a gift from someone who knew your tastes, Kendra. Don't deny it.' He pushed in closer to her, so close that she could barely breathe in his smothering embrace, so close that she could feel his hard-on raking against the wet back of her denim skirt. She could feel the tight shifting and rocking of his hips rucking it up a little at a time. 'Take me for a ride in it, Kendra. Come on, give me a peek at that wild woman who drove me insane with lust back in Santa Monica. I can force the issue, you know?' He released her hair and reached into his pocket. She heard a crisp mechanical click, then felt the cold, sharp edge of a blade against her throat. 'Don't make me start with the knife just yet, sweetheart.' He kissed her ear and nibbled at the lobe. 'I believe in foreplay. Lots and lots of foreplay, and I think our courtship should begin with a ride in a very sexy car. Isn't that what's supposed to happen? Isn't that romantic, Kendra? You and me in the Mustang out on the open road, anticipating all the fun we'll have when the drive ends.' He pressed the knife just hard enough for the blade to sting. 'Now, where are the fucking *keys*?'

'They're in my bag,' she managed, pressing back as tightly against his chest as she could to avoid the bite of the blade.

'Good girl.' He relaxed the tension on the knife just a little. 'Get them, and let's go.'

With hands made awkward by fear, she fumbled in the bag where she'd hung it on the peg next to the door and found the keys, wishing like hell there was something in there, anything she could use for a weapon. There might be a nail file somewhere in the bottom or an ink pen, but she'd never get the chance to use either of them at the moment. *Think, Kendra, think!*

'That's a girl,' he said again as she slowly, carefully pulled the keys from her bag and held them up for him to see. He took them from her hand and pocketed them. 'And now there's only one more thing we need to take care of and then you can take me for a ride.' He reached into her jacket pocket and pulled out the BlackBerry, and her heart sank as he tossed it onto the sofa.

'You won't be needing this anymore, darling. I'm the only one you have to speak to now, and I'll never be more than a blade's edge away.'

'Detectives in Santa Monica say that though the dead man they found in Edge's burnt-out house could have been someone else, it was assumed to be him. Apparently the body was so badly burnt that 100 per cent identification was impossible without DNA testing.' Wade turned off his BlackBerry. His half of the conversation had had everyone's full attention, and now he filled them in on the rest. 'They had no real reason to doubt. Besides, after the body was discovered, there was no sign of the man again. After all, he was dead.' Wade turned his attention to the big screen of the computer and pulled up a satellite map of the North-western US. 'There was no reason to suspect anything, no reason not to think Edge was dead. Fredrick Parks, that's the man's real name, and he's from North Dakota. But look at this.' He zoomed in on the map. 'Two weeks after Edge's supposed death, a liquor store was robbed in Priest Falls, Idaho. Look at the CCTV footage.'

Carla wondered how anyone could get hold of this kind of information. She wasn't sure whether to respect Wade Crittenden or fear him. She was certainly glad he was on her side.

Garrett, who was struggling through construction on I-5, had Kendra's BlackBerry on, listening.

'Sure as hell looks like him,' Harris said.

'But he's dead,' Wade said, 'so no one cares. No one bothers to check. Then –' a few more key strokes '– a couple comes home to Kalispell, Montana after spending the winter in Florida to discover their house on Flathead Lake has been squatted in all winter. Another couple who had rented out the cabin up the lake gave Edge's description. They said he told them he was renting the place for the winter. Since they weren't residents, they had no reason to doubt his story.

'About that same time, a couple from Yakima, Washington came back early from spending the winter in Australia to find their Jeep Cherokee missing. It turned up two months later in a deserted parking garage of a high-rise in Seattle. Again, very grainy CCTV footage shows a man that looks like Edge. The trail goes on, with every incident just far enough apart, time wise and distance wise, so that no one ever quite connects the dots.

'And then, two days ago, a dental hygienist in Nevada comes back from a holiday in Europe to find her Ford Focus stolen. And this was the footage at an all-night supermarket maybe an hour after the incident in the woods behind Ellis's house.'

'Same man,' Ellis said.

'He tried to walk out without paying, not sneaky or anything, the clerk said, but just like his mind was on something else. When the clerk confronted him he paid and made light of it, no problems. But the clerk called it in because he was suspicious. Said the man's jeans were wet up to his thighs and he looked like he'd been rolling in pine needles.'

'OK, I just got through the last of the construction,' Garrett's voice came over the speaker phone. 'I'll be at Kendra's in – Hold on. I'm getting a text. It's from Kendra!'

Everyone gathered around Wade's desk, where the speakers were rigged up.

'What does it say?' Dee asked, pressing in close.

The sound that came from Garrett's end of the phone was a desperate animal cry. 'He's here. That's all it says. He's here.' He cut the connection and all hell broke loose in Wade's boudoir.

Chapter Twenty-seven

Edge held her close to him in the elevator all the way down to the parking garage. The knife was under a jacket he had folded over his arm, and he knew exactly how to ease the point in close and threatening between her ribs. Kendra breathed from her diaphragm like Dee had taught her, like singers were supposed to do. That assured her enough oxygen and kept the knife from piercing her skin. He gave her no room, not an inch, and she yielded, yielded for her own protection. But only physically. Inside she held her ground, inside she'd drawn the line in the sand. She wouldn't allow him the space inside her head. Not this time.

In the parking garage, she walked to the Mustang, with him holding her close to his side like he was the most caring, most tender of lovers. He nodded to the driver's side. 'You drive, darling. I want to sit next to you, bask in your brightness, savour the moment.'

He stood over her while she buckled in, then he brushed the hair away from her forehead and settled a kiss just above the bridge of her nose. She forced herself not to stiffen. 'Don't think you can escape before I get around the car and into my seat.' He breathed the words against her throat. 'I'm as good with a knife from a distance as I am up close and personal. My aim won't be fatal, but I promise it'll be painful, debilitating, and marring. And if I decide I'm bored with the knife, there's always this little baby to make things more interesting ...' He leaned forward and slipped a gun from the waistband of his trousers, just enough for her to get a good view of it. 'And yes, I'm as good with it as I am with the knife. You're mine, Kendra. Best get used to it now, and things will go easier.'

But she wasn't. She wasn't his. She'd never be his. She said the words in her head, enunciating every one clearly over and over like a mantra, reminding herself that she was still in control. That there were things he could never ever take from her. This time she knew that. This time she was certain.

He slid in next to her, handed her the keys, then shifted in the seat expectantly. 'Well, what are you waiting for?'

'Where shall I go?' she asked.

'To my place, sweetheart. I've prepared it especially for you.'

No! she screamed inside her head. No matter what she had to do, she would never go to his place. She knew in her gut if she did, she'd never escape. She didn't mind dying. That was inevitable, but she wasn't about to endure the long suffering and the humiliation he had planned for her before she got there. She knew that ultimately he had been responsible for Lila's death, and she wasn't about to give him time to drive her to such an end. She didn't know what she'd do, but she'd end it all before she got to his place. One way or another.

As she pulled out of the parking garage and made her way toward the freeway, he rested a hand on her thigh and heaved a sigh as he admired the Mustang. 'Don't worry, Kendra, I'll take very good care of it after you're gone. I promise.'

She shivered at the thought, but steeled herself. She had to concentrate. She had to find a way out of this. As she approached the entrance to the freeway, he shook his head.

'Not on the freeways, darling. I hate freeways. They're no way to put a fine car like this through its paces, and really, it would be a shame for me not to let you put this lovely vehicle to the test one last time. We'll take the back roads.'

Garrett recognized the stolen Ford Focus in the parking garage not far from Dee's Audi, and his hopes soared only to crash again when he found the door to her flat unlocked. Kendra would never leave her home so vulnerable. He pushed it open quietly, hoping against hope that they were still inside. But he could tell by the feel that the flat was empty. He gave the door a hard kick with his foot and cursed out loud. Goddamn it, she'd been through enough, and he'd opened her up to all of it, all over again. He grabbed Kendra's BlackBerry from his pocket.

'Wade, they're not here!' he yelled into the phone as soon as he heard it connect. 'They're not fucking here!'

'What do you mean they're not there?' Wade yelled back 'The signal indicates they're right there in her flat.'

'Well they're not. I don't know what the hell's going on and ... Fuck!' Garrett's eye caught the bright plastic of his own BlackBerry where it lay discarded on the couch and suddenly he felt like he was being swallowed alive by the horror of what that meant. 'The BlackBerry.' He forced the words up through the cold fear clenching at his throat. 'She left it. It's on the sofa.'

'What the hell do you mean she left it?' He heard Harris's panicked voice. 'She wouldn't leave it.'

'Only if she were forced to,' Wade replied.

'Goddamn it!' Garrett ran a frantic hand through his hair. 'There has to be something else we can do, there has to be.'

'We've got to have something we can track,' Wade said. 'I can extrapolate from the places where Parks has been spotted, but without some way of tracking her, I can't narrow it down any more than that.'

'Damn it! That means they could be anywhere. He could be taking her anywhere.' Garrett could hear Harris on the speaker phone.

Frantically he looked around the room for something, for anything, and his eyes came to rest on a photo of Kendra dressed in jeans and a black tank top standing next to a bright red Shelby Mustang. 'Wait a minute.' He picked up the photo and squinted at it. 'Can you track a car by that satellite?'

'Only if it has a transponder,' Wade said.

'It's a fucking Shelby Mustang, for Chrissake!' Garrett yelled. Over the phone, he could hear Dee and Harris practically screaming to Wade that it was a gift from Devon Barnet. He talked over them. 'I saw Dee's car in the parking garage, and the Ford Focus was there, but no sign of the Mustang. And Edge mentioned it in the email. Maybe he took it. It's a lot nicer ride than a Focus. Plus, the asshole had to know what it means to her.'

'Wait a minute. Wait a minute.' Wade's voice came in tight little bursts. Garrett could hear his keystrokes against the computer keyboard. 'It's a vintage car, a one-off. I can't imagine there not being a transponder, in case it ever got stolen. Surely Barnet would have given Kendra those details. Hold on, I've got her iPhone here for safe keeping. If it's there, I'll find it.'

'I'll look on her laptop.' Garrett was already trying to navigate Kendra's computer for the information. On both ends of the phone connection, there was complete silence except for the dual tapping of the keyboards.

It seemed like an eternity went by before Wade yelled into the phone, 'I've got it. I've got it! And the Mustang's on the move. I'm transmitting the details to the police.'

'Tell me where they are, Wade,' Garrett yelled. 'I can't be very far behind them.'

'You're not, Wade replied. 'They're off the freeway. It looks like he's taking the slow route, probably to try out the Mustang on the winding roads. I can get you there faster, Garrett. I'm about to become your sat nav. Are you ready?'

Garrett grabbed up both BlackBerries and charged out the door. He didn't wait for the elevator. He bolted down the stairs, the photo still clenched in one hand.

Edge was rattling on and on about how he had suffered without her, how badly she had hurt him, how hard the year had been for him, scheming and planning how he would be with her again. But Kendra was only half listening.

She was thinking of Garrett. She had the rudiments of a plan forming in her mind now, but it was a plan she probably wouldn't survive. That was all right. It had been a good life, and the last few days with Garrett Thorne had been the best ever. He had been the bright spot; he had almost convinced her she could have her happy ever after, and that she could have it with him. If she kept him in her head, if she focused on memories of him, of being in his arms, of laughing with him, of dancing with him, of making love with him, then she could stay safe from the terror with which Edge surrounded her. She could stay focused on what she had to do, and she would have the courage to do it.

She loved him, she loved Garrett Thorne! Suddenly, the darkness that threatened to close around her was run through with the brilliance of that one thought. She loved Garrett Thorne. She loved him with all of her heart, and loving him, being with him, made her more herself than she had ever been in her whole life. She could die knowing that. She could die knowing that he was right, that she could love, that love was as much for her as it was him, or Jessie and Amanda in *Texas Fire*, or Dee and Ellis. Her only regret was that she hadn't allowed herself to realize it while she was still with him, that she hadn't told him. God how she wished she had told him!

She couldn't bear the thought of how he would suffer because of what she was about to do, but she saw no way out. Without the BlackBerry Wade had given her, there was no way they would ever find her in time, and she wasn't brave enough to endure Edge's torture passively and wait, hoping against hope that Garrett would find her before Edge drove her insane. Garrett had people who loved him. He had people who understood how amazing he was, even if he didn't. They would help him heal. And she wanted that for him. She wanted him to heal. God, she wished she could tell him, and now she didn't even have that option left to her. The ache of loss was pushed aside by rage, rage that Edge believed it was his right to take this from her. He might take away her chance to tell Garrett how she felt, he might take away her chance to try for her happy ending, but her rage he couldn't take from her! And, in the end, it would be enough to help her do what she had to, to deny the bastard what he most wanted.

She pressed down a little harder on the accelerator. She'd been doing it gradually since they'd left the apartment so he wouldn't notice. She had the advantage of growing up near here. It meant she knew the place like the back of her hand. She knew where they were and had a pretty good idea of where they were heading. That meant she knew exactly what to do and where. Dee and Harris and she used to put Harris's old beater of a pick-up through its paces out here. The place was hilly, pocked with scrub evergreens struggling on the edge of survival. The main road was paved, but narrow and old, but from it muddied gouges of trails used by motorbikes and four-wheelers snaked off over the rutted hills in all directions. It was also bisected by several disused logging roads. Not far up the road, there was one spot that had just what she needed for her plan to work. She pressed just a little harder on the gas, and Edge whooped.

'Goodness, Bird Woman, you really do know how to fly, don't you?'

'You said you wanted to see what she could do,' Kendra said. 'I've had her long enough to know. Best gift I ever received.' And at the moment, she meant that with all her heart.

'This route should put you out ahead of them,' Wade yelled into Garrett's BlackBerry, which lay on his seat with the speakerphone on. 'But just barely, so you'll have to haul ass. You in the Jeep?'

'I am,' Garrett said. 'Just get me there.'

'You need to make a right just ahead. It's an old logging road, and not much of one, but it'll do the trick.'

'I see it,' Garrett said, sliding into the sharp corner and banking hard to make the turn, barely managing it without turning the Jeep over. The rain had let up for the moment, so it didn't affect the visibility. He sped down the road, bouncing and jostling against the seatbelt 'How am I doing?' he shouted at the device.

'You're fine. You're all right, just don't slow down.'

The words were barely out of Wade's mouth before he hit the first major mud puddle. Water splashed in waves all around him. He cursed and turned on the wipers. 'Christ, Wade, it's a muddy mess up here.' The Jeep slid dangerously to one side, and he felt the back wheel on the driver's side sink.

'Can you drive off the road, on the side?' Wade yelled.

But the wheel dropped with a sickening lurch, and the tire spun.

'No! Goddamn it, no!' Garrett cursed and downshifted. The engine groaned and the wheel spun, slinging mud out in a high arc behind the vehicle.

'Garrett, you've got to go. Now!' Wade yelled. The sound of his voice was drowned out by the revving of the engine as Garrett threw the Jeep into reverse and eased off the gas, struggling like hell to control the panic rising in his chest.

But the Jeep wouldn't budge.

Ignoring Wade's rising panic on the speaker phone, Garrett undid the safety belt and practically threw himself from the driver's seat, frantically looking around in the scrub and deadfall until he found what he needed. He made a mad squelch and lurch of a dash for several limbs about the size of his arm, blow-down from the wind that had accompanied the rain in the early hours. There were plenty of needles still on the branches. Slipping and sliding in the mud, he lunged for them, tugged them with all his strength until they were free from the undergrowth. Then he nearly lost his balance as he slid back to the rear of the Jeep, shoving and stuffing and cramming the branches down into the hole that the spinning of the tire had created, angling just right to create traction. Dear God, it had to work! It just had to! Back in the seat, he belted in and ignored Wade, who was still yelling, along with everyone else in the dungeon. Then he carefully reversed only slightly. It took every ounce of patience to go slow and easy, just enough for the limbs to settle into the hole. Then, even though every nerve in his body was screaming for him to hurry, he eased the Jeep back in gear and carefully, gently pressed on the accelerator. The Jeep jerked hard and sank dishearteningly into the mud with the tire spinning. But, just when Garrett was ready to jump out of the Jeep and run for it, it inched forward, spun, and then juddered and jostled up out of the rut.

'I'm out! I'm out,' he yelled above the roar of the engine. But hope was short-lived as he looked up at the road in front of him to see nothing but a sea of mud. 'Wade, we've got to go cross country. The road's a mud bath.'

'All right.' Wade's voice was tight, his words clipped. Garrett could hear him frantically typing on the keyboard. 'I've got the contour map. It's not too steep or rocky. If you can get through the woods, you can get there, and still join the road just ahead of the Mustang.'

'I can do it.' Garrett made a sharp left off the muddy track and barreled into the woods, bouncing and jolting and dodging trees and roots as best he could.

'The police are on their way,' Wade yelled. 'They're not far behind, but they'll have to take the main road.'

'Just get me there, Wade.' Garrett downshifted and tromped the gas. 'Just get me there before the Mustang.'

She saw the stand of trees, and she nearly wept that they hadn't been cut down as the natural landscape slowly lost the battle to the growing industrial site. They were exactly like she remembered them, if a bit more scraggly. It would be over soon. She could feel his gaze locked on her face, and she did her best to look terrified, stressed – not that hard to do under the circumstances. But hiding her rage was more difficult. She felt her bottom lip tremble and she fought back the tears. He didn't know they were as much tears of rage as they were tears for what she was about to lose, as much as they were tears of fear. He didn't know, and that was good.

'There, there, sweetheart, don't cry. It won't do you any good. I'm not swayed by your tears or your pleading. There was a time I might have been, but don't expect sympathy when you still stink of Garrett Thorne. Don't expect leniency when you deserve everything I can dish out to you and then some.'

Let him lecture, she thought. Let him think what he wanted. She picked out the tree, the perfect tree, and stomped on the accelerator as hard as she could. She hoped it didn't hurt too much. Then she focused everything in her on thoughts of Garrett in her arms.

'What the –?' Those were the last words Edge got out of his mouth before she stepped hard on the gas. She screamed her rage like a banshee as the Mustang ploughed into the tree, and the unbelted Edge went flying through the windshield. With the sickening crunch of metal, the Mustang's front end crumpled into the tree and the engine spluttered and died. The hard jerk of the safety belt forced the breath from her lungs and felt like it would cut her in two. The world went out of focus and wavered, threatened to go dark, and then cleared. Along with the clearing of her vision came the full understanding that she wasn't dead, that her timing had been even more perfect than she could have hoped. She couldn't see how Edge could have possibly survived smashing his way through the windshield into the woods. Surely that alone must have broken his neck. She struggled to get out of the seat belt and out of the car, then slipped on the wet ground, and fell to her knees, squinting to see as the rain set in again. She had just managed to get her feet when a muddied Jeep roared out of the woods and screeched to a stop right in front of her.

For a second, she didn't recognize the man who shoved his way out of the driver's seat covered with almost as much mud as the Jeep was. But then he spoke. 'Kendra! Dear God, Kendra, are you OK?'

She broke into a run toward Garrett, afraid to say his name, afraid to say anything for fear it was all just a dream.

She was never quite sure of what happened next. There were police cars coming up the road. She could hear the sirens like background noise as Garrett pulled her fiercely to him. 'Jesus, woman, I love you. I can't lose you. Don't you know that? I love you! I love you, Kendra Davis. Do you hear me? I love you!'

She was just about to tell him she loved him too, just about to tell him she wanted to be with him more than anything when out of the corner of her eye she saw movement, movement that registered with a cold prickle up the back of her neck. There was a flash of silver through the air, then Garrett yelled like a wildcat and shoved her hard. She landed on the ground with a jolt and rolled, confused, stunned. It was then she saw Garrett lurching, falling to his knees, and there was blood. There was so much blood where the knife lodged in his side. And suddenly Edge stood over him, covered from head to toe in pine straw and mud.

Chapter Twenty-eight

For Kendra, everything downshifted to slow motion. She knew only two things, that Garrett Thorne loved her, and that she would not let this monster take that away from her. Ever!

As Edge drew back to kick Garrett in the stomach, somehow Garrett caught Edge's leg with an arm and unbalanced him. That was all it took. Kendra saw the world through a rage like nothing she'd ever experienced before.

Garrett pulled the knife out of his side with an angry snarl and struggled to pull himself to his feet and take advantage, but she was faster, and she wasn't injured. She launched herself at Edge, screaming at the top of her lungs. 'You sonovabitch! I'm not yours! I'll never be yours!'

She landed a jarring kick in the man's groin, and before he could utter more than a harsh grunt, she followed it with a hard right cross to his jaw. The impact of Kendra's unexpected attack sent him flailing backward, his feet slipping and sliding on the muddy ground before his went down on his back. There was another sharp grunt as the breath left his lungs, then a cry of utter surprise. His eyes teared and his right hand jerked spastically to his chest.

Kendra skidded on the wet pine straw and nearly fell backward, but just as she gathered her balance for another attack she noticed the front of Edge's white T-shirt bloomed bright red, and in the confusion that gripped her, it took her a second to see the jagged, sharpened stake that was the remains of a nearby tree branch broken off by last night's wind and storm. It ran through Edge's chest just below his sternum. He uttered another startled grunt, convulsed once, then his eyes glazed and he didn't move again.

She watched his life's blood drain away with a strange indifference that later might be the stuff of nightmares, but for now she just wanted to be sure he wouldn't come back for more. Then she turned and practically fell onto her knees next to Garrett.

'Call an ambulance!' she shouted as the first police shoved their way out of their cars, guns drawn. 'Damn it, call an ambulance now!' She struggled out of her jacket, barely noticing the cold or the hammering rain. 'You shouldn't have pulled the knife out of the wound,' she heard herself shouting at Garrett, as she pressed the jacket tight against his side to stop the bleeding. 'Damn it, Garrett, you've only got so much blood you, know?' Her words came out as a sob and she struggled to see through the tears.

Garrett winced and grabbed her other hand with a grip that belied the amount of blood he'd lost. 'Jesus, woman, you're bossy to the end, aren't you?'

'No, Garrett,' she sobbed. 'No! This is not the end! I'm gonna be bossy for a long time to come, so you'd better get used to it. Now shut up and stop bleeding!'

His eyelids fluttered and he winced again. His lips were pale and pressed tight in pain but he forced a smile. 'I suppose I could get used to that,' he managed. 'The bossy bit, I mean.' He nodded to the crumpled Mustang. 'How did you do that?'

'Stunt driving course. Gift from another satisfied client.'

'Pity about the Mustang,' he managed.

'It's just a car, Garrett. It's just a car.'

She placed a finger against his lips and her heart nearly broke at his effort to kiss it. 'I love you, Garrett Thorne, and you were right. You were right about me, I do deserve romance, and I want it from you, so stop bleeding, all right, just please stop bleeding, damn it!'

He uttered a little sigh that was some cross between pain and, she hoped, something much happier. 'I'll do my best,' he managed, squeezing her hand hard.

From out of nowhere, Ellis and Dee arrived with Harris and Stacie right behind them, all piling out of Ellis's Jeep. She barely noticed them crowding around. Ellis gently placed his jacket over Kendra's trembling shoulders and Harris knelt next to her with a first aid kit.

'Let me see,' he said, gently easing Kendra aside, just enough that he could tend Garrett's wound. Another one of Harris's outdoor talents was that he was well-trained in first aid.'

Garrett eyed Harris suspiciously. 'You're not going to put the knife back in, are you?'

Harris grunted and bit his lip in concentration. 'I might if you ever do anything to hurt my best friend.'

Garrett forced himself into a half sitting position, leaning heavily against Kendra. 'Your best friend happens to be the woman I love, Walker. I would never hurt her. In fact –' he gave another squeeze of her hand '– I plan to do my best to make her very happy, if she'll let me.'

'See that you do,' Harris said. 'Or this will seem like a little scratch when I get through with you.'

Garrett lost consciousness just as the ambulance arrived and, in spite of Harris assuring her that the wound wasn't as bad as it looked, Kendra couldn't believe it, wouldn't believe it until the emergency room doctor at the hospital had reassured her.

Garrett was lucky, the doctor said. The knife missed both the heart and the lungs. They had kept him in the hospital for observation, and he had been pretty heavily sedated, but not so much that he hadn't called for Kendra in the night, and not so much that he hadn't been aware she was there, in spite of hospital regulations, curled up on the bed next to him. She wasn't about to let him out of her sight again. Dee had brought her fresh clothes, and she had cleaned up as best she could in the bathroom of Garrett's hospital room. In spite of exhaustion, she slept very little, and when she did, she was lulled to sleep by the slow, even in and out of Garrett's breathing, by the steady, powerful beat, beat, beat of his heart, beneath her hand resting gently on his chest.

If anything, the crowd of reporters on the front lawn had swollen. But then the story that Carla Flannery broke about the chase and the ultimate death of Fredrick "Edge" Parks, the stalker of Tess Delaney and other women in the past, had captured everyone's imagination. And what was about to happen next would be even more of a surprise.

Kendra and Garrett stepped out of the limo into rain-washed sunshine. There was a low mumbling among the press and they parted for the couple as they walked up to the porch through the strobe and click of flashing cameras and the myopic focus of television lenses. Don was waiting for them. He gave Kendra a kiss on the cheek and Garrett a gentle pat on the back.

'Are you sure?' Kendra whispered against Garrett's ear, to the click, click, click of cameras capturing their intimate moment for all the world to see. Beyond the porch they could hear a television reporter's excited voice giving her audience the blow by blow, along with a recap of the events of the Tess Delaney saga to date.

'I've never been more sure of anything in my whole life,' Garrett whispered back. He kissed her tenderly and took a deep breath. Then he squared his shoulders and turned to face the press, keeping a tight grip on Kendra's hand.

'I'm sorry you've all had to wait for our statement.' He offered them a teasing smile. 'But we've been recovering at my brother's house for the past two days, and he and his fiancée only just now let us out on good behavior. As far as the attempted abduction of Kendra Davis, and the death of Frederick Parks, who has had a long history of violence, Carla Flannery has pretty well covered those details. That's not what I'm here to talk about.'

Again it was the impatient Mike Pittman who spoke out. 'Kendra Davis? Who is Kendra Davis?'

Garrett and Kendra looked at each other, and Kendra nodded. 'I'm Kendra Davis.'

The press went wild, and it took a few seconds for everyone to calm down again. When they did, Garrett spoke into the enormous silence that followed. 'I hired Kendra Davis to play the part of Tess Delaney because I didn't want her identity made public during the Golden Kiss Awards.'

There was another low murmur of the press and everyone

shuffled closer.

'I thought that was Mr. Bachman's job, to hire help for Ms. Delaney,' Pittman said.

'Ultimately it was Tess's choice,' Garrett answered. 'It has been Tess's choice from the beginning, and it still is.' He shot Kendra an adoring glance that made her knees weak. 'It's impossible for Tess Delaney to allow Kendra Davis to pretend to be her any longer when … Well, when Tess is head over heels in love with Kendra.'

There was a wave of confusion in the crowd as Don stepped forward to flank Garrett, nodding his support. Then Garrett pulled Kendra close, took a deep breath, and found his voice, a voice laced with emotion that surprised Kendra, that made her feel things she never dreamed she would ever feel.

'I'm Tess Delaney,' Garrett said, in a confident voice. He spoke the words carefully, as though he wasn't quite sure how they would feel on his tongue. Then he repeated them into the stunned silence. 'I'm Tess Delaney.'

This time the press erupted into total mayhem, and it took ages to quiet them. It was only when Garrett pulled Kendra into his arms, grunting slightly from the pain of his injury, and lingered to kiss her deeply and tenderly that the press silenced. At last he turned to face them.

'Tess Delaney has always written the deepest, the most sensitive parts of Garrett Thorne's heart. Tess Delaney has always found a way to express what Garrett could never have expressed. She was the secret part of me making itself known through her novels, helping me know myself a little better. I kept her secrets and she kept mine. She always knew what I wanted, better than I did. It wasn't until Kendra Davis came into my life that I understood what Tess was trying to say, what she wanted for me, what I wanted for myself. And now, I don't need Tess to tell me that, any more. I see. I understand.'

The reporter from the *Oregonian* stepped forward. Her eyes looked as though she might have been crying. 'Will Tess Delaney continue to write?'

Garrett smiled at her. 'Tess isn't dead. Of course she'll continue to write. And now she has a new muse.' He smiled at

Kendra. 'A flesh and blood muse. I won't say nothing has changed. Everything has changed. But I will say that for Tess Delaney, at last it really is time to come out into the world and celebrate the love she writes about.' He turned and took Kendra's hands in his. 'And this is the woman I want to celebrate with. This is the woman I want to love and romance for at least the next 50 years or so. If she'll have me.'

And, damn, if she wasn't crying! Kendra Davis, who never shed a tear, Kendra Davis, who had lived her life completely free of romance and love until Garrett Thorne came along. She was crying in front of the whole world. And she was nodding and throwing her arms around his neck. The word "yes" came out, sounding more like a hiccup. She wasn't sure he even understood it. But she made sure when he pulled her close that he heard and understood very clearly her next words. 'I love you, Garrett Thorne. I love you with all of my heart.'